Praise for #1 *New York Times* bestselling author Debbie Macomber

"Debbie Macomber has a gift for evoking the emotions that are at the heart of the genre's popularity."
—*Publishers Weekly*

"Macomber is a master storyteller."
—*RT Book Reviews*

"Bestselling Macomber...sure has a way of pleasing readers."
—*Booklist*

Praise for Caro Carson

"[Caro] Carson's romance is a humorous and heartfelt page-turner from the get-go. Her funny, genuinely touching and vibrant narrative sets the perfect pace with just a touch of Texas twang."
—*RT Book Reviews* on *The Bachelor Doctor's Bride* (4½ stars)

"[Caro] Carson's romance is complex, touching and funny. The Texas catastrophe setting awes, the co-stars shine and the morality tale inspires."
—*RT Book Reviews* on *Not Just a Cowboy* (4½ stars)

Debbie Macomber is a #1 *New York Times* bestselling author and a leading voice in women's fiction worldwide. Her work has appeared on every major bestseller list, with more than 170 million copies in print, and she is a multiple award winner. Hallmark Channel based a television series on Debbie's popular Cedar Cove books. For more information, visit her website, www.debbiemacomber.com.

Despite a no-nonsense background as a West Point graduate, army officer and Fortune 100 sales executive, **Caro Carson** has always treasured the happily-ever-after of a good romance novel. As a RITA® Award–winning Harlequin author, Caro is delighted to be living her own happily-ever-after with her husband and children in Florida, a location which has saved the coaster-loving theme-park fanatic a fortune on plane tickets.

#1 *New York Times* **Bestselling Author**

DEBBIE MACOMBER

YOURS AND MINE

⟨H⟩**HARLEQUIN**®BESTSELLING AUTHOR COLLECTION

ISBN-13: 978-0-373-53783-9

Yours and Mine

Copyright © 2017 by Harlequin Books S.A.

The publisher acknowledges the copyright holders of the individual works as follows:

Yours and Mine
Copyright © 1989 by Debbie Macomber

The Bachelor Doctor's Bride
Copyright © 2014 by Caro Carson

Recycling programs for this product may not exist in your area.

HARLEQUIN®
™ www.Harlequin.com

Printed in U.S.A.

CONTENTS

Also Available from Debbie Macomber

Midnight Sons

VOLUME 1
  (*Brides for Brothers* and
  The Marriage Risk)
VOLUME 2
  (*Daddy's Little Helper* and
  Because of the Baby)
VOLUME 3
  (*Falling for Him, Ending in
  Marriage* and *Midnight Sons
  and Daughters*)

This Matter of Marriage
Montana
Thursdays at Eight
Between Friends
Changing Habits
Married in Seattle
  (*First Comes Marriage* and
  Wanted: Perfect Partner)
Right Next Door
  (*Father's Day* and *The Courtship
  of Carol Sommars*)
Wyoming Brides
  (*Denim and Diamonds* and
  The Wyoming Kid)
Fairy Tale Weddings
  (*Cindy and the Prince* and
  Some Kind of Wonderful)
The Man You'll Marry
  (*The First Man You Meet* and
  The Man You'll Marry)
Orchard Valley Grooms
  (*Valerie* and *Stephanie*)
Orchard Valley Brides
  (*Norah* and *Lone Star Lovin'*)
The Sooner the Better
An Engagement in Seattle
  (*Groom Wanted* and
  Bride Wanted)
Out of the Rain
  (*Marriage Wanted* and
  Laughter in the Rain)
Learning to Love
  (*Sugar and Spice* and
  Love by Degree)

You…Again
  (*Baby Blessed* and
  Yesterday Once More)
The Unexpected Husband
  (*Jury of His Peers* and
  Any Sunday)
Three Brides, No Groom
Love in Plain Sight
  (*Love 'n' Marriage* and
  Almost an Angel)
I Left My Heart
  (*A Friend or Two* and
  No Competition)
Marriage Between Friends
  (*While Lace and Promises* and
  Friends—And Then Some)
A Man's Heart
  (*The Way to a Man's Heart*
  and *Hasty Wedding*)
North to Alaska
  (*That Wintry Feeling* and
  Borrowed Dreams)
On a Clear Day
  (*Starlight* and
  Promise Me Forever)
To Love and Protect
  (*Shadow Chasing* and
  For All My Tomorrows)
Home in Seattle
  (*The Playboy and the Widow*
  and *Fallen Angel*)
Together Again
  (*The Trouble with Caasi* and
  Reflections of Yesterday)
The Reluctant Groom
  (*All Things Considered* and
  Almost Paradise)
A Real Prince
  (*The Bachelor Prince* and
  Yesterday's Hero)
Private Paradise
  (in *That Summer Place*)

*Debbie Macomber's
Cedar Cove Cookbook*
*Debbie Macomber's
Christmas Cookbook*

YOURS AND MINE

Debbie Macomber

For Simone Hartman, the sixteen-year-old German girl who came to live with us to learn about America. Instead, she taught us about love, friendship, Wiener schnitzel and fun... German style. We love you, Simone!

One

"Mom, I forgot to tell you, I need two dozen cup-cakes for tomorrow morning."

Joanna Parsons reluctantly opened her eyes and lifted her head from the soft feather pillow, squinting at the illuminated dial of her clock radio. "Kristen, it's after eleven."

"I know, Mom, I'm sorry. But I've *got* to bring cup-cakes."

"No, you don't," Joanna said hopefully. "There's a package of Oreos on the top shelf of the cupboard. You can take those."

"Oreos! You've been hiding Oreos from me again! Just what kind of mother are you?"

"I was saving them for an emergency—like this."

"It won't work." Crossing her arms over her still-flat chest, eleven-year-old Kristen sat on the edge of the mattress and heaved a loud, discouraged sigh.

"Why not?"

"It's got to be cupcakes, home-baked chocolate ones."

"That's unfortunate, since you seem to have forgotten to mention the fact earlier. And now it's about four hours too late for baking anything. Including chocolate cupcakes." Joanna tried to be fair with Kristen, but being a single parent wasn't easy.

"Mom, I know I forgot," Kristen cried, her young voice rising in panic, "but I've got to bring cupcakes to class tomorrow. It's important! Really important!"

"Convince me." Joanna used the phrase often. She didn't want to seem unyielding and hard-nosed. After all, she'd probably forgotten a few important things in her thirty-odd years, too.

"It's Mrs. Eagleton's last day as our teacher—remember I told you her husband got transferred and she's moving to Denver? Everyone in the whole class hates to see her go, so we're throwing a party."

"Who's *we*?"

"Nicole and me," Kristen answered quickly. "Nicole's bringing the napkins, cups and punch, and I'm supposed to bring homemade cupcakes. Chocolate cupcakes. Mom, I've just got to. Nicole would never forgive me if I did something stupid like bring store-bought cookies for a teacher as wonderful as Mrs. Eagleton."

Kristen had met Nicole almost five months before at the beginning of the school year, and the two girls had been as thick as gnats in August from that time on. "Shouldn't the room mother be organizing this party?" That made sense to Joanna; surely there was an adult who would be willing to help.

"We don't have one this year. Everyone's mother is either too busy or working."

Joanna sighed. Oh, great, she was going to end up baking cupcakes until the wee hours of the morning.

"All right," she muttered, giving in to her daughter's pleading. Mrs. Eagleton *was* a wonderful teacher, and Joanna was as sorry as Kristen to see her leave.

"We just couldn't let Mrs. Eagleton move to Denver without doing something really nice for her," Kristen pressed.

Although Joanna agreed, she felt that Oreos or Fig Newtons should be considered special enough, since it was already after eleven. But Kristen obviously had her heart set on home-baked cupcakes.

"Mom?"

Even in the muted light, Joanna recognized the plea in her daughter's dark brown eyes. She looked so much like Davey that a twinge of anguish worked its way through Joanna's heart. They'd been divorced six years now, but the pain of that failure had yet to fade. Sometimes, at odd moments like these, she still recalled how good it had felt to be in his arms and how much she'd once loved him. Mostly, though, Joanna remembered how naive she'd been to trust him so completely. But she'd come a long way in the six years since her divorce. She'd gained a new measure of independence and self-respect, forging a career for herself at Columbia Basin Savings and Loan. And now she was close to achieving her goal of becoming the first female senior loan officer.

"All right, honey." Joanna sighed, dragging her thoughts back to her daughter. "I'll bake the cupcakes. Only next time, please let me know before we go to bed, okay?"

Kristen's shoulders slumped in relief. "I owe you one, Mom."

Joanna resisted the urge to remind her daughter

that the score was a lot higher than one. Tossing aside the thick warm blankets, she climbed out of bed and reached for her long robe.

Kristen, flannel housecoat flying behind her like a flag unfurling, raced toward the kitchen, eager to do what she could to help. "I'll turn on the oven and get everything ready," she called.

"All right," Joanna said with a yawn as she sent her foot searching under the bed for her slippers. She was mentally scanning the contents of her cupboards, wondering if she had a chocolate cake mix. Somehow she doubted it.

"Trouble, Mom," Kristen announced when Joanna entered the well-lighted kitchen. The eleven-year-old stood on a chair in front of the open cupboards above the refrigerator, an Oreo between her teeth. Looking only mildly guilty, she ate the cookie whole, then shook her head. "We don't have cake mix."

"I was afraid of that."

"I guess we'll have to bake them from scratch," Kristen suggested, reaching for another Oreo.

"Not this late, we won't. I'll drive to the store." There was an Albertson's that stayed open twenty-four hours less than a mile away.

Kristen jumped down from the chair. The pockets of her bathrobe were stuffed full of cookies, but her attempt to conceal them failed. Joanna pointed toward the cookie jar, and dutifully Kristen emptied her pockets.

When Kristen had finished, Joanna yawned again and ambled back into her bedroom.

"Mom, if you're going to the store, I suppose I should go with you."

"No, honey, I'm just going to run in and out. You stay here."

"Okay," Kristen agreed quickly.

The kid wasn't stupid, Joanna thought wryly. Winters in eastern Washington were often merciless, and temperatures in Spokane had been well below freezing all week. To be honest, she wasn't exactly thrilled about braving the elements herself. She pulled on her calf-high boots over two pairs of heavy woolen socks. Because the socks were so thick, Joanna could only zip the boots up to her ankles.

"Mom," Kristen said, following her mother into the bedroom, a thoughtful expression on her face. "Have you ever thought of getting married again?"

Surprised, Joanna looked up and studied her daughter. The question had come from out of nowhere, but her answer was ready. "Never." The first time around had been enough. Not that she was one of the walking wounded, at least she didn't think of herself that way. Instead, her divorce had made her smart, had matured her. Never again would she look to a man for happiness; Joanna was determined to build her own. But the unexpectedness of Kristen's question caught her off guard. Was Kristen telling her something? Perhaps her daughter felt she was missing out because there were only the two of them. "What makes you ask?"

The mattress dipped as she sat beside Joanna. "I'm not exactly sure," she confessed. "But you could remarry, you know. You've still got a halfway decent figure."

Joanna grinned. "Thanks... I think."

"I mean, it's not like you're really old and ugly."

"Coming from you, that's high praise indeed, considering that I'm over thirty."

"I'm sure if you wanted to, you could find another man. Not like Daddy, but someone better."

It hurt Joanna to hear her daughter say things like that about Davey, but she couldn't disguise from Kristen how selfish and hollow her father was. Nor could she hide Davey's roving eye when it came to the opposite sex. Kristen spent one month every summer with him in Seattle and saw for herself the type of man Davey was.

After she'd finished struggling with her boots, Joanna clumped into the entryway and opened the hall cupboard.

"Mom!" Kristen cried, her eyes round with dismay.

"What?"

"You can't go out looking like that!" Her daughter was pointing at her, as though aghast at the sight.

"Like what?" Innocently Joanna glanced down at the dress-length blue wool coat she'd slipped on over her rose-patterned flannel pajamas. Okay, so the bottoms showed, but only a little. And she was willing to admit that the boots would look better zipped up, but she was more concerned with comfort than fashion. If the way she looked didn't bother her, then it certainly shouldn't bother Kristen. Her daughter had obviously forgotten why Joanna was venturing outside in the first place.

"Someone might see you."

"Don't worry, I have no intention of taking off my coat." She'd park close to the front door of the store, run inside, head for aisle three, grab a cake mix and be back at the car in four minutes flat. Joanna didn't exactly feel like donning tights for the event.

"You might meet someone," Kristen persisted.

"So?" Joanna stifled a yawn.

"But your hair… Don't you think you should curl it?"

"Kristen, listen. The only people who are going to be in the grocery store are insomniacs and winos and maybe a couple of pregnant women." It was highly unlikely she'd run into anyone from the bank.

"But what if you got in an accident? The policeman would think you're some kind of weirdo."

Joanna yawned a second time. "Honey, anyone who would consider making cupcakes in the middle of the night has a mental problem as it is. I'll fit right in with everyone else, so quit worrying."

"Oh, all right," Kristen finally agreed.

Draping her bag strap over her shoulder, Joanna opened the front door and shivered as the arctic wind of late January wrapped itself around her. Damn, it was cold. The grass was so white with frost that she wondered, at first, if it had snowed. To ward off the chill, she wound Kristen's purple striped scarf around her neck to cover her ears and mouth and tied it loosely under her chin.

The heater in her ten-year-old Ford didn't have a chance to do anything but spew out frigid air as she huddled over the steering wheel for the few minutes it took to drive to the grocery store. According to her plan, she parked as close to the store as possible, turned off the engine and dashed inside.

Just as she'd predicted, the place was nearly deserted, except for a couple of clerks working near the front, arranging displays. Joanna didn't give them more than a fleeting glance as she headed toward the aisle where baking goods were shelved.

She was reaching for the first chocolate cake mix to come into sight when she heard footsteps behind her.

"Mrs. Parsons! Hello!" The shrill excited voice seemed to ring like a Chinese gong throughout the store.

Joanna hunched down as far as she could and cast a furtive glance over her shoulder. Dear Lord, Kristen had been right. She was actually going to bump into someone who knew her.

"It's me—Nicole. You remember me, don't you?"

Joanna attempted a smile as she turned to face her daughter's best friend. "Hi, there," she said weakly, and raised her right hand to wave, her wrist limp. "It's good to see you again." So she was lying. Anyone with a sense of decency would have pretended not to recognize her and casually looked the other way. Not Nicole. It seemed as though all the world's eleven-year-olds were plotting against her tonight. One chocolate cake mix; that was all she wanted. That and maybe a small tub of ready-made frosting. Then she could return home, get those cupcakes baked and climb back into bed where most sane people were at this very moment.

"You look different," Nicole murmured thoughtfully, her eyes widening as she studied Joanna.

Well, that was one way of putting it.

"When I first saw you, I thought you were a bag lady."

Loosening the scarf that obscured the lower half of her face, Joanna managed a grin.

"What are you doing here this late?" the girl wanted

to know next, following Joanna as she edged her way to the checkout stand.

"Kristen forgot to tell me about the cupcakes."

Nicole's cheerful laugh resounded through the store like a yell echoing in an empty sports stadium. "I was watching 60 Minutes with my dad when I remembered I hadn't bought the juice and stuff for the party. Dad's waiting for me in the car right now."

Nicole's father allowed her to stay up that late on a school night? Joanna did her utmost to hide her disdain. From what Kristen had told her, she knew Nicole's parents were also divorced and her father had custody of Nicole. The poor kid probably didn't know what the word *discipline* meant. No doubt her father was one of those weak-willed liberal parents so involved in their own careers that they didn't have any time left for their children. Imagine a parent letting an eleven-year-old wander around a grocery store at this time of night! The mere thought was enough to send chills of parental outrage racing up and down Joanna's backbone. She placed her arm around Nicole's shoulders as if to protect her from life's harsher realities. The poor sweet kid.

The abrupt whoosh of the automatic door was followed by the sound of someone striding impatiently into the store. Joanna glanced up to discover a tall man, wearing a well-cut dark coat, glaring in their direction.

"Nicole, what's taking so long?"

"Dad," the girl said happily, "this is Mrs. Parsons— Kristen's mom."

Nicole's father approached, obviously reluctant to acknowledge the introduction, his face remote and unsmiling.

Automatically Joanna straightened, her shoulders stiffening with the action. Nicole's father was exactly as she'd pictured him just a few moments earlier. Polished, worldly, and too darn handsome for his own good. Just like Davey. This was exactly the type of man she went out of her way to avoid. She'd been burned once, and no relationship was worth what she'd endured. This brief encounter with Nicole's father told Joanna all she needed to know.

"Tanner Lund," he announced crisply, holding out his hand.

"Joanna Parsons," Joanna said, and gave him hers for a brisk cold shake. She couldn't take her hand away fast enough.

His eyes narrowed as they studied her, and the look he gave her was as disapproving as the one she offered him. Slowly his gaze dropped to the unzipped boots flapping at her ankles and the worn edges of the pajamas visible below her wool coat.

"I think it's time we met, don't you?" Joanna didn't bother to disguise her disapproval of the man's attitude toward child-rearing. She'd had Nicole over after school several times, but on the one occasion Kristen had visited her friend, the child was staying with a babysitter.

A hint of a smile appeared on his face, but it didn't reach his eyes. "Our meeting is long overdue, I agree."

He seemed to be suggesting that he'd made a mistake in allowing his daughter to have anything to do with someone who dressed the way she did.

Joanna's gaze shifted to Nicole. "Isn't it late for you to be up on a school night?"

"Where's Kristen?" he countered, glancing around the store.

"At home," Joanna answered, swallowing the words that said home was exactly where an eleven-year-old child belonged on a school night—or any other night for that matter.

"Isn't she a bit young to be left alone while you run to a store?"

"N-not in the least."

Tanner frowned and his eyes narrowed even more. His disapproving gaze demanded to know what kind of mother left a child alone in the house at this time of night.

Joanna answered him with a scornful look of her own.

"It's a pleasure to meet you, Mr. Lund," she said coolly, knowing her eyes relayed a conflicting message.

"The pleasure's mine."

Joanna was all the more aware of her disheveled appearance. Uncombed and uncurled, her auburn hair hung limply to her shoulders. Her dark eyes were nice enough, she knew, fringed in long curling lashes. She considered them her best asset, and purposely glared at Tanner, hoping her eyes were as cold as the blast from her car heater had been.

Tanner placed his hands on his daughter's shoulders and drew her protectively to his side. Joanna was infuriated by the action. If Nicole needed shielding, it was from an irresponsible father!

Okay, she reasoned, so her attire was a bit outlandish. But that couldn't be helped; she was on a mission that by rights should win her a nomination for the mother-of-the-year award. The way Tanner Lund had implied that *she* was the irresponsible parent was something Joanna found downright insulting.

"Well," Joanna said brightly, "I have to go. Nice to see you again, Nicole." She swept two boxes of cake mix into her arms and grabbed what she hoped was some frosting.

"You, too, Mrs. Parsons," the girl answered, smiling up at her.

"Mr. Lund."

"Mrs. Parsons."

The two nodded politely at each other, and, clutching her packages, Joanna walked regally to the checkout stand. She made her purchase and started back toward the car. The next time Kristen invited Nicole over, Joanna mused on the short drive home, she intended to spend lots of extra time with the girls. Now she knew how badly Nicole needed someone to nurture her, to give her the firm but loving guidance every child deserved.

The poor darling.

Two

Joanna expertly lowered the pressure foot of her sewing machine over the bunched red material, then used both hands to push the fabric slowly under the bobbing needle. Straight pins, tightly clenched between her lips, protruded from her mouth. Her concentration was intense.

"Mom." A breathless Kristen bounded into the room.

Joanna intercepted her daughter with one upraised hand until she finished stitching the seam.

Kristen stalked around the kitchen table several times, like a shark circling its kill. "Mom, hurry, this is really important."

"Wlutt?" Joanna asked, her teeth still clamped on the pins.

"Can Nicole spend the night?"

Joanna blinked. This wasn't the weekend, and Kristen knew the rules; she had permission to invite friends over only on Friday and Saturday nights. Joanna removed the pins from her mouth before she answered. "It's Wednesday."

"I know what day it is." Kristen rolled her eyes towards the ceiling and slapped the heel of her hand against her forehead.

Allowing his daughter to stay over at a friend's house on a school night was exactly the kind of irresponsible parenting Joanna expected from Tanner Lund. Her estimation of the man was dropping steadily, though that hardly seemed possible. Earlier in the afternoon, Joanna had learned that Nicole didn't even plan to tell her father she and Kristen were going to be performing in the school talent show. The man revealed absolutely no interest in his daughter's activities. Joanna felt so bad about Tanner Lund's attitude that she'd volunteered to sew a second costume so Nicole would have something special to wear for this important event. And now it seemed that Tanner was in the habit of farming out his daughter on school nights, as well.

"Mom, hurry and decide. Nicole's on the phone."

"Honey, there's school tomorrow."

Kristen gave her another scornful look.

"The two of you will stay up until midnight chattering, and then in the morning class will be a disaster. The answer is no!"

Kristen's eager face fell. "I promise we won't talk. Just this once, Mom. Oh, please!" She folded her hands prayerfully, and her big brown eyes pleaded with Joanna. "How many times do I ask you for something?"

Joanna stared incredulously at her daughter. The list was endless.

"All right, forget I asked that. But this is important, Mom, real important—for Nicole's sake."

Every request was argued as urgent. But knowing

what she did about the other little girl's home life made refusing all the more difficult. "I'm sorry, Kristen, but not on a school night."

Head drooping, Kristen shuffled toward the phone. "Now Nicole will have to spend the night with Mrs. Wagner, and she hates that."

"Who's Mrs. Wagner?"

Kristen turned to face her mother and released a sigh intended to evoke sympathy. "Her babysitter."

"Her father makes her spend the night at a babysitter's?"

"Yes. He has a business meeting with Becky."

Joanna stiffened and felt a sudden chill. "Becky?"

"His business partner."

I'll just bet! Joanna's eyes narrowed with outrage. Tanner Lund was a lowlife, kicking his own daughter out into the cold so he could bring a woman over. The man disgusted her.

"Mrs. Wagner is real old and she makes Nicole eat health food. She has a black-and-white TV, and the only programs she'll let Nicole watch are nature shows. Wouldn't you hate that?"

Joanna's mind was spinning. Any child would detest being cast from her own bed and thrust upon the not always tender mercies of a babysitter. "How often does Nicole have to spend the night with Mrs. Wagner?"

"Lots."

Joanna could well believe it. "How often is 'lots'?"

"At least twice a month. Sometimes even more often than that."

That poor neglected child. Joanna's heart constricted at the thought of sweet Nicole being ruthlessly handed over to a woman who served soybean burgers.

"Can she, Mom? Oh, please?" Again Kristen folded her hands, pleading with her mother to reconsider.

"All right," Joanna conceded, "but just this once."

Kristen ran across the room and hurled her arms around Joanna's neck, squeezing for all she was worth. "You're the greatest mother in the whole world."

Joanna snorted softly. "I've got to be in the top ten percent, anyway," she said, remembering the cupcakes.

"Absolutely not," Tanner said forcefully as he laid a neatly pressed shirt in his open suitcase. "Nicole, I won't hear of it."

"But, Dad, Kristen is my very best friend."

"Believe me, sweetheart, I'm pleased you've found a soulmate, but when I'm gone on these business trips I need to know you're being well taken care of." And supervised, he added mentally. What he knew about Kristen's mother wasn't encouraging. The woman was a scatterbrain who left her young daughter unattended while she raided the supermarket for nighttime goodies—and then had the nerve to chastise him because Nicole was up a little late. In addition to being a busybody, Joanna Parsons dressed like a fruitcake.

"Dad, you don't understand what it's like for me at Mrs. Wagner's."

Undaunted, Tanner continued packing his suitcase. He wasn't any happier about leaving Nicole than she was, but he didn't have any choice. As a relatively new half owner of Spokane Aluminum, he was required to do a certain amount of traveling. More these first few months than would be necessary later. His business trips were essential, since they familiarized him with the clients and their needs. He would have to absorb this information as quickly as possible in order to determine if the plant was going to achieve his and John Becky's five-year goal. In a few weeks, he expected to hire an assistant who would assume some of this responsibility, but for now the task fell into his hands.

Nicole slumped onto the edge of the bed. "The last time I spent the night at Mrs. Wagner's she served baked beef heart for dinner."

Involuntarily Tanner cringed.

"And, Dad, she made me watch a special on television that was all about fungus."

Tanner gritted his teeth. So the old lady was a bit eccentric, but she looked after Nicole competently, and that was all that mattered.

"Do you know what Kristen's having for dinner?"

Tanner didn't care to guess. It was probably something like strawberry ice cream and caramel-flavored popcorn. "No, and I don't want to know."

"It isn't sweet-and-sour calf liver, I can tell you that."

Tanner's stomach turned at the thought of liver in any kind of sauce. "Nicole, the subject is closed. You're spending the night with Mrs. Wagner."

"It's spaghetti and meatballs and three-bean salad and milk and French bread, that's what. And Mrs. Parsons said I could help Kristen roll the meatballs—but that's all right, I'll call and tell her that you don't want me to spend the night at a home where I won't be properly looked after."

"Nicole—"

"Dad, don't worry about it, I understand."

Tanner sincerely doubted that. He placed the last of his clothes inside the suitcase and closed the lid.

"At least I'm *trying* to understand why you'd send

me to someplace like Mrs. Wagner's when my very best friend *invited* me to spend the night with her."

Tanner could feel himself weakening. It was only one night and Kristen's weird mother wasn't likely to be a dangerous influence on Nicole in that short a time.

"Spaghetti and meatballs," Nicole muttered under her breath. "My all-time favorite food."

Now that was news to Tanner. He'd thought pizza held that honor. He'd never known his daughter to turn down pizza at any time of the day or night.

"And they have a twenty-inch color television set."

Tanner hesitated.

"With remote control."

Would wonders never cease? "Will Kristen's mother be there the entire night?" he asked.

"Of course."

His daughter was looking at him as though he'd asked if Mrs. Parsons were related to ET. "Where will you sleep?"

"Kristen has a double bed." Nicole's eyes brightened. "And we've already promised Mrs. Parsons that we'll go straight to bed at nine o'clock and hardly talk."

It was during times such as this that Tanner felt the full weight of parenting descend upon his shoulders. Common sense told him Nicole would be better off with Mrs. Wagner, but he understood her complaints about the older woman as well. "All right, Nicole, you can stay at Kristen's."

His daughter let out a whoop of sheer delight.

"But just this once."

"Oh, Dad, you're the greatest." Her arms locked around his waist, and she squeezed with all her might, her nose pressed against his flat stomach.

"Okay, okay, I get the idea you're pleased with my decision," Tanner said with a short laugh.

"Can we leave now?"

"Now?" Usually Nicole wanted to linger at the apartment until the last possible minute.

"Yes. Mrs. Parsons really did say I could help roll the meatballs, and you know what else?"

"What?"

"She's sewing me and Kristen identical costumes for the talent show."

Tanner paused—he hadn't known anything about his daughter needing a costume. "What talent show?"

"Oops." Nicole slapped her hand over her mouth. "I wasn't going to tell you because it's on Valentine's Day and I know you won't be able to come. I didn't want you to feel bad."

"Nicole, it's more important that you don't hide things from me."

"But you have to be in Seattle."

She was right. He'd hate missing the show, but he was scheduled to meet with the Foreign Trade Commission on the fourteenth regarding a large shipment of aluminum to Japan. "What talent do you and Kristen have?" he asked, diverting his disappointment for the moment.

"We're lip-synching a song from Heart. You know, the rock group?"

"That sounds cute. A fitting choice, too, for a Valentine's Day show. Perhaps you two can be persuaded to give me a preview before the grand performance."

Her blue eyes became even brighter in her excitement. "That's a great idea! Kristen and I can practice while you're away, and we'll show you when you come back."

It was an acceptable compromise.

Nicole dashed out of his bedroom and returned a couple of minutes later with her backpack. "I'm ready anytime you are," she announced.

Tanner couldn't help but notice that his daughter looked downright cheerful. More cheerful than any of the other times he'd been forced to leave her. Normally she put on a long face and moped around, making him feel guilty about abandoning her to the dreaded Mrs. Wagner.

By the time he picked up his briefcase and luggage, Nicole was waiting at the front door.

"Are you going to come in and say hello to Mrs. Parsons?" Nicole asked when Tanner eased his Mercedes into Kristen's driveway fifteen minutes later. Even in the fading late-afternoon light, he could see that the house was newly painted, white with green shutters at the windows. The lawn and flower beds seemed well maintained. He could almost picture rose bushes in full bloom. It certainly wasn't the type of place he'd associated with Kristen's loony mother.

"Are you coming in or not?" Nicole asked a second time, her voice impatient.

Tanner had to mull over the decision. He wasn't eager to meet that unfriendly woman who wore unzipped boots and flannel pajamas again.

"Dad!"

Before Tanner could answer, the door opened and Kristen came bowling out of the house at top speed. A gorgeous redhead followed sedately behind her. Tanner felt his jaw sag and his mouth drop open. No, it couldn't be! Tall, cool, sophisticated, this woman looked as though she'd walked out of the pages of a fashion magazine. It couldn't be Joanna Parsons—no way. A relative perhaps, but certainly not the woman he'd met in the grocery store that night.

Nicole had already climbed out of the car. She paused as though she'd forgotten something, then ran around to his side of the car. When Tanner rolled down his window, she leaned over and gave him one of her famous bear hugs, hurling her arms around his neck and squeezing enthusiastically. "Bye, Dad."

"Bye, sweetheart. You've got the phone number of my hotel to give Mrs. Parsons?"

Nicole patted her jeans pocket. "It's right here."

"Be good."

"I will."

When Tanner looked up, he noted that Joanna was standing behind her daughter, her hands resting on Kristen's shoulders. Cool, disapproving eyes surveyed him. Yup, it was the same woman all right. Joanna Parsons's gaze could freeze watermelon at a Fourth of July picnic.

Three

"Would you like more spaghetti, Nicole?" Joanna asked for the second time.

"No, thanks, Mrs. Parsons."

"You asked her that already," Kristen commented, giving her mother a puzzled look. "After we've done the dishes, Nicole and I are going to practice our song."

Joanna nodded. "Good idea, but do your homework first."

Kristen exchanged a knowing look with her friend, and the two grinned at each other.

"I'm really glad you're letting me stay the night, Mrs. Parsons," Nicole said, as she carried her empty plate to the kitchen sink. "Dinner was great. Dad tries, but he isn't much of a cook. We get take-out food a lot." She wandered back to the table and fingered the blue-quilted place mat. "Kristen told me you sewed these, too. They're pretty."

"Thank you. The pattern is really very simple."

"They have to be," Kristen added, stuffing the last slice of toasted French bread into her mouth. "'Cause Mom let me do a couple of them."

"You made two of these?"

"Yeah," Kristen said, after she'd finished chewing. Pride beamed from her dark brown eyes. "We've made lots of things together since we bought the house. Do you have any idea how expensive curtains can be? Mom made the entire set in my room—that's why everything matches."

"The bedspread, too?"

"Naturally." Kristen made it sound like they'd whipped up the entire set over a weekend, when the project had actually taken the better part of two weeks.

"Wow."

From the way Nicole was staring at her, Joanna half expected the girl to fall to her knees in homage. She felt a stab of pity for Nicole, who seemed to crave a mother's presence. But she had to admit she was thrilled by her own daughter's pride in their joint accomplishments.

"Mom sews a lot of my clothes," Kristen added, licking the butter from her fingertips. "I thought you knew that."

"I… No, I didn't."

"She's teaching me, too. That's the best part. So I'll be able to make costumes for our next talent show." Kristen's gaze flew from Nicole to her mother then back to Nicole. "I bet my mom would teach you how to sew. Wouldn't you, Mom?"

"Ah…"

"Would you really, Mrs. Parsons?"

Not knowing what else to say, Joanna agreed with a quick nod of her head. "Why not? We'll have fun learning together." She gave an encouraging smile, but she wondered a bit anxiously if she was ready for a project like this.

"That would be great." Nicole slipped her arm around Kristen's shoulders. Her gaze dropped as she hesitated. "Dinner was really good, too," she said again.

"I told you what a great cook my mom is," Kristen boasted.

Nicole nodded, but kept her eyes trained to the floor. "Could I ask you something, Mrs. Parsons?"

"Of course."

"Like I said, Dad tries real hard, but he just isn't a very good cook. Would it be rude to ask you for the recipe for your spaghetti sauce?"

"Not at all. I'll write it out for you tonight."

"Gee, thanks. It's so nice over here. I wish Dad would let me stay here all the time. You and Kristen do such neat things, and you eat real good, too."

Joanna could well imagine the kind of meals Tanner Lund served his daughter. She already knew that he frequently ordered out, and the rest probably came from the frozen-food section of the local grocery. That was if he didn't have an array of willing females who did his cooking for him. Someone like this Becky person, the woman he was with now.

"Dad makes great tacos, though," Nicole was saying. "They're his specialty. He said I might be able to have a slumber party for my birthday in March, and I want him to serve tacos then. But I might ask him to make spaghetti instead—if he gets the recipe right."

"You get to have a slumber party?" Kristen cried, her eyes widening. "That's great! My mom said I could have two friends over for the night on my birthday, but only two, because that's all she can mentally handle."

Joanna pretended an interest in her leftover salad, stirring her fork through the dressing that sat in the bottom of the bowl. It was true; there were limits to her mothering abilities. A house full of screaming eleven- and twelve-year-olds was more than she dared contemplate on a full stomach.

While Nicole finished clearing off the table, Kristen loaded the dishwasher. Working together, the two completed their tasks in only a few minutes.

"We're going to my room now. Okay, Mom?"

"Sure, honey, that's fine," Joanna said, placing the leftovers in the refrigerator. She paused, then decided to remind the pair a second time. "Homework before anything else."

"Of course," answered Kristen.

"Naturally," added Nicole.

Both vanished down the hallway that led to Kristen's bedroom. Watching them, Joanna grinned. The friendship with Nicole had been good for Kristen, and Joanna intended to shower love and attention on Nicole in the hope of compensating her for her unsettled home life.

Once Joanna had finished wiping down the kitchen counters, she made her way to Kristen's bedroom. Dutifully knocking—since her daughter made emphatic comments about privacy these days—she let herself in. Both girls were sitting cross-legged on the bed, spelling books open on their laps.

"Need any help?"

"No, thanks, Mom."

Still Joanna lingered, looking for an excuse to stay

and chat. "I was placed third in the school spelling bee when I was your age."

Kristen glanced speculatively toward her friend. "That's great, Mom."

Warming to her subject, Joanna hurried to add, "I could outspell every boy in the class."

Kristen closed her textbook. "Mrs. Andrews, our new teacher, said the school wasn't going to have a spelling bee this year."

Joanna walked into the room and sat on the edge of the bed. "That's too bad, because I know you'd do well."

"I only got a B in spelling, Mom. I'm okay, but it's not my best subject."

A short uneasy silence followed while both girls studied Joanna, as though waiting for her to either leave or make a formal announcement.

"I thought we'd pop popcorn later," Joanna said, flashing a cheerful smile.

"Good." Kristen nodded and her gaze fell pointedly to her textbook. This was followed by another long moment of silence.

"Mom, I thought you said you wanted us to do our homework."

"I do."

"Well, we can't very well do it with you sitting here watching us."

"Oh." Joanna leapt off the bed. "Sorry."

"That's all right."

"Let me know when you're done."

"Why?" Kristen asked, looking perplexed.

Joanna shrugged. "I...I thought we might all sit around and chat. Girl talk, that sort of thing." Without being obvious about it, she'd hoped to offer Nicole maternal advice and some much needed affection. The thought of the little girl's father and what he was doing that very evening was so distasteful that Joanna had to force herself not to frown.

"Mom, Nicole and I are going to practice our song once we've finished our homework. Remember?"

"Oh, right. I forgot." Sheepishly, she started to walk away.

"I really appreciate your sewing my costume, Mrs. Parsons," Nicole added.

"It's no trouble, Nicole. I'm happy to do it."

"Speaking of the costumes," Kristen muttered, "didn't you say something about wanting to finish them before the weekend?"

"I did?" The look Kristen gave her suggested she must have. "Oh, right, now I remember."

The girls, especially her daughter, seemed relieved when Joanna left the bedroom. This wasn't going well. She'd planned on spending extra time with them, but it was clear they weren't keen on having her around. Taking a deep breath, Joanna headed for the living room, feeling a little piqued. Her ego should be strong enough to handle rejection from two eleven-year-old girls.

She settled in the kitchen and brought out her sewing machine again. The red costumes for the talent show were nearly finished. She ran her hand over the polished cotton and let her thoughts wander. She and Kristen had lived in the house only since September. For the six years following the divorce, Joanna had been forced to raise her daughter in a small apartment. Becoming a home owner had been a major step for her and she was proud of the time and care that had gone into choosing their small one-story house. It had required some repairs, but nothing major, and the sense of accomplishment she'd experienced when she signed her name to the mortgage papers had been well worth the years of scrimping. The house had only two bedrooms, but there was plenty of space in the backyard for a garden, something Joanna had insisted on. She thought that anyone studying her might be amused. On the one hand, she was a woman with basic traditional values, and on the other, a goal-setting businesswoman struggling to succeed in a male-dominated field. Her boss would have found it difficult to understand that the woman who'd set her sights on the position of senior loan officer liked the feel of wet dirt under her fingernails. And he would have been surprised to learn that she could take a simple piece of bright red cotton and turn it into a dazzling costume for a talent show.

An hour later, when Joanna was watching television and finishing up the hand stitching on the costumes, Kristen and Nicole rushed into the living room, looking pleased about something.

"You girls ready for popcorn?"

"Not me," Nicole said, placing her hands over her stomach. "I'm still full from dinner."

Joanna nodded. The girl obviously wasn't accustomed to eating nutritionally balanced meals.

"We want to do our song for you."

"Great." Joanna scooted close to the edge of the sofa, eagerly awaiting their performance. Kristen plugged in her MP3 player, then hurried to her friend's side, striking a pose until the music started.

"I can tell already that you're going to be great," Joanna said, clapping her hands to the lively beat.

She was right. The two did astonishingly well, and when they'd finished Joanna applauded loudly.

"We did okay?"

"You were fabulous."

Kristen and Nicole positively glowed.

When they returned to Kristen's bedroom, Joanna followed them. Kristen turned around and seemed surprised to find her mother there.

"Mom," she hissed between clenched teeth, "what's with you tonight? You haven't been yourself since Nicole arrived."

"I haven't?"

"You keep following us around."

"I do?"

"Really, Mom, we like you and everything, but Nicole and I want to talk about boys and stuff, and we can't very well do that with you here."

"Oh, Mrs. Parsons, I forgot to tell you," Nicole inserted, obviously unaware of the whispered conversation going on between Kristen and her mother. "I told my dad about you making my costume for the talent show, and he said he wants to pay you for your time and expenses."

"You told your dad?" Kristen asked, and whirled around to face her friend. "I thought you weren't going to because he'd feel guilty. Oh, I get it! That's how you got him to let you spend the night. Great idea!"

Joanna frowned. "What exactly does that mean?"

The two girls exchanged meaningful glances and Nicole looked distinctly uncomfortable.

"What does what mean?" Kristen repeated the question in a slightly elevated voice Joanna recognized immediately. Her daughter was up to one of her schemes again.

Nicole stepped in front of her friend. "It's my fault, Mrs. Parsons. I wanted to spend the night here instead of with Mrs. Wagner, so I told Dad that Kristen had invited me."

"Mom, you've got to understand. Mrs. Wagner won't let Nicole watch anything but educational television, and you know there are special shows we like to watch."

"That's not the part I mean," Joanna said, dismissing their rushed explanation. "I want to know what you meant by not telling Mr. Lund about the talent show because he'd feel guilty."

"Oh...that part." The two girls glanced at each other, as though silently deciding which one would do the explaining.

Nicole raised her gaze to Joanna and sighed, her thin shoulders moving up and down expressively. "My dad won't be able to attend the talent show because he's got a business meeting in Seattle, and I knew he'd feel terrible about it. He really likes it when I do things like the show. It gives him something to tell my grandparents about, like I was going to be the next Madonna or something."

"He has to travel a lot to business meetings," Kristen added quickly.

"Business meetings?"

"Like tonight," Kristen went on to explain.

"Dad has to fly someplace with Mr. Becky. He owns half the company and Dad owns the other half. He said it had to do with getting a big order, but I never listen to stuff like that, although Dad likes to explain every little detail so I'll know where he's at and what he's doing."

Joanna felt a numbing sensation creeping slowly up her spine. "Your dad owns half a company?"

"Spokane Aluminum is the reason we moved here from West Virginia."

"Spokane Aluminum?" Joanna's voice rose half an octave. "Your dad owns half of Spokane Aluminum?" The company was one of the largest employers in the Northwest. A shockingly large percentage of their state's economy was directly or indirectly tied to this company. A sick feeling settled in Joanna's stomach. Not only was Nicole's father wealthy, he was socially prominent, and all the while she'd been thinking... Oh, dear heavens. "So your father's out of town tonight?" she asked, feeling the warmth invade her face.

"You knew that, Mom." Kristen gave her mother another one of those searching gazes that suggested Joanna might be losing her memory—due to advanced age, no doubt.

"I...I thought—" Abruptly she bit off what she'd been about to say. When Kristen had said something about Tanner being with Becky, she'd assumed it was a woman. But of course it was *John* Becky, whose name was familiar to everyone in that part of the country. Joanna remembered reading in the *Review* that Becky had taken on a partner, but she hadn't made the connection. Perhaps she'd misjudged Tanner Lund, she reluctantly conceded. Perhaps she'd been a bit too eager to view him in a bad light.

"Before we came to Spokane," Nicole was saying now, "Dad and I had a long talk about the changes the move would make in our lives. We made a list of the good things and a list of the bad things, and then we talked about them. One bad thing was that Dad would be gone a lot, until he can hire another manager. He doesn't feel good about leaving me with strangers, and we didn't know a single person in Spokane other than Mr. Becky and his wife, but they're real old—over forty, anyway. He even went and interviewed Mrs. Wagner before I spent the night there the first time."

The opinion Joanna had formed of Tanner Lund was crumbling at her feet. Evidently he wasn't the irresponsible parent she'd assumed.

"Nicole told me you met her dad in the grocery store when you bought the mix for the cupcakes." Kristen shook her head as if to say she was thoroughly disgusted with her mother for not taking her advice that night and curling her hair before she showed her face in public.

"I told my dad you don't dress that way all the time," Nicole added, then shifted her gaze to the other side of the room. "But I don't think he believed me until he dropped me off tonight."

Joanna began to edge her way toward the bedroom door. "Your father and I seem to have started off on the wrong foot," she said weakly.

Nicole bit her lower lip. "I know. He wasn't real keen on me spending the night here, but I talked him into it."

"Mom?" Kristen asked, frowning. "What did you say to Mr. Lund when you met him at the store?"

"Nothing," she answered, taking a few more retreating steps.

"She asked my dad what I was doing up so late on a school night, and he told me later that he didn't like her attitude," Nicole explained. "I didn't get a chance to tell you that I'm normally in bed by nine thirty, but that night was special because Dad had just come home from one of his trips. His plane was late and I didn't remember to tell him about the party stuff until after we got home from Mrs. Wagner's."

"I see," Joanna murmured, and swallowed uncomfortably.

"You'll get a chance to settle things with Mr. Lund when he picks up Nicole tomorrow night," Kristen stated, and it was obvious that she wanted her mother to make an effort to get along with her best friend's father.

"Right," Joanna muttered, dreading the confrontation. She never had been particularly fond of eating crow.

Four

Joanna was breading pork chops the following evening when Kristen barreled into the kitchen, leaving the door swinging in her wake. "Mr. Lund's here to pick up Nicole. I think you should invite him and Nicole to stay for dinner…and explain about, you know, the other night."

Oh, sure, Joanna mused. She often invited company owners and acting presidents over for an evening meal. Pork chops and mashed potatoes weren't likely to impress someone like Tanner Lund.

Before Kristen could launch into an argument, Joanna shook her head and offered the first excuse that came to mind. "There aren't enough pork chops to ask him tonight. Besides, Mr. Lund is probably tired from his trip and anxious to get home."

"I bet he's hungry, too," Kristen pressed. "And Nicole thinks you're a fabulous cook, and—"

A sharp look from her mother cut her off. "Another night, Kristen!"

Joanna brushed the bread crumbs off her fingertips and untied her apron. Inhaling deeply, she paused long enough to run a hand through her hair and check her reflection in the window above the sink. No one was going to mistake her for Miss America, but her appearance was passable. Okay, it was time to hold her head high, spit the feathers out of her mouth and get ready to down some crow.

Joanna forced a welcoming smile onto her lips as she stepped into the living room. Tanner stood awkwardly just inside the front door, as though prepared to beat a hasty retreat if necessary. "How was your trip?" she ventured, straining to make the question sound cheerful.

"Fine. Thank you." His expression didn't change.

"Do you have time for a cup of coffee?" she asked next, doing her best to disguise her unease. She wondered quickly if she'd unpacked her china cups yet. After their shaky beginning, Joanna wasn't quite sure if she could undo the damage. But standing in the entryway wouldn't work. She needed to sit down for this.

He eyed her suspiciously. Joanna wasn't sure she should even try to explain things. In time he'd learn she wasn't a candidate for the loony bin—just as she'd stumbled over the fact that he wasn't a terrible father. Trying to tell him that she was an upstanding member of the community after he'd seen her dressed in a wool coat draped over pajamas, giving him looks that suggested he be reported to Children's Protective Services, wasn't exactly a task she relished.

Tanner glanced at his wristwatch and shook his head. "I haven't got time to visit tonight. Thanks for the invitation, though."

Joanna almost sighed aloud with relief.

"Did Nicole behave herself?"

Joanna nodded. "She wasn't the least bit of trouble. Nicole's a great kid."

A smile cracked the tight edges of his mouth. "Good."

Kristen and Nicole burst into the room. "Is Mr. Lund going to stay, Mom?"

"He can't tonight…"

"Another time…"

They spoke simultaneously, with an equal lack of enthusiasm.

"Oh." The girls looked at each other and frowned, their disappointment noticeable.

"Have you packed everything, Nicole?" Tanner asked, not hiding his eagerness to leave.

The eleven-year-old nodded reluctantly. "I think so."

"Don't you think you should check my room one more time?" Kristen suggested, grabbing her friend's hand and leading her back toward the hallway.

"Oh, right. I suppose I should." The two disappeared before either Joanna or Tanner could call them back.

The silence between them hummed so loudly Joanna swore she could have waltzed to it. But since the opportunity had presented itself, she decided to get the unpleasant task of explaining her behavior out of the way while she still had her nerve.

"I think I owe you an apology," she murmured, her face flushing.

"An apology?"

"I thought…you know… The night we met, I assumed you were an irresponsible parent because Nicole was up so late. She's now told me that you'd just returned from a trip."

"Yes, well, I admit I did feel the sting of your disapproval."

This wasn't easy. Joanna swallowed uncomfortably and laced her fingers together forcing herself to meet his eyes. "Nicole explained that your flight was delayed and she forgot to mention the party supplies when you picked her up at the babysitter's. She said she didn't remember until you got all the way home."

Tanner's mouth relaxed a bit more. "Since we're both being truthful here, I'll admit that I wasn't overly impressed with you that night, either."

Joanna dropped her gaze. "I can imagine. I hope you realise I don't usually dress like that."

"I gathered as much when I dropped Nicole off yesterday afternoon."

They both paused to share a brief smile and Joanna instantly felt better. It hadn't been easy to blurt all this out, but she was relieved that they'd finally cleared the air.

"Since Kristen and Nicole are such good friends, I thought, well, that I should set things right between us. From everything Nicole's said, you're doing an excellent job of parenting."

"From everything she's told me, the same must be true of you."

"Believe me, it isn't easy raising a preteen daughter," Joanna announced. She rubbed her palms together a couple of times, searching for something brilliant to add.

Tanner shook his head. "Isn't that the truth?"

They laughed then, and because they were still awkward with each other the sound was rusty.

"Now that you mention it, maybe I could spare a few minutes for a cup of coffee."

"Sure." Joanna led the way into the kitchen. While Tanner sat down at the table, she filled a mug from the pot keeping warm on the plate of the automatic coffeemaker and placed it carefully in front of him. Now that she knew him a bit better, she realized he'd prefer that to a dainty china cup. "How do you take it?"

"Just black, thanks."

She pulled out the chair across the table from him, still feeling a little ill at ease. Her mind was whirling. She didn't want to give Tanner a second wrong impression now that she'd managed to correct the first one. Her worry was that he might interpret her friendliness as a sign of romantic interest, which it wasn't. Building a new relationship was low on her priority list. Besides, they simply weren't on the same economic level. She worked for a savings-and-loan institution and he was half owner of the largest employer in the area. The last thing she wanted was for Tanner to think of her as a gold digger.

Joanna's thoughts were tumbling over themselves as she struggled to find a diplomatic way of telling him all this without sounding like some kind of man hater. And without sounding presumptuous.

"I'd like to pay you," Tanner said, cutting into her reflections. His chequebook was resting on the table, Cross pen poised above it.

Joanna blinked, not understanding. "For the coffee?"

He gave her an odd look. "For looking after Nicole."

"No, please." Joanna shook her head dismissively.

"It wasn't the least bit of trouble for her to stay the night. Really."

"What about the costume for the talent show? Surely I owe you something for that."

"No." Once more she shook her head for emphasis. "I've had that material tucked away in a drawer for ages. If I hadn't used it for Nicole's costume, I'd probably have ended up giving it away later."

"But your time must be worth something."

"It was just as easy to sew up two as one. I was happy to do it. Anyway, there'll probably be a time in the future when I need a favor. I'm worthless when it comes to electrical outlets and even worse with plumbing."

Joanna couldn't believe she'd said that. Tanner Lund wasn't the type of man to do his own electrical repairs.

"Don't be afraid to ask," he told her. "If I can't fix it, I'll find someone who can."

"Thank you," she said, relaxing. Now that she was talking to Tanner, she decided he was both pleasant and forthright, not at all the coldly remote or self-important man his wealth might have led her to expect.

"Mom," Kristen cried as she charged into the kitchen, "did you ask Mr. Lund yet?"

"About what?"

"About coming over for dinner some time."

Joanna felt the heat shoot up her neck and face until it reached her hairline. Kristen had made the invitation sound like a romantic tryst the three of them had been planning the entire time Tanner was away.

Nicole, entering the room behind her friend, provided a timely interruption.

"Dad, Kristen and I want to do our song for you now."

"I'd like to see it. Do you mind, Joanna?"

"Of course not."

"Mom finished the costumes last night. We'll change and be back in a minute," Kristen said, her voice high with excitement. The two scurried off. The minute they were out of sight, Joanna stood up abruptly and refilled her cup. Actually she was looking for a way to speak frankly to Tanner, without embarrassing herself—or him. She thought ironically that anyone looking at her now would be hard put to believe she was a competent loan officer with a promising future.

"I think I should explain something," she began, her voice unsteady.

"Yes?" Tanner asked, his gaze following her movements around the kitchen.

Joanna couldn't seem to stand in one place for long. She moved from the coffeepot to the refrigerator, finally stopping in front of the stove. She linked her fingers behind her back and took a deep breath before she trusted herself to speak. "I thought it was important to clear up any misunderstanding between us, because the girls are such good friends. When Nicole's with Kristen and me, I want you to know she's in good hands."

Tanner gave her a polite nod. "I appreciate that."

"But I have a feeling that Kristen—and maybe Nicole, too—would like for us to get to know each other, er, better, if you know what I mean." Oh Lord, that sounded so stupid. Joanna felt herself grasping at straws. "I'm not interested in a romantic relationship, Tanner. I've got too much going on in my life to get involved, and I don't want you to feel threatened by the girls and their schemes. Forgive me for being so blunt, but I'd prefer to have this out in the open." She'd blurted it out so fast, she wondered if he'd understood. "This dinner invitation was Kristen's idea, not mine. I don't want you to think I had anything to do with it."

"An invitation to dinner isn't exactly a marriage proposal."

"True," Joanna threw back quickly. "But you might think... I don't know. I guess I don't want you to assume I'm interested in you—romantically, that is." She slumped back into the chair, pushed her hair away from her forehead and released a long sigh. "I'm only making matters worse, aren't I?"

"No. If I understand you correctly, you're saying you'd like to be friends and nothing more."

"Right." Pleased with his perceptiveness, Joanna straightened. Glad he could say in a few simple words what had left her breathless.

"The truth of the matter is, I feel much the same way," Tanner went on to explain. "I was married once and it was more than enough."

Joanna found herself nodding enthusiastically. "Exactly. I like my life the way it is. Kristen and I are very close. We just moved into this house and we've lots of plans for re-decorating. My career is going nicely."

"Likewise. I'm too busy with this company to get involved in a relationship, either. The last thing I need right now is a woman to complicate my life."

"A man would only come between Kristen and me at this stage."

"How long have you been divorced?" Tanner asked, folding his hands around his coffee mug.

"Six years."

The information appeared to satisfy him, and he nodded slowly, as though to say he trusted what she was telling him. "It's been five for me."

She nodded, too. Like her, he hadn't immediately jumped into another relationship, nor was he looking for one. No doubt he had his reasons; Joanna knew she had hers.

"Friends?" Tanner asked, and extended his hand for her to shake.

"And nothing more," Joanna added, placing her hand in his.

They exchanged a smile.

"Since Mr. Lund can't be here for the talent show on Wednesday, he wants to take Nicole and me out for dinner next Saturday night," Kristen announced. "Nicole said to ask you if it was all right."

"That's fine," Joanna returned absently, scanning the front page of the Saturday evening newspaper. It had been more than a week since she'd spoken to Tanner. She felt good about the way things had gone that afternoon; they understood each other now, despite their rather uncertain start.

Kristen darted back into the kitchen, returning a minute later. "I think it would be best if you spoke to Mr. Lund yourself, Mom."

"Okay, honey." She'd finished reading Dear Abby and had just turned to the comics section, looking for Garfield, her favourite cat.

"Mom!" Kristen cried impatiently. "Mr. Lund's on the phone now. You can't keep him waiting like this. It's impolite."

Hurriedly Joanna set the paper aside. "For heaven's sake, why didn't you say so earlier?"

"I did. Honestly, Mom, I think you're losing it."

Whatever *it* was sounded serious. The minute Joanna was inside the kitchen, Kristen thrust the telephone receiver into her hand.

"This is Joanna," she said.

"This is Tanner," he answered right away. "Don't feel bad. Nicole claims I'm losing *it*, too."

"I'd take her more seriously if I knew what *it* was."

"Yeah, me, too," Tanner said, and she could hear the laughter in his voice. "Listen, is dinner next Saturday evening all right with you?"

"I can't see a problem at this end."

"Great. The girls suggested that ice-cream parlor they're always talking about."

"The Pink Palace," Joanna said, and managed to swallow a chuckle. Tanner was really letting himself in for a crazy night with those two. Last year Kristen had talked Joanna into dinner there for her birthday. The hamburgers had been as expensive as T-bone steaks, and tough as rawhide. The music was so loud it had impaired Joanna's hearing for an entire week afterward. And the place was packed with teenagers. On the bright side, though, the ice cream was pretty good.

"By the way," Joanna said, "Nicole's welcome to stay here when you're away next week."

"Joanna, that's great. I didn't want to ask, but the kid's been at me ever since the last time. She was worried I was going to send her back to Mrs. Wagner."

"It'll work best for her to stay here, since that's the night of the talent show."

"Are you absolutely sure?"

"Absolutely. It's no trouble at all. Just drop her off—and don't worry."

"Right." He sounded relieved. "And don't wear anything fancy next Saturday night."

"Saturday night?" Joanna asked, lost for a moment.

"Yeah. Didn't you just tell me it was all right for the four of us to go to dinner?"

Five

"I really appreciate this, Joanna," Tanner said. Nicole stood at his side, overnight bag clenched in her hand, her eyes round and sad.

"It's no problem, Tanner. Really."

Tanner hugged his daughter tightly. He briefly closed his eyes and Joanna could feel his regret. He was as upset about missing his daughter's talent-show performance as Nicole was not to have him there.

"Be good, sweetheart."

"I will."

"And I want to hear all the details about tonight when I get back, okay?"

Nicole nodded and attempted a smile.

"I'd be there if I could."

"I know, Dad. Don't worry about it. There'll be plenty of other talent shows. Kristen and I were thinking that if we do really good, we might take our act on the road, the way Daisy Gilbert does."

"Daisy who?" Tanner asked, and raised questioning eyes to Joanna, as if he expected her to supply the answer.

"A singer," was the best Joanna could do. Kristen had as many albums as Joanna had runs in her tights. She found it impossible to keep her daughter's favorite rock stars straight. Apparently Tanner wasn't any more knowledgeable than she was.

"Not just *any* singer, Mom," Kristen corrected impatiently. "Daisy's special. She's only a little older than Nicole and me, and if she can be a rock star at fifteen, then so can we."

Although Joanna hated to squelch such optimism, she suspected that the girls might be missing one minor skill if they hoped to find fame and fortune as professional singers. "But you don't sing."

"Yeah, but we lip-synch real good."

"Come on, Nicole," Kristen said, reaching for her friend's overnight bag. "We've got to practice."

The two disappeared down the hallway and Joanna was left alone with Tanner.

"You have the telephone number for the hotel and the meeting place?" he asked.

"I'll call if there's a problem. Don't worry, Tanner, I'm sure everything's going to be fine."

He nodded, but a tight scowl darkened his face.

"For heaven's sake, stop looking so guilty."

His eyes widened in surprise. "It shows?"

"It might as well be flashing from a marquee."

Tanner grinned and rubbed the side of his jaw with his left hand. "There are only two meetings left that I'll have to deal with personally. Becky's promised to handle the others. You know, when I bought into the company and committed myself to these trips, I didn't think leaving Nicole would be this traumatic. We both hate it—at least, she did until she spent the night here with you and Kristen the last time."

"She's a special little girl."

"Thanks," Tanner said, looking suitably proud. It was obvious that he worked hard at being a good father, and Joanna felt a twinge of conscience for the assumptions she'd made about him earlier.

"Listen," she murmured, then took a deep breath, wondering how best to approach the subject of dinner. "About Saturday night…"

"What about it?"

"I thought, well, it would be best if it were just you and the girls."

Already he was shaking his head, his mouth set in firm lines of resolve. "It wouldn't be the same without you. I owe you, Joanna, and since you won't accept payment for keeping Nicole, then the least you can do is agree to dinner."

"But—"

"If you're worried about this seeming too much like a date—don't. We understand each other."

Her responding smile was decidedly weak. "Okay, if that's the way you want it. Kristen and I'll be ready Saturday at six."

"Good."

Joanna was putting the finishing touches to her makeup before the talent show when the telephone rang.

"I'll get it," Kristen yelled, racing down the hallway as if answering the phone before the second ring was a matter of life and death.

Joanna rolled her eyes toward the ceiling at the

importance telephone conversations had recently assumed for Kristen. She half expected the call to be from Tanner, but then she heard Kristen exclaim, "Hi, Grandma!" Joanna smiled softly, pleased that her mother had remembered the talent show. Her parents were retired and lived in Colville, a town about sixty miles north of Spokane. She knew they would have attended the talent show themselves had road conditions been better. In winter, the families tended to keep in touch by phone because driving could be hazardous. No doubt her mother was calling now to wish Kristen luck.

Bits and pieces of the conversation drifted down the hallway as Kristen chatted excitedly about the show, Nicole's visit and their song.

"Mom, it's Grandma!" Kristen yelled. "She wants to talk to you."

Joanna finished blotting her lipstick and hurried to the phone. "Hi, Mom," she said cheerfully. "It's nice of you to call."

"What's this about you going out on a date Saturday night?"

"Who told you that?" Joanna demanded, groaning silently. Her mother had been telling her for years that she ought to remarry. Joanna felt like throttling Kristen for even mentioning Tanner's name. The last thing she needed was for her parents to start pressuring her about this relationship.

"Why, Kristen told me all about it, and sweetie, if you don't mind my saying so, this man sounds just perfect for you. You're both single parents. He has a daughter, you have a daughter, and the girls are best friends. The arrangement is ideal."

"Mother, please, I don't know what Kristen told you, but Tanner only wants to thank me for watching Nicole while he's away on business. Dinner on Saturday night is not a date!"

"He's taking you to dinner?"

"Me and Kristen and his daughter."

"What was his name again?"

"Tanner Lund," Joanna answered, desperate to change the subject. "Hasn't the weather been nasty this week? I'm really looking forward to spring. I was thinking about planting some annuals along the back fence."

"Tanner Lund," her mother repeated, slowly drawling out his name. "Now that has a nice solid feel to it. What's he like, sweetie?"

"Oh, honestly, Mother, I don't know. He's a man. What more do you want me to say?"

Her mother seemed to approve that piece of information. "I find it interesting that that's the way you view him. I think he could be the one, Joanna."

"Mother, please, how many times do I have to tell you? I'm not going to remarry. Ever!"

A short pause followed her announcement. "We'll see, sweetie, we'll see."

"Aren't you going to wear a dress, Mom?" Kristen gave her another of those scathing glances intended to melt a mother's confidence into puddles of doubt. Joanna had deliberated for hours on what to wear for this evening out with Tanner and the girls. If she chose a dress, something simple and classic like the ones she wore to the office, she might look too formal for a casual outing. The only other dresses she owned were party dresses, and those were so outdated they were almost back in style.

Dark wool pants and a wheat-colored Irish cable-knit sweater had seemed the perfect solution. Or so Joanna had thought until Kristen looked at her and frowned.

"Mom, tonight is important."

"We're going to the Pink Palace, not the Spokane House."

"I know, but Mr. Lund is so nice." Her daughter's gaze fell on the bouquet of pink roses on the dining-room table, and she reverently stroked a bloom. Tanner had arranged for the flowers to be delivered to Nicole and Kristen the night of the talent show. "You can't wear slacks to dinner with the man who sent me my first real flowers," she announced in tones of finality.

Joanna hesitated. "I'm sure this is what Mr. Lund expects," she said with far more confidence than she felt.

"You think so?"

She hoped so! She smiled, praying that her air of certainty would be enough to appease her sceptical daughter. Still, she had to agree with Kristen: Tanner *was* nice. More than nice—that was such a weak word. With every meeting, Joanna's estimation of the man grew. He'd called on Friday to thank her for minding Nicole, who'd gone straight home from school on Thursday afternoon since her father was back, and mentioned he was looking forward to Saturday. He was thoughtful, sensitive, personable and a wonderful father. Not to mention one of the best-looking men she'd ever met. It was unfortunate, really, that she wasn't looking for a husband, because Tanner Lund could easily be a prime candidate.

The word *husband* bounced in Joanna's mind like a ricocheting bullet. She blamed her mother for that. What she'd told her was true—Joanna was finished with marriage, finished with love. Davey had taught her how difficult it was for most men to remain faithful, and Joanna had no intention of repeating those painful lessons. Besides, if a man ever did become part of her life again, it would be someone on her own social and economic level. Not like Tanner Lund. But that didn't mean she was completely blind to male charms. On the contrary, she saw handsome men every day, worked with several, and had even dated a few. However, it was Tanner Lund she found herself thinking about lately, and that bothered Joanna. It bothered her a lot.

The best thing to do was nip this near relationship in the bud. She'd go to dinner with him this once, but only this once, and that would be the end of it.

"They're here!" The drape swished back into place as Kristen bolted away from the large picture window.

Calmly Joanna opened the hall closet and retrieved their winter coats. She might appear outwardly composed, but her fingers were shaking. The prospect of seeing Tanner left her trembling, and that fact drained away what little confidence she'd managed to accumulate over the past couple of days.

Both Tanner and Nicole came to the front door. Kristen held out her hands, and Nicole gripped them eagerly. Soon the two were jumping up and down like pogo sticks gone berserk.

"I can tell we're in for a fun evening," Tanner muttered under his breath.

He looked wonderful, Joanna admitted grudgingly. The kind of man every woman dreams about—well, almost every woman. Joanna longed to think of herself as immune to the handsome Mr. Lund. Unfortunately she wasn't.

Since their last meeting, she'd tried to figure out when her feelings for Tanner had changed. The roses had done it, she decided. Ordering them for Kristen and Nicole had been so thoughtful, and the girls had been ecstatic at the gesture.

When they'd finished lip-synching their song, they'd bowed before the auditorium full of appreciative parents. Then the school principal, Mr. Holliday, had stood at their side and presented them each with a beautiful bouquet of long-stemmed pink roses. Flowers Tanner had wired because he couldn't be there to watch their act.

"Are you ready?" Tanner asked, holding open the door for Joanna.

She nodded. "I think so."

Although it was early, a line had already begun to form outside the Pink Palace when they arrived. The minute they pulled into the parking lot, they were accosted by a loud, vibrating rock-and-roll song that might have been an old Jerry Lee Lewis number.

"It looks like we'll have to wait," Joanna commented. "That lineup's getting longer by the minute."

"I had my secretary make reservations," Tanner told her. "I heard this place really grooves on a Saturday night."

"Grooves!" Nicole repeated, smothering her giggles behind her cupped palm. Kristen laughed with her.

Turner leaned his head close to Joanna's. "It's difficult to reason with a generation that grew up without Janis and Jimi!"

Janis Joplin and Jimi Hendrix were a bit before Joanna's time, too, but she knew what he meant.

The Pink Palace was exactly as Joanna remembered. The popular ice-cream parlor was decorated in a fifties theme, with old-fashioned circular booths and outdated jukeboxes. The waitresses wore billowing pink skirts with a French poodle design and roller-skated between tables, taking and delivering orders. Once inside, Joanna, Tanner and the girls were seated almost immediately and handed huge menus. Neither girl bothered to read through the selections, having made their choices in the car. They'd both decided on cheeseburgers and banana splits.

By the time the waitress, chewing on a thick wad of bubble gum, skated to a stop at their table, Joanna had made her selection, too.

"A cheeseburger and a banana split," she said, grinning at the girls.

"Same here," Tanner said, "and coffee, please."

"I'll have a cup, too," Joanna added.

The teenager wrote down their order and glided toward the kitchen.

Joanna opened her purse and brought out a small wad of cotton wool.

"What's that for?" Tanner wanted to know when she pulled it apart into four fluffy balls and handed two of them to him, keeping the other pair for herself.

She pointed to her ears. "The last time I was here,

I was haunted for days by a ringing in my ears that sounded suspiciously like an old Elvis tune."

Tanner chuckled and leaned across the table to shout, "It does get a bit loud, doesn't it?"

Kristen and Nicole looked from one parent to the other then shouted together, "If it's too loud, you're too old!"

Joanna raised her hand. "Guilty as charged."

Tanner nodded and shared a smile with Joanna. The smile did funny things to her stomach, and Joanna pressed her hands over her abdomen in a futile effort to quell her growing awareness of Tanner. A warning light flashed in her mind, spelling out danger.

Joanna wasn't sure what had come over her, but whatever it was, she didn't like it.

Their meal arrived, and for a while, at least, Joanna could direct her attention to that. The food was better than she remembered. The cheeseburgers were juicy and tender and the banana splits divine. She promised herself she'd eat cottage cheese and fruit every day at lunch for the next week to balance all the extra calories from this one meal.

While Joanna and Tanner exchanged only the occasional remark, the girls chattered happily throughout dinner. When the waitress skated away with the last of their empty plates, Tanner suggested a movie.

"Great idea!" Nicole cried, enthusiastically seconded by Kristen.

"What do you think, Joanna?" asked Tanner.

She started to say that the evening had been full enough—until she found two eager young faces looking hopefully at her. She couldn't finish her sentence; it just wasn't in her to dash their good time.

"Sure," she managed instead, trying to insert a bit of excitement into her voice.

"*Teen Massacre* is showing at the mall," Nicole said, shooting a glance in her father's direction. "Donny Rosenburg saw it and claims it scared him out of his wits, but then Donny doesn't have many."

Kristen laughed and nodded, apparently well-acquainted with the witless Donny.

Without the least bit of hesitation, Tanner shook his head. "No way, Nicole."

"Come on, Dad, everyone's seen it. The only reason it got an adult rating is because of the blood and gore, and I've seen that lots of times."

"Discussion is closed." He spoke without raising his voice, but the authority behind his words was enough to convince Joanna she'd turn up the loser if she ever crossed Tanner Lund. Still, she knew she wouldn't hesitate if she felt he was wrong, but in this case she agreed with him completely.

Nicole's lower lip jutted out rebelliously, and for a minute Joanna thought the girl might try to argue her case. But she wasn't surprised when Nicole yielded without further argument.

Deciding which movie to see involved some real negotiating. The girls had definite ideas of what was acceptable, as did Tanner and Joanna. Like Tanner, Joanna wasn't about to allow her daughter to see a movie with an adult rating, even if it was "only because of the blood and gore."

They finally compromised on a comedy that starred a popular teen idol. The girls thought that would be "all right," but they made it clear that *Teen Massacre* was their first choice.

Half an hour later they were inside the theater, and Tanner asked, "Anyone for popcorn?"

"Me," Kristen said.

"Me, too, and could we both have a Coke and chocolate-covered raisins, too?" Nicole asked.

Tanner rolled his eyes and, grinning, glanced toward Joanna. "What about you?"

"Nothing." She didn't know where the girls were going to put all this food, but she knew where it would end up if she were to consume it. Her hips! She sometimes suspected that junk food didn't even pass through her stomach, but attached itself directly to her hip bones.

"You're sure?"

"Positive."

Tanner returned a moment later with three large boxes of popcorn and other assorted treats.

As soon as they'd emptied Tanner's arms of all but one box of popcorn, the girls started into the auditorium.

"Hey, you two, wait for us," Joanna called after them, bewildered by the way they'd hurried off without waiting for her and Tanner.

Kristen and Nicole stopped abruptly and turned around, a look of pure horror on their young faces.

"You're not going to sit with us, are you, Mom?" Kristen wailed. "You just can't!"

"Why not?" This was news to Joanna. Sure, it had been a while since she'd gone to a movie with her daughter, but Kristen had always sat with her in the past.

"Someone might see us," her daughter went on to

explain, in tones of exaggerated patience. "No one sits with their parents anymore. Not even woosies."

"Woosies?"

"Sort of like nerds, only worse!" Kristen said.

"Sitting with us is obviously a social embarrassment to be avoided at all costs," Tanner muttered.

"Can we go now, Mom?" Kristen pleaded. "I don't want to miss the previews."

Joanna nodded, still a little stunned. She enjoyed going out to a movie now and again, usually accompanied by her daughter and often several of Kristen's friends. Until tonight, no one had openly objected to sitting in the same row with her. However, now that Joanna thought about it, Kristen hadn't been interested in going to the movies for the past couple of months.

"I guess this is what happens when they hit sixth grade," Tanner said, holding the auditorium door for Joanna.

She walked down the center aisle and paused by an empty row near the back, checking with Tanner before she entered. Neither of them sat down, though, until they'd located the girls. Kristen and Nicole were three rows from the front and had slid down so far that their eyes were level with the seats ahead of them.

"Ah, the joys of fatherhood," Tanner commented, after they'd taken their places. "Not to mention motherhood."

Joanna still felt a little taken aback by what had happened. She thought she had a close relationship with Kristen, and yet her daughter had never said a word about not wanting to be anywhere near her in a movie theater. She knew this might sound like a trivial concern to some, but she couldn't help worrying that the solid foundation she'd spent a decade reinforcing had started to crumble.

"Joanna?"

She turned to Tanner and tried to smile, but the attempt was unconvincing.

"What's wrong?"

Joanna fluttered her hand weakly, unable to find her voice. "Nothing." That came out sounding as though she might burst into tears any second.

"Is it Kristen?"

She nodded wildly.

"Because she didn't want to sit with us?"

Her hair bounced against her shoulders as she nodded again.

"The girls wanting to be by themselves bothers you?"

"No... Yes. I don't know what I'm feeling. She's growing up, Tanner, and I guess it just hit me right between the eyes."

"It happened to me last week," Tanner said thoughtfully. "I found Nicole wearing a pair of tights. Hell, I didn't even know they made them for girls her age."

"They do, believe it or not," Joanna informed him. "Kristen did the same thing."

He shook his head as though he couldn't quite grasp the concept. "But they're only eleven."

"Going on sixteen."

"Has Kristen tried pasting on those fake fingernails yet?" Tanner shuddered in exaggerated disgust.

Joanna covered her mouth with one hand to hold back an attack of giggles. "Those press-on things turned up every place imaginable for weeks afterward."

Tanner turned sideways in his seat. "What about makeup?" he asked urgently.

"I caught her trying to sneak out of the house one morning last month. She was wearing the brightest eye shadow I've ever seen in my life. Tanner, I swear if she'd been standing on a shore, she could have guided lost ships into port."

He smiled, then dropped his gaze, looking uncomfortable. "So you do let her wear makeup?"

"I'm holding off as long as I can," Joanna admitted. "At the very least, she'll have to wait until seventh grade. That was when my mother let me. I don't think it's so unreasonable to expect Kristen to wait until junior high."

Tanner relaxed against the back of his seat and nodded a couple of times. "I'm glad to hear that. Nicole's been after me to 'wake up and smell the coffee,' as she puts it, for the past six months. Hell, I didn't know who to ask about these things. It really isn't something I'm comfortable discussing with my secretary."

"What about her mother?"

His eyes hardened. "She only sees Nicole when it's convenient, and it hasn't been for the past three years."

"I...I didn't mean to pry."

"You weren't. Carmen and I didn't exactly part on the best of terms. She's got a new life now and apparently doesn't want any reminders of the past—not that I totally blame her. We made each other miserable. Frankly, Joanna, my feelings about getting married again are the same as yours. One failed marriage was enough for me."

The theater lights dimmed then, and the sound track

started. Tanner leaned back and crossed his long legs, balancing one ankle on the opposite knee.

Joanna settled back, too, grateful that the movie they'd selected was a comedy. Her emotions were riding too close to the surface this evening. She could see herself bursting into tears at the slightest hint of sadness—for that matter, joy. Bambi traipsing through the woods would have done her in just then.

Joanna was so caught up in her thoughts that when Tanner and the others around her let out a boisterous laugh, she'd completely missed whatever had been so hilarious.

Without thinking, she reached over and grabbed a handful of Tanner's popcorn. She discovered that the crunchiness and the buttery, salty flavor suited her mood. Tanner held the box on the arm between them to make sharing easier.

The next time Joanna sent her fingers digging, they encountered Tanner's. "Sorry," she murmured, pulling her hand free.

"No problem," he answered, tilting the box her way.

Joanna munched steadily. Before she knew it, the popcorn was gone and her fingers were laced with Tanner's, her hand firmly clasped in his.

The minute he reached for her hand, Joanna lost track of what was happening on the screen. Holding hands seemed such an innocent gesture, something teenagers did. He certainly didn't mean anything by it, Joanna told herself. It was just that her emotions were so confused lately, and she wasn't even sure why.

She liked Tanner, Joanna realised anew, liked him very much. And she thoroughly enjoyed Nicole. For the first time since her divorce, she could imagine getting involved with another man, and the thought frightened her. All right, it terrified her. This man belonged to a different world. Besides, she wasn't ready. Good grief, six years should have given her ample time to heal, but she'd been too afraid to lift the bandage.

When the movie was over, Tanner drove them home. The girls were tired, but managed to carry on a lively backseat conversation. The front seat was a different story. Neither Tanner nor Joanna had much to say.

"Would you like to come in for coffee?" Joanna asked when Tanner pulled into her driveway, although she was silently wishing he'd decline. Her nerves continued to clamor from the hand holding, and she wanted some time alone to organise her thoughts.

"Can we, Dad? Please?" Nicole begged. "Kristen and I want to watch the Saturday night videos together."

"You're sure?" Tanner looked at Joanna, his brow creased with concern.

She couldn't answer. She wasn't sure of anything just then. "Of course," she forced herself to say. "It'll only take a minute or two to brew a pot."

"All right, then," Tanner said, and the girls let out whoops of delight.

Occasionally Joanna wondered if their daughters would ever get tired of one another's company. Probably, although they hadn't shown any signs of it yet. As far as she knew, the two girls had never had a serious disagreement.

Kristen and Nicole disappeared as soon as they got into the house. Within seconds, the television could be heard blaring rock music, which had recently become a familiar sound in the small one-storey house.

Tanner followed Joanna into the kitchen and stood leaning against the counter while she filled the automatic coffeemaker with water. Her movements were jerky and abrupt. She felt awkward, ungraceful—as though this was the first time she'd ever been alone with a man. And that was a ridiculous way to feel, especially since the girls were practically within sight.

"I enjoyed tonight," Tanner commented, as she removed two cups from the cupboard.

"I did, too." She tossed him a lazy smile over her shoulder. But Tanner's eyes held hers, and it was as if she was seeing him for the first time. She half turned toward him, suddenly aware of how tall and lean he was, how thick and soft his dark hair. With an effort, Joanna looked from those mesmerising blue eyes and returned to the task of making coffee, although her fingers didn't seem willing to cooperate.

She stood waiting for the dark liquid to filter its way into the glass pot. Never had it seemed to take so long.

"Joanna."

Judging by the loudness of his voice, Tanner was standing directly behind her. A beat of silence followed before she turned around to face him.

Tanner's hands grasped her shoulders. "It's been a long time since I've sat in a movie and held a girl's hand."

She lowered her eyes and nodded. "Me, too."

"I felt like a kid again."

She'd been thinking much the same thing herself.

"I want to kiss you, Joanna."

She didn't need an analyst to inform her that kissing Tanner was something best avoided. She was about to tell him so when his hands gripped her waist and pulled her away from the support of the kitchen counter. A little taken aback, Joanna threw up her hands, as if to ward him off. But the minute they came into contact with the muscled hardness of his chest, they lost their purpose.

The moment Tanner's warm mouth claimed her lips, she felt an excitement that was almost shocking in its intensity. Her hands clutched the collar of his shirt as she eagerly gave herself up to the forgotten sensations. It had been so long since a man had kissed her like this.

The kiss was over much too soon. Far sooner than Joanna would have liked. The fire of his mouth had ignited a response in her she'd believed long dead. She was amazed at how readily it had sprung back to life. When Tanner dropped his arms and released her, Joanna felt suddenly weak, barely able to remain upright.

Her hand found her chest and she heaved a giant breath. "I...don't think that was a good idea."

Tanner's brows drew together, forming a ledge over his narrowed eyes. "I'm not sure I do, either, but it seemed right. I don't know what's happening between us, Joanna, and it's confusing the hell out of me."

"You? I'm the one who made it abundantly clear from the outset that I wasn't looking for a romantic involvement."

"I know, and I agree, but—"

"I'm more than pleased Kristen and Nicole are good friends, but I happen to like my life the way it is, thank you."

Tanner's frown grew darker, his expression both baffled and annoyed. "I feel the same way. It was a kiss, not a suggestion we live in sin."

"I...really wish you hadn't done that, Tanner."

"I apologize. Trust me, it won't happen again," he muttered, and buried his hands deep inside his pockets. "In fact it would probably be best if we forgot the entire incident."

"I agree totally."

"Fine then." He stalked out of the kitchen, but not before Joanna found herself wondering if she *could* forget it.

Six

A kiss was really such a minor thing, Joanna mused, slowly rotating her pencil between her palms. She'd made a criminal case out of nothing, and embarrassed both Tanner and herself.

"Joanna, have you had time to read over the Osborne loan application yet?" her boss, Robin Simpson asked, strolling up to her desk.

"Ah, no, not yet," Joanna said, her face flushing with guilt.

Robin frowned as he studied her. "What's been with you today? Every time I see you, you're gazing at the wall with a faraway look in your eye."

"Nothing's wrong." Blindly she reached toward her In basket and grabbed a file, although she hadn't a clue which one it was.

"If I didn't know better, I'd say you were daydreaming about a man."

Joanna managed a short, sarcastic laugh meant to deny everything. "Men are the last thing on my mind," she said flippantly. It was a half-truth. Men in the plural didn't interest her, but *man*, as in Tanner Lund, well, that was another matter.

Over the years Joanna had gone out of her way to avoid men she was attracted to—it was safer. She dated occasionally, but usually men who might be classified as pleasant, men for whom she could never feel anything beyond a mild friendship. Magnetism, charm and sex appeal were lost on her, thanks to a husband who'd possessed all three and systematically destroyed her faith in the possibility of a lasting relationship. At least, those qualities hadn't piqued her interest again, until she met Tanner. Okay, so her dating habits for the past few years had been a bit premeditated, but everyone deserved a night out now and again. It didn't seem fair to be denied the pleasure of a fun evening simply because she wasn't in the market for another husband. So she'd dated, not a lot, but some and nothing in the past six years had affected her as much as those few short hours with Nicole's father.

"Joanna!"

She jerked her head up to discover her boss still standing beside her desk. "Yes?"

"The Osborne file."

She briefly closed her eyes in a futile effort to clear her thoughts. "What about it?"

Robin glared at the ceiling and paused, as though pleading with the light fixture for patience. "Read it and get back to me before the end of the day—if that isn't too much to ask?"

"Sure," she grumbled, wondering what had put Robin in such a foul mood. She picked up the loan application and was halfway through it before she realized the name on it wasn't Osborne. Great! If her day continued like this, she could blame Tanner Lund for getting her fired.

When Joanna arrived home three hours later she was exhausted and short-tempered. She hadn't been herself all day, mainly because she'd been so preoccupied with thoughts of Tanner Lund and the way he'd kissed her. She was overreacting—she'd certainly been kissed before, so it shouldn't be such a big deal. But it was. Her behaviour demonstrated all the maturity of someone Kristen's age, she chided herself. She'd simply forgotten how to act with men; it was too long since she'd been involved with one. The day wasn't a complete waste, however. She'd made a couple of important decisions in the last few hours, and she wanted to clear the air with her daughter before matters got completely out of hand.

"Hi, honey."

"Hi."

Kristen's gaze didn't waver from the television screen where a talk-show host was interviewing a man whose brilliant red hair was so short on top it stuck straight up and so messy in front it fell over his face, almost reaching his left eye and part of his nose.

"Who's that?"

Kristen gave a deep sigh of wonder and adolescent love. "You mean you don't know? I've been in love with Ed Sheeran for a whole year and you don't even know him when you see him?"

"No, I can't say that I do."

"Oh, Mom, honestly, get with it."

There *it* was again. First she was losing *it* and now she was supposed to get with *it*. Joanna wished her daughter would decide which she wanted.

"We need to talk."

Kristen reluctantly dragged her eyes away from her idol. "Mom, this is important. Can't it wait?"

Frustrated, Joanna sighed and muttered, "I suppose."

"Good."

Kristen had already tuned her out. Joanna strolled into the kitchen and realised she hadn't taken the hamburger out of the freezer to thaw. Great. So much for the tacos she'd planned to make for dinner. She opened and closed cupboard doors, rummaging around for something interesting. A can of tuna fish wasn't likely to meet with Kristen's approval. One thing about her daughter that the approach of the teen years hadn't disrupted was her healthy appetite.

Joanna stuck her head around the corner. "How does tuna casserole sound for dinner?"

Kristen didn't even look in her direction, just held out her arm and jerked her thumb toward the carpet.

"Soup and sandwiches?"

Once more Kristen's thumb headed downward, and Joanna groaned.

"Bacon, lettuce and tomato on toast with chicken noodle soup," she tried. "And that's the best I can do. Take it or leave it."

Kristen sighed. "If that's the final offer, I'll take it. But I thought we were having tacos."

"We were. I forgot to take out the hamburger."

"All right, BLTs," Kristen muttered, reversing the direction of her thumb.

Joanna was frying the bacon when Kristen joined her, sitting on a stool while her mother worked. "You wanted to talk to me about something?"

"Yes." Joanna concentrated on spreading mayonnaise over slices of whole-wheat toast, as she made an effort to gather her scattered thoughts. She cast about for several moments, trying to come up with a way of saying what needed to be said without making more of it than necessary.

"It must be something big," Kristen commented. "Did my teacher phone you at work or something?"

"No, should she have?" She raised her eyes and scrutinised Kristen's face closely.

Kristen gave a quick denial with a shake of her head. "No way. I'm a star pupil this year. Nicole and I are both doing great. Just wait until report-card time, then you'll see."

"I believe you." Kristen had been getting top marks all year, and Joanna was proud of how well her daughter was doing. "What I have to say concerns Nicole and—" she hesitated, swallowing tightly "—her father."

"Mr. Lund sure is good-looking, isn't he?" Kristen said enthusiastically, watching for Joanna's reaction.

Reluctantly Joanna nodded, hoping to sound casual. "I suppose."

"Oh, come on, Mom, he's a hunk."

"All right," Joanna admitted slowly. "I'll grant you that Tanner has a certain amount of...appeal."

Kristen grinned, looking pleased with herself.

"Actually it was Mr. Lund I wanted to talk to you about," Joanna continued, placing a layer of tomato slices on the toast.

"Really?" The brown eyes opened even wider.

"Yes, well, I wanted to tell you that I...I don't think

it would be a good idea for the four of us to go on doing things together."

Abruptly Kristen's face fell with surprise and disappointment. "Why not?"

"Well…because he and I are both really busy." Even to her own ears, the statement sounded illogical, but it was difficult to tell her own daughter that she was frightened of her attraction to the man. Difficult to explain why nothing could come of it.

"Because you're both busy? Come on, Mom, that doesn't make any sense."

"All right, I'll be honest." She wondered whether an eleven-year-old could grasp the complexities of adult relationships. "I don't want to give Nicole's dad the wrong idea," she said carefully.

Kristen leaned forward, setting her elbows on the kitchen counter and resting her face in both hands. Her gaze looked sharp enough to shatter diamonds. "The wrong idea about what?" she asked.

"Me," Joanna said, swallowing uncomfortably.

"You?" Kristen repeated thoughtfully, a frown creasing her smooth brow. She relaxed then and released a huge sigh. "Oh, I see. You think Mr. Lund might think you're in the marriage market."

Joanna pointed a fork at her daughter. "Bingo!"

"But, Mom, I think it would be great if you and Nicole's dad got together. In fact, Nicole and I were talking about it just today. Think about all the advantages. We could all be a real family, and you could have more babies… I don't know if I ever told you this, but I'd really like a baby brother, and so would Nicole. And if you married Mr. Lund we could take family vacations together. You wouldn't have to work, because…

I don't know if you realize this, but Mr. Lund is pretty rich. You could stay home and bake cookies and sew and stuff."

Joanna was so surprised that it took her a minute to find her voice. Openmouthed, she waved the fork jerkily around. "No way, Kristen." Joanna's knees felt rubbery, and before she could slip to the floor, she slumped into a chair. All this time she'd assumed she was a good mother, giving her daughter everything she needed physically and emotionally, making up to Kristen as much as she could for her father's absence. But she apparently hadn't done enough. And Kristen and Nicole were scheming to get Joanna and Tanner together. As in married!

Something had to be done.

She decided to talk to Tanner, but an opportunity didn't present itself until much later that evening when Kristen was in bed, asleep. At least Joanna hoped her daughter was asleep. She dialled his number and prayed Nicole wouldn't answer.

Thankfully she didn't.

"Tanner, it's Joanna," she whispered, cupping her hand over the mouthpiece, taking no chance that Kristen could overhear their conversation.

"What's the matter? Have you got laryngitis?"

"No," she returned hoarsely, straining her voice. "I don't want Kristen to hear me talking to you."

"I see. Should I pretend you're someone else so Nicole won't tell on you?" he whispered back.

"Please." She didn't appreciate the humor in his voice. Obviously he had yet to realize the seriousness of the situation. "We need to talk."

"We do?"

"Trust me, Tanner. You have no idea what I just learned. The girls are planning on us getting married."

"Married?" he shouted.

That, Joanna had known, would get a reaction out of him.

"When do you want to meet?"

"As soon as possible." He still seemed to think she was joking, but she couldn't blame him. If the situation were reversed, no doubt she would react the same way. "Kristen said something about the two of them swimming Wednesday night at the community pool. What if we meet at Denny's for coffee after you drop Nicole off?"

"What time?" He said it as though they were planning a reconnaissance mission deep into enemy territory.

"Seven ten." That would give them both a few extra minutes to make it to the restaurant.

"Shall we synchronise our watches?"

"This isn't funny, Tanner."

"I'm not laughing."

But he was, and Joanna was furious with him. "I'll see you then."

"Seven-ten, Wednesday night at Denny's," he repeated. "I'll be there."

On the evening of their scheduled meeting, Joanna arrived at the restaurant before Tanner. She already regretted suggesting they meet at Denny's, but it was too late to change that now. There were bound to be other customers who would recognise either Tanner or her, and Joanna feared that word of their meeting could somehow filter back to the girls. She'd been guilty of underestimating them before; she wouldn't make the same mistake a second time. If Kristen and Nicole did hear about this private meeting, they'd consider it justification for further interference.

Tanner strolled into the restaurant and glanced around. He didn't seem to recognise Joanna, and she moved her sunglasses down her nose and gave him an abrupt wave.

He took one look at her, and even from the other side of the room she could see he was struggling to hold in his laughter.

"What's with the scarf and sunglasses?"

"I'm afraid someone might recognize us and tell the girls." It made perfect sense to her, but obviously not to him. Joanna forgave him since he didn't know the extent of the difficulties facing them.

But all he said was, "I see." He inserted his hands in the pockets of his overcoat and walked lazily past her, whistling. "Should I sit here or would you prefer the next booth?"

"Don't be silly."

"I'm not going to comment on that."

"For heaven's sake," Joanna hissed, "sit down before someone notices you."

"Someone notices me? Lady, you're wearing sunglasses at night, in the dead of winter, and with that scarf tied around your chin you look like an old woman."

"Tanner," she said, "this is not the time to crack jokes."

A smile lifted his features as he slid into the booth opposite her. He reached for a menu. "Are you hungry?"

"No." His attitude was beginning to annoy her. "I'm just having coffee."

"Nicole cooked dinner tonight, and frankly I'm starving."

When the waitress appeared he ordered a complete dinner. Joanna asked for coffee.

"Okay, what's up, Sherlock?" he asked, once the coffee had been poured.

"To begin with I...I think Kristen and Nicole saw you kiss me the other night."

He made no comment, but his brow puckered slightly.

"It seems the two of them have been talking, and from what I gather they're interested in getting us, er, together."

"I see."

To Joanna's dismay, Tanner didn't seem to be the slightest bit concerned by her revelation.

"That troubles you?"

"Tanner," she said, leaning toward him, "to quote my daughter, 'Nicole and I have been talking and we thought it would be great if you and Mr. Lund got together. You could have more babies and we could go on vacations and be a real family and you could stay home and bake cookies and stuff.'" She waited for his reaction, but his face remained completely impassive.

"What kind of cookies?" he asked finally.

"Tanner, if you're going to turn this into a joke, I'm leaving." As far as Joanna was concerned, he deserved to be tormented by two dedicated eleven-year-old matchmakers! She started to slide out of the booth, but he stopped her with an upraised hand.

"All right, I'm sorry."

He didn't sound too contrite, and she gave a weak sigh of disgust. "You may consider this a joking matter, but I don't."

"Joanna, we're both mature adults," he stated calmly. "We aren't going to let a couple of eleven-year-old girls manipulate us!"

"Yes, but—"

"From the first, we've been honest with each other. That isn't going to change. You have no interest in re-marriage—to me or anyone else—and I feel the same way. As long as we continue as we are now, the girls don't have a prayer."

"It's more than that," Joanna said vehemently. "We need to look past their schemes to the root of the problem."

"Which is?"

"Tanner, obviously we're doing something wrong as single parents."

He frowned. "What makes you say that?"

"Isn't it obvious? Kristen, and it seems equally true for Nicole, wants a complete family. What Kristen is really saying is that she longs for a father. Nicole is telling you she'd like a mother."

The humour drained out of Tanner's eyes, replaced with a look of real concern. "I see. And you think this all started because Kristen and Nicole saw us kissing?"

"I don't know," she murmured, shaking her head. "But I do know my daughter, and when she wants something, she goes after it with the force of a bull-dog and won't let up. Once she's got it in her head that you and I are destined for each other, it's going to be pretty difficult for her to accept that all we'll ever be is friends."

"Nicole can get that way about certain things," he said thoughtfully.

The waitress delivered his roast beef sandwich and refilled Joanna's coffee cup.

Maybe she'd overreacted to the situation, but she couldn't help being worried. "I suppose you think I'm making more of a fuss about this than necessary," she said, flustered and a little embarrassed.

"About the girls manipulating us?"

"No, about the fact that we've both tried so hard to be good single parents, and obviously we're doing something wrong."

"I will admit that part concerns me."

"I don't mind telling you, Tanner, I've been in a panic all week, wondering where I've failed. We've got to come to terms with this. Make some important decisions."

"What do you suggest?"

"To start with, we've got to squelch any hint of personal involvement. I realize a certain amount of contact will be unavoidable with the girls being such close friends." She paused and chewed on her bottom lip. "I don't want to disrupt their relationship."

"I agree with you there. Being friends with Kristen has meant a good deal to Nicole."

"You and I went months without talking to each other," Joanna said, recalling that they'd only recently met. "There's no need for us to see each other now, is there?"

"That won't work."

"Why not?"

"Nicole will be spending the night with you again next Thursday—that is, unless you'd rather she didn't."

"Of course she can stay."

Tanner nodded, looking relieved. "To be honest, I don't think she'd go back to Mrs. Wagner's anymore without raising a big fuss."

"Taking care of Nicole is one thing, but the four of us doing anything together is out of the question."

Once more he nodded, but he didn't look pleased with the suggestion. "I think that would be best, too."

"We can't give them any encouragement."

Pushing his plate aside, Tanner reached for his water glass, cupping it with both hands. "You know, Joanna, I think a lot of you." He paused, then gave her a teasing smile. "You have a habit of dressing a little oddly every now and then, but other than that I respect your judgment. I'd like to consider you a friend."

She decided to let his comment about her choice of clothing slide. "I'd like to be your friend, too," she told him softly.

He grinned, and his gaze held hers for a long uninterrupted moment before they both looked away. "I know you think that kiss the other night was a big mistake, and I suppose you're right, but I'm not sorry it happened." He hesitated, as though waiting for her to argue with him, and when she didn't, he continued. "It's been a lot of years since I held a woman's hand at a movie or kissed her the way I did you. It was good to feel that young and innocent again."

Joanna dropped her gaze to her half-filled cup. It had felt right for her, too. So right that she'd been frightened out of her wits ever since. She could easily fall in love with Tanner, and that would be the worst possible thing for her. She just wasn't ready to take those risks again. They came from different worlds, too, and she'd never fit comfortably in his. Yet every time she thought about that kiss, she started to shake from the inside out.

"In a strange sort of way we need each other," Tanner went on, his look thoughtful. "Nicole needs a strong loving woman to identify with, to fill a mother's role, and she thinks you're wonderful."

"And Kristen needs to see a man who can be a father, putting the needs of his family before his own."

"I think it's only natural for the two of them to try to get us together," Tanner added. "It's something we should be prepared to deal with in the future."

"You're right," Joanna agreed, understanding exactly what he meant. "We need each other to help provide what's lacking in our daughters' lives. But we can't get involved with each other." She didn't know any other way to say it but bluntly.

"I agree," he said, with enough conviction to lay aside any doubt Joanna might still hold.

They were silent for a long moment.

"Why?"

Strangely, Joanna knew immediately what he was asking. She had the same questions about what had happened between him and Nicole's mother.

"Davey was—is—the most charming personable man I've ever met. I was fresh out of college and so in love with him I didn't stop to think." She paused and glanced away, not daring to look at Tanner. Her voice had fallen so low it was almost a whisper. "We were engaged when my best friend, Carol, told me Davey had made a pass at her. Fool that I was, I didn't believe her. I thought she was jealous that Davey had chosen me to love and marry. I was sick that my friend would stoop to anything so underhand. I always knew Carol found him attractive—most women did—and I was devastated that she would lie that way. I trusted Davey so completely that I didn't even ask him about the incident. Later, after we were married, there were a lot of times when he said he was working late, a lot of unexplained absences, but I didn't question those, either. He was building his career in real estate, and if he had to put in extra hours, well, that was understandable. All those nights I sat alone, trusting him when he claimed he was working, believing with all my heart that he was doing his utmost to build a life for us…and then learning he'd been with some other woman."

"How'd you find out?"

"The first time?"

"You mean there was more than once?"

She nodded, hating to let Tanner know how many times she'd forgiven Davey, how many times she'd taken him back after he'd pleaded and begged and promised it would never happen again.

"I was blind to his wandering eye for the first couple of years. What they say about ignorance being bliss is true. When I found out, I was physically sick. When I realised how I'd fallen for his lies, it was even worse, and yet I stuck it out with him, trusting that everything would be better, everything would change…someday. I wanted so badly to believe him, to trust him, that I accepted anything he told me, no matter how implausible it sounded.

"The problem was that the more I forgave him, the lower my self-esteem dropped. I became convinced it was all my fault. I obviously lacked something, since he…felt a need to seek out other women."

"You know now that's not true, don't you?" His voice was so gentle, so caring, that Joanna battled down a rush of emotion.

"There'd never been a divorce in my family," she told him quietly. "My parents have been married nearly forty years, and my brothers all have happy marriages. I think that was one of the reasons I held on so long. I just didn't know how to let go. I'd be devastated and crushed when I learned about his latest affair, yet I kept coming back for more. I suppose I believed Davey would change. Something magical would happen and all our problems would disappear. Only it never did. One afternoon—I don't even know what prompted it… All I knew was that I couldn't stay in the marriage any longer. I packed Kristen's and my things and walked out. I've never been back, never wanted to go back."

Tanner reached for her hand, and his fingers wrapped warmly around hers. A moment passed before he spoke, and when he did, his voice was tight with remembered pain. "I thought Carmen was the sweetest, gentlest woman in the world. As nonsensical as it sounds, I think I was in love with her before I even knew her name. She was a college cheerleader and a homecoming queen, and I felt like a nobody. By chance, we met several years after graduation when I'd just begun making a name for myself. I'd bought my first company, a small aluminum window manufacturer back in West Virginia. And I was working night and day to see it through those first rough weeks of transition.

"I was high on status," Tanner admitted, his voice filled with regret. "Small-town boy makes good—that kind of stuff. She'd been the most popular girl in my college year, and dating her was the fulfilment of a fantasy. She'd recently broken up with a guy she'd been involved with for two years and had something to prove herself, I suppose." He focused his gaze away from Joanna. "Things got out of hand and a couple of months later Carmen announced she was pregnant. To be honest, I was happy about it, thrilled. There was never any question whether I'd marry her. By then I was so in love with her I couldn't see straight. Eight months after the wedding, Nicole was born…" He hesitated, as though gathering his thoughts. "Some women are meant to be mothers, but not Carmen. She didn't even like to hold Nicole, didn't want anything to do with her. I'd come home at night and find that Carmen had neglected Nicole most of the day. But I made excuses for her, reasoned everything out in my own mind—the unexplained bruises on the baby, the fear I saw in Nicole's eyes whenever her mother was around. It got so bad that I started dropping Nicole off at my parents', just so I could be sure she was being looked after properly."

Joanna bit the corner of her lip at the raw pain she witnessed in Tanner's eyes. She was convinced he didn't speak of his marriage often, just as she rarely talked about Davey, but this was necessary if they were to understand each other.

"To be fair to Carmen, I wasn't much of a husband in those early months. Hell, I didn't have time to be. I was feeling like a big success when we met, but that didn't last long. Things started going wrong at work and I damn near lost my shirt.

"Later," he continued slowly, "I learned that the entire time I was struggling to hold the company together, Carmen was seeing her old boyfriend, Sam Dailey."

"Oh, Tanner."

"Nicole's my daughter, there was no doubting that. But Carmen had never really wanted children, and she felt trapped in the marriage. We separated when Nicole was less than three years old."

"I thought you said you'd only been divorced five years?"

"We have. It took Carmen a few years to get around to the legal aspect of things. I wasn't in any rush, since I had no intention of ever marrying again."

"What's happened to Carmen since? Did she remarry?"

"Eventually. She lived with Sam for several years, and the last thing I heard was they'd split up and she married a professional baseball player."

"Does Nicole ever see her mother?" Joanna remembered that he'd said his ex-wife saw Nicole only when it was convenient.

"She hasn't in the past three years. The thing I worry about most is having Carmen show up someday, demanding that Nicole come to live with her. Nicole doesn't remember anything about those early years—thank God—and she seems to have formed a rosy image of her mother. She keeps Carmen's picture in her bedroom and every once in a while I'll see her staring at it wistfully." He paused and glanced at his watch. "What time were we supposed to pick up the kids?"

"Eight."

"It's five after now."

"Oh, good grief." Joanna slung her bag over her shoulder as they slid out of the booth and hurried toward the cash register. Tanner insisted on paying for her coffee, and Joanna didn't want to waste time arguing.

They walked briskly toward their cars, parked beside each other in the lot. "Joanna," he called, as she fumbled with her keys. "I'll wait a couple of minutes so we don't both arrive at the same time. Otherwise the girls will probably guess we've been together."

She flashed him a grateful smile. "Good thinking."

"Joanna." She looked at him questioningly as he shortened the distance between them. "Don't misunderstand this," he said softly. He pulled her gently into the circle of his arms, holding her close for a lingering moment. "I'm sorry for what Davey did to you. The man's a fool." Tenderly he brushed his lips over her forehead, then turned and abruptly left her.

It took Joanna a full minute to recover enough to get into her car and drive away.

Seven

"Mom," Kristen screeched, "the phone's for you."

Joanna was surprised. A call for her on a school night was rare enough, but one that actually got through with Kristen and Nicole continually on the line was a special occasion.

"Who is it, honey?" No doubt someone interested in cleaning her carpets or selling her a cemetery plot.

"I don't know," Kristen said, holding the phone to her shoulder. She lowered her voice to whisper, "But whoever it is sounds weird."

"Hello." Joanna spoke into the receiver as Kristen wandered toward her bedroom.

"Can you talk?" The husky male voice was unmistakably Tanner's.

"Y-yes." Joanna looked toward Kristen's bedroom to be certain her daughter was out of earshot.

"Can you meet me tomorrow for lunch?"

"What time?"

"Noon at the Sea Galley."

"Should we synchronize our watches?" Joanna couldn't resist asking. It had been a week since she'd last talked to Tanner. In the meantime she hadn't heard a word from Kristen about getting their two families together again. That in itself was suspicious, but Joanna had been too busy at work to think about it.

"Don't be cute, Joanna. I need help."

"Buy me lunch and I'm yours." She hadn't meant that quite the way it sounded and was grateful Tanner didn't comment on her slip of the tongue.

"I'll see you tomorrow then."

"Right."

A smile tugged at the edges of her mouth as she replaced the telephone receiver. Her hand lingered there for a moment as an unexpected tide of happiness washed over her.

"Who was that, Mom?" Kristen asked, poking her head around her bedroom door.

"A...friend, calling to ask if I could meet...her for lunch."

"Oh." Kristen's young face was a study in scepticism. "For a minute there I thought it sounded like Mr. Lund trying to fake a woman's voice."

"Mr. Lund? That's silly," Joanna said with a forced little laugh, then deftly changed the subject. "Kristen, it's nine thirty. Hit the hay, kiddo."

"Right, Mom. 'Night."

"'Night, sweetheart."

"Enjoy your lunch tomorrow."

"I will."

Joanna hadn't had a chance to walk away from the phone before it pealed a second time. She gave a guilty start and reached for it.

"Hello," she said hesitantly, half expecting to hear Tanner's voice again.

But it was her mother's crisp clear voice that rang over the wire. "Joanna, I hope this isn't too late to call."

"Of course not, Mom," Joanna answered quickly. "Is everything all right?"

Her mother ignored the question and asked one of her own instead. "What was the name of that young man you're dating again?"

"Mother," Joanna said with an exasperated sigh, "I'm not seeing anyone. I told you that."

"Tanner Lund, wasn't it?"

"We went out to dinner *once* with both our daughters, and that's the extent of our relationship. If Kristen let you assume anything else, it was just wishful thinking on her part. One dinner, I swear."

"But, Joanna, he sounds like such a nice young man. He's the same Tanner Lund who recently bought half of Spokane Aluminum, isn't he? I saw his name in the paper this morning and recognised it right away. Sweetie, your dad and I are so pleased you're dating such a famous successful man."

"Mother, please!" Joanna cried. "Tanner and I are friends. How many times do I have to tell you, we're not dating? Kristen and Tanner's daughter, Nicole, are best friends. I swear that's all there is to—"

"Joanna," her mother interrupted. "The first time you mentioned his name, I heard something in your voice that's been missing for a good long while. You may be able to fool yourself, but not me. You like this Tanner." Her voice softened perceptively.

"Mother, nothing could possibly come of it even if I was attracted to him—which I'm not." Okay, so that last part wasn't entirely true. But the rest of it certainly was.

"And why couldn't it?" her mother insisted.

"You said it yourself. He's famous, in addition to being wealthy. I'm out of his league."

"Nonsense," her mother responded in a huff.

Joanna knew better than to get into a war of words with her stubborn parent.

"Now don't be silly. You like Tanner Lund, and I say it's about time you let down those walls you've built around yourself. Joanna, sweetie, you've been hiding behind them for six years now. Don't let what happened with Davey ruin your whole life."

"I'm not going to," Joanna promised.

There was a long pause before her mother sighed and answered, "Good. You deserve some happiness."

At precisely noon the following day, Joanna drove into the Sea Galley parking lot. Tanner was already there, waiting for her by the entrance.

"Hi," she said with a friendly grin, as he walked toward her.

"What, no disguises?"

Joanna laughed, embarrassed now by that silly scarf and sunglasses she'd worn when they met at Denny's. "Kristen doesn't know anyone who eats here."

"I'm grateful for that."

His smile was warm enough to tunnel through snow drifts, and as much as Joanna had warned herself not to be affected by it, she was.

"It's good to see you," Tanner added, taking her arm to escort her into the restaurant.

"You, too." Although she hadn't seen him in almost a week, Tanner was never far from her thoughts. Nicole had stayed with her and Kristen when Tanner flew to New York for two days in the middle of the previous week. The Spokane area had been hit by a fierce snowstorm the evening he left. Joanna had felt nervous the entire time about his traveling in such inclement weather, yet she hadn't so much as asked him about his flight when he arrived to pick up Nicole. Their conversation had been brief and pleasantly casual, but her relief that he'd got home safely had kept her awake for hours. Later, she'd been furious with herself for caring so much.

The Sea Galley hostess seated them right away and handed them thick menus. Joanna ordered a shrimp salad and coffee. Tanner echoed her choice.

"Nicole's birthday is next week," he announced, studying her face carefully. "She's handing out the party invitations today at school."

Joanna smiled and nodded. But Tanner's eyes held hers, and she saw something unidentifiable flicker there.

"In a moment of weakness, I told her she could have a slumber party."

Joanna's smile faded. "As I recall, Nicole did mention something about this party," she said, trying to sound cheerful. The poor guy didn't know what he was in for. "You're obviously braver than I am."

"You think it was a bad move?"

Joanna made a show of closing her eyes and nodding vigorously.

"I was afraid of that," Tanner muttered, and he rearranged the silverware around his place setting a couple of times. "I know we agreed it probably wouldn't be a good idea for us to do things together. But I need some advice—from a friend."

"What can I do?"

"Joanna, I haven't the foggiest idea about entertaining a whole troop of girls. I can handle contract negotiations and make split-second business decisions, but I panic at the thought of all those squealing little girls sequestered in my apartment for all those hours."

"How do you want me to help?"

"Would you consider…" He gave her a hopeful look, then shook his head regretfully. "No. I can't ask that of you. Besides, we don't want to give the girls any more ideas about the two of us. What I really need is some suggestions for keeping all these kids occupied. What do other parents do?"

"Other parents know better."

Tanner wiped a lock of dark brown hair from his brow and frowned. "I was afraid of that."

"What time are the girls supposed to arrive?"

"Six."

"Tanner, that's too early."

"I know, but Nicole insists I serve my special tacos, and she has some screwy idea about all the girls crowding into the kitchen to watch me."

Now it was Joanna's turn to frown. "That won't work. You'll end up with ten different pairs of hands trying to help. There'll be hamburger and cheese from one end of the place to the other."

"I thought as much. Good Lord, Joanna, how did I get myself into this mess?"

"Order pizza," she tossed out, tapping her index finger against her bottom lip. "Everyone loves that."

"Pizza. Okay. What about games?"

"A scavenger hunt always comes in handy when

things get out of hand. Release the troops on your unsuspecting neighbours."

"So far we've got thirty minutes of the first fourteen hours filled."

"Movies," Joanna suggested next. "Lots of movies. You can go on Netflix and browse for something, maybe pick an old favourite like *Pretty in Pink*, and the girls will be in seventh heaven."

His eyes brightened. "Good idea."

"And if you really feel adventurous, take them roller-skating."

"Roller-skating? You think they'd like that?"

"They'd love it, especially if word leaked out that they were going to be at the rink Friday night. That way, several of the boys from the sixth-grade class can just happen to be there, too."

Tanner nodded, and a smile quirked the corners of his mouth. "And you think that'll keep everyone happy?"

"I'm sure of it. Wear 'em out first, show a movie or two second, with the lights out, of course, and I guarantee you by midnight everyone will be sound asleep."

Their salads arrived and Tanner stuck his fork into a fat succulent shrimp, then paused. "Now what was it you said last night about buying you lunch and making you mine?"

"It was a slip of the tongue," she muttered, dropping her gaze to her salad.

"Just my luck."

They laughed, and it felt good. Joanna had never had a relationship like this with a man. She wasn't on her guard the way she normally was, fearing that her date would put too much stock in an evening or two out. Because their daughters were the same age, they had a lot in common. They were both single parents doing their damnedest to raise their daughters right. The normal dating rituals and practised moves were unnecessary with him. Tanner was her friend, and it renewed Joanna's faith in the opposite sex to know there were still men like him left. Their friendship reassured her—but the undeniable attraction between them still frightened her.

"I really appreciate your suggestions," he said, after they'd both concentrated on their meals for several moments. "I've had this panicky feeling for the past three days. I suppose it wasn't a brilliant move on my part to call you at home, but I was getting desperate."

"You'll do fine. Just remember, it's important to keep the upper hand."

"I'll try."

"By the way, when *is* Hell Night?" She couldn't resist teasing him.

He gave a heartfelt sigh. "Next Friday."

Joanna slowly ate a shrimp. "I think Kristen figured out it was you on the phone last night."

"She did?"

"Yeah. She started asking questions the minute I hung up. She claimed my 'friend' sounded suspiciously like Mr. Lund faking a woman's voice."

Tanner cleared his throat and answered in a high falsetto. "That should tell you how desperate I was."

Joanna laughed and speared another shrimp. "That's what friends are for."

Eight

"Mom, hurry or we're going to be late." Kristen paced the hallway outside her mother's bedroom door while Joanna finished dressing.

"Have you got Nicole's gift?"

"Oh." Kristen dashed into her bedroom and returned with a gaily wrapped oblong box. They'd bought the birthday gift the night before, a popular board game, which Kristen happened to know Nicole really wanted.

"I think Mr. Lund is really nice to let Nicole have a slumber party, don't you?"

"Really brave is a more apt description. How many girls are coming?"

"Fifteen."

"Fifteen!" Joanna echoed in a shocked voice.

"Nicole originally invited twenty, but only fifteen could make it."

Joanna slowly shook her head. He'd had good reason to feel panicky. With all these squealing, giddy preadolescent girls, the poor man would be certifiable by the end of the night. Either that or a prime candidate for extensive counseling.

When they arrived, the parking area outside Tanner's apartment building looked like the scene of a rock concert. There were enough parents dropping off kids to cause a minor traffic jam.

"I can walk across the street if you want to let me out here," Kristen suggested, anxiously eyeing the group of girls gathering outside the building.

"I'm going to find a parking place," Joanna said, scanning the side streets for two adjacent spaces— so that she wouldn't need to struggle to parallel park.

"You're going to find a place to leave the car? Why?" Kristen wanted to know, her voice higher pitched and more excited than usual. "You don't have to come in, if you don't want. I thought you said you were going to refinish that old chair Grandpa gave us last summer."

"I was," Joanna murmured with a short sigh, "but I have the distinct impression that Nicole's father is going to need a helping hand."

"I'm sure he doesn't, Mom. Mr. Lund is a really organized person. I'm sure he's got everything under control."

Kristen's reaction surprised Joanna. She would have expected her daughter to encourage the idea of getting the two of them together.

She finally found a place to park and they hurried across the street, Kristen apparently deep in thought.

"Actually, Mom, I think helping Mr. Lund might be a good idea," she said after a long pause. "He'll probably be grateful."

Joanna wasn't nearly as confident by this time. "I have a feeling I'm going to regret this later."

"No, you won't." Joanna could tell Kristen was

about to launch into another one of her little speeches about babies, vacations and homemade cookies. Thankfully she didn't get the chance, since they'd entered the building and encountered a group of Kristen's other friends.

Tanner was standing in the doorway of his apartment, already looking frazzled when Joanna arrived. Surprise flashed through his eyes when he saw her.

"I've come to help," she announced, peeling off her jacket and pushing up the sleeves of her thin sweater. "This group is more than one parent can reasonably be expected to control."

He looked for a moment as though he wanted to fall to the ground and kiss her feet. "Bless you."

"Believe me, Tanner, you owe me for this." She glanced around at the chaos that dominated the large apartment. The girls had already formed small groups and were arguing loudly with each other over some subject of earth-shattering importance—like Adam Levine's age, or the real color of Niall Horan's hair.

"Is the pizza ready?" Joanna asked him, raising her voice in order to be heard over the din of squeals, shouts and rock music.

Tanner nodded. "It's in the kitchen. I ordered eight large ones. Do you think that'll be enough?"

Joanna rolled her eyes. "I suspect you're going to be eating leftover pizza for the next two weeks."

The girls proved her wrong. Never had Joanna seen a hungrier group. They were like school of piranha attacking a hapless victim, and within fifteen minutes everyone had eaten her fill. There were one or two slices left of four of the pizzas, but the others had vanished completely.

"It's time for a movie," Joanna decided, and while the girls voted on which film to see first Tanner started dumping dirty paper plates and pop cans into a plastic garbage sack. When the movie was finished, Joanna calculated, it would be time to go skating.

Peace reigned once Tom Cruise appeared on the television screen and Joanna joined Tanner in the bright cheery kitchen.

He was sitting dejectedly at the round table, rubbing a hand across his forehead. "I feel a headache coming on."

"It's too late for that," she said with a soft smile. "Actually I think everything is going very well. Everyone seems to be having a good time, and Nicole is a wonderful hostess."

"You do? She is?" He gave her an astonished look. "I keep having nightmares about pillow fights and lost dental appliances."

"Hey, it isn't going to happen." Not while they maintained control. "Tanner, I meant what I said about the party going well. In fact, I'm surprised at how smoothly everything is falling into place. The kids really are having a good time, and as long as we keep them busy there shouldn't be any problems."

He grinned, looking relieved. "I don't know about you, but I could use a cup of coffee."

"I'll second that."

He poured coffee into two pottery mugs and carried them to the table. Joanna sat across from him, propping her feet on the opposite chair. Sighing, she leaned back and cradled the steaming mug.

"The pizza was a good idea." He reached for a piece and shoved the box in her direction.

Now that she had a chance to think about it, Joanna realized she'd been so busy earlier, serving the girls, she hadn't managed to eat any of the pizza herself. She straightened enough to reach for a napkin and a thick slice dotted with pepperoni and spicy Italian sausage.

"What made you decide to give up your evening to help me out?" Tanner asked, watching her closely. "Kristen told Nicole that you had a hot date tonight. You were the last person I expected to see."

Joanna wasn't sure what had changed her mind about tonight and staying to help Tanner. Pity, she suspected. "If the situation were reversed, you'd lend me a hand," she replied, more interested in eating than conversation at the moment.

Tanner frowned at his pizza. "You missed what I was really asking."

"I did?"

"I was trying to be subtle about asking if you had a date tonight."

Joanna found that question odd. "Obviously I didn't."

"It isn't so obvious to me. You're a single parent, so there aren't that many evenings you can count on being free of responsibility. I would have thought you'd use this time to go out with someone special, flap your wings and that sort of thing." His frown grew darker.

"I'm too old to flap my wings," she said with a soft chuckle. "Good grief, I'm over thirty."

"So you aren't dating anyone special?"

"Tanner, you know I'm not."

"I don't know anything of the sort." Although he didn't raise his voice, Joanna could sense his disquiet.

"All right, what's up?" She didn't like the looks he was giving her. Not one bit.

"Nicole."

"Nicole?" she repeated.

"She was telling me that other day that you'd met someone recently. 'A real prince' is the phrase she used. Someone rich and handsome who was crazy about you—she claimed you were seeing a lot of this guy. Said you were falling madly in love."

Joanna dropped her feet to the floor with a loud thud and bolted upright so fast she nearly tumbled out of the chair. She was furiously chewing her pepperoni-and-sausage pizza, trying to swallow it as quickly as she could. All the while, her finger was pointing, first toward the living room where the girls were innocently watching *Top Gun* and then at Tanner who was staring at her in fascination.

"Hey, don't get angry with me," he said. "I'm only repeating what Kristen supposedly told Nicole and what Nicole told me."

She swallowed the piece of pizza in one huge lump. "They're plotting again, don't you see? I should have known something was up. It's been much too quiet lately. Kristen and Nicole are getting devious now, because the direct approach didn't work." Flustered, she started pacing the kitchen floor.

"Settle down, Joanna. We're smarter than a couple of school kids."

"That's easy for you to say." She pushed her hair away from her forehead and continued to pace. Little wonder Kristen hadn't been keen on the idea of her helping Tanner tonight. Joanna whirled around to face him. "Well, aren't you going to say something?"

To her dismay, she discovered he was doing his best not to chuckle. "This isn't a laughing matter, Tanner Lund. I wish you'd take this seriously!"

"I am."

Joanna snorted softly. "You are not!"

"We're mature adults, Joanna. We aren't going to allow two children to dictate our actions."

"Is that a fact?" She braced both hands against her hips and glared at him. "I'm pleased to hear you're such a tower of strength, but I'll bet a week's pay that it wasn't your idea to have this slumber party. You probably rejected the whole thing the first time Nicole suggested it, but after having the subject of a birthday slumber party brought up thirty times in about thirty minutes you weakened, and that was when Nicole struck the fatal blow. If your daughter is anything like mine, she probably used every trick in the book to talk you into this party idea. Knowing how guilty you felt about all those business trips, I suppose Nicole brought them up ten or twelve times. And before you knew what hit you, there were fifteen little girls spending the night at your apartment."

Tanner paled.

"Am I right?" she insisted.

He shrugged and muttered disparagingly, "Close enough."

Slumping into the chair, Joanna pushed the pizza box aside and forcefully expelled her breath. "I don't mind telling you, I'm concerned about this. If Kristen and Nicole are plotting against us, then we've got to form some kind of plan of our own before they drive us out of our minds. We can't allow them to manipulate us like this."

"I think you may be right."

She eyed him hopefully. "Any suggestions?" If he was smart enough to manage a couple of thousand employees, surely he could figure out a way to keep two eleven-year-olds under control.

Slouched in his chair, his shoulders sagging, Tanner shook his head. "None. What about you?"

"Communication is the key."

"Right."

"We've got to keep in touch with each other and keep tabs on what's going on with these two. Don't believe a thing they say until we check it out with the other."

"We've got another problem, Joanna," Tanner said, looking in every direction but hers.

"What?"

"It worked."

"What worked?" she asked irritably. Why was he speaking in riddles?

"Nicole's telling me that you'd been swept off your feet by this rich guy."

"Yes?" He still wasn't making any sense.

"The purpose of that whole fabrication was to make me jealous—and it worked."

"It worked?" An icy numb feeling swept through her. Swallowing became difficult.

Tanner nodded. "I kept thinking about how much I liked you. How much I enjoyed talking to you. And then I decided that when this slumber party business was over, I was going to risk asking you out to dinner."

"But I've already told you I'm not interested in a romantic relationship. One marriage was more than enough for me."

"I don't think that's what bothered me."

"Then what did?"

It was obvious from the way his eyes darted around the room that he felt uncomfortable. "I kept thinking about another man kissing you, and frankly, Joanna, that's what bothered me most."

The kitchen suddenly went so quiet that Joanna was almost afraid to breathe. The only noise was the faint sound of the movie playing in the other room.

Joanna tried to put herself in Tanner's place, wondering how she'd feel if Kristen announced that he'd met a gorgeous blonde and was dating her. Instantly she felt her stomach muscles tighten. There wasn't the slightest doubt in Joanna's mind that the girls' trick would have worked on her, too. Just the thought of Tanner's kissing another woman produced a curious ache, a pain that couldn't be described—or denied.

"Kissing you that night was the worst thing I could have done," Tanner conceded reluctantly. "I know you don't want to talk about it. I don't blame you—"

"Tanner," she interjected in a low hesitant voice, which hardly resembled her own. "It would have worked with me, too."

His eyes were dark and piercing. "Are you certain?"

She nodded, feeling utterly defeated yet strangely excited. "I'm afraid so. What are we going to do now?"

The silence returned as they stared at one another.

"The first thing I think we should do is experiment a little," he suggested in a flat emotionless voice. Then he released a long sigh. "Almost three weeks have passed since the night we took the girls out, and we've both had plenty of time to let that kiss build in our minds. Right?"

"Right," Joanna agreed. She'd attempted to put that kiss completely out of her mind, but it hadn't worked, and there was no point in telling him otherwise.

"It seems to me," Tanner continued thoughtfully, "that we should kiss again, for the sake of research, and find out what we're dealing with here."

She didn't need him to kiss her again to know she was going to like it. The first time had been ample opportunity for her to recognise how strongly she was attracted to Tanner Lund, and she didn't need another kiss to remind her.

"Once we know, we can decide where to go from there. Agreed?"

"Okay," she said impulsively, ignoring the small voice that warned of danger.

He stood up and held out his hand. She stared at it for a moment, uncertain. "You want to kiss right now?"

"Do you know of a better time?"

She shook her head. Good grief, she couldn't believe she was doing this. Tanner stretched out his arms and she walked into them with all the finesse of tumbleweed. The way she fit so snugly, so comfortably into his embrace worried her already. And he hadn't even kissed her yet.

Tanner held her lightly, his eyes wide and curious as he stared down at her. First he cocked his head to the right, then abruptly changed his mind and moved it to the left.

Joanna's movements countered his until she was certain they looked like a pair of ostriches who couldn't make up their minds.

"Are you comfortable?" he asked, and his voice was slightly hoarse.

Joanna nodded. She wished he'd hurry up and do it before one of the girls came crashing into the kitchen and found them. With their luck, it would be either Kristen or Nicole. Or both.

"You ready?" he asked.

Joanna nodded again. He was looking at her almost anxiously as though they were waiting for an imminent explosion. And that was exactly the way it felt when Tanner's mouth settled on hers, even though the kiss was infinitely gentle, his lips sliding over hers like a soft summer rain, barely touching.

They broke apart, momentarily stunned. Neither spoke, and then Tanner kissed her again, moving his mouth over her parted lips in undisguised hunger. His hand clutched the thick hair at her nape as she raised her arms and tightened them around his neck, leaning into him, absorbing his strength.

Tanner groaned softly and deepened the kiss until it threatened to consume Joanna. She met his fierce urgency with her own, arching closer to him, holding onto him with everything that was in her.

An unabating desire flared to life between them as he kissed her again and again, until they were both breathless and shaking.

"Joanna," he groaned, and dragged in several deep breaths. After taking a long moment to compose himself, he asked, "What do you think?" The question was murmured into her hair.

Joanna's chest was heaving, as though she'd been running and was desperate for oxygen. "I…I don't know," she lied, silently calling herself a coward.

"I do."

"You do?"

"Good Lord, Joanna, you taste like heaven. We're in trouble here. Deep trouble."

Nine

The pop music at the roller-skating rink blared from huge speakers and vibrated around the room. A disc jockey announced the tunes from a glass-fronted booth and joked with the skaters as they circled the polished hardwood floor.

"I can't believe I let you talk me into this," Joanna muttered, sitting beside Tanner as she laced up her rented high-top white skates.

"I refuse to be the only one over thirty out there," he replied, but he was smiling, obviously pleased with his persuasive talents. No doubt he'd take equal pleasure in watching her fall flat on her face. It had been years since Joanna had worn a pair of roller skates. *Years.*

"It's like riding a bicycle," Tanner assured her with that maddening grin of his. "Once you know how, you never forget."

Joanna grumbled under her breath, but she was actually beginning to look forward to this. She'd always loved roller-skating as a kid, and there was something about being with Tanner that brought out the little girl in her. *And the woman*, she thought, remembering their kiss.

Nicole's friends were already skating with an ease that made Joanna envious. Slowly, cautiously, she joined the crowd circling the rink.

"Hi, Mom." Kristen zoomed past at the speed of light.

"Hi, Mrs. Parsons," Nicole shouted, following her friend.

Staying safely near the side, within easy reach of the handrail, Joanna concentrated on making her feet work properly, wheeling them back and forth as smoothly as possible. But instead of the gliding motion achieved by the others, her movements were short and jerky. She didn't acknowledge the girls' greetings with anything more than a raised hand and was slightly disconcerted to see the other skaters giving her a wide berth. They obviously recognized danger when they saw it.

Tanner glided past her, whirled around and deftly skated backward, facing Joanna. She looked up and threw him a weak smile. She should have known Tanner would be as confident on skates as he seemed to be at everything else—except slumber parties for eleven-year-old girls. Looking at him, one would think he'd been skating every day for years, although he claimed it was twenty years since he'd been inside a rink. It was clear from the expert way he soared across the floor that he didn't need to relearn anything—unlike Joanna, who felt as awkward as a newborn foal attempting to stand for the first time.

"How's it going?" he asked, with a cocky grin.

"Great. Can't you tell?" Just then, her right foot jerked out from under her and she groped desperately for the rail, managing to get a grip on it seconds before she went crashing to the floor.

Tanner was by her side at once. "You okay?"

"About as okay as anyone who has stood on the edge and looked into the deep abyss," she muttered.

"Come on, what you need is a strong hand to guide you."

Joanna snorted. "Forget it, fellow. I'll be fine in a few minutes, once I get my sea legs."

"You're sure?"

"Tanner, for heaven's sake, at least leave me with my pride intact!" Keeping anything intact at the moment was difficult, with her feet flaying wildly as she tried to pull herself back into an upright position.

"Okay, if that's what you want," he said shrugging, and sailed away from her with annoying ease.

Fifteen minutes later, Joanna felt steady enough to join the main part of the crowd circling the rink. Her movements looked a little less clumsy, a little less shaky, though she certainly wasn't in complete control.

"Hey, you're doing great," Tanner said, slowing down enough to skate beside her.

"Thanks," she said breathlessly, studying her feet in an effort to maintain her balance.

"You've got a gift for this," he teased.

She looked up at him and laughed outright. "Isn't that the truth! I wonder if I should consider a new career as a roller-skating waitress at the Pink Palace."

Amusement lifted the edge of his sensuous mouth. "Has anyone ever told you that you have an odd sense of humor?"

Looking at Tanner distracted Joanna, and her feet

floundered for an instant. "Kristen does at least once a day."

Tanner chuckled. "I shouldn't laugh. Nicole tells me the same thing."

The disc jockey announced that the next song was for couples only. Joanna gave a sigh of relief and aimed her body toward the nearest exit. She could use the break; her calf muscles were already protesting the unaccustomed exercise. She didn't need roller-skating to remind her she wasn't a kid.

"How about it, Joanna?" Tanner asked, skating around her.

"How about what?"

"Skating together for the couples' dance. You and me and fifty thousand preteens sharing center stage." He offered her his hand. The lights had dimmed and a mirrored ball hanging in the middle of the ceiling cast speckled shadows over the floor.

"No way, Tanner," she muttered, ignoring his hand.

"I thought not. Oh well, I'll see if I can get Nicole to skate with her dear old dad." Effortlessly he glided toward the group of girls who stood against the wall flirtatiously challenging the boys on the other side with their eyes.

Once Joanna was safely off the rink, she found a place to sit and rest her weary bones. Within a couple of minutes, Tanner lowered himself into the chair beside her, looking chagrined.

"I got beat out by Tommy Spenser," he muttered.

Joanna couldn't help it—she was delighted. Now Tanner would understand how she'd felt when Kristen announced she didn't want her mother sitting with her at the movies. Tanner looked just as dejected as Joanna had felt then.

"It's hell when they insist on growing up, isn't it?" she said, doing her best not to smile, knowing he wouldn't appreciate it.

He heaved an expressive sigh and gave her a hopeful look before glancing out at the skating couples. "I don't suppose you'd reconsider?"

The floor was filled with kids, and Joanna knew the minute she moved onto the hardwood surface with Tanner, every eye in the place would be on them.

He seemed to read her mind, because he added, "Come on, Joanna. My ego has just suffered a near-mortal wound. I've been rejected by my own flesh and blood."

She swallowed down a comment and awkwardly rose to her feet, struggling to remain upright. "When my ego got shot to bits at the movie theatre, all you did was share your popcorn with me."

He chuckled and reached for her hand. "Don't complain. This gives me an excuse to put my arm around you again." His right arm slipped around her waist, and she tucked her left hand in his as they moved side by side. She had to admit it felt incredibly good to be this close to him. Almost as good as it had felt being in his arms for those few moments in his kitchen.

Tanner must have been thinking the same thing, because he was unusually quiet as he directed her smoothly across the floor to the strains of a romantic ballad. They'd circled the rink a couple of times when Tanner abruptly switched position, skating backward and holding onto her as though they were dancing.

"Tanner," she said, surprise widening her eyes as he

swept her into his arms. "The girls will start thinking…
things if we skate like this."

"Let them."

His hands locked at the base of her spine and he
pulled her close. Very close. Joanna drew a slow breath,
savoring the feel of Tanner's body pressed so intimately
against her own.

"Joanna, listen," he whispered. "I've been thinking."

So had she. Hard to do when she was around Tanner.

"Would it really be such a terrible thing if we were
to start seeing more of each other? On a casual basis—
it doesn't have to be anything serious. We're both mature adults. Neither of us is going to allow the girls to
manipulate us into anything we don't want. And as
far as the past is concerned, I'm not Davey and you're
not Carmen."

Why, Joanna wondered, was the most important
discussion she'd had in years taking place in a roller-
skating rink with a top-forty hit blaring in one ear and
Tanner whispering in the other? Deciding to ignore
the thought, she said, "But the girls might start making assumptions, and I'm afraid we'd only end up dis-
appointing them."

Tanner disagreed. "I feel our seeing each other
might help more than it would hinder."

"How do you mean?" Joanna couldn't believe she
was actually entertaining this suggestion. Entertaining
was putting it mildly; her heart was doing somersaults
at the prospect of seeing Tanner more often. She was
thrilled, excited…and yet hesitant. The wounds Davey
had inflicted went very deep.

"If we see each other more often we could include
the girls, and that should lay to rest some of the fears

we've had over their matchmaking efforts. And spending time with you will help satisfy Nicole's need for a strong mother figure. At the same time, I can help Kristen, by being a father figure."

"Yes, but—"

"The four of us together will give the girls a sense of belonging to a whole family," Tanner added confidently.

His arguments sounded so reasonable, so logical. Still, Joanna remained uncertain. "But I'm afraid the girls will think we're serious."

Tanner lifted his head enough to look into her eyes, and Joanna couldn't remember a time they'd ever been bluer or more intense. "I am serious."

She pressed her forehead against his collarbone and willed her body to stop trembling. Their little kissing experiment had affected her far more than she dared let him know. Until tonight, they'd both tried to disguise or deny their attraction for each other, but the kiss had exposed everything.

"I haven't stopped thinking about you from the minute we first met," he whispered, and touched his lips to her temple. "If we were anyplace else right now, I'd show you how crazy I am about you."

If they'd been anyplace else, Joanna would have let him. She wanted him to kiss her, needed him to, but she was more frightened by her reaction to this one man than she'd been by anything else in a very long while. "Tanner, I'm afraid."

"Joanna, so am I, but I can't allow fear to rule my life." Gently he brushed the loose wisps of curls from the side of her face. His eyes studied her intently. "I didn't expect to feel this way again. I've guarded against letting this happen, but here we are, and Joanna, I don't mind telling you, I wouldn't change a thing."

Joanna closed her eyes and listened to the battle raging inside her head. She wanted so badly to give this feeling between them a chance to grow. But logic told her that if she agreed to his suggestion, she'd be making herself vulnerable again. Even worse, Tanner Lund wasn't just any man—he was wealthy and successful, the half owner of an important company. And she was just a loan officer at a small local bank.

"Joanna, at least tell me what you're feeling."

"I…I don't know," she hedged, still uncertain.

He gripped her hand and pressed it over his heart, holding it there. "Just feel what you do to me."

Her own heart seemed about to hammer its way out of her chest. "You do the same thing to me."

He smiled ever so gently. "I know."

The music came to an end and the lights brightened. Reluctantly Tanner and Joanna broke apart, but he still kept her close to his side, tucking his arm around her waist.

"You haven't answered me, Joanna. I'm not going to hurt you, you know. We'll take it nice and easy at first and see how things develop."

Joanna's throat felt constricted, and she couldn't answer him one way or the other, although it was clear that he was waiting for her to make a decision.

"We've got something good between us," he continued, "and I don't want to just throw it away. I think we should find out whether this can last."

He wouldn't hurt her intentionally, Joanna realised,

but the probability of her walking away unscathed from a relationship with this man was remote.

"What do you think?" he pressed.

She couldn't refuse him. "Maybe we should give it a try," she said after a long pause.

Tanner gazed down on her, bathing her in the warmth of his smile. "Neither of us is going to be sorry."

Joanna wasn't nearly as confident. She glanced away and happened to notice Kristen and Nicole. "Uh-oh," she murmured.

"What's wrong?"

"I just saw Kristen zoom over to Nicole and whisper into her ear. Then they hugged each other like long-lost sisters."

"I can deal with it if you can," he said, squeezing her hand.

Tanner's certainty lent her courage. "Then so can I."

Ten

Joanna didn't sleep well that night, or the following two. Tanner had suggested they meet for dinner the next weekend. It seemed an eternity, but there were several problems at work that demanded his attention. She felt as disappointed as he sounded that their first real date wouldn't take place for a week.

Joanna wished he hadn't given her so much time to think about it. If they'd been able to casually go to a movie the afternoon following the slumber party, she wouldn't have been so nervous about it.

When she arrived at work Monday morning, her brain was so muddled she felt as though she were walking in a fog. Twice during the weekend she'd almost called Tanner to suggest they call the whole thing off.

"Morning," her boss murmured absently, hardly looking up from the newspaper. "How was your weekend?"

"Exciting," Joanna told Robin, tucking her purse into the bottom drawer of her desk. "I went roller-skating with fifteen eleven-year-old girls."

"Sounds adventurous," Robin said, his gaze never leaving the paper.

Joanna poured herself a cup of coffee and carried it to her desk to drink black. The way she was feeling, she knew she'd need something strong to clear her head.

"I don't suppose you've been following what's happening at Spokane Aluminum?" Robin asked, refilling his own coffee cup.

It was a good thing Joanna had set her mug down when she did, otherwise it would have tumbled from her fingers. "Spokane Aluminum?" she echoed.

"Yes." Robin sat on the edge of her desk, allowing one leg to dangle. "There's another news item in the paper this morning on Tanner Lund. Six months ago, he bought out half the company from John Becky. I'm sure you've heard of John Becky?"

"Of…course."

"Apparently Lund came into this company and breathed new life into its sagging foreign sales. He took over management himself and has completely changed the company's direction…all for the better. I've heard nothing but good about this guy. Every time I turn around, I'm either reading how great he is, or hearing people talk about him. Take my word, Tanner Lund is a man who's going places."

Joanna couldn't agree more. And she knew for a fact where he was going Saturday night. He was taking her to dinner.

"Mr. Lund's here," Kristen announced the following Saturday, opening Joanna's bedroom door. "And does he ever look handsome!"

A dinner date. A simple dinner date, and Joanna

was more nervous than a college graduate applying for her first job. She smoothed her hand down her red-and-white flowered dress and held in her breath so long her lungs ached.

Kristen rolled her eyes. "You look fine, Mom."

"I do?"

"As nice as Mr. Lund."

For good measure, Joanna paused long enough to dab more cologne behind her ears, then she squared her shoulders and turned to face the long hallway that led to the living room. "Okay, I'm ready."

Kristen threw open the bedroom door as though she expected royalty to emerge. By the time Joanna had walked down the hallway to the living room where Tanner was waiting, her heart was pounding and her hands were shaking. Kristen was right. Tanner looked marvellous in a three-piece suit and silk tie. He smiled when she came into the room, and stood up, gazing at her with an expression of undisguised delight.

"Hi."

"Hi." Their eyes met, and everything else faded away. Just seeing him again made Joanna's pulse leap into overdrive. No week had ever dragged more.

"Sally's got the phone number of the restaurant, and her mother said it was fine if she stayed here late," Kristen said, standing between them and glancing from one adult to the other. "I don't have any plans myself, so you two feel free to stay out as long as you want."

"Sally?" Joanna forced herself to glance at the baby-sitter.

"Yes, Mrs. Parsons?"

"There's salad and leftover spaghetti in the refrigerator for dinner, and some microwave popcorn in the cupboard for later."

"Okay."

"I won't be too late."

"But, Mom," Kristen cut in, a slight whine in her voice, "I just got done telling you that it'd be fine if you stayed out till the wee hours of the morning."

"We'll be back before midnight," Joanna informed the babysitter, ignoring Kristen.

"Okay," the girl said, as Kristen sighed expressively. "Have a good time."

Tanner escorted Joanna out to the car, which was parked in front of the house, and opened the passenger door. He paused, his hand still resting on her shoulder. "I'd like to kiss you now, but we have an audience," he said, nodding toward the house.

Joanna chanced a look and discovered Kristen standing in the living-room window, holding aside the curtain and watching them intently. No doubt she was memorising everything they said and did to report back to Nicole.

"I couldn't believe it when she agreed to let Sally come over. She's of the opinion lately that she's old enough to stay by herself."

"Nicole claims the same thing, but she didn't raise any objections about having a babysitter, either."

"I guess we should count our blessings."

Tanner drove to an expensive downtown restaurant overlooking the Spokane River, in the heart of the city.

Joanna's mouth was dry and her palms sweaty when the valet opened her door and helped her out. She'd never eaten at such a luxurious place in her life. She'd heard that their prices were outrageous. The amount

Tanner intended to spend on one meal would probably outfit Kristen for an entire school year. Joanna felt faint at the very idea.

"Chez Michel is an exceptionally nice restaurant, Tanner, if you get my drift," she muttered under her breath after he handed the car keys to the valet. As a newcomer to town, he might not have been aware of just how expensive this place actually was.

"Yes, that's why I chose it," he said nonchalantly. "I was quite pleased with the food and the service when I was here a few weeks ago." He glanced at Joanna and her discomfort must have shown. "Consider it a small token of my appreciation for your help with Nicole's birthday party," he added, offering her one of his bone-melting smiles.

Joanna would have been more than content to eat at Denny's, and that thought reminded her again of how different they were.

She wished now that she'd worn something a little more elegant. The waiters seemed to be better dressed than she was. For that matter, so were the menus.

They were escorted to a table with an unobstructed view of the river. The maître d' held out Joanna's chair and seated her with flair. The first thing she noticed was the setting of silverware, with its bewildering array of forks, knives and spoons. After the maître d' left, she leaned forward and whispered to Tanner, "I've never eaten at a place that uses three teaspoons."

"Oh, quit complaining."

"I'm not, but if I embarrass you and use the wrong fork, don't blame me."

Unconcerned, Tanner chuckled and reached for the shiny gold menu.

Apparently Chez Michel believed in leisurely dining, because nearly two hours had passed by the time
they were served their after-dinner coffee. The entire
meal was everything Joanna could have hoped for, and
more. The food was exceptional, but Joanna considered Tanner's company the best part of the evening.
She'd never felt this much at ease with a man before.
He made her smile, but he challenged her ideas, too.
They talked about the girls and about the demands of
being a parent. They discussed Joanna's career goals
and Tanner's plans for his company. They covered a
lot of different subjects, but didn't focus their conversation on any one.

Now that the meal was over, Joanna was reluctant to
see the evening end. She lifted the delicate china cup,
admiring its pattern, and took a sip of fragrant coffee.
She paused, her cup raised halfway to her mouth, when
she noticed Tanner staring at her. "What's wrong?" she
asked, fearing part of her dessert was on her nose or
something equally disastrous.

"Nothing."

"Then why are you looking at me like that?"

Tanner relaxed, leaned back in his chair, and
grinned. "I'm sorry. I was just thinking how lovely
you are, and how pleased I am that we met. It seems
nothing's been the same since. I never thought a woman
could make me feel the way you do, Joanna."

She looked quickly down, feeling a sudden shy-
ness—and a wonderful warmth. Her life had changed,
too, and she wasn't sure she could ever go back to the
way things had been before. She was dreaming again,
feeling again, trusting again, and it felt so good. And
so frightening.

"I'm pleased, too," was her only comment.

"You know what the girls are thinking, don't you?"

Joanna could well imagine. No doubt those two would have them engaged after one dinner date. "They're probably expecting us to announce our marriage plans tomorrow morning," Joanna said, trying to make a joke of it.

"To be honest, I find some aspects of married life appealing."

Joanna smiled and narrowed her eyes suspiciously. "Come on, Tanner, just how much wine have you had?"

"Obviously too much, now that I think about it," he said, grinning. Then his face sobered. "All kidding aside, I want you to know how much I enjoy your company. Every time I'm with you, I come away feeling good about life—you make me laugh again."

"I'd make anyone laugh," she said, "especially if I'm wearing a pair of roller skates." She didn't know where their conversation was leading, but the fact that Tanner spoke so openly and honestly about the promise of their relationship completely unnerved her. She felt exactly the same things, but didn't have the courage to voice them.

"I'm glad you agreed we should start seeing each other," Tanner continued.

"Me, too." But she fervently hoped her mother wouldn't hear about it, although Kristen had probably phoned her grandmother the minute Joanna was out the door. Lowering her gaze, Joanna discovered that a bread crumb on the linen tablecloth had become utterly absorbing. She carefully brushed it onto the floor, an inch at a time. "It's worked out fine...so far. Us dating, I mean." It was more than fine. And now he was telling her how she'd brightened his life, as though *he* was the lucky one. That someone like Tanner Lund would ever want to date her still astonished Joanna.

She gazed up at him, her heart shining through her eyes, telling him without words what she was feeling.

Tanner briefly shut his eyes. "Joanna, for heaven's sake, don't look at me like that."

"Like what?"

"Like…that."

"I think you should kiss me," Joanna announced, once again staring down at the tablecloth. The instant the words slipped out she longed to take them back. She couldn't believe she'd said something like that to him.

"I beg your pardon?"

"Never mind," she said quickly, grateful he hadn't heard her.

He had. "Kiss you? Now? Here?"

Joanna shook her head, forcing a smile. "Forget I said that. It just slipped out. Sometimes my mouth disconnects itself from my brain."

Tanner didn't remove his gaze from hers as he raised his hand. Their waiter appeared almost immediately, and still looking at Joanna, he muttered, "Check, please."

"Right away, sir."

They were out of the restaurant so fast Joanna's head was spinning. Once they were seated in the car, Tanner paused, frowning, his hands clenched on the steering wheel.

"What's the matter?" Joanna asked anxiously.

"We goofed. We should have shared a babysitter."

The thought had fleetingly entered her mind earlier,

but she'd discounted the idea because she didn't want to encourage the girls' scheming.

"I can't take you back to my place because Nicole will be all over us with questions, and it'll probably be the same story at your house with Kristen."

"You're right." Besides, her daughter would be sorely disappointed if they showed up this early. It wasn't even close to midnight.

"Just where am I supposed to kiss you, Joanna Parsons?"

Oh Lord, he'd taken her seriously. "Tanner…it was a joke."

He ignored her comment. "I don't know of a single lookout point in the city."

"Tanner, please." Her voice rose in embarrassment, and she could feel herself blushing.

Tanner leaned over and brushed his lips against her cheek. "I've got an idea for something we can do, but don't laugh."

"An idea? What?"

"You'll see soon enough." He eased his car onto the street and drove quickly through the city to the freeway on-ramp and didn't exit until they were well into the suburbs.

"Tanner?" Joanna said, looking around her at the unfamiliar streets. "What's out here?" Almost as soon as she'd spoken a huge white screen appeared in the distance. "A drive-in?" she whispered in disbelief.

"Have you got any better ideas?"

"Not a one." Joanna chuckled; she couldn't help it. He was taking her to a drive-in movie just so he could kiss her.

"I can't guarantee this movie. This is its opening

weekend, and if I remember the ad correctly, they're showing something with lots of blood and gore."

"As long as it isn't *Teen Massacre*. Kristen would never forgive me if I saw it when she hadn't."

"If the truth be known, I don't plan to watch a whole lot of the movie." He darted an exaggerated leer in her direction and wiggled his eyebrows suggestively.

Joanna returned his look by demurely fluttering her lashes. "I don't know if my mother would approve of my going to a drive-in on a first date."

"With good reason," Tanner retorted. "Especially if she knew what I had in mind."

Although the weather had been mild and the sky was cloudless and clear, only a few cars were scattered across the wide lot.

Tanner parked as far away from the others as possible. He connected the speaker, but turned the volume so low it was almost inaudible. When he'd finished, he placed his arm around Joanna's shoulders, pulling her closer.

"Come here, woman."

Joanna leaned her head against his shoulder and pretended to be interested in the cartoon characters leaping across the large screen. Her stomach was playing jumping jacks with the dinner she'd just eaten.

"Joanna?" His voice was low and seductive.

She tilted her head to meet his gaze, and his eyes moved slowly over her upturned face, searing her with their intensity. The openness of his desire stole her breath away. Her heart was pounding, although he hadn't even kissed her yet. One hungry look from Tanner and she was melting at his feet.

Her first thought was to crack a joke. That had saved

her in the past, but whatever she might have said or done was lost as Tanner lowered his mouth and tantalized the edges of her trembling lips, teasing her with soft, tempting nibbles, making her ache all the way to her toes for his kiss. Instinctively her fingers slid up his chest and around the back of his neck. Tanner created such an overwhelming need in her that she felt both humble and elated at the same time. When her hands tightened around his neck, his mouth hardened into firm possession.

Joanna thought she'd drown in the sensations that flooded her. She hadn't felt this kind of longing in years, and she trembled with the wonder of it. Tanner had awakened the deep womanly part of her that had lain dormant for so long. And suddenly she felt all that time without love come rushing up at her, overtaking her. Years of regret, years of doubt, years of rejection all pressed so heavily on her heart that she could barely breathe.

A sob was ripped from her throat, and the sound of it broke them apart. Tears she couldn't explain flooded her eyes and ran unheeded down her face.

"Joanna, what's wrong? Did I hurt you?"

She tried to break away, but Tanner wouldn't let her go. He brushed the hair from her face and tilted her head to lift her eyes to his, but she resisted.

He must have felt the wetness on her face, because he paused and murmured, "You're crying," in a tone that sounded as shocked as she felt. "Dear Lord, what did I do?"

Wildly she shook her head, unable to speak even if she'd been able to find the words to explain.

"Joanna, tell me, please."

"J-just hold me." Even saying that much required all her reserves of strength.

He did as she asked, wrapping his arms completely around her, kissing the crown of her head as she buried herself in his strong, solid warmth.

Still, the tears refused to stop, no matter how hard she tried to make them. They flooded her face and seemed to come from the deepest part of her.

"I can't believe I'm doing this," she said between sobs. "Oh, Tanner, I feel like such a fool."

"Go ahead and cry, Joanna. I understand."

"You do? Good. You can explain it to me."

She could feel his smile as he kissed the corner of her eye. She moaned a little and he lowered his lips to her cheek, then her chin, and when she couldn't bear it any longer, she turned her face, her mouth seeking his. Tanner didn't disappoint her, kissing her gently again and again until she was certain her heart would stop beating if he ever stopped holding her and kissing her.

"Good Lord, Joanna," he whispered after a while, gently extricating himself from her arms and leaning against the car seat, his eyes closed. His face was a picture of desire struggling for restraint. He drew in several deep breaths.

Joanna's tears had long since dried on her face and now her cheeks flamed with confusion and remorse.

A heavy silence fell between them. Joanna searched frantically for something witty to say to break the terrible tension.

"Joanna, listen—"

"No, let me speak first," she broke in, then hesitated. Now that she had his attention, she didn't know what to say. "I'm sorry, Tanner, really sorry. I don't know what came over me, but you weren't the one responsible for my tears. Well, no, you were, but not the way you think."

"Joanna, please," he said and his hands bracketed her face. "Don't be embarrassed by the tears. Believe me when I say I'm feeling the same things you are, only they come out in different ways."

Joanna stared up at him, not sure he could possibly understand.

"It's been so long for you—it has for me, too," Tanner went on. "I feel like a teenager again. And the drive-in has nothing to do with it."

Her lips trembled with the effort to smile. Tanner leaned his forehead against hers. "We need to take this slow. Very, very slow."

That was a fine thing for him to say, considering they'd been as hot as torches for each other a few minutes ago. If they continued at this rate, they'd end up in bed together by the first of the week.

"I've got a company party in a couple of weeks—I want you there with me. Will you do that?"

Joanna nodded.

Tanner drew her closer to his side and she tucked her head against his chest. His hand stroked her shoulder, as he kissed the top of her head.

"You're awfully quiet," he said after several minutes. "What are you thinking?"

Joanna sighed and snuggled closer, looping one arm around his middle. Her free hand was laced with his. "It just occurred to me that for the first time in my life I've met a real prince. Up until now, all I've done is make a few frogs happy."

Eleven

Kneeling on the polished linoleum floor of the kitchen, Joanna held her breath and tentatively poked her head inside the foam-covered oven. Sharp, lemon-scented fumes made her grimace as she dragged the wet sponge along the sides, peeling away a layer of blackened crust. She'd felt unusually ambitious for a Saturday and had worked in the yard earlier, planning her garden. When she'd finished that, she'd decided to tackle the oven, not questioning where this burst of energy had come from. Spring was in the air, but instead of turning her fancy to thoughts of love, it filled her mind with zucchini seeds and rows of tomato seedlings.

"I'm leaving now, Mom," Kristen called from behind her.

Joanna jerked her head free, gulped some fresh air and twisted toward her daughter. "What time will you be through at the library?" Kristen and Nicole were working together on a school project, and although they complained about having to do research, they'd come to enjoy it. Their biggest surprise was discovering all the cute junior-high boys who sometimes visited the library. In Kristen's words, it was an untapped gold mine.

"I don't know when we'll be through, but I'll call. And remember, Nicole is coming over afterwards."

"I remember."

Kristen hesitated, then asked, "When are you going out with Mr. Lund again?"

Joanna glanced over at the calendar. "Next weekend. We're attending a dinner party his company's sponsoring."

"Oh."

Joanna rubbed her forearm across her cheek, and glanced suspiciously at her daughter. "What does that mean?"

"What?"

"That little 'oh.'"

Kristen shrugged. "Nothing... It's just that you're not seeing him as often as Nicole and I think you should. You like Mr. Lund, don't you?"

That was putting it mildly. "He's very nice," Joanna said cautiously. If she admitted to anything beyond a casual attraction, Kristen would assume much more. Joanna wanted her relationship with Tanner to progress slowly, one careful step at a time, not in giant leaps—though slow and careful didn't exactly describe what had happened so far!

"Nice?" Kristen exclaimed.

Her daughter's outburst caught Joanna by surprise.

"Is that all you can say about Mr. Lund?" Kristen asked, hands on her hips. "I've given the matter serious consideration and I think he's a whole lot more than just nice. Really, Mother."

Taking a deep breath, Joanna plunged her head back inside the oven, swiping her sponge furiously against the sides.

"Are you going to ignore me?" Kristen demanded.

Joanna emerged again, gasped and looked straight at her daughter. "Yes. Unless you want to volunteer to clean the oven yourself."

"I would, but I have to go to the library with Nicole."

Joanna noted the soft regret that filled her daughter's voice and gave her a derisive snort. The kid actually sounded sorry that she wouldn't be there to do her part. Kristen was a genius at getting out of work, and she always managed to give the impression of really wishing she could help her mother—if only she could fit it into her busy schedule.

A car horn beeped out front. "That's Mr. Lund," Kristen said, glancing toward the living room. "I'll give you a call when we're done."

"Okay, honey. Have a good time."

"I will."

With form an Olympic sprinter would envy, Kristen tore out of the kitchen. Two seconds later, the front door slammed. Joanna was only mildly disappointed that Tanner hadn't stopped in to chat. He'd phoned earlier and explained that after he dropped the girls off at the library; he was driving to the office for a couple of hours. An unexpected problem had arisen, and he needed to deal with it right away.

Actually Joanna had to admit she was more grateful than disappointed that Tanner hadn't stopped in. It didn't look as though she'd get a chance to see him before the company party. She needed this short separation to pull together her reserves. Following their dinner date and the drive-in movie afterward, Joanna felt dangerously close to falling in love with Tanner. Every time he came to mind, and that was practically every minute of every day, a rush of warmth and happiness followed. Without too much trouble, she could envision them finding a lifetime of happiness together. For the first time since her divorce she allowed herself the luxury of dreaming again, and although the prospect of remarriage excited and thrilled her, it also terrified her.

Fifteen minutes later, with perspiration beaded on her forehead and upper lip, Joanna heaved a sigh and sat back on her heels. The hair she'd so neatly tucked inside a scarf and tied at the back of her head, had fallen loose. She swiped a grimy hand at the auburn curls that hung limply over her eyes and ears. It was all worth it, though, since the gray-speckled sides of the oven, which had been encrusted with black grime, were now clearly visible and shining.

Joanna emptied the bucket of dirty water and hauled a fresh one back to wipe the oven one last time. She'd just knelt down when the doorbell chimed.

"Great," she muttered under her breath, casting a glance at herself. She looked like something that had crawled out of the bog in some horror movie. Pasting a smile on her face, she peeled off her rubber gloves and hurried to the door.

"Davey!" Finding her ex-husband standing on the porch was enough of a shock to knock the breath from Joanna's lungs.

"May I come in?"

"Of course." Flustered, she ran her hand through her hair and stepped aside to allow him to pass. He looked good—really good—but then Davey had never lacked in the looks department. From the expensive cut of his three-piece suit, she could tell that his real-estate business must be doing well, and of course that was precisely the impression he wanted her to have. She was pleased for him; she'd never wished him ill. They'd gone their separate ways, and although both the marriage and the divorce had devastated Joanna, she shared a beautiful child with this man. If he had come by to tell her how successful he was, well, she'd just smile and let him.

"It's good to see you, Joanna."

"You, too. What brings you to town?" She struggled to keep her voice even and controlled, hoping to hide her discomfort at being caught unawares.

"I'm attending a conference downtown. I apologize for dropping in unexpectedly like this, but since I was going to be in Spokane, I thought I'd stop in and see how you and Kristen are doing."

"I wish you'd phoned first. Kristen's at the library." Joanna wasn't fooled—Davey hadn't come to see their daughter, although he meant Joanna to think so. It was all part of the game he played with her, wanting her to believe that their divorce had hurt him badly. Not calling to let her know he planned to visit was an attempt to catch her off guard and completely unprepared—which, of course, she was. Joanna knew Davey, knew him well. He'd often tried to manipulate her this way.

"I should have called, but I didn't know if I'd have the time, and I didn't want to disappoint you if I found I couldn't slip away."

Joanna didn't believe that for a minute. It wouldn't have taken him much time or trouble to phone before he left the hotel. But she didn't mention the fact, couldn't see that it would have done any good.

"Come in and have some coffee." She led him into the kitchen and poured him a mug, automatically adding the sugar and cream she knew he used. She handed it to him and was rewarded with a dazzling smile. When he wanted, Davey Parsons could be charming, attentive and generous. The confusing thing about her ex-husband was that he wasn't all bad. He'd gravely wounded her with his unfaithfulness, but in his own way he'd loved her and Kristen—as much as he could possibly love anybody beyond himself. It had taken Joanna a good many years to distance herself enough to appreciate his good points and to forgive him for the pain he'd caused her.

"You've got a nice place here," he commented, casually glancing around the kitchen. "How long have you lived here now?"

"Seven months."

"How's Kristen?"

Joanna was relieved that the conversation had moved to the only subject they still had in common—their daughter. She talked for fifteen minutes nonstop, telling him about the talent show and the other activities Kristen had been involved in since the last time she'd seen her father.

Davey listened and laughed, and then his gaze softened as he studied Joanna. "You're looking wonderful."

She grinned ruefully. "Sure I am," she scoffed. "I've just finished working in the yard and cleaning the oven."

"I wondered about the lemon perfume you were wearing."

They both laughed. Davey started to tease her about their early years together and some of the experimental meals she'd cooked and expected him to eat and praise. Joanna let him and even enjoyed his comments, for Davey could be warm and funny when he chose. Kristen had inherited her friendly, easygoing confidence from her father.

The doorbell chimed and still chuckling, Joanna stood up. "It's probably one of the neighborhood kids. I'll just be a minute." She never ceased to be astonished at how easy it was to be with Davey. He'd ripped her heart in two, lied to her repeatedly, cheated on her and still she couldn't be around him and not laugh. It always took him a few minutes to conquer her reserve, but he never failed. She was mature enough to recognise her ex-husband's faults, yet appreciate his redeeming qualities.

For the second time that day, Joanna was surprised by the man who stood on her front porch. "Tanner."

"Hi," he said with a sheepish grin. "The girls got off okay and I thought I'd stop in for a cup of coffee before heading to the office." His eyes smiled softly into hers. "I heard you laughing from out here. Do you have company? Should I come back later?"

"N-no, come in," she said, her pulse beating as hard and loud as jungle drums. Lowering her eyes, she automatically moved aside. He walked into the living room and paused, then raised his hand and gently touched her cheek in a gesture so loving that Joanna longed to fall into his arms. Now that he was here, she found herself craving some time alone with him.

Tanner's gaze reached out to her, but Joanna had

trouble meeting it. A frown started to form, and his eyes clouded. "This is a bad time, isn't it?"

"No…not really." When she turned around, Davey was standing in the kitchen doorway watching them. The smile she'd been wearing felt shaky as she stood between the two men and made the introductions. "Davey, this is Tanner Lund. Tanner, this is Davey— Kristen's father."

For a moment, the two men glared at each other like angry bears who had claimed territory and were prepared to do battle to protect what was theirs. When they stepped towards each other, Joanna held her breath for fear neither one would make the effort to be civil.

Stunned, she watched as they exchanged hand- shakes and enthusiastic greetings.

"Davey's in town for a real-estate conference and thought he'd stop in to see Kristen," Joanna explained, her words coming out in such a rush that they nearly stumbled over themselves.

"I came to see you, too, Joanna," Davey added in a low sultry voice that suggested he had more on his mind than a chat over a cup of coffee.

She flashed him a heated look before marching into the kitchen, closely followed by both men. She walked straight to the cupboard, bringing down another cup, then poured Tanner's coffee and delivered it to the table.

"Kristen and my daughter are at the library," Tan- ner announced in a perfectly friendly voice, but Joanna heard the undercurrents even if Davey didn't.

"Joanna told me," Davey returned.

The two men remained standing, smiling at each

other. Tanner took a seat first, and Davey promptly did the same.

"What do you do?" her ex-husband asked.

"I own half of Spokane Aluminum."

It was apparent to Joanna that Davey hadn't even bothered to listen to Tanner's reply because he immediately fired back in an aggressive tone, "I recently opened my own real-estate brokerage and have plans to expand within the next couple of years." He announced his success with a cocky slant to his mouth.

Watching the change in Davey's features as Tanner's identity began to sink in was so comical that Joanna nearly laughed out loud. Davey's mouth sagged open, and his eyes flew from Joanna to Tanner and then back to Joanna.

"Spokane Aluminum," Davey repeated slowly, his face unusually pale. "I seem to remember reading something about John Becky taking on a partner."

Joanna almost felt sorry for Davey. "Kristen and Tanner's daughter, Nicole, are best friends. They were in the Valentine's Day show together—the one I was telling you about…"

To his credit, Davey regrouped quickly. "She gets all that performing talent from you."

"Oh, hardly," Joanna countered, denying it with a vigorous shake of her head. Of the two of them, Davey was the entertainer—crowds had never intimidated him. He could walk into a room full of strangers, and anyone who didn't know better would end up thinking Davey Parsons was his best friend.

"With the girls being so close, it seemed only natural for Joanna and me to start dating," Tanner said, turning to smile warmly at Joanna.

"I see," Davey answered. He didn't appear to have recovered from Tanner's first announcement.

"I sincerely hope you do understand," Tanner returned, all pretence of friendliness dropped.

Joanna resisted rolling her eyes toward the ceiling. Both of them were behaving like immature children, battling with looks and words as if she were a prize to be awarded the victor.

"I suppose I'd better think about heading out," Davey said after several awkward moments had passed. He stood up, noticeably eager to make his escape.

As a polite hostess, Joanna stood when Davey did. "I'll walk you to the door."

He sent Tanner a wary smile. "That's not necessary."

"Of course it is," Joanna countered.

To her dismay, Tanner followed them and stood conspicuously in the background while Davey made arrangements to phone Kristen later that evening. The whole time Davey was speaking, Joanna could feel Tanner's eyes burning into her back. She didn't know why he'd insisted on following her to the door. It was like saying he couldn't trust her not to fall into Davey's arms the minute he was out of sight, and that irritated her no end.

Once her ex-husband had left, she closed the door and whirled around to face Tanner. The questions were jammed in her mind. They'd only gone out on one date, for heaven's sake, and here he was, acting as though... as though they were engaged.

"I thought he broke your heart," Tanner said, in a cutting voice.

Joanna debated whether or not to answer him, then decided it would be best to clear the air. "He did."

"I heard you laughing when I rang the doorbell. Do you often have such a good time with men you're supposed to hate?"

"I don't hate Davey."

"Believe me, I can tell."

"Tanner, what's wrong with you?" That was a silly question, and she regretted asking it immediately. She already knew what was troubling Tanner. He was jealous. And angry. And hurt.

"Wrong with me?" He tossed the words back at her. "Nothing's wrong with me. I happen to stumble upon the woman I'm involved with cozying up to her ex-husband, and I don't mind telling you I'm upset. But nothing's wrong with me. Not one damn thing. If there's something wrong with anyone, it's you, lady."

Joanna held tightly onto her patience. "Before we start arguing, let's sit down and talk this out." She led him back into the kitchen, then took Davey's empty coffee mug and placed it in the sink, removing all evidence of his brief visit. She searched for a way to reassure Tanner that Davey meant nothing to her anymore. But she had to explain that she and her ex-husband weren't enemies, either; they couldn't be for Kristen's sake.

"First of all," she said, as evenly as her pounding heart would allow, "I could never hate Davey the way you seem to think I should. As far as I'm concerned, that would only be counterproductive. The people who would end up suffering are Kristen and me. Davey is incapable of being faithful to one woman, but he'll always be Kristen's father, and if for no other reason than that, I prefer to remain on friendly terms with him."

"But he cheated on you…used you."

"Yes." She couldn't deny it. "But, Tanner, I lived a lot of years with Davey. He's not all bad—no one is—and scattered between all the bad times were a few good ones. We're divorced now. What good would it do to harbor ill will toward him? None that I can see."

"He let it be known from the moment I walked into this house that he could have you back any time he wanted."

Joanna wasn't blind; she'd recognized the looks Davey had given Tanner, and the insinuations. "He'd like to believe that. It helps him deal with his ego."

"And you let him?"

"Not the way you're implying."

Tanner mulled that over for a few moments. "How often does he casually drop in unannounced like this?"

She hesitated, wondering whether she should answer his question. His tone had softened, but he was obviously still angry. She could sympathize, but she didn't like having to defend herself or her attitude toward Davey. "I haven't seen him in over a year. This is the first time he's been to the house."

Tanner's hands gripped the coffee mug so tightly that Joanna was amazed it remained intact. "You still love him, don't you?"

The question hit her square between the eyes. Her mouth opened and closed several times as she struggled for the words to deny it. Then she realized she couldn't. Lying to Tanner about this would be simple enough and it would keep the peace, but it would wrong them both. "I suppose in a way I do," she began slowly. "He's the father of my child. He was my first love, Tanner. And the only lover I've ever had. Although I'd like to tell you I don't feel a thing for him, I can't do that and be completely honest. But please, try to understand—"

"You don't need to say anything more." He stood abruptly, his back stiff. "I appreciate the fact that you told me the truth. I won't waste any more of your time. I wish you and Kristen a good life." With that he stalked out of the room, headed for the door.

Joanna was shocked. "Tanner...you make it sound like I'll never see you again."

"I think that would be best for everyone concerned," he replied, without looking at her.

"But...that's silly. Nothing's changed." She snapped her mouth closed. If Tanner wanted to act so childishly and ruin everything, she wasn't about to argue with him. He was the one who insisted they had something special, something so good they shouldn't throw it away because of their fears. And now he was acting like this! Fine. If that was the way he wanted it. It was better to find out how unreasonable he could be before anything serious developed between them. Better to discover now how quick-tempered he could be, how hurtful.

"I have no intention of becoming involved with a woman who's still in love with her loser of an ex-husband," he announced, his hands clenched at his sides. His voice was calm, but she recognized the tension in it. And the resolve.

Unable to restrain her anger any longer, Joanna marched across the room and threw open the front door. "Smart move, Tanner," she said, her words coated with sarcasm. "You made a terrible mistake getting involved with a woman who refuses to hate." Now that she had a better look at him, she decided he wasn't a prince after all, only another frog.

Tanner didn't say a word as he walked past her, his strides filled with purpose. She closed the door and leaned against it, needing the support. Tears burned in her eyes and clogged her throat, but she held her head high and hurried back into the kitchen, determined not to give in to the powerful emotions that racked her, body and soul.

She finished cleaning up the kitchen, and took a long hot shower afterward. Then she sat quietly at the table, waiting for Kristen to phone so she could pick up the two girls. The call came a half hour later, but by that time she'd already reached for the cookies, bent on self-destruction.

On the way home from the library, Joanna stopped off at McDonald's and bought the girls cheeseburgers and chocolate milk shakes to take home for dinner. Her mind was filled with doubts. In retrospect, she wished she'd done a better job of explaining things to Tanner. The thought of never seeing him again was almost too painful to endure.

"Aren't you going to order anything, Mom?" Kristen asked, surprised.

"Not tonight." Somewhere deep inside, Joanna found the energy to smile.

She managed to maintain a lighthearted facade while Kristen and Nicole ate their dinner and chattered about the boys they'd seen at the library and how they were going to shock Mrs. Andrews with their well-researched report.

"Are you feeling okay?" Kristen asked, pausing in midsentence.

"Sure," Joanna lied, looking for something to occupy her hands. She settled for briskly wiping down the kitchen counters. Actually, she felt sick to her stomach, but she couldn't blame Tanner; she'd done that to herself with all those stupid cookies.

It was when she was putting the girls' empty McDonald's containers in the garbage that the silly tears threatened to spill over. She did her best to hide them and quickly carried out the trash. Nicole went to get her MP3 player from Kristen's bedroom, but Kristen followed her mother outside.

"Mom, what's wrong?"

"Nothing, sweetheart."

"You have tears in your eyes."

"It's nothing."

"You never cry," Kristen insisted.

"Something must have got into my eye to make it tear like this," she said, shaking her head. The effort to smile was too much for her. She straightened and placed her hands on Kristen's shoulders, then took a deep breath. "I don't want you to be disappointed if I don't see Mr. Lund again."

"He did this?" Kristen demanded, in a high shocked voice.

"No," Joanna countered immediately. "I already told you, I got something in my eye."

Kristen studied her with a frown, and Joanna tried to meet her daughter's gaze. If she was fool enough to make herself vulnerable to a man again, then she deserved this pain. She'd known better than to get involved with Tanner, but her heart had refused to listen.

A couple of hours later, Tanner arrived to pick up

Nicole. Joanna let Kristen answer the door and stayed in the kitchen, pretending to be occupied there.

When the door swung open, Joanna assumed it was her daughter and asked, "Did Nicole get off all right?"

"Not yet."

Joanna jerked away from the sink at the husky sound of Tanner's voice. "Where are the girls?"

"In Kristen's room. I want to talk to you."

"I can't see how that would do much good."

"I've reconsidered."

"Bravo for you. Unfortunately so have I. You're absolutely right about it being better all around if we don't see each other again."

Tanner dragged his fingers through his hair and stalked to the other side of the room. "Okay, I'll admit it. I was jealous as hell when I walked in and found you having coffee with Davey. I felt you were treating him like some conquering hero returned from the war."

"Oh, honestly, it wasn't anything like that."

"You were laughing and smiling."

"Grievous sins, I'm sure."

Tanner clamped down his jaw so hard that the sides of his face went white. "All I can do is apologise, Joanna. I've already made a fool of myself over one woman who loved someone else, and frankly that caused me enough grief. I'm not looking to repeat the mistake with you."

A strained silence fell between them.

"I thought I could walk away from you and not feel any regrets, but I was wrong," he continued a moment later. "I haven't stopped thinking about you all afternoon. Maybe I overreacted. Maybe I behaved like a jealous fool."

"Maybe?" Joanna challenged. "Maybe? You were unreasonable and hurtful and…and I ate a whole row of Oreo cookies over you."

"What?"

"You heard me. I stuffed down a dozen cookies and now I think I'm going to be sick and it was all because of you. I've come too far to be reduced to that. One argument with you and I was right back into the Oreos! If you think you're frightened—because of what happened with Carmen—it's nothing compared to the fears I've been facing since the day we met. I can't deal with your insecurities, Tanner. I've got too damn many of my own."

"Joanna, I've already apologized. If you can honestly tell me there isn't any chance that you'll ever get back together with Davey, I swear to you I'll drop the subject and never bring it up again. But I need to know that much. I'm sorry, but I've got to hear you say it."

"I had a nice quiet life before you paraded into it," she went on, as though she hadn't heard him.

"Joanna, I asked you a question." His intense gaze cut straight through her.

"You must be nuts! I'd be certifiably insane to ever take Davey back. Our marriage—our entire relationship—was over the day I filed for divorce, and probably a lot earlier than that."

Tanner relaxed visibly. "I wouldn't blame you if you decided you never wanted to see me again, but I'm hoping you'll be able to forget what happened this afternoon so we can go back to being…friends again."

Joanna struggled against the strong pull of his magnetism for as long as she could, then nodded, agreeing to place this quarrel behind them.

Tanner walked toward her and she met him halfway, slipping easily into his embrace. She felt as if she belonged here, as if he were the man she would always be content with. He'd once told her he wouldn't ever hurt her the way her ex-husband had, but caring about him, risking a relationship with him, left her vulnerable all over again. She'd realised that this afternoon, learned again what it was to give a man the power to hurt her.

"I reduced you to gorging yourself with Oreos?" Tanner whispered the question into her hair.

She nodded wildly. "You fiend. I didn't mean to eat that many, but I sat at the table with the Oreos package and a glass of milk and the more I thought about what happened, the angrier I became, and the faster I shoved those cookies into my mouth."

"Could this mean you care?" His voice was still a whisper.

She nodded a second time. "I hate fighting with you. My stomach was in knots all afternoon."

"Good Lord, Joanna," he said, dropping several swift kisses on her face. "I can't believe what fools we are."

"We?" She tilted back her head and glared up at him, but her mild indignation drained away the moment their eyes met. Tanner was looking down at her with such tenderness, such concern, that every negative emotion she'd experienced earlier that afternoon vanished like rain falling into a clear blue lake.

He kissed her then, with a thoroughness that left her in no doubt about the strength of his feelings. Joanna rested against this warmth, holding on to him with everything that was in her. When he raised his head, she looked up at him through tear-filled eyes and blinked furiously in a futile effort to keep them at bay.

"I'm glad you came back," she said, when she could find her voice.

"I am, too." He kissed her once more, lightly this time, sampling her lips, kissing the tears from her face. "I wasn't worth a damn all afternoon." Once more he lowered his mouth to hers, creating a delicious sensation that electrified Joanna and sent chills racing down her spine.

Tanner's arms tightened as loud voices suddenly erupted from the direction of the living room.

"I never want to see you again," Joanna heard Kristen declare vehemently.

"You couldn't possibly want to see me any less than I want to see you," Nicole returned with equal volume and fury.

"What's that all about?" Tanner asked, his eyes searching Joanna's.

"I don't know, but I think we'd better find out."

Tanner led the way into the living room. They discovered Kristen and Nicole standing face to face, glaring at each other in undisguised antagonism.

"Kristen, stop that right now," Joanna demanded. "Nicole is a guest in our home and I won't have you talking to her in that tone of voice."

Tanner moved to his daughter's side. "And you're Kristen's guest. I expect you to be on your best behaviour whenever you're here."

Nicole crossed her arms over her chest and darted a venomous look in Kristen's direction. "I refuse to be friends with her ever again. And I don't think you should have anything more to do with Mrs. Parsons."

Joanna's eyes found Tanner's.

"I don't want my mother to have anything to do with Mr. Lund, either." Kristen spun around and glared at Tanner and Nicole.

"I think we'd best separate these two and find out what happened," Joanna suggested. She pointed toward Kristen's bedroom. "Come on, honey, let's talk."

Kristen averted her face. "I have nothing to say!" she declared melodramatically and stalked out of the room without a backward glance.

Joanna raised questioning eyes to Tanner, threw up her hands and followed her daughter.

Twelve

"Kristen, what's wrong?" Joanna sat on the end of her daughter's bed and patiently waited for the eleven-year-old to repeat the list of atrocities committed by Nicole Lund.

"Nothing."

Joanna had seen her daughter wear this affronted look often enough to recognize it readily, and she felt a weary sigh work its way through her. Hell hath no fury like a sixth-grader done wrong by her closest friend.

"I don't ever want to see Nicole again."

"But, sweetheart, she's your best friend."

"*Was* my best friend," Kristen announced theatrically. She crossed her arms over her chest with all the pomp of a queen who'd made her statement and expected unquestioning acquiescence.

With mounting frustration, Joanna folded her hands in her lap and waited, knowing better than to try to reason with Kristen when she was in this mood. Five minutes passed, but Kristen didn't utter another word. Joanna wasn't surprised.

"Does your argument have to do with something

that happened at school?" she asked as nonchalantly as possible, examining the fingernails on her right hand.

Kristen shook her head. She pinched her lips as if to suggest that nothing Joanna could say would force the information out of her.

"Does it involve a boy?" Joanna persisted.

Kristen's gaze widened. "Of course not."

"What about another friend?"

"Nope."

At the rate they were going, Joanna would soon run out of questions. "Can't you just tell me what happened?"

Kristen cast her a look that seemed to question her mother's intelligence. "No!"

"Does that mean we're going to sit here all night while I try to guess?"

Kristen twisted her head and tilted it at a lofty angle, then pantomimed locking her lips.

"All right," Joanna said with an exaggerated sigh, "I'll simply have to ask Nicole, who will, no doubt, be more than ready to tell all. Her version should be highly interesting."

"Mr. Lund made you cry!" Kristen mumbled, her eyes lowered.

Joanna blinked back her astonishment. "You mean to say this whole thing has to do with Tanner and me?"

Kristen nodded once.

"But—"

"Nicole claims that whatever happened was obviously your fault, and as far as I'm concerned that did it. From here on out, Nicole is no longer my friend and I don't think you should have anything to do with... with that man, either."

"That man?"

Kristen sent her a sour look. "You know very well who I mean."

Joanna shifted farther onto the bed, brought up her knees and rested her chin on them. She paused to carefully measure her words. "What if I told you I was beginning to grow fond of 'that man'?"

"Mom, no!" Her daughter's eyes widened with horror, and she cast her mother a look of sheer panic. "That would be the worst possible thing to happen. You might marry him and then Nicole and I would end up being sisters!"

Joanna made no attempt to conceal her surprise. "But, Kristen, from the not-so-subtle hints you and Nicole have been giving me and Mr. Lund, I thought that was exactly what you both wanted. What you'd planned."

"That was before."

"Before what?"

"Before...tonight, when Nicole said those things she said. I can't forgive her, Mom, I just can't."

Joanna stayed in the room a few more silent minutes, then left. Tanner and Nicole were talking in the living room, and from the frustrated look he gave her, she knew he hadn't been any more successful with his daughter than Joanna had been with hers.

When he saw Joanna, Tanner got to his feet and nodded toward the kitchen, mutely suggesting they talk privately and compare stories.

"What did you find out?" she asked the minute they were alone.

Tanner shrugged, then gestured defeat with his

hands. "I don't understand it. She keeps saying she never wants to see Kristen again."

"Kristen says the same thing. Adamantly. She seems to think she's defending my honour. It seems this all has to do with our misunderstanding earlier this afternoon."

"Nicole seems to think it started when you didn't order anything at McDonalds," Tanner said, his expression confused.

"What?" Joanna's question escaped on a short laugh.

"From what I can get out of Nicole, Kristen claims you didn't order a Big Mac, which is supposed to mean something. Then later, before I arrived, there was some mention of your emptying the garbage when it was only half-full?" He paused to wait for her to speak. When she simply nodded, he continued, "I understand that's unusual for you, as well?"

Once more Joanna nodded. She'd wanted to hide her tears from the girls, so taking out the garbage had been an excuse to escape for a couple of minutes while she composed herself.

Tanner wiped his hand across his brow in mock relief. "Whew! At least neither of them learned about the Oreos!"

Joanna ignored his joke and slumped against the kitchen counter with a long slow sigh of frustration. "Having the girls argue is a problem neither of us anticipated."

"Maybe I should talk to Kristen and you talk to Nicole?" Tanner suggested, all seriousness again.

Joanna shook her head. "Then we'd be guilty of interfering. We'd be doing the same thing they've done to us—and I don't think we'd be doing them any favors."

"What do you suggest then?" Tanner asked, looking more disgruntled by the minute.

Joanna shrugged. "I don't know."

"Come on, Joanna, we're intelligent adults. Surely we can come up with a way to handle a couple of pre-adolescent egos."

"Be my guest," Joanna said, and laughed aloud at the comical look that crossed Tanner's handsome face.

"Forget it."

Joanna brushed the hair away from her face. "I think our best bet is to let them work this matter out between themselves."

Tanner's forehead creased in concern, then he nodded, his look reluctant. "I hope this doesn't mean you and I can't be friends." His tender gaze held hers.

Joanna was forced to lower her eyes so he couldn't see just how important his friendship had become to her. "Of course we can."

"Good." He walked across the room and gently pulled her into his arms. He kissed her until she was weak and breathless. When he raised his head, he said in a husky murmur, "I'll take Nicole home now and do as you suggest. We'll give these two a week to settle their differences. After that, you and I are taking over."

"A week?" Joanna wasn't sure that would be long enough, considering Kristen's attitude.

"A week!" Tanner repeated emphatically, kissing her again.

By the time he'd finished, Joanna would have agreed to almost anything. "All right," she managed. "A week."

"How was school today?" Joanna asked Kristen on Monday evening while they sat at the dinner table.

She'd waited as long as she could before asking. If either girl was inclined to make a move toward reconciliation, it would be now, she reasoned. They'd both had ample time to think about what had happened and to determine the value of their friendship.

Kristen shrugged. "School was fine, I guess."

Joanna took her time eating her salad, focusing her attention on it instead of her daughter. "How'd you do on the math paper I helped you with?"

Kristen rolled her eyes. "You showed me wrong."

"Wrong!"

"The answers were all right, but Mrs. Andrews told me they don't figure out equations that way anymore."

"Oh. Sorry about that."

"You weren't the only parent who messed up."

That was good to hear.

"A bunch of other kids did it wrong. Including Nicole."

Joanna slipped her hand around her water glass. Kristen sounded far too pleased that her ex-friend had messed up the assignment. That wasn't encouraging. "So you saw Nicole today?"

"I couldn't very well not see her. Her desk is across the aisle from mine. But if you're thinking what I think you're thinking, you can forget it. I don't need a friend like Nicole Lund."

Joanna didn't comment on that, although she practically had to bite her tongue. She wondered how Tanner was doing. Staying out of this argument between the two girls was far more difficult than she'd imagined. It was obvious to Joanna that Kristen was miserable without her best friend, but saying as much would hurt her case more than help it. Kristen needed to recognize the fact herself.

The phone rang while Joanna was finishing up the last of the dinner dishes. Kristen was in the bath, so Joanna grabbed the receiver, holding it between her hunched shoulder and her ear while she squirted detergent into the hot running water.

"Hello?"

"Joanna? Good Lord, you sounded just like Kristen there. I was prepared to have the phone slammed in my ear," Tanner said. "How's it going?"

Her heart swelled with emotion. She hadn't talked to him since Saturday, and it felt as though months had passed since she'd heard his voice. It wrapped itself around her now, warm and comforting. "Things aren't going too well. How are they at your end?"

"Not much better. Did you know Kristen had the nerve to eat lunch with Nora this afternoon? In case you weren't aware of this, Nora is Nicole's sworn enemy."

"Nora?" Joanna could hardly believe her ears. "Kristen doesn't even like the girl." If anything, this war between Kristen and Nicole was heating up.

"I hear you bungled the math assignment," Tanner said softly, amused.

"Apparently you did, too."

He chuckled. "Yeah, this new math is beyond me." He paused, and when he spoke, Joanna could hear the frustration in his voice. "I wish the girls would hurry and patch things up. Frankly, Joanna, I miss you like crazy."

"It's only been two days." She should talk—the last forty-eight hours had seemed like an eternity.

"It feels like two years."

"I know," she agreed softly, closing her eyes and savoring Tanner's words. "But we don't usually see each other during the week anyway." At least not during the past couple of weeks.

"I've been thinking things over and I may have come up with an idea that will put us all out of our misery."

"What?" By now, Joanna was game for anything.

"How about a movie?" he asked unexpectedly, his voice eager.

"But Tanner—"

"Tomorrow night. You can bring Kristen and I'll bring Nicole, and we could accidentally-on-purpose meet at the theater. Naturally there'll be a bit of acting on our part and some huffing and puffing on theirs, but if things work out the way I think they will, we won't have to do a thing. Nature will take its course."

Joanna wasn't convinced this scheme of his would work. The whole thing could blow up in their faces, but the thought of being with Tanner was too enticing to refuse. "All right," she agreed. "As long as you buy the popcorn and promise to hold my hand."

"You've got yourself a deal."

On Tuesday evening, Kristen was unusually quiet over dinner. Joanna had fixed one of her daughter's favorite meals—macaroni-and-cheese casserole—but Kristen barely touched it.

"Do you feel like going to a movie?" Joanna asked, her heart in her throat. Normally Kristen would leap at the idea, but this evening Joanna couldn't predict anything.

"It's a school night, and I don't think I'm in the mood to see a movie."

"But you said you didn't have any homework, and it sounds like a fun thing to do…and weren't you saying something about wanting to see Tom Cruise's latest film?" Kristen's eyes momentarily brightened, then faded. "And don't worry," Joanna added cheerfully, "you won't have to sit with me."

Kristen gave a huge sigh. "I don't have anyone else to sit with," she said, as though Joanna had suggested a trip to the dentist.

It wasn't until they were in the parking lot at the theater that Kristen spoke. "Nicole likes Tom Cruise, too."

Joanna made a noncommittal reply, wondering how easily the girls would see through her and Tanner's scheme.

"Mom," Kristen cried. "I see Nicole. She's with her dad. Oh, no, it looks like they're going to the same movie."

"Oh, no," Joanna echoed, her heart acting like a Ping-Pong ball in her chest. "Does this mean you want to skip the whole thing and go home?"

"Of course not," Kristen answered smugly. She practically bounded out of the car once Joanna turned off the engine, glancing anxiously at Joanna when she didn't walk across the parking lot fast enough to suit her.

They joined the line, about eight people behind Tanner and Nicole. Joanna was undecided about what to do next. She wasn't completely sure that Tanner had even seen her. If he had, he was playing his part perfectly, acting as though this whole thing had happened by coincidence.

Kristen couldn't seem to stand still. She peeked around the couple ahead of them several times, loudly humming the song of Heart's that she and Nicole had performed in the talent show.

Nicole whirled around, standing on her tiptoes and staring into the crowd behind her. She jerked on Tanner's sleeve and, when he bent down, whispered something in his ear. Then Tanner turned around, too, and pretended to be shocked when he saw Joanna and Kristen.

By the time they were inside the theater, Tanner and Nicole had disappeared. Kristen was craning her neck in every direction while Joanna stood at the refreshment counter.

"Do you want any popcorn?"

"No. Just some of those raisin things. Mom, you said I didn't have to sit with you. Did you really mean that?"

"Yes, honey, don't worry about it, I'll find a place by myself."

"You're sure?" Kristen looked only mildly concerned.

"No problem. You go sit by yourself."

"Okay." Kristen collected her candy and was gone before Joanna could say any more.

Since it was still several minutes before the movie was scheduled to start, the theater auditorium was well lit. Joanna found a seat toward the back and noted that Kristen was two rows from the front. Nicole sat in the row behind her.

"Is this seat taken?"

Joanna smiled up at Tanner as he claimed the seat next to her, and had they been anyplace else she was sure he would have kissed her. He handed her a bag of popcorn and a cold drink.

"I sure hope this works," he muttered under his breath, "because if Nicole sees me sitting with you, I could be hung as a traitor." Mischief brightened his eyes. "But the risk is worth it. Did anyone ever tell you how kissable your mouth looks?"

"Tanner," she whispered frantically and pointed toward the girls. "Look."

Kristen sat twisted around and Nicole leaned forward. Kristen shook a handful of her chocolate-covered raisins into Nicole's outstretched hand. Nicole offered Kristen some popcorn. After several of these exchanges, both girls stood up, moved from their seats to a different row entirely, sitting next to each other.

"That looks promising," Joanna whispered.

"It certainly does," Tanner agreed, slipping his arm around her shoulder.

They both watched as Kristen and Nicole tilted their heads toward each other and smiled at the sound of their combined giggles drifting to the back of the theater.

Thirteen

After their night at the movies, Joanna didn't give Tanner's invitation to the dinner party more than a passing thought until she read about the event on the society page of Wednesday's newspaper. The *Review* described the dinner, which was being sponsored by Spokane Aluminum, as the gala event of the year. Anyone who was anyone in the eastern half of Washington state would be attending. Until Joanna noticed the news article, she'd thought it was a small intimate party; that was the impression Tanner had given her.

From that moment on, Joanna started worrying, though she wasn't altogether sure why. As a loan officer, she'd attended her share of business-related social functions...but never anything of this scope. The problem, she decided, was one she'd been denying since the night of Nicole's slumber party. Tanner's social position and wealth far outdistanced her own. He was an important member of their community, and she was just a spoke in the wheel of everyday life.

Now, as she dressed for the event, her uneasiness grew, because she knew how important this evening was to Tanner—although he hadn't told her in so many words. The reception and dinner were all part of his becoming half owner of a major corporation and, according to the newspaper article, had been in the planning stages for several months after his arrival. All John Becky's way of introducing Tanner to the community leaders.

Within the first half hour of their arrival, Joanna recognized the mayor and a couple of members from the city council, plus several other people she didn't know, who nonetheless looked terribly important.

"Here," Tanner whispered, stepping to her side and handing her a glass of champagne.

Smiling up at him, she took the glass and held the dainty stem in a death grip, angry with herself for being so unnerved. It wasn't as though she'd never seen the mayor before—okay, only in pictures, but still... "I don't know if I dare have anything too potent," she admitted.

"Why not?"

"If you want the truth, I feel out of it at this affair. I'd prefer to fade into the background, mingle among the draperies, get acquainted with the wallpaper. That sort of thing."

Tanner's smile was encouraging. "No one would know it to look at you."

Joanna had trouble believing that. The smile she wore felt frozen on her lips, and her stomach protested the fact that she'd barely managed to eat all day. Tonight was important, and for Tanner's sake she'd do what she had to.

The man who owned the controlling interest in Columbia Basin Savings and Loan strolled past them and paused when he recognized her. Joanna nodded her recognition, and when he continued on she swallowed the entire glass of champagne in three giant gulps.

"I feel better," she announced.

"Good."

Tanner apparently hadn't noticed how quickly she'd downed the champagne, for which Joanna was grateful.

"Come over here. There are some people I want you to meet."

More people! Tanner had already introduced her to so many that the names were swimming around in her head like fish crowded in a small pond. She'd tried to keep them all straight, and it had been simple in the beginning when he'd started with his partner, John Becky, and John's wife, Jean, but from that point on her memory had deteriorated steadily.

Tanner pressed his hand to the middle of her spine and steered her across the room to where a small group had gathered.

Along the way, Joanna picked up another glass of champagne, just so she'd have something to do with her hands. The way she was feeling, she had no intention of drinking it.

The men and women paused in the middle of their conversation when Tanner approached. After a few words of greeting, introductions were made.

"Pleased to meet all of you," Joanna said, forcing some life into her fatigued smile. Everyone seemed to be looking at her, expecting something more. She nodded toward Tanner. "Our daughters are best friends."

The others smiled.

"I didn't know you had a daughter," a voluptuous blonde said, smiling sweetly up at Tanner.

"Nicole just turned twelve."

The blonde seemed fascinated with this information. "How very sweet. My niece is ten and I know she'd just love to meet Nicole. Perhaps we could get the two of them together. Soon."

"I'm sure Nicole would like that."

"It's a date then." She sidled as close to Tanner as she possibly could, practically draping her breast over his forearm.

Joanna narrowed her gaze and took a small sip of the champagne. The blonde, whose name was—she searched her mind—Blaise, couldn't have been any more obvious had she issued an invitation to her bed.

"Tanner, there's someone you must meet—that is, if I can drag you away from Joanna for just a little minute." The blonde cast a challenging look in Joanna's direction.

"Oh, sure." Joanna gestured with her hand as though to let Blaise know Tanner was free to do as he wished. She certainly didn't have any claims on him.

Tanner frowned. "Come with us," he suggested.

Joanna threw him what she hoped was a dazzling smile. "Go on. You'll only be gone a little minute," she said sweetly, purposely echoing Blaise's words.

The two left, Blaise clinging to Tanner's arm, and Joanna chatted with the others in the group for a few more minutes before fading into the background. Her stomach was twisted in knots. She didn't know why she'd sent Tanner off like that, when it so deeply upset her. Something in her refused to let him know that; it was difficult enough to admit even to herself.

Hoping she wasn't being obvious, her gaze followed Tanner and Blaise until she couldn't endure it any longer, and then she turned and made her way into the ladies' room. Joanna was grateful that the outer room was empty, and she slouched onto the sofa. Her heart was slamming painfully against her rib cage, and when she pressed her hands to her cheeks her face felt hot and feverish. Joanna would gladly have paid the entire three hundred and fifteen dollars in her savings account for a way to gracefully disappear.

It was then that she knew.

She was in love with Tanner Lund. Despite all the warnings she'd given herself. Despite the fact that they were worlds apart, financially and socially.

With the realisation that she loved Tanner came another. The night had only begun—they hadn't even eaten yet. The ordeal of a formal dinner still lay before her.

"Hello again," Jean Becky said, strolling into the ladies' room. She stopped for a moment, watching Joanna, then sat down beside her.

"Oh, hi." Joanna managed the semblance of a smile to greet the likeable older woman.

"I just saw Blaise Ferguson walk past clinging to Tanner. I hope you're not upset."

"Oh heavens, no," Joanna lied.

"Good. Blaise, er, has something of a reputation, and I didn't want you to worry. I'm sure Tanner's smart enough not to be taken in by someone that obvious."

"I'm sure he is, too."

"You're a sensible young woman," Jean said, looking pleased.

At the moment, Joanna didn't feel the least bit sensible. The one emotion she was experiencing was fear. She'd fallen in love again, and the first time had been so painful she had promised never to let it happen again. But it had. With Tanner Lund, yet. Why couldn't she have fallen for the mechanic who'd worked so hard repairing her car last winter, or someone at the office? Oh, no, she had to fall—and fall hard—for the most eligible man in town. The man every single woman in the party had her eye on this evening.

"It really has been a pleasure meeting you," Jean continued. "Tanner and Nicole talk about you and your daughter so often. We've been friends of Tanner's for several years now, and it gladdens our hearts to see him finally meet a good woman."

"Thank you." Joanna wasn't sure what to think about being classified as a "good woman." It made her wonder who Tanner had dated before he'd met her. She'd never asked him about his social life before he'd moved to Spokane—or even after. She wasn't sure she wanted to know. No doubt he'd made quite a splash when he came to town. Rich, handsome, available men were a rare commodity these days. It was a wonder he hadn't been snatched up long before now.

Five minutes later, Joanna had composed herself enough to rejoin the party. Tanner was at her side within a few seconds, noticeably irritable and short-tempered.

"I've been searching all over for you," he said, frowning heavily.

Joanna let that remark slide. "I thought you were otherwise occupied."

"Why'd you let that she-cat walk off with me like that?" His eyes were hot with fury. "Couldn't you tell I wanted out? Good Lord, woman, what do I have to do, flash flags?"

"No." A waiter walked past with a loaded tray, and Joanna deftly reached out and helped herself to another glass of champagne.

Just as smoothly, Tanner removed it from her fingers. "I think you've had enough."

Joanna took the glass back from him. She might not completely understand what was happening to her this evening, but she certainly didn't like his attitude. "Excuse me, Tanner, but I am perfectly capable of determining my own limit."

His frown darkened into a scowl. "It's taken me the last twenty minutes to extract myself from her claws. The least you could have done was stick around instead of doing a disappearing act."

"No way." Being married to Davey all those years had taught her more than one valuable lesson. If her ex-husband, Tanner, or any other man, for that matter, expected her to make a scene over another woman, it wouldn't work. Joanna was through with those kinds of destructive games.

"What do you mean by that?"

"I'm just not the jealous type. If you were to go home with Blaise, that'd be fine with me. In fact, you could leave with her right now. I'll grab a cab. I'm really not up to playing the role of a jealous girlfriend because another woman happens to show some interest in you. Nor am I willing to find a flimsy excuse to extract you from her clutches. You look more than capable of doing that yourself."

"You honestly want me to leave with Blaise?" His words were low and hard.

Joanna made a show of shrugging. "It's entirely up

to you—you're free to do as you please. Actually you might be doing me a favor."

Joanna couldn't remember ever seeing a man more angry. His eyes seemed to spit fire at her. His jaws clamped together tightly, and he held himself with such an unnatural stiffness, it was surprising that something in his body didn't crack. She observed all this in some distant part of her mind, her concentration focused on preserving her facade of unconcern.

"I'm beginning to understand Davey," he said, his tone as cold as an arctic wind. "Has it ever occurred to you that your ex-husband turned to other women out of a desperate need to know you cared?"

Tanner's words hurt more than any physical blow could have. Joanna's breath caught in her throat, though she did her best to disguise the pain his remark had inflicted. When she was finally able to breathe, the words tumbled from her lips. "No. Funny, I never thought of that." She paused and searched the room. "Pick a woman then, any woman will do, and I'll slug it out with her."

"Joanna, stop it," Tanner hissed.

"You mean you don't want me to fight?"

He closed his eyes as if seeking patience. "No."

Dramatically, Joanna placed her hand over her heart. "Thank goodness. I don't know how I'd ever explain a black eye to Kristen."

Dinner was about to be served, and, tucking his hand under her elbow, Tanner led Joanna into the banquet room, which was quickly filling up.

"I'm sorry, I didn't mean that about Davey," Tanner whispered as they strolled toward the dining room. "I realize you're nervous, but no one would ever know it—except me. We'll discuss this Blaise thing later."

Joanna nodded, feeling subdued now, accepting his apology. She realized that she'd panicked earlier, and not because this was an important social event, either. She'd attended enough business dinners in her career to know she hadn't made a fool of herself. What disturbed her so much was the knowledge that she'd fallen in love with Tanner.

To add to Joanna's dismay, she discovered that she was expected to sit at the head table between Tanner and John Becky. She trembled at the thought, but she wasn't about to let anyone see her nervousness.

"Don't worry," Tanner said, stroking her hand after they were seated. "Everyone who's met you has been impressed."

His statement was meant to lend her courage; unfortunately it had the opposite effect. What had she said or done to impress anyone?

When the evening was finally over, Tanner appeared to be as eager to escape as she was. With a minimum of fuss, they made their farewells and were gone.

Once in the car, Tanner didn't speak. But when he parked in front of the house, he turned off the car engine and said quietly, "Invite me in for coffee."

It was on the tip of Joanna's tongue to tell him she had a headache, which was fast becoming the truth, but delaying the inevitable wouldn't help either of them.

"Okay," she mumbled.

The house was quiet, and Sally was asleep on the sofa. Joanna paid her and waited on the front porch while the teenager ran across the street to her own house. Gathering her courage, she walked into the kitchen. Tanner had put the water and ground coffee into the machine and taken two cups down from the cupboard.

"Okay," he said, turning around to face her, "I want to know what's wrong."

The bewilderment in his eyes made Joanna raise her chin an extra notch. Then she remembered Kristen doing the same thing when she'd questioned her about her argument with Nicole, and the recollection wasn't comforting.

Joanna was actually surprised Tanner had guessed anything was wrong. She thought she'd done a brilliant job of disguising her distress. She'd done her best to say and do all the right things. When Tanner had stood up, after the meal, to give his talk, she'd whispered encouragement and smiled at him. Throughout the rest of the evening, she'd chatted easily with both Tanner and John Becky.

Now she had to try to explain something she barely understood herself.

"I don't think I ever realized what an important man you are," she said, struggling to find her voice. "I've always seen you as Nicole's father, the man who was crazy enough to agree to a slumber party for his daughter's birthday. The man who called and disguised his voice so Kristen wouldn't recognise it. That's the man I know, not the one tonight who stood before a filled banquet room and promised growth and prosperity for our city. Not the man who charts the destiny of an entire community."

Tanner glared at her. "What has that got to do with anything?"

"You play in the big league. I'm in the minors."

Tanner's gaze clouded with confusion. "I'm talking about our relationship and you're discussing baseball!"

Pulling out a kitchen chair, Joanna sat in it and took a deep breath. The best place to start, she decided, was the beginning. "You have to understand that I didn't come away from my marriage without a few quirks."

Tanner started pacing, clearly not in the mood to sit still. "Quirks? You call what happened with Blaise a quirk? I call it loony. Some woman I don't know from Adam comes up to me—"

"Eve," Joanna inserted, and when he stared at her, uncomprehending, she elaborated. "Since Blaise Ferguson's a woman, you don't know her from Eve."

"Whatever!"

"Well, it does make a difference." The coffee had finished filtering into the pot, so Joanna got up and poured them each a cup. Holding hers in both hands, she leaned against the counter and took a tentative sip.

"Some woman I don't know from Eve," Tanner tried again, "comes up to me, and you act as if you can't wait to get me out of your hair."

"*You* acted as if you expected me to come to your rescue. Honestly, Tanner, you're a big boy. I assumed you could take care of yourself."

"You looked more than happy to see me go with her."

"That's not true. I was content where I was." Joanna knew they were sidestepping the real issue, but this other business seemed to concern Tanner more.

"You were content to go into hiding."

"If you're looking for someone to fly into a jealous rage every time another woman winks at you, you'll need to look elsewhere."

Tanner did some more pacing, his steps growing longer and heavier with each circuit of the kitchen. "Explain what you meant when you said you didn't come away from your marriage without a few quirks."

"It's simply really," she said, making light of it. "Davey used to get a kick out of introducing me to his women friends. Everyone in the room knew what he was doing, except me. I was so stupid, so blind, that I just didn't know any better. Once the scales fell from my eyes, I was astonished at what a complete fool I'd been. But when I became wise to his ways, it was much worse. Every time he introduced me to a woman, I'd be filled with suspicion. Was Davey involved with her, or wasn't he? The only thing left for me to do was hold my head high and smile." Her voice was growing tighter with every word, cracking just as she finished.

Tanner walked toward her and reached out his hands as though to comfort her. "Joanna, listen—"

"No." She set her coffee aside and wrapped her arms around her middle. "I feel honored, Tanner, that you would ask me to attend this important dinner with you tonight. I think we both learned something valuable from the experience. At least, I know I did."

"Joanna—"

"No," she cut in again, "let me finish, please. Although it's difficult to say this, it needs to be said. We're not right for each other. We've been so caught up in everything we had in common and what good friends the girls are and how wonderful it felt to…be together, we didn't stop to notice that we live in different worlds." She paused and gathered her resolve before continuing. "Knowing you and becoming your friend has been wonderful, but anything beyond that just isn't going to work."

"The only thing I got carried away with was you, Joanna. The girls have nothing to do with it."

"I feel good that you would say that, I really do, but we both lost sight of the fact that neither one of us wants to become involved. That had never been our intention. Something happened, and I'm not sure when or why, but suddenly everything is so intense between us. It's got to stop before we end up really hurting each other."

Tanner seemed to mull over her words. "You're so frightened of giving another man the power to hurt you that you can't see anything else, can you?" His brooding, confused look was back. "I told you this once, but it didn't seem to sink into that head of yours—I'm never going to do the things Davey did. We're two entirely different men, and it's time you realized that."

"What you say may very well be true, Tanner, but I don't see what difference it's going to make. Because I have no intention of involving myself in another relationship."

"In case you hadn't noticed, Joanna, we're already involved."

"Roller-skating in the couples round doesn't qualify as being involved to me," she said, in a futile attempt at humor. It fell flat.

Tanner was the first to break the heavy silence that followed. "You've obviously got some thinking to do," he said wearily. "For that matter, so do I. Call me, Joanna, when you're in the mood to be reasonable."

Fourteen

"Hi, Mom," Kristen said, slumping down on the sofa beside Joanna. "I hope you know I'm bored out of my mind," she said, and sighed deeply.

Joanna was busy counting the stitches on her knitting needle and didn't pause to answer until she'd finished. "What about your homework?"

"Cute, Mom, real cute. It's spring break—I don't have any homework."

"Right. Phone Nicole then. I bet she'll commiserate with you." And she might even give Kristen some information about Tanner. He'd walked out of her house, and although she'd thought her heart would break she'd let him go. Since then, she'd reconsidered. She was dying to hear something from Tanner. Anything. But she hadn't—not since the party more than a week earlier, and each passing day seemed like a lifetime.

"Calling Nicole is a nothing idea."

"I could suggest you clean your room."

"Funny, Mom, real funny."

"Gee, I'm funny and cute all in one evening. How'd I get so lucky?"

Not bothering to answer, Kristen reached for a magazine and idly thumbed through the pages, not finding a single picture or article worth more than a fleeting glance. She set it aside and reached for another. By the time she'd gone through the four magazines resting on top of the coffee table, Joanna was losing her patience.

"Call Nicole."

"I can't."

"Why not?"

"Because I can't."

That didn't make much sense to Joanna. And suggesting that Kristen phone Nicole was another sign of her willingness to settle this rift between her and Tanner. It had been so long since she'd last seen or heard from him. Ten interminable days, and with each one that passed she missed him more. She'd debated long and hard about calling him, wavering with indecision, battling with her pride. What she'd told him that night had been the truth—they did live in different worlds. But she'd overreacted at the dinner party, and now she felt guilty about how the evening had gone. When he'd left the house, Tanner had suggested she call him when she was ready to be reasonable. Well, she'd been ready the following morning, ready to acknowledge her fault. And her need. But pride held her back. And with each passing day, it became more difficult to swallow that pride.

"You know I can't call Nicole," Kristen whined.

"Why not? Did you have another argument?" Joanna asked without looking at her daughter. Her mind was preoccupied with counting stitches. She always knitted when she was frustrated with herself; it was a form of self-punishment, she suspected wryly.

"We never fight. Not anymore. Nicole's in West Virginia."

Joanna paused and carefully set the knitting needles down on her lap. "Oh? What's she doing there?"

"I think she went to visit her mother."

"Her mother?" It took some effort to keep her heart from exploding in her throat. According to Tanner, Nicole hadn't seen or heard from Carmen in three years. His biggest worry, he'd told her, was that someday his ex-wife would develop an interest in their daughter and steal her away from him. "Nicole is with her mother?" Joanna repeated, to be certain she'd heard Kristen correctly.

"You knew that."

"No, I didn't."

"Yes, you did. I told you she was leaving last Sunday. Remember?"

Vaguely, Joanna recalled the conversation—she'd been peeling potatoes at the sink—but for the last week, every time Kristen mentioned either Tanner or Nicole, Joanna had made an effort to tune her daughter out. Now she was hungry for information, starving for every tidbit Kristen was willing to feed her.

The eleven-year-old straightened and stared at her mother. "Didn't Mr. Lund mention Nicole was leaving?"

"Er, no."

Kristen sighed and threw herself against the back of the sofa. "You haven't been seeing much of him lately, have you?"

"Er, no."

Kristen picked up Joanna's hand and patted it gently. "You two had a fight?"

"Not exactly."

Her daughter's hand continued its soothing action. "Okay, tell me all about it. Don't hold back a single thing—you need to talk this out. Bare your soul."

"Kristen!"

"Mom, you need this. Releasing your anger and frustration will help. You've got to work out all that inner agitation and responsive turbulence. It's disrupting your emotional poise. Seriously, Mom, have you ever considered Rolfing?"

"Emotional poise? Responsive turbulence? Where'd you hear about that? Where'd you hear about Rolfing?"

Kristen blinked and cocked her head to one side, doing her best to look concerned and sympathetic. "Oprah Winfrey."

"I see," Joanna muttered, and rolled her eyes.

"Are you or are you not going to tell me all about it?"

"No, I am not!"

Kristen released a deep sigh that expressed her keen disappointment. "I thought not. When it comes to Nicole's dad, you never want to talk about it. It's like a deep dark secret the two of you keep from Nicole and me. Well, that's all right—we're doing our best to understand. You don't want us to get our hopes up that you two might be interested in each other. I can accept that, although I consider it grossly unfair." She stood up and gazed at her mother with undisguised longing, then loudly slapped her hands against her sides. "I'm perfectly content to live the way we do...but it sure would be nice to have a baby sister to dress up. And you know how I've *always* wanted a brother."

"Kristen!"

"No, Mom." She held up her hand as though she

were stopping a freight train. "Really, I do understand. You and I get along fine the way we are. I guess we don't need to complicate our lives with Nicole and her dad. That could even cause real problems."

For the first time, her daughter was making sense.

"Although heaven knows, I can't remember what it's like to be part of a *real* family."

"Kristen, that's enough," Joanna cried, shaking her head. Her daughter was invoking so much guilt that Joanna was beginning to hear violins in the background. "You and I *are* a real family."

"But, Mom, it could be so much better." Kristen sank down beside Joanna again and crossed her legs. Obviously her argument had long since been prepared, and without pausing to breathe between sentences, she proceeded to list the advantages of joining the two families.

"Kristen—"

Once more her daughter stopped her with an outstretched hand, as she started on her much shorter list of possible disadvantages. There was little Joanna could do to stem the rehearsed speech. Impatiently she waited for Kristen to finish.

"I don't want to talk about Tanner again," Joanna said in a no-nonsense tone of voice reserved for instances such as this. "Not a single word. Is that clearly understood?"

Kristen turned round sad eyes on her mother. The fun and laughter seemed to drain from her face as she glared back at Joanna. "Okay—if that's what you really want."

"It is, Kristen. Not a single word."

Banning his name from her daughter's lips and banning his name from her own mind were two entirely different things, Joanna decided an hour later. The fact that Nicole was visiting Carmen concerned her—not that she shared Tanner's worries. But knowing Tanner, he was probably beside himself worrying that Carmen would want their daughter to come and live with her.

It took another half hour for Joanna to build up enough courage to phone Tanner. He answered on the second ring.

"Hello, Tanner...it's Joanna." Even that was almost more than she could manage.

"Joanna." Just the way he said her name revealed his delight in hearing from her.

Joanna was grateful that he didn't immediately bring up the dinner party and the argument that had followed. "How have you been?"

"Good. How about you?"

"Just fine," she returned awkwardly. She leaned against the wall, crossing and uncrossing her ankles. "Listen, the reason I phoned is that Kristen told me Nicole was with her mother, and I thought you might be in need of a divorced-parent prep talk."

"What I really need is to see you. Lord, woman, it took you long enough. I thought you were going to make me wait forever. Ten days can be a very long time, Joanna. Ten whole days!"

"Tanner—"

"Can we meet someplace?"

"I'm not sure." Her mind struggled with a list of excuses, but she couldn't deny how lonely and miserable she'd been, how badly she wanted to feel his arms around her. "I'd have to find someone to sit with

Kristen, and that could be difficult at the last minute like this."

"I'll come to you then."

It was part question, part statement, and again, she hesitated. "All right," she finally whispered.

The line went oddly silent. When Tanner spoke again there was a wealth of emotion in his words, although his voice was quiet. "I'm glad you phoned, Joanna."

She closed her eyes, feeling weak and shaky. "I am, too," she said softly.

"I'll be there within half an hour."

"I'll have coffee ready."

When she replaced the receiver, her hand was trembling, and it was as though she were twenty-one again. Her heart was pounding out of control just from the sound of his voice, her head swimming with the knowledge that she'd be seeing him in a few minutes. How wrong she'd been to assume that if she put him out of her sight and mind she could keep him out of her heart, too. How foolish she'd been to deny her feelings. She loved this man, and it wouldn't matter if he owned the company or swept the floors.

Joanna barely had time to refresh her makeup and drag a brush through her hair. Kristen had been in her room for the past hour without a sound; Joanna sincerely hoped she was asleep.

She'd just poured water into the coffeemaker when the doorbell chimed.

The bedroom door flew open, and Kristen appeared in her pajamas, wide awake. "I'll get it," she yelled.

Joanna started to call after her, but it was too late.

With a resigned sigh, she stood in the background and waited for her daughter to admit Tanner.

Kristen turned to face her mother, wearing a grin as wide as the Mississippi River. "It's that man whose name I'm not supposed to mention ever again."

"Yes, I know."

"You know?"

Joanna nodded.

"Good. Talk it out with him, Mom. Relieve yourself of all that inner stuff. Get rid of that turmoil before it eats you alive."

Joanna cast a weak smile in Tanner's direction, then turned her attention to Kristen. "Isn't it your bedtime, young lady?"

"No."

Joanna's eyes narrowed. "Yes, it is."

"But, Mom, it's spring break, so I can sleep in tomorrow—Oh, I get it, you want me out of here."

"In your room reading or listening to music should do nicely."

Kristen beamed her mother a broad smile. "'Night, Mom. 'Night... Nicole's dad."

"'Night."

With her arms swinging at her sides, Kristen strolled out of the living room. Tanner waited until they heard her bedroom door shut, then he started across the carpet toward Joanna. He stopped suddenly, frowning. "She wasn't supposed to say my name?"

Joanna gave a weak half shrug, her gaze holding his. No man had ever looked better. His eyes seemed to caress her with a tenderness and aching hunger that did crazy things to her equilibrium.

"It's so good to see you," she said, her voice unsteady. She took two steps towards him.

When Tanner reached for her, a heavy sigh broke from his lips and the tension left his muscles. "Dear Lord, woman, ten days you left me dangling." He said more, but his words were muffled in the curve of her neck as he crushed her against his chest.

Joanna soaked up his warmth, and when his lips found hers she surrendered with a soft sigh of joy. Being in Tanner's arms was like coming home after a long journey and discovering the comfort in all that's familiar. It was like walking in sunshine after a bad storm, like holding the first rose of summer in her hand.

Again and again his mouth sought hers in a series of passionate kisses, as though he couldn't get enough of the taste of her.

The creaky sound of a bedroom door opening caused Joanna to break away from him. "It's Kristen," she murmured, her voice little more than a whisper.

"I know, but I don't care." Tanner kept her close for a moment longer. "Okay," he breathed, and slowly stroked the top of her head with his chin. "We need to settle a few things. Let's talk."

Joanna led him into the kitchen, since they were afforded the most privacy there. She automatically took down two cups and poured them each some coffee. They sat at the small table, directly across from each other, but even that seemed much too far.

"First, tell me about Nicole," she said, her eyes meeting his. "Are you worried now that she's with Carmen?"

A sad smile touched the edges of Tanner's mouth. "Not particularly. Carmen, who prefers to be called

Rama Sheba now, contacted my parents at the end of last week. According to my mother, the reason we haven't heard from her in the past three years is that Carmen's been on a long journey in India and Nepal. Apparently Carmen went halfway around the world searching for herself. I guess she found what she was looking for, because she's back in the United States and inquiring about Nicole."

"Oh, dear. Do you think she wants Nicole to come live with her?"

"Not a chance. Carmen, er, Rama Sheba, doesn't want a child complicating her life. She never did. Nicole wanted to see her mother and that's understandable, so I sent her back to West Virginia for a visit with my parents. While she's there, Carmen will spend an afternoon with her."

"What happened to... Rama Sheba and the baseball player?"

"Who knows? He may have joined her in her wanderings, for all I know. Or care. Carmen plays such a minor role in my life now that I haven't the energy to second-guess her. She's free to do as she likes, and I prefer it that way. If she wants to visit Nicole, fine. She can see her daughter—she has the right."

"Do you love her?" The question sounded abrupt and tactless, but Joanna needed to know.

"No," he said quickly, then grinned. "I suppose I feel much the same way about her as you do about Davey."

"Then you don't hate her?" she asked next, not looking at him.

"No."

Joanna ran a fingertip along the rim of her cup and smiled. "Good."

"Why's that good?"

She lifted her eyes to meet his and smiled a little shyly. "Because if you did have strong feelings for her it would suggest some unresolved emotion."

Tanner nodded. "As illogical as it sounds, I don't feel anything for Carmen. Not love, not hate—nothing. If something bad were to happen to her, I suppose I'd feel sad, but I don't harbor any resentments toward her."

"That's what I was trying to explain to you the afternoon you dropped by when Davey was here. Other people have a hard time believing this, especially my parents, but I honestly wish him success in life. I want him to be happy, although I doubt he ever will be." Davey wasn't a man who would ever be content. He was always looking for something more, something better.

Tanner nodded.

Once more, Joanna dropped her gaze to the steaming coffee. "Calling you and asking about Nicole was only an excuse, you know."

"Yes. I just wish you'd come up with it a few days earlier. As far as I'm concerned, waiting for you to come to your senses took nine days too long."

"I—"

"I know, I know," Tanner said before she could list her excuses. "Okay, let's talk."

Joanna managed a smile. "Where do we start?"

"How about with what happened the night of the party?"

Instantly Joanna's stomach knotted. "Yes, well, I guess I should be honest and let you know I was intimidated by how important you are. It shook me, Tanner, really shook me. I'm not used to seeing you as chairman of the board. And then later, when you strolled off with Blaise, those old wounds from my marriage with Davey started to bleed."

"I suppose I did all the wrong things. Maybe I should have insisted you come with me when Blaise dragged me away, but—"

"No, that wouldn't have worked, either."

"I should have guessed how you'd feel after being married to Davey."

"You had no way of knowing." Now came the hard part. "Tanner," she began, and was shocked at how thin and weak her voice sounded, "I was so consumed with jealousy that I just about went crazy when Blaise wrapped her arms around you. It frightened me to have to deal with those negative emotions again. I know I acted like an idiot, hiding like that, and I'd like to apologize."

"Joanna, it isn't necessary."

She shook her head. "I don't mean this as an excuse, but you need to understand why I was driven to behave the way I did. I'd thought I was beyond that— years beyond acting like a jealous fool. I promised myself I'd never allow a man to do it to me again." In her own way, Joanna was trying to tell him how much she loved him, but the words weren't coming out right.

He frowned at that. "Jealous? You were jealous? Good Lord, woman, you could have fooled me. You handed me over to Blaise without so much as a hint of regret. From the way you were behaving, I thought you *wanted* to be rid of me."

The tightness in Joanna's throat made talking difficult. "I already explained why I did that."

"I know. The way I acted when I saw your ex here

was the other kind of jealous reaction—the raging-bull kind. I think I see now where *your* kind of reaction came from. I'm not sure which one is worse, but I think mine is." He smiled ruefully, and a silence fell between them.

"Could this mean you have some strong feelings for me, Joanna Parsons?"

A smile quirked at the corners of her mouth. "You're the only man I've ever eaten Oreos over."

The laughter in Tanner's eyes slowly faded. "We could have the start of something very important here, Joanna. What do you think?"

"I...I think you may be right."

"Good." Tanner looked exceedingly pleased with this turn of events. "That's exactly what I wanted to hear."

Joanna thought—no, hoped—that he intended to lean over and kiss her. Instead his brows drew together darkly over brooding blue eyes. "Okay, where do we go from here?"

"Go?" Joanna repeated, feeling uncomfortable all of a sudden. "Why do we have to go anywhere?"

Tanner looked surprised. "Joanna, for heaven's sake, when a man and a woman feel about each other the way we do, they generally make plans."

"What do you mean 'feel about each other the way we do'?"

Tanner's frown darkened even more. "You love me."

Only a few moments before, Joanna would have willingly admitted it, but silly as it sounded, she wanted to hear Tanner say the words first. "I... I..."

"If you have to think about it, then I'd say you obviously don't know."

"But I do know," she said, lifting her chin a notch higher. "I'm just not sure this is the time to do anything about it. You may think my success is insignificant compared to yours, but I've worked damn hard to get where I am. I've got the house I saved for years to buy, and my career is starting to swing along nicely, and Robin—he's my boss—let me know that I was up for promotion. My goal of becoming the first female senior loan officer at the branch is within sight."

"And you don't want to complicate your life right now with a husband and second family?"

"I didn't say that."

"It sure sounded like it to me."

Joanna swallowed. The last thing in the world she wanted to do was argue with Tanner. Craziest of all, she wasn't even sure what they were arguing about. They were in love with each other and both just too damn proud. "I don't think we're getting anywhere with this conversation."

Tanner braced his elbows on the table and folded his hands. "I'm beginning to agree with you. All week, I've been waiting for you to call me, convinced that once you did, everything between us would be settled. I wanted us to start building a life together, and all of a sudden you're Ms. Career Woman, and about as independent as they come."

"I haven't changed. You just didn't know me."

His lips tightened. "I guess you're right. I don't know you at all, do I?"

"Mom, Mom, come quick!"

Joanna's warm cozy dream was interrupted by Kristen's shrieks. She rolled over and glared at the digital readout on her clock radio. Five. In the morning. "Kristen?" She sat straight up in bed.

"Mom!"

The one word conveyed such panic that Joanna's heart rushed to her throat and she threw back her covers, running barefoot into the hallway. Almost immediately, her feet encountered ice-cold water.

"Something's wrong," Kristen cried, hopping up and down. "The water won't stop."

That was the understatement of the year. From the way the water was gushing out of the bathroom door and into the hallway, it looked as though a dam had burst.

"Grab some towels," Joanna cried, pointing toward the hallway linen closet. The hems of her long pajamas were already damp. She scooted around her daughter, who was standing in the doorway, still hopping up and down like a crazed kangaroo.

Further investigation showed that the water was escaping from the cabinet under the sink.

"Mom, Mom, here!" Dancing around, Kristen threw her a stack of towels that separated in midair and landed in every direction.

"Kristen!" Joanna snapped, squatting down in front of the sink. She opened the cabinet and was immediately hit by a wall of foaming bubbles. The force of the flowing water had knocked over her container of expensive bubble bath and spilled its contents. "You were in my bubble bath!" Joanna cried.

"I… How'd you know?"

"The cap's off, and now it's everywhere!"

"I just used a little bit."

Three bars of Ivory soap, still in their wrappers,

floated past Joanna's feet. Heaven only knew what else had been stored under the sink or where it was headed now.

"I'm sorry about the bubble bath," Kristen said defensively. "I figured you'd get mad if you found out, but a kid needs to know what luxury feels like, too, you know."

"It's all right, we can't worry about that now." Joanna waved her hands back and forth trying to disperse the bubbles enough to assess the damage. It didn't take long to determine that a pipe had burst. With her forehead pressing against the edge of the sink, Joanna groped inside the cabinet for the knob to turn off the water supply. Once she found it, she twisted it furiously until the flowing water dwindled to a mere trickle.

"Kristen!" Joanna shouted, looking over her shoulder. Naturally, when she needed her, her daughter disappeared. "Get me some more towels. Hurry, honey!"

A couple of minutes later, Kristen reappeared, her arms loaded with every towel and washcloth in the house. "Yuck," she muttered, screwing her face into a mask of sheer disgust. "What a mess!"

"Did any water get into the living room?"

Kristen nodded furiously. "But only as far as the front door."

"Great." Joanna mumbled under her breath. Now she'd need to phone someone about coming in to dry out the carpet.

On her hands and knees, sopping up as much water as she could, Joanna was already soaked to the skin herself.

"You need help," her daughter announced.

The child was a master of observation. "Change

out of those wet things first, Kristen, before you catch your death of cold."

"What about you?"

"I'll dry off as soon as I get some of this water cleaned up."

"Mom—"

"Honey, just do as I ask. I'm not in any mood to argue with you."

Joanna couldn't remember ever seeing a bigger mess in her life. Her pajamas were soaked; bubbles were popping around her head—how on earth had they got into her hair? She sneezed violently, and reached for a tissue that quickly dissolved in her wet hands.

"Here, use this."

The male voice coming from behind her surprised Joanna so much that when she twisted around, she lost her footing and slid down into a puddle of the coldest water she'd ever felt.

"Tanner!" she cried, leaping to her feet. "What are you doing here?"

Fifteen

Dumbfounded, Joanna stared at Tanner, her mouth hanging open and her eyes wide.

"I got this frantic phone call from Kristen."

"Kristen?"

"The one and only. She suggested I hurry over here before something drastic happened." Tanner took one step toward her and lovingly brushed a wet tendril away from her face. "How's it going, Tugboat Annie?"

"A pipe under the sink broke. I've got it under control now—I think." Her pajamas hung limply at her ankles, dripping water onto her bare feet. Her hair fell in wet spongy curls around her face, and Joanna had never felt more like bursting into tears in her life.

"Kristen shouldn't have phoned you," she said, once she found her voice.

"I'm glad she did. It's nice to know I can be useful every now and again." Heedless of her wet state, he wrapped his arms around Joanna and brought her close, gently pressing her damp head to his chest.

A chill went through her and she shuddered. Tanner felt so warm and vital, so concerned and loving. She'd let him think she was this strong independent woman, and normally she was, but when it came to broken pipes and floods and things like that, she crumbled into bite-sized pieces. When it came to Tanner Lund, well...

"You're soaked to the skin," he whispered, close to her ear.

"I know."

"Go change. I'll take over here."

The tears started then, silly ones that sprang from somewhere deep inside her and refused to be stopped. "I can't get dry," she sobbed, wiping furiously at the moisture that rained down her face. "There aren't any dry towels left in this entire house."

Tanner jerked his water-blotched tan leather jacket off and placed it around her shoulders. "Honey, don't cry. Please. Everything's going to be all right. It's just a broken pipe, and I can have it fixed for you before noon—possibly sooner."

"I can't help it," she bellowed, and to her horror, hic-cuped. She threw a hand over her mouth and leaned her forehead against his strong chest. "It's five o'clock in the morning, my expensive Giorgio bubble bath is ruined, and I'm so much in love I can't think straight."

Tanner's hands gripped her shoulders and eased her away so he could look her in the eye. "What did you just say?"

Joanna hung her head as low as it would go, bracing her weight against Tanner's arms. "My Giorgio bubble bath is ruined." The words wobbled out of her mouth like a rubber ball tumbling down stairs.

"Not that. I want to hear the other part, about being so much in love."

Joanna sniffled. "What about it?"

"What about it? Good Lord, woman, I was here not more than eight hours ago wearing my heart on my sleeve like a schoolboy. You were so casual about everything, I thought you were going to open a discussion on stock options."

"*You* were the one who was so calm and collected about everything, as if what happened between us didn't really matter to you." She rubbed her hand under her nose and sniffled loudly. "Then you made everything sound like a foregone conclusion and—"

"I was nervous. Now, shall we give it another try? I want to marry you, Joanna Parsons. I want you to share my life, maybe have my babies. I want to love you until we're both old and gray. I've even had fantasies about us traveling around the country in a mobile home to visit our grandchildren!"

"You want grandkids?" Timidly, she raised her eyes to his, almost afraid to believe what he was telling her.

"I'd prefer to take this one step at a time. The first thing I want to do is marry you. I couldn't have made that plainer than I did a few hours ago."

"But—"

"Stop right now, before we get sidetracked. First things first. Are you and Kristen going to marry me and Nicole?"

"I think we should," the eleven-year-old said excitedly from the hallway, looking smugly pleased with the way things were going. "I mean, it's been obvious to Nicole and me for ages that you two were meant to be together." Kristen sighed and slouched against the wall, crossing her arms over her chest with the sophistication that befitted someone of superior intelligence. "There's only one flaw in this plan."

"Flaw?" Joanna echoed.

"Yup," Kristen said, nodding with unquestionable confidence. "Nicole is going to be mad as hops when she finds out she missed this."

Tanner frowned, and then he chuckled. "Oh, boy. I think Kristen could be right. We're going to have to stage a second proposal."

Feeling slightly piqued, Joanna straightened. "Listen, you two, I never said I was going to marry anybody— yet."

"Of course you're going to marry Mr. Lund," Kristen inserted smoothly. "Honestly, Mom, now isn't the time to play hard to get."

"W-what?" Stunned, Joanna stood there staring at her daughter. Her gaze flew from Kristen to Tanner and then back to Kristen.

"She's right, you know," said Tanner.

"I can't believe I'm hearing this." Joanna was standing in a sea of wet towels, while her daughter and the man she loved discussed her fate as though she was to play only a minor role in it.

"We've got to think of a way to include Nicole," Tanner said thoughtfully.

"I am going to change my clothes," Joanna murmured, eager to escape.

"Good idea," Tanner answered, without looking at her.

Joanna stomped off to her bedroom and slammed the door. She discarded her pajamas and, shivering, reached for a thick wool sweater and blue jeans.

Tanner and Kristen were still in the bathroom doorway, discussing details, when Joanna reappeared. She moved silently around them and into the kitchen, where she made a pot of coffee. Then she gathered up the wet towels, hauled them onto the back porch, threw them into the washer and started the machine. By the time she returned to the kitchen, Tanner had joined her there.

"Uh-oh. Trouble," he said, watching her abrupt angry movements. "Okay, tell me what's wrong now."

"I don't like the way you and my daughter are planning my life," she told him point-blank. "Honestly, Tanner, I haven't even agreed to marry you, and already you and Kristen have got the next ten years all figured out."

He stuck his hands in his pants pockets. "It's not that bad."

"Maybe not, but it's bad enough. I'm letting you know right now that I'm not about to let you stage a second proposal just so Nicole can hear it. To be honest, I'm not exactly thrilled about Kristen being part of this one. A marriage proposal is supposed to be private. And romantic, with flowers and music, not... not in front of a busted pipe with bath bubbles popping around my head and my family standing around applauding."

"Okay, what do you suggest?"

"I don't know yet."

Tanner looked disgruntled. "If you want the romance, Joanna, that's fine. I'd be more than happy to give it to you."

"Every woman wants romance."

Tanner walked toward her then and took her in his arms, and until that moment Joanna had no idea how much she did, indeed, want it.

Her eyes were drawn to his. Everything about Tanner Lund fascinated her, and she raised her hand to lightly caress the proud strong line of his jaw. She really did love this man. His eyes, blue and intense, met hers, and a tiny shiver of awareness went through her. His arms circled her waist, and then he lifted her off the ground so that her gaze was level with his own.

Joanna gasped a little at the unexpectedness of his action. Smiling, she looped her arms around his neck.

Tanner kissed her then, with a hunger that left her weak and clinging in its aftermath.

"How's that?" he asked, his voice husky.

"Better. Much better."

"I thought so." Once more his warm mouth made contact with hers. Joanna was startled and thrilled at the intensity of his touch. He kissed her again and again, until she thought that if he released her, she'd fall to the floor and melt at his feet. Every part of her body was heated to fever pitch.

"Joanna—"

She planted warm moist kisses across his face, not satisfied, wanting him until her heart felt as if it might explode. Tanner had awoken the sensual part of her nature, buried all the years since her divorce, and now that it had been stirred back to life, she felt starved for a man's love—this man's love.

"Yes," she breathed into his mouth. "Yes, yes, yes."

"Yes what?" he asked in a breathless murmur.

Joanna paused and smiled gently. "Yes, I'll marry you. Right now. Okay? This minute. We can fly somewhere... find a church... Oh, Tanner," she pleaded, "I want you so much."

"Joanna, we can't." His words came out in a groan, forced from deep inside him.

She heard him, but it didn't seem to matter. She kissed him and he kissed her. Their kiss continued as he lowered her to the floor, her body sliding intimately down his.

Suddenly Joanna realized what she'd just said, what she'd suggested. "We mustn't. Kristen—"

Tanner shushed her with another kiss, then said, "I know, love. This isn't the time or place, but I sure wish…"

Joanna straightened, and broke away. Shakily, she said, "So do I…and, uh, I think we should wait a while for the wedding. At least until Nicole gets back."

"Right."

"How long will that be?"

"The end of the week."

Joanna nodded and closed her eyes. It sounded like an eternity.

"What about your job?"

"I don't want to work forever, and when we decide to start a family I'll probably quit. But I want that promotion first." Joanna wasn't sure exactly why that was so important to her, but it was. She'd worked years for this achievement, and she had no intention of walking away until she'd become the first female senior loan officer.

Tanner kissed her again. "If it makes you happy keep your job as long as you want."

At that moment, however, all Joanna could think about were babies, family vacations and homemade cookies.

"That's her plane now," Tanner said to Kristen, pointing toward the Boeing jet that was approaching the long narrow landing strip at Spokane International.

"I get to tell her, okay?"

"I think Tanner should do it, sweetheart," Joanna suggested gently.

"But Nicole and I are best friends. You can't expect me to keep something like this from her, something we planned since that night we all went to the Pink Palace. If it weren't for us, you two wouldn't even know each other."

Kristen's eyes were round and pleading as she stared up at Tanner and Joanna.

"You two would have been cast adrift in a sea of loneliness if it hadn't been for me and Nicole," she added melodramatically.

"All right, all right," Tanner said with a sigh. "You can tell her."

Poised at the railing by the window of the terminal, Kristen eagerly studied each passenger who stepped inside. The minute Nicole appeared, Kristen flew into her friend's arms as though it had been years since they'd last seen each other instead of a week.

Joanna watched the unfolding scene with a quiet sense of happiness. Nicole let out a squeal of delight and gripped her friend around the shoulders, and the two jumped frantically up and down.

"From her reaction, I'd guess that she's happy about our decision," Tanner said to Joanna.

"Dad, Dad!" Nicole raced up to her father, and hugged him with all her might. "It's so good to be home. I missed you. I missed everyone," she said, looking at Joanna.

Tanner returned the hug. "It's good to have you home, cupcake."

"But everything exciting happened while I was

away," she said, pouting a little. "Gee, if I'd known you were finally going to get rolling with Mrs. Parsons, I'd never have left."

Joanna smiled blandly at the group of people standing around them.

"Don't be mad," Kristen said. "It was a now-or-never situation, with Mom standing there in her pajamas and everything."

Now it was Tanner's turn to notice the interested group of onlookers.

"Yes, well, you needn't feel left out. I saved the best part for you," Tanner said, taking a beautiful solitaire diamond ring out of his pocket. "I wanted you to be here for this." He reached for Joanna's hand, looking into her eyes, as he slowly, reverently, slipped it onto her finger. "I love you, Joanna, and I'll be the happiest man alive if you marry me."

"I love you, Tanner," she said in a soft voice filled with joy.

"Does this mean we're going to be sisters from now on?" Kristen shrieked, clutching her best friend's hand.

"Yup," Nicole answered. "It's what we always wanted."

With their arms wrapped around one another's shoulders, the girls headed toward the baggage-claim area.

"Yours and mine," Joanna said, watching their two daughters.

Tanner slid his arm around her waist and smiled into her eyes.

* * * * *

THE BACHELOR DOCTOR'S BRIDE

Caro Carson

For Katie and William,
the two brightest lights in my life.

Acknowledgments

With many thanks to my family,
who are getting very good at ignoring me
when my headphones are in and
I'm typing madly in my own little world.

And with gratitude for Kay Clark's quick reading
and sharp eye, for T. Elliott Brown's savvy
critiques, and for Catherine Kean,
who casually stirred her tea one day
and said two magical words that made my story
fall into place: sock puppets.

One

A black-tie gala on a summer night ought to be the perfect setting for happiness. Glamour, romance, excitement—everything Diana Connor thought a person's life should have. So far, she was having a ball at this particular ball.

Downtown Austin's historic hotel, the Driskill, had pulled out all the stops, making the most out of its Victorian gilding by adding a crystal candelabra to the center of every table. Each one added prisms of real candlelight to the night. Diana couldn't remember the last time she'd seen real flames reflected through real crystal. Parties usually got their sparkle from plastic sequins and tiny LED lights—not that there was anything wrong with that. Diana enjoyed festive settings of any kind, but there was something extra special about tonight's real flames. Their movement echoed the dancing of the human glitterati on the dance floor.

The gala had attracted everyone who was anyone in central Texas, and the ballroom, the smaller parlor rooms, and the grand mezzanine were all part of the flow as everyone made their rounds, dancing and dining, seeing and being seen. All this glittering happiness benefited West Central Texas Hospital's new pediatric research project, making the evening a perfectly delightful way to raise money for a good cause.

Diana's boss hadn't thought so. The single thousand-dollar ticket he'd bought was the minimum he could donate to make his real estate company look marginally philanthropic. One after another, the top agents at the office had declined the use of the lone ticket to the hospital gala. When the ticket had made its way down to Diana, the ninth-best agent out of ten, she'd jumped at the chance to use it. Being solo was no problem; parties were meant for making new friends.

Her boss had given her gruff instructions with the ticket: *Give your business card to every doctor you meet, and tell them you sold that house to the MacDowells.* Diana had nodded politely, but she didn't waste precious space in her adorably tiny purse on business cards. If Lana and Braden MacDowell wanted to pass her name on to their friends, they would.

As it turned out, the MacDowells were here tonight—hardly a surprise, since they were both doctors at West Central. The surprise was that Diana knew them at all. Fate must have played a role when she'd first met Lana at a flower shop. Diana had spotted Lana, an eye-catching woman with jet-black hair, looking as harried as only a physician moving to Austin from out of state while starting a new job and planning a wedding could look.

Pretty darn harried.

Diana had offered to give Lana a second opinion on the bridal bouquets that seemed to be overwhelming her. When Lana had asked her if she knew a good DJ, too, Diana had been able to help, since dancing was her favorite thing to do on a Friday night. Lana had laughingly asked her if she could magically produce a dream home for her. Diana had been carrying her business cards that day. Fate was a wonderful thing.

Amazingly enough, helping a woman choose wedding flowers gave a person a good idea of what she might like in a house. Diana had found Lana and her husband their perfect home.

The MacDowells danced under the permanently blue sky painted on the ballroom's domed ceiling, a light and smiling couple in love. Later tonight, country-Western stars were going to entertain this high-paying crowd, but for now, the big band orchestra seemed like the right music for the MacDowells, a perfect match for them.

All around the chandeliered space, Diana saw good things. Laughing faces, liveliness, shimmer and shine. Everyone looked happy and satisfied. Everyone except...

Her gaze was drawn again to the one man who seemed utterly still in a room full of motion. His matte black tux drew the light in and kept it. He was supposed to reflect the light, didn't he know?

Champagne sips provided some discreet cover as Diana kept an eye on him, waiting for his date or his wife to return. The song ended, the dance floor cleared, and still, he brooded alone, sitting at an empty table near the dance floor while everyone else was mingling.

Diana frowned into her bubbly. She didn't like to see this man so unhappy. Then again, she didn't like to see anyone unhappy, and she was pretty good at cheering people up, so she and her champagne headed over.

It's going to be like cheering up James Bond.

Not a hardship, really. Handsome man in a tux?

I choose to accept this mission.

While she was grinning at her own silly thought, James Bond cut his gaze to her. Just, *bam*. One second he'd been brooding at the dance floor, the next, she'd been caught in a green-eyed, intense stare.

Oh, my.

She hadn't expected such sea-green eyes from a man with such richly brown hair. Handsome? Holy cow, handsome.

Those sea-green eyes stayed on her, but otherwise, the man didn't move a muscle. Handsome as all get-out, yes, but not happy at a happy party. She had a job to do.

"Hi," she said, while she was still a few feet away. The faintest lift of his brow revealed his surprise that she was headed for him. "Thanks for saving me a seat."

She gave the hem of her bright green dress a tug to be sure it wouldn't ride up and expose her derriere, then sat in the chair next to his. The dress was a little too short, but she'd fallen in love with its layers of fringe. Even when she moved only the tiniest bit, the fringe looked like she was dancing. Still, she was showing a lot more skin than usual. In an effort to look less like a '60s go-go girl and more like a flapper from the '20s, Diana had twisted her brownish—well, mostly red—hair into something resembling a short bob, secured with a jeweled brooch on the side. That had been another great reason to use her stingy boss's single ticket: the chance to play dress-up.

Oh, yes, it was a great ball. Time for James Bond to enjoy it, too.

First things first. She angled her chair toward his with a little scoot. She stuck her hand practically into his torso, so he had little choice but to shake it. "My name is Diana."

"Quinn," he said, then released her hand. His voice was somber. The poor man was serious from the inside out.

He glanced away from her, but she kept her gaze on him and saw muscles bunch a little as he clenched his jaw, quite a tense reaction to something. She followed his gaze. He was unhappy about... Lana MacDowell.

Uh-oh

"I'm sorry to tell you," Diana said, "but she's married. Happily."

"Pardon?"

He said it like a cowboy, with just a touch of Texas twang, but the way he looked at her was purely upper-class offended dignity. He wore polished black cowboy boots with his tuxedo, as did probably half the men at this Austin ball, but he had "exclusive club" written all over him. Ivy League education, for certain.

Diana had to raise her voice as the music resumed. Who'd have guessed that a dozen people making up an orchestra could be as loud as any DJ with massive speakers? "She's married. Don't give her another thought."

"I wasn't," he said, without taking his eyes off Lana.

"Sure, you weren't."

Mr. Bond brooded on.

Diana sighed and sipped her champagne. "I hate to dash anyone's hopes, but that's one marriage that is going to last."

That got his attention. Those sea-green eyes looked directly at her again. Better at her than a married woman, she supposed.

"How do you know?" he asked.

"Lana and I are friends." For some reason, she added, "And business associates."

Business associates? It sounded like she was trying to say she was as accomplished as Dr. Lana Mac-Dowell, but Diana was most definitely not med school material. Not Ivy League. Not even community college. Why did she want James Bond to think she was?

She wasn't his type. It was a simple fact. She could tell, at a glance, that this man would squarely put her in the buddy category. Maybe little sister—annoying little sister.

I'm not annoying, I'm friendly. Her heart was in the right place, so she wasn't worried if his initial impression was "annoying." She was going to be his buddy before the party was over, the gal pal who encouraged a guy to get out there and live. It was a role she fell into all the time. People liked her that way.

The poor man continued glowering as he watched Braden and Lana dance. "You're being a little too obvious," she said. "What is your name again?"

"Quinn." From his tone, she guessed he didn't like having to repeat himself.

Diana snapped her fingers. "Now I know who you are. I saw you on the hospital's bachelor calendar, didn't I?" She laughed out loud. "I didn't recognize you tonight with your clothes on."

"What?" He sounded baffled—or annoyed. Baffled was nicer, so she went with baffled.

"It's a joke. I've only seen you in your doctor duds, the green scrubs. Didn't recognize you tonight with your real clothes on, get it?"

He didn't laugh, just sent a faint, polite smile in the direction of the dance floor. He probably preferred to get his humor from *The New Yorker*. Intellectual humor, not party joke humor.

Well, she was here to change all that. "Look, I'm good at matchmaking, so let's find someone else for you to think about. We need to salvage your evening."

That green gaze returned to her. "Do we? I wasn't aware I was so dangerously near rock bottom."

"You need to find the right woman for you. Lana isn't it."

He dropped his gaze, which meant he looked at her bare thighs being tickled by green fringe. Then he looked away, frowning faintly.

She tugged at her hem, relieved that he wasn't ogling her. She hated when guys mistook her friendliness as a sign that she wanted to party horizontally.

It was hard to imagine that anyone had persuaded this man to pose for a fund-raising man-candy calendar. Diana remembered the photo, though. He'd been glowering in that one, too, as if daring the camera to make him take his surgeon's garb off. She'd thought it was a shame the photographer hadn't succeeded.

"Lana and I are only friends," he said. "I'm well aware that she isn't available."

"And she never will be."

"The divorce rate among doctors is astronomical."

"The MacDowells are rock solid. Just put Lana out

of your mind while we find you someone super special."

Despite the loud music, Diana could almost hear his snort of derision.

She pretended not to notice. Men often acted tough and grouchy when they were really sad and lonely. She'd rescued enough homeless dogs to recognize the gruff defense. "The good news is, you're far from a hopeless case. For starters, you're a man, so we don't have to work too hard to get you on the dance floor."

"I don't understand, Miss...?"

"Just call me Diana, please. 'Miss Connor' would be ridiculously stuffy."

"Miss Connor. What makes you think I'm in need of your matchmaking assistance?"

"Because you're sitting here sulking. Like a child."

Being blunt had the desired effect. The look on his face made her want to laugh. He couldn't even frown at her, she'd shocked him so greatly.

She nudged his shoulder with hers. "Don't take yourself so seriously—or me, either, for that matter. I'm friends with Lana, you're friends with Lana, so that makes us friends, too. As your friend, I'm here to help you get your party on."

He leaned back in his chair and crossed his arms over his chest. At least she had his attention—totally, this time—and he looked like he was actually close to smiling. "How fortunate for me. I thought I'd never manage to get my party on. It was worrying me considerably."

"Glad to hear we agree. Now, I was saying that you are at a big advantage because you're a man."

"Is that right?"

YOUR PARTICIPATION IS REQUESTED!

Dear Debbie Macomber Fan,

Since you are a lover of our books – we would like to get to know you!

Inside you will find a short Reader's Survey. Sharing your answers with us will help our editorial staff understand who you are and what activities you enjoy.

To thank you for your participation, we would like to send you 2 books and 2 gifts – **ABSOLUTELY FREE!**

Enjoy your gifts with our appreciation,

Pam Powers

SEE INSIDE FOR READER'S SURVEY

For Your Reading Pleasure...

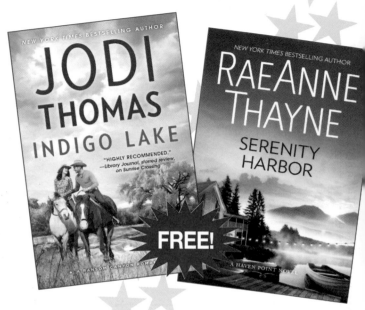

We'll send you 2 books and 2 gifts
ABSOLUTELY FREE
just for completing our Reader's Survey!

YOUR READER'S SURVEY
"THANK YOU" FREE GIFTS INCLUDE:
- ▶ 2 FREE books
- ▶ 2 lovely surprise gifts

"You can ask a girl to dance. You have no idea what a luxury that is. This would be much harder if you were a woman. If you saw a likely candidate, you'd have to strategically stand where he could see you, make a little eye contact, flirt a little, and hope he asked you to dance."

"I doubt you are saying this from experience. You don't strike me as a wallflower."

"I never ask the man to dance. I only approached you because you were so obviously in need of a little coaching."

"Thank you."

"You'll thank me later, trust me," she said, answering his sarcasm with sauciness. "Now, what kind of woman do you think you want?"

He looked toward the dance floor, but Lana and Braden weren't there. They'd probably gotten a hotel room—they were practically on their honeymoon.

Diana sighed dramatically. "Okay, okay. You think Lana is the perfect woman. Then let's find you a woman like Lana." Diana scanned the crowd. "Gosh, everyone is so beautiful. The whole ballroom is beautiful. Isn't it great?"

When he made no comment, she turned to him. "Don't you think it's a great night?"

He shrugged, an uncaring movement of masculine shoulders under fine black wool.

"Well, it is. Everyone's so sparkly. And happy." She poked his lapel, earning herself another raised eyebrow. "And you're going to be happy tonight, too."

"What makes you think I'm not happy?"

Diana started to laugh, but she had the sudden intuition he was asking a sincere question. The man needed to take a good look in the mirror.

Diana decided to be that mirror. She crossed her arms over her chest and scowled, hard. Dropping her voice to the lowest bass she could manage, she said, "What makes you think I'm not happy?"

Quinn scowled back at her for a good, long while. Then he uncrossed his arms and looked away with a little shake of his head. "That bad?"

"That bad, but not for long. Let me just find you the perfect partner."

"Do you often perform your matchmaking services for total strangers?"

"All the time." Every weekend, in fact, but she wasn't going to tell James Bond that. Every weekend, she volunteered at an animal shelter where she matched total strangers with the perfect pets.

This Quinn-in-a-tuxedo wouldn't appreciate that her skills had been honed on dogs, but people weren't much different. It was all a matter of finding complementing temperaments, something Diana had found success at by relying less on talking and more on facial expressions and body language.

Diana trusted her mad matchmaking skills. Lana would never have been right for Quinn, even if she'd been available, but Quinn would never believe Diana. Perhaps she should let him figure it out for himself. "Look—there's a Lana look-alike for you. Go ask her to dance."

When he didn't budge, she put her hand on his shoulder and pushed.

Quinn shook his head as he stood. "I can't believe I'm going to do this."

But he did. The woman was petite and slender, with shiny, straight black hair and an air of confidence about her. Diana watched her graciously present her hand to Quinn, so he could lead her to the dance floor. Like so many men in Texas, men who grew up leading women in the Texas two-step and country waltzes, Quinn was obviously a confident dancer. He and his partner looked elegant together, dancing to a Frank Sinatra standard.

Still, Diana wasn't surprised when Quinn returned after only one dance. The Lana-type wasn't what he needed.

"Well?" she prompted him as he sat next to her once more.

"She was the perfect woman—just ask her. She's chairing the board at whichever museum she said, and she's running a gardening gig, all out of the kindness of her heart."

"Charity work sounds like something Lana would do."

"She wouldn't brag about it."

"True, true. Your Lana look-alike was too old for you, anyway." Diana had a feeling this man would too easily retire into a sedate, settled lifestyle if she let him. Well, not if she herself let him, but if he were matched with the wrong woman, he'd find himself talking politics with gray-haired gentleman at a prestigious club in no time. Quinn was probably only thirty or so. He ought to be surfing or mountain-climbing, not serving on museum boards with a society wife.

"I'm afraid you're mistaken, my dear matchmaker," he said. "Lana's only two years older than I."

"She's taken. Get over it." Really, some cases

needed a little tough love. Diana patted his arm, though, to soften her direct words. "Okay, at your three o'clock. Blonde in the sheath dress. A knock-out and still in her twenties. She might enjoy bungee jumping."

Suave Mr. Bond was apparently caught off guard by that. He gave away his surprise with a discreet cough, a polite clearing of the throat. "Is bungee jumping the criteria now?"

"Go."

Humoring her, which Diana took to be a sign of progress already, Quinn walked over and struck up a conversation. Diana watched his nod toward the dance floor, watched the woman light up and say yes. Who wouldn't?

It only lasted one dance. After a polite thank-you nod to the woman, Quinn returned to Diana.

"No?" she asked.

"No."

"Give me something to go on."

"She still lives at home with Daddy. Rich Daddy. She wanted to know if I thought a trip to Europe would really be more educational than a trip to the Caribbean. Daddy thinks it would be."

"Not Lana-like at all, you're right. You want someone more educated, then?"

"I want someone who is less into money. Lana's no gold digger."

Diana felt her first little zip of irritation toward him. She doubted he'd meant to insult her, but there it was. "I would never have matched you with a gold digger."

"I assure you, Daddy's Girl would be one very expensive entanglement."

From their side-by-side chairs, they could easily

see the woman with her group of friends. She'd just dropped her gem-studded clutch. She made absolutely no move to pick it up, but pouted down at it, as if the purse had somehow misbehaved. Diana watched with amusement as another woman in her circle picked up the clutch and handed it back.

"That's not a gold digger, Quinn. She expects expensive things and an easy life, but only because she's always been given them. Always, from day one, and most definitely by Daddy. She just assumes everyone around her is rich, like she is. That's not the same thing as a gold digger. Those women calculate which man in the room has the most money and then go after him."

Quinn had started to take a breath to argue with her before she'd even finished her point, but to his credit, he stopped. Diana enjoyed one lovely, long moment of staring into his green, green eyes before they crinkled just a bit in what was precariously close to a smile.

"You're right. There is a difference. I stand corrected." He leaned close to Diana's ear and said, "But I'm still not interested."

His voice was warm. His tone was very assured, very in charge, but she could hear that touch of humor that lay just under the surface.

Diana felt...well, she felt antsy. There was something about Quinn that made her feel restless. The prospect of spending more time watching him dance with other women was not appealing. She needed to find a suitable partner for serious Quinn, and then she needed to get back to her mixing and her mingling.

That was all she'd come for tonight. Just a lovely, fun evening. She hadn't come to pass out business cards, and she certainly hadn't come to start brooding over a man who wouldn't stop brooding over Lana MacDowell.

The band struck up a song with a livelier beat. Diana stood, and when Quinn didn't follow, she grabbed his hand and practically hauled him out of his chair.

"Don't worry, Quinn, we're getting closer."

"I wasn't worried."

"Two o'clock, white dress. Guaranteed not to live at home with Daddy. Looks like she's terribly educated, but still young enough to go bungee jumping with you."

"Haven't I danced with enough women?"

"Third time's the charm. She looks perfect for you."

Quinn looked toward the woman Diana had picked out. Diana studied his face, feeling some smug satisfaction as Quinn raised that eyebrow in reluctant approval. "Very well," he said, and he walked away.

Diana watched. Of course, the woman said hello graciously. Of course, the woman was soon smiling. Of course, the woman walked onto the dance floor and into Quinn's arms.

This time, Quinn looked like he was enjoying the conversation. His partner looked self-possessed and confident, which was excellent, because she wasn't going to be Quinn's girlfriend for long. Diana had just found him his rebound girl, the one who would help him get past this Lana phase.

The lady in white looked like she'd be able to handle it. She and Quinn would share some lovely evenings and mutual interests in the meantime, and then...

And then, when that phase was over and Lana was firmly out of Quinn's system, would he be open to a different kind of woman? One, say, with a love of parties and a passion for homeless pups?

Diana gave herself a mental shake. She was not a plotter and planner. She was the spontaneous girl who trusted her senses, and she'd sensed right away that this man needed a little fun in his life. That was what had drawn her to him, the desire to help a fellow human being enjoy life. Nothing more.

The woman he was dancing with was the one. Diana could see it in everything about their body language. They looked right together.

Mission accomplished.

Diana toasted herself with a sip of her champagne. It still looked pretty in the glass, but it had grown warm and kind of flat.

She looked around the room, hoping to see someone with whom to strike up a conversation. It would be nice to enjoy herself with a man the way the woman in the white dress was enjoying herself with Quinn.

I'm the gal pal. Again.

Diana knew her role. There was always a character like her in movies and TV shows. Once the gal pal helped the guy decide to go for it, she exited, stage left.

Diana tapped her tiny purse against her thigh as she took one more look around at the crystal and the flames. They were pretty, but they didn't need her to continue brightening the night. Neither did Quinn.

Diana headed for the grand mezzanine. Maybe someone there was just waiting for a push in the right direction.

Two

Quinn MacDowell, M.D., was enjoying himself. His family would be surprised.

He was enjoying himself at a mandatory-attendance gala for the hospital. Forget his family's surprise; Quinn found himself somewhat astonished.

The reason he was enjoying himself was a bold and playful woman with hair the color of whiskey and a green dress that tantalized him with her every move. And that was—

Well, it was…

Unsettling.

At thirty-one years old, Quinn knew himself. He was a cardiologist. He dealt in physics, in measurable pressures and electrical impulses that powered the human body. He served on the board that governed the hospital his father had founded. He visited his mother on the homestead ranch, he badgered his brothers for getting married and tying themselves down, and he dated women who were polished, professional and career-oriented.

He knew himself.

If a complete stranger ordered him to dance with other women at a black-tie gala, then he, Quinn Mac-Dowell, M.D., would never comply.

Never.

Yet here he was.

The woman in his arms purred her words in a cultured, educated voice. "It's so refreshing to have real music to dance to, not that auto-tuned nonsense, don't you think?"

She was stunningly beautiful. Every woman Diana had chosen for him had been so. As a matchmaker, Diana actually was good. Quinn had been exaggerating the flaws of his partners after each dance, but Diana had definitely picked out women in whom he'd normally be interested.

He'd fine-tuned his criteria over years of trial and error, and knew exactly the type of woman who fit into the lifestyle that his career as a cardiologist dictated. Long-term relationships saved time and effort when it came to dating, so Quinn generally dated a woman for a half-year or more. Eventually, the girlfriend would announce the need to move on, typically after reporting that her biological clock was ticking, or because she wanted to move into the ranks of the society matrons and needed to find someone with marriage in mind. With no hard feelings, they kissed goodbye.

His last kiss had been quite a while ago.

West Central Hospital had been floundering under poor leadership, and it had taken all of Quinn's efforts to keep the ship afloat. Despite his aversion for corporate politics, he'd found himself incapable of standing by and watching his father's legacy flounder, so he'd joined the hospital board. There'd been very little time for female companionship this year, not while he'd been the only MacDowell still in town.

The hospital was going to survive. With some manipulation on Quinn's part, his oldest brother had left Manhattan to return to Austin, and a more competent CEO for West Central was hard to imagine. His brother's wife, Lana, the woman whom Diana claimed was her business associate, was rebuilding the research division. Quinn's youngest brother had finished his years of service in the army and now worked in the emergency department, and had just announced that he would take over as department chair in the fall.

All of which left Quinn with less of a professional burden to bear. He supposed the time was right for the next woman in his life. In fact, while he'd been watching Braden and Lana dance, he'd been thinking just that: something was missing in his life. Then Diana had appeared out of nowhere.

Now here he was, dancing with an entirely eligible woman, someone familiar to him as an acquaintance of an acquaintance. Tonight's rounds on the dance floor were tantamount to announcing that he was available, something that managed to get around his social circles with quiet efficiency. Appropriate women, like the one in his arms, would find him. Quinn would make a choice, and everything would proceed smoothly.

Diana Connor's matchmaking mission had been unnecessary.

Still, it was amazing, really, that a perfect stranger like Diana could take one glance at him, another glance around a crowded ballroom, and choose matches for him as well as he could have himself. By every measurable criterion, the woman Diana had chosen, the woman in white who was so smoothly following his lead on the dance floor, was perfect for him.

Yet, something wasn't quite right. He ought to be more interested in his dance partner. She pressed a little closer, causing her very well-supported, very expensively clad, very tastefully revealed cleavage to swell a bit against his chest.

He ought to be very interested, indeed.

But tonight, he was finding one thing utterly distracting: Diana herself. It was hard to focus on the woman in his arms when green fringe kept shimmying in his mind, shimmying its way over a curvy body that nearly crackled with energy.

To dance with her, to hold that woman in his arms, a woman so vibrant with her enthusiasm for life…

There was no hope for it. Diana had caught his attention completely, and no amount of cultured, educated, wealthy women that she threw his way could divert him.

Diana wasn't his type. He'd probably never run into her again after tonight. They didn't move in the same circles, despite her claim to be a business associate of his sister-in-law, Lana. After all, *he* was a business associate of Lana's. Diana did not work at West Central, that much Quinn knew.

There were other businesses besides medicine, of course, but there was nothing businesslike about Diana's behavior. She was too forward in her manner, too familiar in the way she spoke to a perfect stranger.

But she made him laugh. She poked and prodded him—literally—and he was certain that she had no idea that she was physically appealing in a way that was slowly sending him out of his mind. He'd spent the past half hour waiting for that green fringe to travel that last inch up her thighs.

Life had been all work and no play for too long. He was not going to let a curvaceous, vivacious woman with whiskey-colored hair slip through his fingers without a dance.

And if she refused to dance with him, but insisted he ask someone else of her choosing? Then Miss Diana Connor, the woman who seemed to think he had no idea how to pursue a woman, would find herself on the receiving end of all the charm Quinn MacDowell could muster.

He smiled.

The elegant woman in his arms thought it was meant for her.

Quinn changed directions in time to the music, a move designed to return his partner's focus to her feet rather than the smile on his face. He glanced toward the chairs he and Diana had been sharing.

She was gone.

"Strike three."

The deep voice caused Diana to stutter midstep. She whirled around, a quick pirouette in her smooth-soled sandals on the polished mezzanine floor. Quinn caught her elbow, stopping her so she squarely faced him. He stepped closer as he steadied her, so she found herself caught with just inches between a cold pillar at her back and a hot man at her front.

"Strike three?" she asked, leaning away from the pillar. Hot man in a tuxedo was infinitely preferable. Still, she was a bit baffled that he'd come to tell her his partner hadn't worked out. She'd left him with a woman who fit him perfectly.

What was more, Quinn didn't look very upset at striking out.

"What was the problem?" Diana asked.

"Let's go back to our seats." Quinn gestured toward the ballroom, and fell into place beside her. She half-expected him to offer her his arm in an old-fashioned way, but he didn't. Without touching, they walked side by side along the row of pillars. They'd definitely become buddies, just as she'd predicted.

Okay, Quinn, spill your guts to your gal pal.

Diana gave him the opening she knew he needed. "You can't tell me she wasn't educated enough. I could tell she was terribly educated just by looking at her."

"Terribly educated is right. She can't see why the Nobel committee overlooked the contributions of two scientists I've never heard of who discovered some molecular entity I've never heard of. And I'm a doctor, mind you."

Oh, he was most definitely a doctor. She knew this from the calendar, of course, but Quinn's career explained so much about him. Diana did not envy doctors. They were too often grim, too often facing long odds in their line of work. Someone had to do it, of course. Someone had to pit their skills against illness and injury, but Diana was glad to leave the life-and-death work to others.

Diana was satisfied with her matchmaking calling. To bring in money, she matched people with homes. In her spare time, she matched people with dogs. And tonight, she'd taken it upon herself to match this doctor with a person who could help him lighten up.

"Here's the bright side, Quinn," she said, as she snagged a glass of champagne from one of the circulating waiters, "at least she knew how to say 'molecular entity.'"

That drew another smile from him. Diana was pleased that he'd stopped being stingy with the smiles. She was good at this, helping people enjoy themselves. In any group, Diana was the one who bubbled and chatted and smoothed over any awkwardness.

Sometimes, she wondered what would happen if she stopped. If she let herself have a bad day, if she groused at a neighbor or frowned at a stranger, was there another Diana out there who would try to cheer her up? If she wore a plain black dress and sat alone in a corner, would anyone notice she existed?

Diana never intended to find out. She'd continue making people happy, and they'd continue to include her in their world, the way Quinn was including her in his. One of her mother's best pieces of advice had been to follow the Scout philosophy of leaving the world a better place than you found it. Diana had taken that to heart, and always tried to leave people happier than she found them.

She returned his smile brightly. "We'll keep looking until we find the right one for you tonight."

Diana turned in a slow circle, eyeing the crowd over the rim of her champagne flute, gauging all the eligible women, taking in at a glance how they dressed, how they held themselves, how they smiled—or didn't. How they might match with Quinn.

"How about the girl in the red dress?"

"She's not very pretty. If we're going for someone like Lana, she'd have to be quite attractive."

"I'd tell you to get over the physical looks, but chemistry is everything. When you take the right woman in your arms tonight, you'll know. Since she'll be getting James Bond, it's only fair that she be a knockout, too."

"James Bond?"

"Ooh—I see a good one. At your six. Turn around casually."

"I haven't experienced this level of espionage since high school."

In his deadpan way, he was cracking jokes. Really, he was quite charming. Diana found herself laughing with him because she liked his sense of humor, no longer because she wanted him to follow her lead and lighten up. He was more of a serious person than she was, sure, but that gruff demeanor had softened into something more genuine. Maybe her mission had been accomplished despite his lack of a dancing partner.

Diana handed him her champagne flute. "Here, you need a drink after making small talk with strangers for the past three songs."

He took a sip. "It's warm."

"It's free. It's all included in this wonderful party. You've got to remember to look at the bright side of things."

The expression on his face changed just a tiny bit. Less critical, more thoughtful. "You're right, of course. Excuse me for a moment. Don't disappear." He left—with her champagne glass.

Diana entertained herself by awarding imaginary scores for the best gowns. When she spotted one young woman nervously tugging up her strapless dress and standing with her shoulders self-consciously stooped, Diana wanted to run over and hug her. It was obvious the young person had no idea just how pretty she was. If only Diana could tell her to throw her shoulders back and smile.

Diana had learned during her school years that she couldn't hug everyone. For one thing, it alarmed people, sometimes, to have strangers offer advice. She'd learned to approach people the way she approached new dogs, with a positive attitude and a hand outstretched in a nonthreatening way. She had yet to meet a dog that wouldn't be her friend, and humans were pretty much the same way.

Even people like her James Bond. Quinn seemed independent and self-sufficient, but Diana sensed that he was a lonely man. Subconsciously, he must know it, too. It was why he was accepting her help tonight, wasn't it?

The shy girl in the strapless gown that didn't quite fit would have to wait. Quinn was headed her way again, debonair in his black tuxedo, standing an inch taller than most of the men, moving easily through the sea of partygoers.

Look at the bright side. He's part of the party now, no longer standing alone.

He was part of the festive atmosphere, light reflecting off his dark hair as he nodded at acquaintances. He didn't stop walking to talk to anyone, however. He was heading directly back to her.

Diana twirled a piece of her fringe around one finger. Too bad they weren't each other's type. He was a damned good-looking guy.

"I'm sorry to have left you alone, but it was necessary if you were going to insist that we drink champagne." Quinn held up a bottle painted with flowers in one hand, then set a pair of empty flutes down on the table nearest them. He grabbed an unused napkin from a place setting and snapped it out of its elegant knot. With a twist, he tucked it around the champagne bottle.

He had good hands.

"Were you a waiter?" she asked.

Quinn glanced up from his pouring.

Diana nodded toward the flutes. "You do this very well."

And that simple compliment finally, finally, broke through the last of Quinn's reserve. The suave smile turned into something more.

He laughed.

Diana went still.

This is the man for me.

A man who laughed, a man who enjoyed life, now *that* was the kind of man who could be a perfect match for her, Ivy League or community college be damned.

If only he weren't on the rebound…if only he didn't want a woman like Lana…a woman nothing like Diana.

Diana took the champagne he offered, glad for the excuse to get back in motion, grateful for the sharp bubbles that woke up her taste buds. "It does taste better cold. You were right."

He lifted his own glass to his lips with a grin, and Diana felt her heart trip a little in the middle of its usually quick rhythm. He was lovesick over Lana MacDowell. She needed to remember that. The next woman he dated would only be a phase, a transition to his next serious relationship.

Being this man's rebound girl would be crushing for someone like her. It was better to just be friends.

"I agree champagne is better cold," Quinn was saying, "but it's also better when it's actually champagne."

"I'm not sure what you mean."

"Champagne has to actually come from a part of France called 'Champagne.'"

The way he said it, all French-sounding with extra syllables, made her want to swoon. Diana had never swooned in her life, over anything. This man was positively dangerous.

"The waiters have been handing out some domestic swill. Sparkling wine, if you want to be kind."

"Oh." Diana glanced at the wrapped bottle.

"The effervescence in this champagne has more bite to it, but the fruit is smooth." He topped off her glass. "Try it again and tell me what you think."

What she thought? What she thought was that she was not in this man's league. She could see the beauty in the crystal and flames, but she could also enjoy the sequins and the LED lights. Quinn, she realized, was from a strictly crystal lifestyle.

They were not a match, no matter how much she was attracted to him.

For one thing, he was scoffing at the champagne at this beautiful party, something she would never do. It bothered her.

And so, for the first time that night—heck, for the first time in weeks—Diana frowned. She raised an eyebrow at him disapprovingly. "I think you can overdo the biting part. When someone offers you free champagne at a party, you should just relax and enjoy it, not critique it. Life is sweeter that way."

He raised an eyebrow right back at her—with ten times the withering effect that she could muster.

"Are you criticizing me for being critical?" he asked. Then, once more, he smiled. "I do believe there is a certain amount of irony there."

"No. Well...yes." Darn it, his smile was something dazzling. It was probably best if she moved on for the night. Diana looked around for the girl with the stooped shoulders.

"Miss Connor, would it be too critical of me to point out that you were just handed cold *and* free *and* genuine champagne?" He clinked his glass with hers, and sabotaged her resolve with another smile. "You are right. We have no choice but to relax and enjoy it."

Well. The man was obviously relaxed enough to start turning the charm on. If she directed him toward the right woman and he gave her that smile, Diana's mission would be accomplished. She took another sip. It really did taste special. She surreptitiously moved the napkin away from the bottle's label with one finger. One never knew when the name of a good champagne might be handy.

She took one more sip, and hoped she could fake some enthusiasm for finding Quinn someone to dance with. "All right, Quinn. Back to business. While we've got champagne, real champagne, to cover our movements, this is an easy time to check out the other people in the room. You never gave me your opinion on the knockout in the red dress."

Quinn took the champagne glass out of her hand and set it down methodically, precisely next to his. He looked rather stern. "I'm not interested."

"Don't give up. The night is still young. We'll find you someone worth dancing with."

"The bottom line is this, Diana Connor. The only

woman I want to dance with, or talk to, or drink champagne with, is you."

"Me?"

Her heart skipped around in her chest, as crazy and out of sync as the fringe on her dress, shivering with the shaky breath she sucked in.

"You. May I have this dance?"

The orchestra began the opening strains of "Moonlight Serenade." It was all so perfect. The champagne, the man, the music, the night.

Diana felt a little shiver of fear. Dancing with Quinn seemed dangerous. Risky, somehow. What if life was never this perfect again?

It takes courage to be happy. Her mother's mantra had become her own. Diana had been doing her best to live a courageous life, seizing happiness when it came her way, just as she'd seized the ticket to this lovely gala. She could dance one perfect dance with a perfect man to a perfect song. It wouldn't change her life. It would be a happy memory to hold when the dark ones threatened.

"I love this song," she said to Quinn.

The corners of his eyes crinkled as his expression went from serious to something softer. Then a woman's voice called to him from behind Diana. "There you are, Quinn MacDowell. I thought for sure you would have ducked out by now. Being quite the trouper tonight, are you?"

Quinn's gaze flicked to someone beyond Diana's shoulder. Diana turned to see who was speaking. A woman, tall and confident, stepped in to kiss Quinn on the cheek.

Two facts warred for attention in Diana's mind.

One, this woman could be a good match for Quinn. She was only a few inches taller than Diana, but her hair had been professionally and intricately piled on top of her head in a striking style that made her seem positively statuesque—and very confident. She wore a floor-length gown, one spectacular drape of blue cloth with a high, choker-style collar, a design only a woman with an elegant, long neck could wear.

Diana was not that woman.

Her second thought was more upsetting: Quinn's last name was MacDowell.

MacDowell. He's a MacDowell. He can't be in love with Lana. That would be horrible, in love with your relative's wife. Just horrible for him.

It was nearly enough to make Diana happy that the woman in blue would be a good match.

The woman trailed an entourage behind her, women who seemed lost in her wake. One was much older, dressed in a severe jacket over a floor-length, straight skirt, and one was much younger—the girl with the stooped shoulders. Diana smiled at her and nodded encouragingly.

The woman in blue, done kissing Quinn, set her purse on the table next to Diana's, and seemed ready to settle in for a chat. Diana took a step to the side to give her room, and felt the brush of the tablecloth against her bare leg.

Bare legs. She was completely underdressed for this event, something she'd noticed as soon as she'd arrived, but something she'd dismissed as being no more than an "oops." Next to this elegant friend of Quinn's, however, she wished for just a second that she'd worn a long gown. Too bad she didn't own a long gown. Formal balls weren't her usual Friday night.

"Thank God you're still here," the woman said to Quinn. "There isn't anyone worth talking to. Dance with me."

Quinn did the raised-eyebrow thing to her, but without any real animosity. The pair were obviously old friends. "As charmingly worded as that invitation was, I've asked Diana to dance."

Quinn nodded her way, and suddenly, Diana was the focus of attention. "Diana, this is Patricia Cargill."

Patricia looked her up and down, once, lingering for a millisecond on Diana's hemline.

Yes, I know everyone else is in a gown.

Quinn continued his introductions. "And, Patricia, this is Diana Connor. She's a friend of Lana's."

"A friend of Lana's." Patricia seemed mildly surprised at this. "From med school?"

Diana fought not to blush. This portion of her evening was rapidly coming to a close. His friends had found him; Quinn no longer needed her. Not even as a dance partner to wile away a song or two.

"I was Lana's real estate agent." She dared a quick glance at Quinn, then looked down to the tablecloth and her nearly empty champagne glass. There was nothing wrong with being a real estate agent, of course, but when she'd met Quinn, she'd said she was Lana's business associate. Had he thought she was a business associate from the world of medicine? Had he assumed she was a doctor or nurse when he'd asked her to dance?

Regardless, he surely had not assumed she paid her bills from the sale of Lana's house.

"Moonlight Serenade" was in full swing without her.

Diana stifled a sigh and turned to the other two women. She stuck her hand out so the stooped-shoulder girl would have to take it.

"My name is Diana. Isn't this a great ball?"

Three

Quinn kept one eye on Diana as she led the quiet girl into the ballroom's far corner. The other woman with Patricia had been introduced as Karen Weaver, the new director of the Austin-area's branch of Texas Rescue and Relief. Quinn kept Diana in his peripheral vision while he greeted Karen and said all the appropriate things about Texas Rescue's importance in times of crisis. He almost wished Diana could hear him, so she'd know he wasn't always as curt as he'd been when she'd first spoken to him. He had the requisite social graces. His mother had raised him right.

Karen Weaver said all the right things in return, complimenting Patricia on the quality of volunteers she recruited for Texas Rescue, physicians like Quinn.

Quinn had long volunteered with Texas Rescue and Relief, a home state organization that stood ready to offer medical help should natural disaster strike anywhere in Texas. Last summer, they'd sweltered in makeshift tents near the border of Oklahoma in order to provide medical care after tornados had torn through a small town.

"Yes, of course I'm committed to another year of service," Quinn assured the new director. "Let's hope the summer is hot, dry and boring."

He made a toasting gesture with his champagne flute, and Patricia tugged at his sleeve. "Do get me some champagne, would you?"

Quinn flagged a passing waiter to stop. Patricia took a flute as Karen declined, their momentary fuss giving Quinn the opportunity to focus on Diana. She was practically hiding behind a potted palm with the new girl.

"Who is the young lady you're dragging along?" he asked Patricia.

"My father's second wife's stepdaughter, or some such nonsense. I refuse to introduce her as a Cargill. She goes by the ironically perky name Becky." She hadn't taken a sip of her glass, but instead dumped the sparkling wine into the empty flute that sat on the table. Diana's empty flute.

"I thought your father was on his third wife now," Quinn said, sliding Diana's now-full flute closer to himself. "And this glass was in use, by the way."

Patricia shrugged. "I sincerely doubt your real estate agent will care what it was refilled with. And wife number three is exactly why I had no idea I'd be forced to babysit number two's offspring." She held her glass in front of Quinn. "Do pour a girl something halfway decent."

Quinn could hardly refuse her, although he'd planned on putting that bottle to better use. He filled her glass. "You make a terrible wingman."

"Do I?" Patricia laughed. "Don't tell me Dr. Quinn MacDowell of the West Central MacDowells needs help landing a real estate agent for the evening, especially one dressed so... Or are you Cowboy Quinn of the River Mack Ranch tonight?"

Quinn hadn't tried to flaunt either side of himself, actually. Diana had talked to him as a complete stranger, without introduction. It was, he realized, unusual. Refreshing. Perfect strangers were perfect equals.

"Either way, she's not your type." Patricia slipped her arm through his.

"I'm in a better position than you to know my type." Quinn said it mildly. He included Karen in their conversation. "Don't worry. Your recruiter and I are not having a lover's spat. Patricia is merely the annoying sister I never had."

Still, being told Diana wasn't his type didn't sit well with him. Having an identifiable type seemed uninspiring. Monotonous. Was he required to stay within this restricted social circle of the hospital, Texas Rescue, and the ranch owner associations?

Haven't I dated all the available women in that pool?

They were all starting to blur together in his memory. It hadn't been hard to stay unattached this past year.

Tonight, he was suddenly obsessing about his own love life. It was ludicrous, when the only reason he'd attended this ball was specifically to fulfill his duties to the hospital as a board member. Meeting the new director of Texas Rescue was an efficient use of the evening, as well. Worrying about female companionship? Not on the radar. Not an issue. Not important.

He resisted the urge to look toward Diana's corner of the ballroom.

"Have you seen Marcel around?" Patricia asked, referring to her current escort. "He's so easy to lose. Oh, Lord—your redhead and my ex-step-in-law are on their way back. I can't take it. Quick, top off my glass."

Quinn only raised an eyebrow at her. To refill her glass would imply that he agreed that Patricia's gloomy girl and the bubbly Diana were burdens best borne with the help of alcohol. Quinn didn't know the girl, of course, but Diana's company didn't require a dose of alcohol. She was not a part of their usual circle, but being with her was no burden.

Diana emerged from the corner, talking and laughing, looking colorful and alive and wonderfully modern against her Victorian surroundings. The solemn girl she'd dragged off with her was laughing, as well. Quinn had to look twice to be sure she was Patricia's step-whatever. Becky, who had all but disappeared in Patricia's shadow, was now walking confidently, eagerly answering a question Diana asked, and generally looking happy.

Had being around Diana done as much for him tonight? He suspected it had. Being around Diana lifted people's spirits. And he, for all his medical training and his business acumen, had no idea how she did it.

She fascinated him.

Quinn wished he'd had a chance to dance with her, but she'd clearly moved on to a new protégée for the evening.

"We're back," Diana said brightly.

Patricia cast a critical eye in her step-whatever's

direction, then took a dramatically deep drink from her flute.

Quinn watched the young lady deflate a little, as if Patricia were the kryptonite to Diana's superpower. It was hardly young Becky's fault that Patricia's father's second wife had dumped her into Patricia's hands.

He smiled sympathetically at Diana's protégée. Becky would be all right. Diana had clearly taken her under her wing, and she'd have her dancing in no time.

The new Texas Rescue director was speaking. Her plans for the coming year were important, and her need for financial and facility support from the hospital were legitimate. Quinn could only lend her half an ear, however. The rest of him was distracted by details from his earlier conversations with Diana.

This would be much harder if you were a woman... you'd have to hope he asked you to dance.

It wasn't always good to have a mind that held details, endless details like Diana's description of the challenges faced by a woman who wanted to be asked to dance. When piecing together a medical puzzle, Quinn was grateful for his memory. Right now, it tugged at his conscience.

Patricia set her flute down and turned to him. "Now, would you dance with me?" she asked in her prettiest voice. She could be delightful company when she chose, but Quinn had known her too long and too well to be interested in more than friendship.

"Since your date is heading this way, I think he'll want this dance." It was a complete lie, of course, since Quinn hadn't caught sight of the missing Marcel, but damn it, Patricia had caused her ex-stepsister's spirits to droop, undoing Diana's good deed.

Quinn held out his hand toward the timid Becky. "Would you care to dance?"

The young lady brightened up once more and placed her hand in his. It wasn't the hand he wanted to be holding, and she wasn't the woman he wanted to dance with. But he'd made her happy by asking her to dance, which had in turn made Diana beam at him in approval. She even bounced on her toes, the tiniest of motions, reminding him of a kid at Christmas.

As Quinn led his partner onto the dance floor, he smiled. He'd made Diana happy, and damn if that didn't make him feel dangerously close to happy, too.

"Becky is a very nice person."

Diana waited for a reply, but Quinn's elegant friend barely made a polite noise of agreement.

Diana tried again. "Have you known each other long?"

Patricia Cargill, the woman who could be a match for Quinn, speared her with one direct look. "Long enough."

Not for Quinn.

Oh, Quinn could handle her, of that Diana had no doubt. In fact, Patricia needed a strong man like Quinn, someone she couldn't bully and intimidate. But Diana didn't want Quinn to have to spend his whole life shaping another woman's personality into something it naturally wasn't. Patricia reminded Diana too much of a striking but strong-headed Dalmatian they'd had a terrible time placing at the animal shelter. Eventually, a professional dog trainer had volunteered to work with families that expressed an interest in the dog, until they found one that could provide her the consistent discipline she needed without breaking her spirit.

I don't want Quinn to have to work that hard.

Quinn MacDowell was a nice guy. Diana hadn't even had to drop a hint, and Quinn had known right away that dancing with Becky would help make the ball beautiful for her.

Diana looked for her champagne glass, wanting a sip to privately toast Quinn, but the glasses were out of place.

"This one," Patricia said, and slid a flute toward her.

Diana took a sip. It was warm. And flat.

It was not real champagne.

She didn't like it. What a horrible realization, to know that forever more, she would not enjoy fake champagne. Quinn had introduced her to something better, and she couldn't undo that experience. Every interaction with every person left its mark, of course, so spending time with Quinn had been bound to affect her, but still...

Look on the bright side. You only got spoiled for champagne.

It could have been worse. She could have danced with Quinn.

It was a lucky thing that Patricia's arrival had saved her from having a taste of being Quinn's date for the night. Diana had never danced with a handsome man who wore a tuxedo as if it were a regular part of his wardrobe. A man who laughed as he poured champagne at a glorious gala.

She wouldn't miss what she'd never had.

Nothing had changed. Nothing at all. "Moonlight

Serenade" had ended two songs earlier. Quinn was surrounded by friends, Becky was enjoying herself, and it was time for Diana to move on. Patricia would surely claim the next dance, and Karen looked like she was ready to talk business all night. Diana was feeling distinctly like the third wheel, now that Quinn was no longer a lone figure, brooding silently at a party.

Diana took another sip of the "domestic sparkling wine," as Quinn had called it, determined to be satisfied.

Patricia watched her. Her words were civil and smooth, but every muscle in her elegant body was tense. "You must have friends who are wondering where you are. Perhaps you should go back to them."

"I will," Diana said, fighting fire with friendliness, always her best chance at success. "I'll just say goodbye to Becky and Quinn and then I'll be on my way."

Patricia leveled a direct look on her, one that would have made many a puppy at the pound drop its gaze in submission. Diana kept smiling, anyway. Patricia looked away, toward the far side of the dance floor. "I see Quinn and Becky have joined a group of my friends. Karen, let me introduce you." She was already in motion before she casually spoke to Diana. "Do excuse us."

"Of course," Diana said, her smile firmly in place. *Easy girl, I'm not going to fight you for that bone. See how friendly I am? I'm just the buddy.*

But the buddy could hardly stand to watch, so Diana scooped up her tiny purse and retreated to the mezzanine once more, but not before topping off her sparkling wine with a tiny bit of the real champagne.

* * *

The buzzing of his cell phone gave Quinn the perfect excuse to leave Becky with a few of the young med school students who'd spent a month interning in his cardiology practice.

He stepped away from the group as he pulled the cell phone from his pocket. The first digits of the phone number indicated that it came from one of the hospital lines.

"MacDowell," he said, turning his back on the orchestra.

"Quinn, it's Brian. Irene Caulsky passed away about twenty minutes ago. Thought you'd like to know."

"An MI?" Quinn knew it had to have been a heart attack, but he asked. It bought him a few seconds, the moments he needed to let that first punch of failure pass.

"Yes. She'd been sedated, but the nurses saw it happening on telemetry. I was on the floor when they called for the crash cart, so I stepped in. I think the nurses were relieved I was there to call it. Everyone could see this was the end."

"Of course. I'm glad she wasn't awake and aware." Modern medicine had its limits. The patient had already survived two heart attacks. Given her age and health, the odds of Irene surviving a third were practically nonexistent, but the hospital's floor staff didn't have the legal authority to declare a patient dead. They had to keep attempting to resuscitate a hopeless case until a physician could make the call. Since Quinn's new partner, Brian, had been present, everyone—including Irene's fragile, expired body—had been spared significant stress.

The orchestra finished its song, and the crowd applauded. Quinn hunched his shoulders to block out the sound as Brian told him the family had taken the news well. "They specifically asked me to thank you for taking care of their grandma."

Taking care of her. What had he done? He'd placed some stents in her arteries after the first heart attack. That had bought the octogenarian a few more years, until a second heart attack had brought her to West Central this morning, where Quinn had admitted her for an overnight stay in the critical care unit.

During those few years, she'd been a regular patient at the office as Quinn monitored the medicines he'd prescribed. She'd left his staff smiling after each appointment, because she called their boss "sonny boy" and she told all the women how beautiful and young they were. She'd never failed to ask Quinn how his mother fared.

He passed a hand over his eyes briefly. He'd have to call his mother tomorrow and break the news that her beloved fourth-grade teacher had passed away.

Brian's voice was clear as the orchestra struck up another song. "I'm sorry to bother you on your weekend off, but I thought you'd want to know about Irene."

"Thank you. I'm glad you were there, Brian."

"Me, too. I'll see you Monday."

Quinn disconnected the call, slid the cell phone back into his pocket and waited. The feeling of being punched would pass. It always did.

The human body cannot last indefinitely. This was a fact. It would always be a fact, no matter what cures were discovered and which diseases were eradicated. *Death is part of any medical practice.* His earliest mentors had impressed that upon him. He'd chosen this profession knowing he would see death, up close and personal.

The patient died, but I did not fail to do my best. That was an important one. Quinn knew he'd done everything right. Everything was sometimes not enough. After all, the human body could not last indefinitely.

The loop of logical statements ran through his mind again, as they always did when he lost a patient, as they always did until his mind muted his emotions.

Quinn reached up to rub the back of his neck. This punch had been powerful, because Irene had been a special patient. The hurt wasn't subsiding at its usual pace. He focused on his surroundings, and realized he was staring at the potted palm trees Diana had hidden behind.

Diana. Quinn pictured her green dress and her shapely legs. For once, it was good to be able to recall the details: the way she'd bounced on toes that were polished in red and peeking through silver sandal straps. Impractical. Feminine. Sexy.

Diana—lively, lovely Diana. Quinn wanted to be with her. He wanted to hold her.

"Damn it, we were supposed to dance." He said the words under his breath as he turned back to the room, angry at himself for letting anything dissuade him from his earlier goal of dancing with Diana. With an intensity he could feel over and above the punch of losing a patient, Quinn wanted his hands on Diana. He wanted to feel that fringe in his fingers. He wanted to know the smell of her hair and the softness of her skin. He wanted that dance.

He looked toward the table where he'd left her

standing with Patricia and the director of Texas Rescue. Only the champagne bottle remained.

She was gone. Again.

Four

Diana had barely reached the doors to the mezzanine when she ran into Dr. Lana MacDowell, the woman Quinn had been studying so longingly when Diana had first spotted him. Lana looked simply smashing in her evening gown, glowing like the bride she was as she walked next to Braden MacDowell.

Poor Quinn.

Diana held out her hand, ready to shake Lana's like a proper business associate, but Lana kissed her on the cheek and, to Diana's surprise, the always business-like Braden did, too. They'd barely gotten past their hellos when a gentleman asked Lana to dance. Braden turned to Diana, and for the first time that night, she found herself on the dance floor, partnered by a hand-some man in a tuxedo.

It was lovely. Diana enjoyed it for what it was. Lovely—but not romantic. Even if Braden had been single, Diana would not have felt a spark with him. They were simply not a match.

She didn't recognize the song the band was play-ing. She wondered how Braden and Quinn were related—and she worried how Braden would feel if he knew Quinn was in love with his wife. She worried that Quinn would never get over his unrequited feelings for Lana. She worried—

"Are you having a good time tonight?" Braden asked.

"Yes, thank you."

Braden looked at her more closely. "Is anything wrong? That was the most lukewarm thing I've ever heard you say."

Diana felt herself blush a bit. This whole gala was to benefit the hospital that Braden's father had founded, the hospital he now ran as CEO. She'd gone and made him worry that she didn't like the evening.

She tried harder. "Nothing's wrong. Nothing *could* be wrong tonight. Your gala is absolutely beautiful, down to the last detail."

"Thank you, but I can't take credit for planning any of this. I only approved the final proposal." Braden smiled faintly at her praise, but he was still studying her too closely.

Diana seized on the subject of party planning and kept up a bright stream of chatter. She didn't doubt that she was rambling a bit, but people didn't mind in general, as long as she was friendly and undemanding.

The song ended, and they rejoined Lana just as Quinn walked up to their little group. Diana's bright chatter petered out. She couldn't talk around the lump in her throat as Quinn greeted Lana with a kiss on the cheek. When Quinn and Braden stood side by side, Diana knew they had to be brothers.

Oh, God, poor Quinn—in love with his brother's

wife. It made for dramatic movies, but in real life, she could hardly imagine a worse situation.

Braden introduced her to Quinn.

"Brothers?" Diana confirmed, then cleared her throat a little. "The green eyes threw me off. I should have seen the resemblance earlier."

"Earlier? You two have already met?" Lana squeezed Quinn's arm. "Diana's more than a real estate agent. She's a magician."

"She's already tried to perform a little magic with me tonight," Quinn said with mock severity. "Brace yourself. I've been dancing."

"No!" Lana laughed.

Quinn winked at Diana.

Two things hit Diana in rapid succession.

One, Quinn was not in love with Lana. It was evident in his body language, in his tone of voice, in his relaxed manner. Nope, not in love, not the least little bit.

Two, Diana was overwhelmingly relieved. Absurdly so. She wanted to laugh, to float, to hug everyone.

Quinn didn't need time to nurse a broken heart. He didn't need a transition girl.

He could—

What? Decide she was his perfect match? Choose her over all these elegant women as the one he wanted in his life?

Not very likely.

Her bubble burst. Diana tapped her purse impatiently against her bare thigh. It took courage to be happy, her mother had said. But experience had taught Diana that life was easier when you didn't expect too much. When you didn't long for things you couldn't have. When you enjoyed the sparkling wine, and didn't compare it to champagne.

What would one taste of Quinn be like?

She really should be going. It was time to move on. The MacDowells were catching up with each other. If she gave Lana a little friendly wave, if she nodded toward Quinn, then she could head to the mezzanine.

As she raised her hand for that wave, Quinn cupped her elbow. He stepped close to her, very close, and she was overwhelmed at the height and the heat of him, at his masculine body clad in a civilized tuxedo crowding into her personal space.

"You can't leave yet."

She looked up at him in surprise.

He smiled, a subtle lifting of one corner of his mouth. "I haven't had the privilege of dancing with you tonight."

Oh, this was delicious, this shiver his voice sent through her body. He sounded almost like he was giving her an order, but his words were so courteous. *The privilege of dancing with you...* She could get lost in a romantic fantasy if she weren't careful.

"That's okay. I've been forcing you to dance enough as is." She lightly socked him in the arm with her purse, as much to remind herself that she was his pal as for any other reason.

"I think my stamina is up to the task. Let's dance. This song fits you too well for us to stand here, talking."

Diana listened for a moment. Quinn thought "The Way You Look Tonight" fit her? This handsome man, the brother of people she liked and respected, liked the way she looked.

Life might never be this perfect again, her conscience reminded her. *You can't miss what you've never had.*

It takes courage to be happy. Diana remembered her mother's words. When in doubt, she always tried to follow her mother's advice. She placed her hand in Quinn's, and let him lead her onto the dance floor.

Quinn was a wonderful dancer, holding her properly with one strong arm across her back, just under her shoulder blades, making it easy for her to rest her entire arm along his. He held her other hand out to the side, keeping their arms extended like real ballroom dancers. Her hand rested easily in his. He held her with just the right amount of squeeze to make her feel secure.

Secure. Special. In sync. *Right.* Dancing with Quinn felt right. She looked up a bit, wanting to see his expression. Did he think they were a match?

"You were trying to escape again, weren't you?" he said, as they moved forward in time to the music.

With every step, her bare legs brushed the black wool covering his. Each and every step. She was aware of her relative nakedness in a way that made talking difficult. Or perhaps, it made talking imperative.

"You didn't need me any longer. Patricia was obviously your next dance partner."

"She is not the one I asked. You are."

Diana enjoyed that delicious shiver once more, before the implications set in. "So poor Becky is stuck with Patricia again? Oh—I don't mean your friend is someone to be stuck with."

"You meant exactly that, and you are exactly right." Quinn gave her a little extra spin at the edge of the dance floor, before they merged into the dance floor traffic once more. "Patricia can make a plant wither with one look, if she wishes. Never fear. I left Becky with some of West Central's med school students. They are much closer to her age, and they were fighting over the chance to dance with someone who isn't a professor's wife."

"That's wonderful. What a good idea."

She felt his fingers sift through the fringe that fell from her shoulder.

"Thank you," he said. "I'm not the magician you are, though. I'd like to know your secret. How did you change Becky's outlook so completely?"

Diana jumped at the chance to talk about something so silly. Remaining quiet as he toyed with the fringe of her dress was too much to ask of herself. Talking would distract her from this awareness of how they moved, how they meshed, how they made magic—at least in her mind. Oh, but did he feel it, too?

Talk. He asked about Becky.

She tapped his shoulder with her purse. "To my boss's dismay, this purse is too small for me to waste room on things like business cards, but I always find space for critical items like safety pins. Becky's dress was just a size too big. She couldn't relax, because her top was loose. A few safety pins along the seams —"

"Strategically placed while you chatted behind a palm tree?"

"Bingo. You can really dance once you know your dress won't come off."

Quinn laughed, but this time the laugh had a slightly different undertone. A little more bass to it.

"Since you're dancing with me, you must feel very certain that your dress is not going to come off."

She leaned back just enough to smile with him, but he wasn't smiling.

He turned them once more. "Your dress will stay on no matter what I try?"

The possibility that he was talking about more than dancing was hard to ignore.

Quinn spoke intimately into her ear. "I find myself tempted to test that theory."

He smiled at her, but it was something of a pirate's smile. "Just how certain are you that your dress won't be coming off tonight?"

Diana hoped her smile didn't slip. Apparently, she'd gone and done it again. A man had mistaken friendliness for something else. Something looser. Easier.

Sleazier.

She never saw herself that way. It always disappointed her when other people did. It just about killed her that Quinn did.

Darn it, she'd wanted him to be different.

She was curvy. She smiled a lot. Tonight, she was pretty much flashing all the leg she owned in a dress that was just a teensy bit too small. Could she blame Quinn for thinking she was less of a matchmaker and more of an easy bed partner?

She'd been thinking about finding magic, about making perfect matches. He was thinking about getting her naked. Tonight. His hand slid lower, leaving her upper back cold as he curved his arm around her waist.

The disappointment was crushing.

She started to let go. At the same moment she loosened her hold, he tightened his, and then she found herself bent backward in a dip, breathless and disoriented, despite being held securely by his strong arms.

The last notes of the song faded away. She focused on his green eyes, the crystal and the flames and the music all a blur beyond him.

He smiled that disarming, charming half smile. "You were quite right. Your dress is secure. It's safe to dance the next song with me." He stood her up and gave her hand a friendly squeeze.

She was such an idiot. She was the one who'd jumped to all the wrong conclusions. They'd been talking about safety pins. Quinn hadn't been thinking of her in a sexual way; he'd been joking with her. Of course he had been—she was the buddy.

Quinn held her lightly, waiting for her to say she'd dance with him.

Diana called up her smile. She forced herself to laugh. She placed her hand on his shoulder and smacked her other hand in his, in a move that resembled a high five. "Let's dance. We can scope out your perfect partner over each other's shoulders."

Quinn knew he'd screwed up.

Thirty seconds, that was all it had taken. He'd been dancing with Diana, having a genuinely interesting and lighthearted conversation on a topic unfamiliar to him—how to fix a girl's dress and thereby a girl's evening—and then he'd lost Diana's spark. She was still dancing with him, moving in time to the music, but she was no longer *with* him.

He needed that spark. Without any conscious effort

on her part, without knowing he was hurting from the passing of Irene Caulsky, she'd made him feel better. Balanced, like there was enough light in the world to offset the dark.

But somehow, he'd blown it. Hell, she was even looking for another woman again, someone else for him to dance with.

Quinn was familiar with situations that went sour in a moment. As a cardiologist, he'd had patients chatting groggily with him as they waited for their sedation to take effect suddenly go into full cardiac arrest. As a rancher, he'd seen livestock ambling across a dry creek bed, kicking up dust, suddenly be swept away in a roaring torrent of water, a deadly flash flood from some faraway rainstorm.

When situations turned, Quinn turned them back. He threaded wires into hearts and opened blocked arteries. He gave chase on horseback and lassoed swimming cattle.

What did he do with Diana?

Situations with women didn't turn so rapidly. Women liked being with him, and he with them. If a woman was upset, it was generally because he hadn't been able to keep a date—which usually meant a patient had taken one of those sudden turns for the worse. Although the circumstances that kept him from showing up were beyond his control, women liked an apology. They liked their apologies best when he showed up bearing a gift, generally wine and roses, or a tasteful piece of gold jewelry. No gemstones. He liked his relationships exclusive, but without expectations of permanence.

He wasn't in a relationship with Diana, and he

hadn't failed to show up for this dance, but since women loved apologies...

"I'm sorry," he said.

Diana frowned slightly, making a little wrinkle appear between her brows. She really had a fascinating face, open and expressive. He wanted that genuine spark of hers to come back.

"I'm very sorry," he said, more emphatically.

"For what?" she asked.

That nearly made him pause in the middle of the dance floor. Women didn't ask that. They accepted his apology, took the wine and roses, and stayed with him.

Diana was different.

"For what?" he repeated, aware that he had no answer.

She met his gaze, and he noticed that although her eyes were brown, they had a touch of gold to them, or perhaps it was closer to copper, a bit of rose color to match her hair.

"All you did was dip me," Diana said. "Very nicely. You didn't even come close to dropping me."

They danced in silence while the band's singer crooned a few lines. Quinn thought back, trying to pinpoint where the tone of the evening had changed. "Perhaps I didn't give you enough warning? No one likes to be startled."

Her laugh sounded forced to him. "Seriously, Quinn, you've got nothing to apologize for. Look, there's that woman in the red dress again. No, don't look—that's too obvious. I'm looking for you. I don't think she's with any man in particular. You could dance us closer to her side of the floor, and then when the song ends—"

"I warned you, right before the dip, that I was going to test whether or not your dress was secure enough for dancing."

Diana abruptly fell silent. She studied the orchestra, keeping her face turned away from him.

Details. Quinn needed to remember the details. "I said… Aw, hell. I said I was going to try to get you out of your dress. That's it, isn't it? I didn't mean it that way, Diana. I'm sorry—truly sorry."

She looked at him for a second, but she seemed embarrassed, and she looked back at the band.

"I didn't mean it that way," he said, as lame an excuse as he'd ever given in his life.

"I know you didn't." She shrugged and spoke to his lapel. "I'm an idiot."

"Why are you the idiot? I'm the one who said something stupid." Quinn didn't like the way Diana seemed to assume she'd done something wrong. They'd stopped moving across the dance floor and were marking time, swaying to the music in one place. He tried to lighten the moment. "My mother would tan my hide if she heard me say such a thing."

"I took it the wrong way." She ventured a glance at him, embarrassment written all over her hide-nothing face.

Something in Quinn's gut twisted. "It was perfectly reasonable for you to have taken it that way. I imagine you've heard plenty of lines from plenty of men."

She blushed in the glow of the orchestra's stage lighting. "I know. My dress is too short, and I tend to touch people too much." She touched his shoulder with her purse, just one weak thump, a pale imitation of her earlier playfulness. "I give guys the wrong impression."

Quinn stopped cold, right there on the dance floor. "No. I meant nothing like that."

The song finished and couples all around them stepped apart. Their polite applause faded away as the band leader spoke. Diana dropped Quinn's hand and stepped back.

Damn it, he'd just told her she was wrong. He'd probably scared her with his intensity. This wasn't a hospital operating room. He didn't need to bark out corrections.

Diana was facing the band leader, looking interested in his words. Quinn stepped closer to her, so he could keep their conversation private. "The only impression you've given anyone tonight is that you are open and friendly."

Quinn had underestimated Diana, that much was certain. He'd thought she was an open book, unguarded almost to a fault, but she obviously had her past hurts and secrets. He tried, once more, to restore their lighter mood. "If I were making a pass at you, I would deserve a good, swift kick for a stupid line like 'bet I can get your dress off tonight.'"

"But you weren't making a pass at me, because we're just friends."

You weren't making a pass at me. She said it as though it were impossible for him to be interested. That she could miss his attraction to her was astounding.

Or perhaps, she did not want to see it, because she did not feel attracted to him. *We're just friends.* She'd made a point of saying that.

If a woman was not interested, then Quinn was not interested. After all, if the woman in white was not available, then the woman in blue or red would be. It had been so for as long as he could remember—since one cheerleader had broken his teenaged heart and two others had vied for the chance to make it whole. It made no sense for a man to hang all his hopes on one particular woman.

Unless that woman was one of a kind. Effervescent. Irresistible.

Diana tipped her chin toward a cluster of people grouped around a table. "I think you'll regret it for the rest of the weekend if you don't ask the woman in the red dress to dance at least once. The band leader just announced this was their last song."

She wanted him to find a new partner. Quinn felt that punch again. Loss. Diana Connor had no desire to get to know him better.

She was smiling at him, chatting away in that pleasant way of hers as she backed away. "I'm so glad I got to meet you tonight. I can honestly say I've never met a MacDowell I didn't like. Good luck with the lady in red. Now hurry, go."

He watched her as she began threading her way through the crowd around the edge of the dance floor. He remained stoic, waiting for cool logic to counter that hot stab of regret. The rationalizations began automatically: nothing lasted indefinitely. Endings were part of life. This loss hadn't occurred because he'd failed to do his best.

Quinn stopped the loop right there. Did he even know what his best was when it came to a woman? An apology. A piece of gold jewelry. A relationship with finite expectations. A civilized parting of ways after six months or twelve. That was the endless loop of his relationships, and it all required so little effort.

How could he let Diana walk away, when he didn't know what his best was?

Five

She wasn't going to cry. At least, not in public, she wasn't. Diana batted her eyelashes rapidly, heading for the mezzanine and the ladies' room, and nearly ran into the man in front of her.

He steadied her with a hand at her elbow.

Quinn. She knew it the instant before he spoke. "I meant it when I said you were the only woman I cared to dance with this evening, Diana. May I have the last dance?"

Quinn started guiding her onto the dance floor without waiting for her answer. Diana didn't try to resist. She'd never be the same after this ball, anyway. She'd never forget Quinn MacDowell, so she might as well enjoy the feeling of moving in time with him for a few minutes more.

She blinked her wet eyelashes some more, and gestured vaguely toward the spot where she'd left him. "How did you get in front of me?"

"You were going around the edges of the square, so I took the hypotenuse."

He was holding her with just the right amount of

squeeze, moving the two of them easily to the music, and Diana felt like she could breathe without any danger of a sob coming out. Her smile was real. "Did you just use the word *hypotenuse* at a party?"

Quinn smiled, a full smile, the kind that lifted both sides of his mouth. *Dear Lord, he has a dimple on one side.*

"It's the shortest distance between two points," he said.

Diana rolled her eyes. "I can't believe your brain really works that way."

"Blame my father. I grew up on a ranch, and he taught me to ride at a forty-five degree angle to whatever path a runaway steer was taking."

She could be offended that he was comparing her to a steer, but it was too fascinating to imagine him as a boy on horseback.

"To cut off the steer's trajectory," he said, as if her silence meant he hadn't explained very well. "You can't chase behind them, you need to get in front of them, so they'll change direction and go back to the herd."

"You don't use a lasso?" Heck, if she was going to imagine Quinn as a cowboy, she might as well go all the way.

"That takes practice. I wasn't very good at it yet when my dad first took me on a round-up." Quinn shifted his arm, pulling her closer. "I doubt I'm good at it anymore, either. I spend all my time at the hospital."

"Your dad is a cowboy who taught you to think about a hypotenuse? He sounds very unique."

"He was. He's passed away."

"Oh, I'm so sorry." She squeezed his hand, the one he was holding in their ballroom dancing pose.

"Thank you. It's been years, I'm sad to say." He brought their joined hands closer to their chests, brushing his knuckles briefly over the curve of her cheek. "May I ask you why you were crying?"

Diana sucked in a quick breath at his caress, sorry he'd noticed her tears. She was supposed to make parties fun for everyone. "I wasn't crying."

"Technically, I suppose you weren't." He tucked their hands against his chest. The black satin of his lapel soothed the back of her hand as they danced, in silence. The music was beautiful, the lights were low, and her partner kept her secure as they danced smoothly, slowly, swaying to the sounds of an orchestra in a ballroom that had seen more than a hundred years of celebrations. It was one of the perfect moments of her life, and Diana knew it.

Gosh darn it, it was going to make her cry.

"Diana?"

She tilted her head back, looking at the blue sky that was permanently painted on the vaulted ceiling, as she blinked away more pesky salt water. "It's just a great evening, isn't it?"

"Yes, it is. That's making you sad?"

"I'm not sad. Beauty can make you cry."

They danced in silence a while longer, then Quinn spoke. This close, she could feel the deep bass of his voice in his chest.

"Were you experiencing great beauty as you left me so that I would dance with the woman in the red dress?"

"Oh, no fair. That's a hard question."

"It's a good question."

Diana tried to glare at him from under her wet lashes, but he seemed pretty unflappable. Darned doctor He probably got training in that.

"Why don't you answer my good question? I'm very interested."

Honestly, how was a girl supposed to deal with a man like Quinn? *Honestly*, she supposed. The problem was, she wasn't really sure what was behind her tears. She did what she always did when faced with a dilemma, and started talking it out.

"My mother loved the performing arts. Ballet, symphony, plays." Diana could picture the list as her mother had written it, with loops for the tails of the letter *y* that were a work of art in themselves. "She said they were moments of perfection, and she was sorry I hadn't witnessed them with her, because they would never happen exactly the same way again. But she said I should go and find my own moments of beauty, and to have the courage to be happy, even knowing that happiness might only be a moment in time."

Quinn said nothing. The orchestra played, a beautiful blend of instruments. He held her against his polished tuxedo for the longest time, and then Diana felt him rest his cheek against her hair.

The song ended.

Diana closed her eyes, and tried not to care that a tear—or two, or three—fell from her lashes.

Mother knows best.

That last, sweet dance with Quinn had been special. Perfect. Her mother had been right: it was a moment in time that would never happen again, and it was all the more precious because of it. Diana wanted to quit while she was ahead.

She wanted to take her perfect memory of the perfect dance and go home, tuck both it and herself into bed, and relive it over and over. She'd even told Quinn she wasn't staying for the country-Western concert that was about to begin in the spacious mezzanine because she had to work this weekend. It was barely past ten o'clock, and Diana didn't have to be at the animal shelter at any particular time on Saturday, but she was expected, and it was work.

Before she left him, she had one more beautiful moment in mind, like something out of the movies. She envisioned herself leaving Quinn with a kiss, with one perfectly sweet press of her lips on his. Then she'd walk away, alone. But while she stared at his mouth, thinking about that kiss, his lips formed words she'd never expected.

"Where are you parked?"

She was undone by his practicality. She wasn't going to quit while she was ahead, after all. Quinn insisted on escorting her to her car, which seemed so very *Quinn* of him, Diana had not bothered trying to refuse. He'd already changed her image of the ideal man, setting the bar higher than she'd thought possible before tonight. She might as well take his arm and stroll outside on a summer night. It was a terrible risk, because no other summer night might ever be so special.

Quinn led the way through the crush in the mezzanine, nodding at acquaintances and subtly clearing the way as the crowd jockeyed for positions around the temporary stage. Diana spotted Becky Cargill, who was laughing as a young man boosted her onto a table for a better view as the evening's first star began his country-Western hit.

Diana smiled at Becky's happiness. There, at least, she'd lived up to her mother's standards. She was leaving someone at this ball better off than she'd found her.

Quinn kept Diana close behind him as they headed down to the lobby on the crowded, carpeted staircase. They were stopped by every other person, it seemed, people who wanted to greet Dr. MacDowell. Clearly, he was more important to the hospital than she knew. It was a sobering reminder that he was destined for a woman like Patricia Cargill, or the lady in red, or the woman in white. In the future, someone elegant and educated would accompany Quinn through event after elegant event.

Will she help him enjoy each party?

"Dr. MacDowell!"

Diana and Quinn turned simultaneously toward the woman who had called his name. There was something in the way she said his name, a tone of shock, that gave Diana chills.

"What are you doing here?" the woman asked, staring up at Quinn from the bottom of the staircase as if she couldn't believe her eyes.

Quinn hesitated, almost imperceptibly. Diana might have missed it if she hadn't had her hand on his shoulder, keeping her balance as she stood one step above him. Then, with his usual decisiveness, he led Diana down the last two stairs, pulled her out of the main stream of partygoers, and asked her to wait for him.

Diana watched him approach the woman. It was easy to see that he was saying "I'm sorry."

Everything about the woman's stiff posture expressed her shock. She kept looking from the phone in her hand to Quinn's face. "I just heard. You weren't there?" she said, her voice carrying easily above the motion and murmur of the lobby crowd. "But you're her doctor. You've always been her doctor. She loved you."

Quinn answered her, but he kept his voice too low for Diana to hear. Diana thought that was wise. She could tell in a glance that this woman was teetering on an emotional edge, and if Quinn raised his voice to match hers, she'd be high-pitched and howling in no time.

"You put her in the hospital and then you came to a *party*? You weren't there when she died?" The woman's words bounced off the marble and wood, drawing attention from those nearby, some of whom stopped and whispered to their fellows.

Diana's heart bled—for both the woman and Quinn. The woman was clearly distraught, but Quinn had to have been cut by that accusation, cut deeply. Still, he was staying calm, speaking seriously, giving the woman all his attention.

She jerked away from him. As she strode past Diana, she practically spat her words over her shoulder at Quinn. "I'm going to the hospital. You enjoy your evening, Dr. MacDowell. You just enjoy yourself."

Quinn said a few words to the man who'd been standing with her, who then headed after the woman.

Quinn remained where he was, looking calm and unfazed, when he couldn't possibly be. People began to resume their own conversations. Diana thought she should give him a minute, perhaps, to let him recover from the scene in his own way.

To heck with that.

Diana scooted around the people still lingering, perhaps waiting for more drama, and hugged Quinn's arm as soon as she reached his side. "I'm so sorry," she said.

He turned that neutral expression on her, then dropped his gaze to his sleeve, where she clung with both hands as she pressed against him. "For what? You have nothing to be sorry for."

"I'm sorry you had to hear such bitter words. She was in pain."

"Yes, she was. Her grandmother passed away this evening."

He sounded so matter-of-fact, but it was all so upsetting. Diana wished she could give Quinn a proper hug, but they were in a busy hotel lobby. At a black-tie gala.

Quinn covered one of Diana's hands with his. "It's an occupational hazard. I'm fine. Death is part of any doctor's practice. The human body can't last indefinitely. I did all I could."

"But—"

"Ready to leave?" Quinn turned toward the Sixth Street exit, as if he'd merely offered Diana his arm as a gentleman, not as if he had a woman clinging to him in sympathy.

She kept one hand tucked into his elbow. They were silent as they walked through the leaded glass door and down the steps to the sidewalk. The hotel anchored a corner of Sixth Street, a street lined with bar after restaurant after pub, each with its own musician spilling live music out its door. Diana was about to gesture one way, toward her car, when Quinn began walking her in the opposite direction.

It was Friday night, so the sidewalk was busy, filled with young people, hyper, happy, hollering, a striking contrast to the formal crowd in the hotel that loomed over them.

Quinn remained as he'd been all evening, calm, cool and collected in his tuxedo, walking with un-hurried steps down Sixth Street, then down one of the main cross streets, but Diana was now certain his cool was all an act. Quinn MacDowell was upset: he'd forgotten to ask her which way to her car.

They lived different lives. They had nothing in common, not friends, careers or lifestyles. Diana would never have matched them together. It would have been as doomed as matching a Yorkie with a rancher. No matter how fond they were of each other, it was not a good pairing. As a couple, she and Quinn wouldn't last.

But tonight, he was more vulnerable than the world knew, and he had no one but her to care. He'd been alone when she found him, alone and brooding, and she wouldn't leave him just as badly off as she'd found him. Quinn MacDowell, M.D., needed her. And that, to her, was a thing of beauty.

Diana let him lead the way, content to go in the wrong direction with the right man.

Six

I did not fail to do my best.

No matter what her granddaughter had accused him of, Quinn had taken all the right steps with Irene. Quinn had assured her granddaughter that Irene hadn't suffered, although it would take time for that truth to sink in and bring comfort.

Quinn had done his best. It was a fact that the human body could not last indefinitely...

Diana rested her cheek on his shoulder, interrupting his thoughts and slowing his steps. Her simple act seemed tender. Sweet—to cancel out the bitterness.

If Quinn allowed himself to think about that, he'd lose what calm he commanded.

Yet, he was glad she was by his side. As her hair brushed his cheek, he could abandon logic and loss, and lose himself in the sensation of having a woman so willingly pressed against him. She smelled good, damned good, a mix of flowers and spices, a feast for the senses. Quinn allowed himself to breathe more deeply, long, slow inhalations that matched their un-hurried steps. More spicy than floral, he decided, like the best wine in his collection.

Quinn glanced down, taking in the view of her legs from this angle. They stepped in unison over each crack in the sidewalk, the metallic straps of her sandals reflecting the neon lights of the bars they passed. The rhythmic flashes of her bare legs and the flexing of her toned thighs had a hypnotic effect that silenced the endless loop of his thoughts.

They were alive, she and he. The human body had its limits, but it also had its pleasures, and hers was a pleasure to view. From the first moment she'd sat next to him and he'd watched that green hemline settle dangerously high on her thighs, Quinn had been enjoying the view.

For hours, he'd watched as she'd smiled and laughed, beautifully enjoying her life. And Quinn? Hell, he'd had to be told that a ball was made for dancing, that sparkling wine was worth drinking, that a man should find the right woman.

The right woman. What did that mean? A woman whose willingness to be happy made those around her happier. A woman with childish delight in a party. A woman with a wise appreciation of the ephemeral quality of beauty. A woman who outshone the shimmer of her own silk-fringed dress.

Watching her was no longer enough. Not nearly enough.

The night was still young, and Quinn was wasting this time with her, settling for a glimpse of leg, a whiff of fragrance, a hand on his arm. It was all too little, a drop of water on the tongue of a man who'd just realized he was dying of thirst.

He dropped his arm, sliding it around her waist to pull her closer. Better. They kept walking as she slid her arm around his waist, too, and he turned to kiss her temple, savoring the warmth as he pressed his mouth to her skin. She pressed her whole body against him in response, and the last of Quinn's reason took a hike.

They'd reached his building. Thank God. It would only be minutes before he could satisfy his craving for Diana. The elevator was mirrored, and it would soon be filled with reflections of tan legs and red-gold hair. He'd get his hands on all that green fringe, get his mouth on hers. They'd lose his jacket, shred the tie, and by the time the elevator stopped on his floor, he could have her in his condo and on his bed in—

He stopped at the lobby doors, pulled her into his arms, and kissed her on the sidewalk, because the elevator was too far away. Her mouth was perfect, hot and moist and as eager as his. He pulled her body against his, and her arm felt strong around his waist. They were alive. They were together.

Her other hand slid over his collar and secured a fistful of his hair.

Hell, yes.

The crowd on the sidewalk approved, too. The wolf whistles barely registered, but when male voices got too close and too crude, a sense of protectiveness made Quinn break off the kiss. Diana's expression was perfect. Panting, a bit dazed, she looked at him with something close to wonder—exactly how he felt.

Awed.

"You are...my God, Diana, you are everything worth having. Kissing you, it's..."

"It's magic," she whispered. "I know."

He pushed open the glass door to his building and waited for the security guard to recognize his face and buzz him through the inner set of doors.

"Why are we going in here?" Diana asked.

"I live here."

"Good."

She grabbed him by the lapels and kissed him hard. She was a great kisser, matching him in intensity, meeting him all the way. When the buzzer sounded, Quinn backed into the inner door, dragging Diana into the lobby with him before he dragged his mouth away from hers.

That elevator seemed a mile away. As they crossed the carpeted lobby, he grabbed one end of his bowtie and jerked it loose. The elevator doors opened with a soft chime. He took one step inside, managing—just barely—not to yank her into the mirrored interior. He forced himself to turn and place a hand on the door to prevent it from sliding shut.

Diana hadn't stepped in when the door opened. She was looking over her shoulder, taking in the artwork, which was set off by the dramatic architecture of the lobby. With his eyes on her legs, he saw her bounce, just once, on her toes. "This is a beautiful place."

Control. He needed control over himself. He took her hand, brought it to his lips, and kissed the flawless, smooth skin. "I can't see it. I only see you." It was sappy. He'd never been more serious.

She looked at him, her brown eyes serious, too. "Let's make some magic," she whispered.

He didn't move.

"Now."

He yanked her into the mirrored car and slammed

the side of his fist on the *close door* button. She didn't
need to regain her balance, because he lifted her high
against him as the doors slid shut. He devoured her
mouth as he cupped her perfectly rounded backside
in his greedy hands. Her purse hit the floor and her
hands dug into his shoulders as she wrapped one leg
around him, and he felt the heel of her silver sandal
pressing into the back of his thigh.

He tore his mouth away from hers, struggling to
slow the pace—he was not going to take her in the
elevator, no matter what his body demanded—but
when he opened his eyes, he saw Diana everywhere,
every angle, wrapped around him like a dream come to
life. The green dress had finally, finally ridden above
the perfect curve of her backside, and his hands were
spread over hot-pink satin. Color, vibrant color. That
was Diana, beautiful, vibrant Diana.

The chime sounded again, and she quickly let go of
him to slide down his body until her toes touched the
ground again. People were waiting outside. Quinn instinctively stepped in front of Diana, although he was
aware that the mirrors probably hid nothing.

"Quinn," one of his neighbors greeted him, getting
on without waiting for Quinn to get off.

He could feel Diana wriggling behind him to pull
her dress down as two more guys stepped inside.

"You going to the roof party?" one asked.

"No," Quinn said, and he hit the *door open* button while the look on his neighbor's face registered
a big moment of enlightenment as Diana slid into a
deep knee bend to pick up her purse, using Quinn's
leg for balance.

"Right," the man said. "Catch you later."

They left, Quinn keeping Diana close behind him in the hallway as the elevator continued without them.

"Are you okay?" he asked. The words "I'm sorry" were on his lips when he realized Diana was laughing.

And so, suddenly, was he. Life was good. This night was perfect. This woman was amazing.

He scooped Diana into his arms and carried her down the hall to his door. She pulled her jeweled barrette out of her hair, and shook out surprisingly long hair. Quinn managed to open his door as he cradled her to his chest, because she was unbuttoning the studs of his tuxedo shirt, and there was no way in heaven or hell he'd stop her from doing that.

Quinn carried her over his threshold and, without pausing, straight into his bedroom. They didn't need to discuss anything. Shoes were kicked off, protection was grabbed from a drawer and Diana pushed him down on his own bed to finish undressing him. He lay on his back, drowning in a sensual feast of spice and flowers, held captive under the fall of her hair. She didn't make him wait before she straddled him, and he, with a lift of his hips, was desperately, insanely grateful to bury himself in the welcoming warmth of this woman.

And later, much later, as he drifted off to sleep with Diana in his arms, Quinn knew Diana had worked her magic.

For this moment in time, he was truly, unreservedly happy.

"You're running away again, aren't you?"

Diana froze in the middle of pulling on her sandal, achieving a moment of perfect balance on one foot, something that would have made any yoga instructor proud. Then she finished tugging her ankle strap into place with a precarious hop. Darn it, she'd been so quiet, gathering up her clothes and tiptoeing into the living room to get dressed, buying time while she tried to figure out what the proper morning-after etiquette ought to be.

Her time to decide was up. She straightened and faced Quinn. He was standing in the archway that separated the hall from the living room, leaning with one arm high against the wall, as if he'd been there, watching her get dressed, for some time. He was very nearly naked. Stunningly, wonderfully nude, except for skintight black boxer-briefs that did almost nothing to hide his athletic body. His half-aroused, athletic body.

She couldn't help but gaze for a moment at thick calves, hard abs and sculpted biceps, amazed that she'd had a man like that at her mercy, even for one night. When she finally looked at his face, his knowing expression made her blush.

She turned her back to him, although her dress was unzipped in the back, so her move revealed more of her body, not less. In the cold light of day, it was hard to feel like a woman who could make demands of a man. She was just Diana Connor, small-potatoes real estate agent, matchmaker at the dog pound, everybody's favorite pal.

Last night had been a breathtaking experience, one of those beautiful moments in time, and she was glad she'd had the courage to enjoy it while she could. She started to fumble with her zipper, trying not to cringe at her own thoughts. Her mother had undoubtedly never intended her *it takes courage to be happy* philosophy to apply to sex with a stranger.

He is a MacDowell, though, Lana's brother-in-law. He isn't really some stranger from a bar.

She yanked at her zipper, feeling defensive against her own accusations.

"Let me help you with that." Quinn walked up behind her and stilled her awkward hands with his own. He began zipping her dress, but stopped in the middle of her back to scoop her long hair out of his way with sure hands, the hands of a doctor, hands that had twisted a napkin around a champagne bottle before teaching her how good something could taste.

He took his time smoothing her uncombed hair over her shoulder. Diana held very still, melting under that soothing touch. The touch of a cowboy? She felt like a skittish horse.

"Where were you going?" he asked.

"Remember, I told you at the Driskill that I had to leave because I had work today?"

He took her by the shoulders, gently, and dropped a kiss on the nape of her neck. "You were going to leave without saying goodbye."

She shivered, and she knew he felt it. "Isn't that how it's done? No expectations, no strings attached, no embarrassing morning-after moments?"

For the teeniest, tiniest piece of a second, she thought she felt his fingers tighten on her shoulders, but he sounded perfectly calm and certain when he spoke. "Not after a night like ours. You told me there were moments of beauty that could make you cry. Believe me, Diana, you had me as close to tears as I've ever been." He turned her to face him. "You don't sneak out after a night like that."

He was so ridiculously handsome, so confident in everything he said. How could he expect so much from her?

"I didn't know that rule. I don't do one-night stands." She gestured to her dress apologetically. "I know you might find that hard to believe."

He narrowed his gaze, causing lines to form at the corners of his eyes. They weren't laugh lines. "What do you mean, I'd find that hard to believe?"

Diana couldn't bear the scrutiny of that green gaze. She stepped away. "I don't usually show this much skin. I was trying to look glamorous, like I belonged at the gala, maybe like I was rich." She gestured at the modern space of his living room, with its sky-high ceilings and industrial beams.

She'd seen condos in this building hit the real estate listings. They started just under a million. She'd never shown one to any of her clients. This wasn't her world. She hadn't even known what she was pretending to be.

"But I didn't look glamorous, did I? Not like your friends in their gowns. I just made myself look like a girl who...will. And I did."

Diana studied Quinn's million-dollar modern industrial designer fireplace until she couldn't take the silence and looked at him. He'd crossed his arms over his chest, but was otherwise scrutinizing her the same way as before, green eyes, serious expression. She let her own gaze drop to his chest, with its defined muscles, and to his flexed arms. Already, it seemed incredible to her that she'd ever made love to a man that looked like that. That she'd made a man like him gasp and shudder at her touch. She couldn't have missed what she'd never had, but now that she'd been with Quinn, how would she fantasize about anyone else, ever again?

Quinn abruptly uncrossed his arms and closed the space between them. "Okay, let's get two things sorted out. First, you do not look like the kind of girl that guys think *will*. You look like the kind of girl that guys *wish* would, but they know won't. There is an innocence about you that's as obvious as your beauty."

He turned her around, she assumed in order to finish tugging up her zipper. Instead, she felt him run one finger over her bra strap. "Do you know what I was thinking right now, watching you put on this pink underwear? It looks like one of those old-fashioned bathing suits from the World War Two era. That fits you perfectly. You're the kind of girl men painted on their bombers, the kind of girl that would give a man a reason to fight to get home. Sexy, but smiling. You're a bombshell, Diana, but with that girl-next-door friendliness. I am very, very lucky to be with you. Do we have that straight?"

She nodded, speechless around the lump in her throat. She loved the image of herself he'd just painted. Loved it.

"Good, then are you ready to address the second thing?" He zipped up her dress in one efficient move.

She faced him, waiting. He didn't look so stern now.

"You don't do one-night stands. I don't, either." He imitated her earlier gesture, the one she'd made to indicate her short dress, brushing his hand over his own bare thighs. "I really don't, although I know you may find that hard to believe, considering how I'm dressed."

He smiled at her then, and surprised a laugh out of Diana. Really, he was so charming when he wasn't brooding.

"This isn't a one-night stand yet," he said. "It will be if you leave and never see me again. For the sake of not ruining our track records, we should stay together for a while longer, don't you agree?"

He pulled her into his arms, and she hugged him, fitting against his body easily. He kissed her, a leisurely taste as different from their aggressive passion as day from night. Different, but wonderful all the same. Last night, he'd been in a civilized tuxedo, but he'd been more demanding. Today, he was all bared body, but a gentleman.

His mouth left hers to trail along her jawline, to nuzzle aside her hair, until he whispered in her ear. "If we make love today, then last night wasn't a one-time thing. And if we promise to make love tomorrow, then we can say we've been dating, and no one will think we're shallow."

"Or sleazy," she said, whispering in his ear.

"No, we don't want to be sleazy. Anything but that."

He lowered her zipper, gave her dress a tug so that it fell to the floor. She stood there, feeling glamorous and glorious in her bombshell bathing suit underwear.

With an almost unbearably light touch, Quinn traced one finger over the contours of her pink bra, from her shoulder to the tip of her breast. As he slid his palm slowly over the satin covering her backside, she whispered her next words over his lips.

"We better get started. I want to be sure I'm a respectable woman by the time I get to work at the shelter."

Seven

The animal shelter was Quinn's idea of hell. Sheer, unadulterated, headache-inducing, noisy hell. And it smelled bad, too.

Diana seemed oblivious to her horrible surroundings. She'd just left the building with a family of four whose youngest son was cradling a dog that weighed as much as he did. It was quite possibly the ugliest dog that Quinn had ever seen, but the boy was pampering it like it might win a blue ribbon at the Westminster, and Diana was beaming like—well, like the successful matchmaker she was.

She didn't even get paid for this. She just liked it.

How could anyone like this? The cinder block reception building had a red door that led to the parking lot and a blue door that led to a long walkway lined with kennels for the larger dogs. Quinn loathed that blue door. The moment it opened, every dog erupted into a barking frenzy. He'd given up trying to speak after the first two rounds. It took at least eight long minutes for the dogs to calm down, every time. He'd timed it.

There was one dog that never calmed down. For two hours, he'd listened to either that one dog barking, or fifteen. Quinn had missed hearing his own phone ring, something that was more than an irritation. He was a cardiologist. He was on staff at a hospital. He served with Texas Rescue. His calls were no joke.

Granted, Brian was on call this weekend to handle his private practice patients, but that didn't mean Quinn could go off the grid and be completely unreachable. Whether he wore a tuxedo or scrubs or today's jeans and cowboy boots, he was a doctor, and he had responsibilities. Always. He'd tried to return a missed call from Brian three times, but each time he hit the call button, someone would touch that damned blue door, and the frenzy would begin.

He'd tried standing outside to place calls in the nearly one-hundred-degree heat, but the dog kennels were open-aired. Shaded, but open to the air, and noisy as hell. At least the lobby was air-conditioned and noisy as hell.

He leaned back in the plastic patio chair that served as lobby furniture, tempted to bang his head on the cinder block wall behind him, until he realized silence reigned. The dogs had finally calmed down, now that Diana had taken the family and their large creature out to the baking-hot parking lot. The solo barker had even gone silent. Quinn quickly got out his cell phone.

No sooner had he tapped Brian's name to initiate the call than a volunteer, a teenager who didn't appear to be the sharpest knife in the drawer, meandered to the blue door and reached for the knob.

"Don't touch that damned door."

The teen barely flinched, but he did glare at Quinn

as he shoved his hand into the front pocket of his shredded jeans. "Dude, you need to chill."

Quinn came out of his chair, and the teen showed some normal sense of self-preservation, backing away from six feet of grown man in his prime. Angry grown man.

"Dr. MacDowell here," he barked into the phone when his practice's answering service picked up. He considered standing in front of the door in case the surly teen wanted to make a second, defiant attempt at the knob, but the kid retreated to the side room that held a wall of stacked kennels for little dogs.

Good. Let him sit in there and listen to the Chihuahuas yip.

Just as the answering service relayed Brian's message to him, Diana came in from the parking lot. The opening of the red door meant the blue door rattled at the incoming rush of hot summer air, and the dogs went berserk again.

"Another happy family," Diana announced.

Quinn cursed under his breath and tossed his phone on the counter.

Diana looked only slightly less wary of him than the teenager had. "Where's Stewy?" she asked.

"He's in with the little dogs."

"Shoot. I asked him to start leashing the dogs that were due for their walk."

Quinn had undoubtedly stopped him from doing just that.

The dogs were only one minute into their eight-minute frenzy. He scrubbed his jaw with one hand. Ol' Stewy had been right. He needed to chill, because he was stuck. He'd offered to drive Diana here, so he couldn't leave until her shift was over.

He shouldn't have driven her here. After this morning's lovemaking, another round of sex so perfect it was humbling, he'd been right to drive her to her car, of course. Then he'd followed her to her house, one of the funky 1940s bungalows that made up various Austin streets. Diana's street had been a mix of decrepit buildings and absurdly cute restorations. Her unique house had been in transition from one to the other.

While she dressed for the day, he'd waited in a living room the size of a postage stamp. He'd begun handling the day's requirements by calling his mother to break the news of Irene Caulsky's passing. His mother had assumed he was calling to find out if she needed anything for the afternoon's family get-together.

He'd forgotten all about it. It wasn't like him to forget a commitment, but his body was conveniently ruling his brain, he supposed. He started mentally adjusting his plans. It took an hour to drive to the ranch, plus he'd need to stay for two hours. Add in the hour return, and he'd lose four hours out of the weekend he'd planned to spend not having a one-night stand with Diana Connor.

Taking her to the ranch with him was out of the question. Introduce a girlfriend to his mother? He might as well buy a diamond ring if he was going to raise everyone's expectations that way. He had to be particularly careful with Diana. She wasn't from his usual crowd. She might not understand that a professional with a career like his had no time—and no desire—to be anything other than a bachelor.

No, if he couldn't spend the whole day in bed with

her, then a straightforward dinner date and a return to his place would be the right thing to do. Keep it clear. Keep it simple.

Then Diana had emerged from her bedroom. She'd been telling the truth when she'd said that she didn't usually show as much skin as she had at the gala, but that didn't mean she wasn't as sexy as hell in her casual Saturday clothes.

Her red denim shorts were nearly knee-length, but they were skintight. Her short-sleeved button-down shirt, white with cherries printed all over it, was tucked firmly into her waistband and buttoned up high enough so it didn't show a hint of what he knew from firsthand experience was first-class cleavage. Despite the casual white canvas sneakers on her feet, her shirt sparkled with red sequins, one in the middle of each cherry. The red rhinestone sunglasses perched on her head were overkill, but even so, Diana looked like one of those 1940s pinup-girl posters. A poster that some kid had glued sequins all over, but still a picture to fuel a man's fantasies.

Quinn had taken one look and known he wasn't willing to say goodbye for four hours. Not yet.

They'd eaten a quick lunch at a food truck on the way to her beloved animal shelter. He'd planned on stealing touches and kisses and enjoying more of the way Diana had teased him at the gala. Instead, he'd gotten a headache from the dogs and the chaos, and he'd resented each and every person who'd taken Diana's time and attention away from him.

The dogs launched into their second minute of noise. Six more to go.

He hadn't expected to be unable to work. He hadn't expected that Diana would do nothing *but* work.

"I stopped Stewy as he was going to leash them up," he said, using a voice that would carry over the barking. "My fault. I needed him to hold off so that I could get one phone call in. One."

Just one godforsaken phone call in this madhouse.

Diana walked straight to him and gave him a hug.

Damn. It was a little alarming, the way she did that, but he had to admit it was an effective way to break the tension that had been stretching between them for the past two hours.

Quinn hugged her back, and the feel of her body against his lightened his mood considerably. Hadn't she taught him to look on the bright side? He'd make love to this woman tonight—and tomorrow, too. They had a commitment to that much, and despite this canine chaos being her idea of fun, he wanted to uphold his end of that bargain. Badly.

She let go of him and picked up the first leash. With that uncanny prescience she had, she correctly interpreted his pain from the cacophony of dogs. "You hate the noise, I can tell, but don't worry. They'll be quieter after their walk."

As she gathered up the rest of the leashes, he enjoyed looking at her fully clothed, knowing what she looked like naked. It was an incredible turn-on to know that those white sneakers hid pretty toes, painted red. Anyone could see that she had a nicely curved backside in her red denim, but he'd actually felt the smooth skin, felt the muscle flex beneath his hand.

The red door opened again, the blue door rattled and the dogs went crazy, a welcome distraction for once, since Quinn's thoughts had been about to cause a physical reaction that would be distinctly uncomfortable right now.

Another man entered the shelter. With her back to him, Diana didn't see the older man checking her out, but Quinn caught it. He retrieved his phone, slid it into his pocket, and then stood with his arms crossed over his chest, staring the man down. It took less than two seconds to make his point silently. Quinn had inherited his dad's build, as had his brothers. It was useful.

The door opened again—the dogs kept up their cacophony—and more people entered, Austin hipsters by the look of them. Diana had warned him that Saturday was their busiest day. The men in this new group also did a double take at Diana. Quinn kept his stance, acting like her bodyguard.

He wasn't really irritated with other men looking. It was impossible not to look at someone as pretty as Diana. But judging from her insecurity this morning, men had obviously made comments in the past, comments that embarrassed her, and that would not happen while Quinn was around.

She seemed oblivious to her appeal. Quinn watched her give instructions to the man who'd arrived alone, who was yet another volunteer. Diana was surprisingly organized, or perhaps it was only that she was experienced. Either way, she displayed a competence he hadn't expected with her party-loving persona. In fact, for the past two hours, she'd seemed like the only competent worker here. Her patience with the other volunteers amazed him, although he found that less surprising. After all, she'd been amazingly patient with him as he'd glowered at the gala.

"Now that Bill is here, would you like to walk the dogs with me?" she asked Quinn. "We could get them all done at once. The sooner they're walked, the sooner I'll be done for the day."

Quinn began leashing up barking dogs.

They only walked about fifty yards to a fenced area where the dogs were to run free. Some valiant, heat-defying cedar elm trees provided shade. At the park, Quinn hated to unleash the dogs after the amount of time they'd spent getting them on the leashes, but he did.

Diana took the leashes from his hand and hung them on the gate. Her whiskey-colored hair looked more red today, perhaps because of the cherries and the red sunglasses. Perhaps it was an effect of the June sunlight. Quinn had a sudden desire to make love to her while the sun was high in the sky, just to experience her at her most vibrant color.

"I didn't realize you weren't a dog person," she said. The way she studied the leashes, refusing to make eye contact, belied her casual tone. She was frowning. Quinn realized that while he'd kept his mind firmly on their physical compatibility, she'd been thinking about something else completely.

He should have realized what was at stake here. Dogs were important to her. Hating what a woman loved was not the way to convince someone to get naked under a hot summer sun.

"I don't hate dogs," he said automatically. He wished the words back immediately. They were so obviously a knee-jerk response, and they were in contrast to the way he'd been acting for the past two hours.

She made a sound, a *tch* of disappointment, or disapproval, or even anger, that made Quinn feel cold. Had he just lied to her? He wasn't the kind of desperate guy that would say anything to get a woman into bed. He wasn't.

He watched the pack of ecstatic mutts. They looked like they were in a normal environment, running free like this. More like the dogs he'd grown up with. He needed to dig a little deeper, if he wanted Diana to believe him.

"I've always had dogs, but they're free to roam the ranch."

"Like a pack of wild animals?"

"No. Like ranch dogs." Quinn didn't want her to think so poorly of him. He reached for some details, the kind of details a dog lover would care about. "You almost can't have a ranch without some good dogs. One or two always choose to live in the barn. They keep the horses calm. Sometimes, a particular horse and dog will get on so well, they become a constant pair. The dog comes along every time you take the horse out."

"Like animal best friends? That's adorable."

Quinn didn't think any cowboy had thought of a barn-dwelling dog in those terms. Still, Diana wasn't frowning any longer. He kept talking.

"We had one dog we called the porch dog. He decided that was where he belonged. Mom liked him, because he kept the armadillos out of her flower beds. Most of the dogs are self-appointed patrolmen, though. They almost never barked, so when they did, you took notice. It meant a stranger was coming—or once, we went to see what they were barking at, and found a horse had broken his leg in the pasture and was struggling like mad. My dad had to put him down." Jeez, he hadn't thought about that in years. It had been a hard day in his boyhood.

She squeezed his arm, a little hug. "You do like dogs. It's the barking that gets to you. The kennels must have been hard today."

"Of course that noise was irritating. I couldn't make any calls. I got zero work done."

"My guess is that somewhere inside you is a boy who was raised to know that barking meant danger. It must have driven you crazy to hear dogs bark for two hours. I'm so sorry to have put you through that."

He'd never dated a woman so soft, so sympathetic. It was sweet, but once more, she was apologizing for something that wasn't her fault. It bothered him now as it had last night. "I would have left and come back later if it really was that bad. The truth is, no matter how annoying that barking was, I wanted to stay with you."

"Really?"

She seemed very happy with him now, and Quinn felt good, too. Damned good. Being around Diana could get addicting.

"I'm flattered that you and the little boy you once were wanted to be with me that much." She kissed him then, sweetly, but with her pinup-girl body pressed against the arm she was hugging.

Quinn broke off the kiss first. "I have to warn you, there's nothing boyish about what I want to do with you, but if flattery gets me anywhere, by all means, be flattered." He took the red glasses off her face and angled in for a better, closer kiss. Harder. One with more passion, one that led him to press her back to the fence.

Her passionate response blinded him, all heat, all sunshine, until a dog jumped on her, dirty paws on her white cherry blouse. Quinn had him off in a second with a snap of his fingers and a sharp verbal command.

"Wow, you did that like a pro," Diana said, taking her sunglasses back from his hand.

Quinn snapped a leash on the dog, then whistled to see which others would respond. It was all coming back to him. He hid a smile as two more dogs ran up, tails wagging as he leashed them. "I told you, I don't hate dogs. I've got lots on my ranch."

Diana made little kissing noises to get a few more dogs to come her way for their leashes. "It sounds wonderful. A real ranch, then."

"As opposed to what kind?"

"Some people say they live on a ranch, but what they mean is they live in a ranch-style house on a two-acre lot."

"This is a real ranch. The dogs there all have a purpose. I think that makes them content."

"You're so, so right. Even city dogs need a purpose. These guys might not have ranching skills, but they'd love the job of being a companion. They just need the right person to make them happy."

All the dogs had been leashed but one. Quinn could tell that mischief-maker wasn't going to come, no matter how much he whistled or Diana smooched. Quinn knew what was coming next. "I suppose I'm supposed to chase him down like I'm in a greased pig contest?"

Diana laughed at that. "We can just wait. He'll wear himself out sooner or later, the way he's running around."

"How long does that usually take?"

"Half an hour or so."

Quinn suspected she winked at him when she said that, but she'd put her sunglasses on. Visions of making love in the sun flashed through his rather one-track mind. He had to get to the ranch soon, but if the dog didn't waste half an hour, maybe he could put that time to good use first.

"I'll catch him," he said, properly motivated by the possibilities.

What ensued, however, was the rather humbling adventure of trying to corner a smart dog who thought this was all a grand game. It would have been hellish, except for the fact that Quinn had the sexiest cheerleader in cherries rooting for him.

"Hypotenuse, Quinn!" she shouted. "Take the hypotenuse!"

He laughed as he slipped and slid, changing directions until he actually cornered the beast—who proceeded to slobber affection all over him.

Diana could dish out the sarcasm as well as his brothers could. She'd love his brothers. Or rather, she'd love Jamie, the one she hadn't met yet. Braden already thought she was something special. Diana would go crazy for the ranch dogs. She'd love his mom's sweet tea. She'd love his ranch.

As his innocent pinup girl laughed at him under a clear blue sky, nothing seemed more reasonable than sticking to his original plan of spending the whole day with her. Diana would love the ranch. Why not take her there?

It would be no big deal to bring his first girl home to the River Mack Ranch—and to Mom.

Eight

"This is such a big deal," Quinn's mother whispered fiercely. "If I'd known you were bringing a girl home, I would have made a cake, at least."

"This isn't a big deal, Mom." But Quinn had been delusional to think otherwise. "I just wanted Diana to meet the dogs. Maybe the horses. I don't know if she likes horses."

"Go ask her. Show her the barn. You have plenty of time before we eat."

Despite the fact that he'd given his mother no warning about bringing a guest, she was delighted with him. He didn't have the heart to tell her, once more, that this was just a date, not a commitment of any kind, in any form.

Diana, at least, was taking it all in stride. She'd been happy to see Lana and Braden, pleased to meet Kendry and Jamie. Quinn walked her through the stables and out the far side, and then he kept walking with her, because they were talking and there didn't seem to be any reason to stop. Diana had liked the horses, but she'd made a bigger fuss over Jamie's baby, Sam.

It was Quinn's mother, however, that seemed to have made the biggest impression on her.

"She's so very pretty at her age, don't you think? Of course you must think so. But your mom really is. I love her apron, and the sweet tea. You're so lucky, having a good cook for a mom. Do you come out here every weekend? I would, just for the food."

They walked on, staying along the fence line and the hundred-year-old live oaks. It was hot, but not stifling, and Quinn found himself seeing the ranch through her eyes, really looking at it for the first time in years. In a decade. The house was behind them, easy to spot where it stood on its slight elevation, a beacon of white symmetry with a wraparound porch. The stable was aged wood, almost as large as the house. The pastures were green, but they'd turn brown when they baked all summer long in the ovenlike heat of Central Texas.

This was his heritage, this ground they strolled over. The ranch dogs served as a distant escort, running away to check on some smell, returning to see how far the humans had progressed. It had always been so, Quinn realized. He'd never walked the ranch alone, but always had dogs nearby. He'd taken that canine company for granted.

He could have a dog in his condo. There was plenty of room for one of Diana's strays, and he had no doubt she'd match him up with a dog of the right temperament. As soon as he thought it, cool logic countered the thought. He had room, yes, but he had a doctor's unpredictable schedule. As the owner of a private practice, he worked far more than a forty-hour workweek. Between office hours and hospital rounds, between board meetings and cardiac caths, he worked closer to seventy hours, on average.

He could not have a dog, even if he wanted one. He wouldn't be so inconsiderate, to have another life depending on him for companionship he couldn't give on a daily basis.

As they walked under the oaks, Quinn watched for roots that could trip them. Diana looked around, silent after singing his mother's praises, with a bit of her ever-present smile on her lips. Her lips were made for kissing. He'd like to have her around for kissing on a daily basis.

Cool logic intruded once more. He didn't have time for a girlfriend, either. It would be difficult to find time for Diana next weekend. He could visualize his calendar, remember the details. Two weeks from now, his Saturday was clear.

Two weeks without Diana sounded bleak. Gray.

He'd been right to worry that being with Diana was addicting. It would take some rescheduling, but they could see each other sooner than two weeks from now. If she was amenable, of course, to staying with him beyond tomorrow.

A firm date for the weekend after next would be best. Otherwise, she had a tendency to disappear when he turned his back. He'd had to track her down twice last night at the gala, and he'd had to catch her before she'd tiptoed out of his condo this morning. It would be good to know exactly when and where he'd see her again.

Diana bent to pick up a stick and flung it for the dog that had circled back to check on them. The sun that broke through the branches highlighted the red in her hair.

Quinn didn't want her to disappear. Forget setting one date. He should formalize their relationship. He'd had that conversation often enough in the past ten or so years. Women liked the security they got from a frank discussion of their relationship. As always, he'd make it clear that they were to be exclusive for as long as they were together. That they'd be together on weekends, and on weeknights when schedules permitted. That she was always welcome to spend the entire night, or he'd drive her back to her place. Her choice. Women always found it very generous of him to let them store some cosmetics at his place.

Patricia Cargill had opined on the very subject last summer, when they'd been thrown together for days on end, working with Texas Rescue and Relief on the Oklahoma border. Without electricity and cell service, people tended to talk. A lot.

Bethany Valrez made a point of letting everyone know that she keeps her things at your place.

Why would that be a topic of conversation?

Don't be obtuse. She's merely boasting that she's your girlfriend. I confess, I'm impressed that you let her keep a toothbrush at your place. For a commitment-phobic bachelor, it's really very generous of you. As your friend, though, I advise you to be careful. It could give some women the wrong impression.

I'm obviously not commitment-phobic, not when I've got one and only one woman keeping a toothbrush at my place.

For how long?

For as long as it makes sense for us to be together.

You are as romantic as a computer, Quinn Mac-Dowell. Don't ever change.

He and Bethany had ended their relationship shortly after that, actually, although he couldn't recall why. Then his commitment to the hospital and his new appointment to the board had led to his year-long hiatus from dating. From women. From sex.

Diana ran a little way ahead, chasing a dog. Quinn watched her with a definitely male feeling of satisfaction. He'd ended a year's fast with a feast better than any he'd known. She would have been worth a five-year fast. Ten. She made him feel *that* good. He felt alive today, alive in every way.

The dog led Diana into the old graveyard. Quinn didn't miss the irony.

Diana came to an abrupt halt. The dog—Quinn did not know this one's name, although he was undoubtedly the descendent of an earlier blue heeler named Patch—barked at Diana, wanting her to play hide-and-seek among the tombstones. Quinn ruffled the top of the dog's head, feeling nostalgic because he recognized the black patch of fur over the dog's right eye and ear.

The memories came out of nowhere, crystal clear and bittersweet. Patch had been the ideal stable dog, herding the horses in from pasture at the same time every day, as if he'd had a perfectly working canine clock inside his brindled gray body. Quinn wanted to tell Diana about him, but when he looked at her face as she looked at the grave markers, he knew something was wrong.

"This is the ranch cemetery," he said, just to have something to say. It was a nondescript cluster of eight plain tombstones, none of them particularly old, only from the 1930s, and none of them particularly recent. The newest one, he remembered from his boyhood explorations, was from 1957.

Diana ran her fingertips slowly, reverently, over the top of one tombstone. "I didn't know ranches had cemeteries."

"A lot do." He watched her run her fingers over a second tombstone as she walked in a slow grapevine between the graves. "If you worked and lived out here on all this land, it wouldn't make sense to be carted into town and buried in the city. That's what my dad told us."

"Oh." She lifted her finger immediately and turned to him. "Is your dad buried on your ranch?"

He shook his head. "No, he's in a cemetery near the hospital. He didn't want us to face the hassle of legal permits and bringing heavy equipment out here. That's why you don't see many graves on a ranch anymore."

She began moving down the second row. "These are all men's names. Only the years of their deaths." Diana was clearly upset, and she'd resumed her methodical touching of each tombstone.

Quinn wasn't sure what to say. Facts seemed safe. "They were ranch hands. Probably itinerant cowboys who would go from one ranch to another, looking for different kinds of work at different times of the year."

"Did these men work for your family?"

"No, my parents bought this ranch in 1980."

"So, no one knows anymore who Skip Laredo was? Where he was from?" She touched the marker, which bore only the date of death. "How old was he when he died?"

"I don't know, Diana."

Quinn had been around enough death to know that Diana was feeling that punch of grief. She'd gone from a sunny walk along a split-rail fence to grieving in a matter of minutes. It was the damnedest thing. It worried him.

He talked her through that punch. "The human body can't last indefinitely, but they may have lived a very long time. Death is a part of—"

He had to stop there. His usual logic didn't quite fit. Or maybe it did. "Death is part of many jobs. Ranching can be dangerous, but they must have loved it, to have worked on ranches until their last days."

His attempt at comfort backfired. Diana began crying tears, real tears, and they were definitely not a reaction to a perfect, beautiful moment. Quinn felt helpless. She was genuinely distressed at the thought of the men who'd been forgotten.

He'd never been with a woman so tenderhearted. No wine, no roses, no tasteful gold bracelet would soothe this kind of hurt. Quinn had none of those available, anyway. He had only himself. So, for what it was worth, he offered that to Diana. He touched her tentatively with one hand, and held his other arm open. "Would you like to cry on my shoulder, maybe?"

She turned into him. Without her high heels, she felt smaller, more vulnerable. He held her more tightly.

"I'm the last one of my family," she said, after a minute. She used the heel of one hand to wipe her cheeks, but he noticed she kept her other arm firmly around his waist. "The very last one."

Now her tears made sense. Quinn could handle discussions about mortality. He'd had dozens of patients ask him if they were going to die, and when. "You're afraid you'll be forgotten when you die. That is a painful thought."

Quinn felt a certain sense of relief at Diana's explanation. He took over the tear-wiping duties, using his thumb to smooth the wetness across her perfect cheek. The dry summer heat would evaporate the rest in no time. "I don't think you'll be the last of your family. Don't you see yourself being married someday, having children of your own?"

She shrugged. "I suppose. It could happen."

But, Quinn realized, she didn't really believe it would, although he couldn't imagine why she didn't. A woman like Diana Connor seemed cut out for motherhood. She was friendly, and beautiful to boot. Some man would get to know her well, become her husband, share her life.

Right now, he was the man who knew her. He was the one who knew what lay under her most superficial layers of sequins and smiles. But someday, it would be some other man, and that man would know her far better. He'd know what color her hair was in the frost as well as the sun. He'd know what she was like when she was round with pregnancy. He'd know what she was like when she was old.

Quinn felt a stab of envy for that unknown man.

He cleared his throat, heading into unfamiliar territory. "A matchmaker like you will find her own match. You will be married someday. You won't be forgotten when you pass away."

"It's not me I'm worried about. When that time comes, I won't care, will I? But I can't stand the thought that if I died tomorrow, no one would be left to know who my mother was. No one will visit her grave. She'll be just like these men. A name and a date. Nothing more."

Quinn was ready for fresh tears, but Diana stepped away from him and turned her face up to the branches of the shade tree. She flapped her hands in front of her cheeks and blinked her eyes a few times.

"I can't go back to the house so upset," she said. "It will just upset everyone else."

Quinn pictured his sisters-in-law. His mother. Jamie and Braden. "I think everyone could handle it, honestly."

"There's a quote my mother liked that I think is very true. 'There's enough misery in the world without you adding yours to it.' She wouldn't want me crying over her, not while I'm on a very nice date with a very nice man, and I don't want to be the guest that brings misery to your family picnic. Just give me a minute to get myself together."

She fluttered her hands with more determination. Quinn wished he could do more. He hated standing by helplessly, but no matter what poets or preachers said, pain couldn't be shared. When he'd been a kid and lost his grandmother, even his own mother's hugs could only do so much. He'd worked off a lot of his grief in the stables, shoveling out old hay, forking in new, with Patch as his constant companion.

Of course. Quinn whistled, hoping any of the dogs would come running. They all did. Within seconds, Diana couldn't keep fanning her face, because the dogs were licking her salty, wet hands. Her smile returned as she buried her hands in his dogs' ruffs, as she cooed "good boy" and found another stick to throw.

Quinn watched it all with a powerful, unfamiliar feeling in his chest. As a cardiologist, he knew emotions couldn't affect the size of the heart, but if he were less educated, if he'd lived in a long-ago, superstitious century, he might say his heart swelled as he watched Diana Connor playing with Patch the Second.

Nine

They arrived back at the house after the food had already been blessed and the potato salad passed. They washed up and took their places at the picnic table on the flagstone back porch.

Diana bore no resemblance to the woman who'd mourned the forgotten ranch hands. Quinn supposed a backyard cookout was the same as a party, and Diana was in her element, sparkling and happy. Her joy in the meal was infectious, and Quinn watched his whole family benefit from Diana being at their table.

She knew Lana well enough to encourage her to recount her tales of the bridal worries she'd experienced the day before her wedding. Quinn hadn't had any idea that Lana, the coolly competent director of research and development at West Central Texas Hospital, had worried about such frivolous things as the width of ribbons. Lana couldn't seem to believe how stressed out she'd been over it herself. Her obsession seemed normal and amusing, though, once Diana shared stories of other brides she'd known.

Diana was a dream guest to have at a gathering, the

one who made everyone feel at ease, even when the guests were family who'd known each other their entire lives. His mother had caught his eye several times and directed all sorts of approving pantomimes at him.

He ate brisket, he laughed with everyone else and he watched Diana. As he had at the gala, Quinn wondered what was behind Diana's magic. Trained to pay attention to details, he started to notice a pattern.

Diana brought out the best in everyone by finding out what they needed in order to relax and be themselves. Last night, he'd needed to stop his self-imposed no-play-and-all-work policy, now that the hospital was going to survive the damage done by its former CEO. Becky Cargill had needed to be able to literally let go of her loose dress and dance. Quinn never would have guessed that Lana needed to be able to laugh at her temporary wedding madness. If anyone stayed in Diana's vicinity long enough, she'd find a way to make him or her feel better about themselves.

So that's how she does it. Her "magic" could be analyzed and elucidated, which made him respect her abilities all the more. Even when meeting strangers, she had an uncanny instinct about what people needed. When baby Sammy was passed to Diana for some time in her lap, his mother Kendry had no more than glanced at the red sunglasses perched on Diana's head before Diana had taken them off and set them out of the baby's sight. Kendry sat back to talk to her husband, and only then did Quinn realize that she'd been poised on the edge of her seat, ready to intervene if Sammy should make a grab for those red glasses.

Diana was a keen observer, and she used that skill to please others. But when it came to Diana, who observed her? Who found out what she needed? She made it impossible by appearing to have no cares of her own.

The meal was over and everyone was lingering over brownies when Quinn's mother asked Diana what she'd seen on her walk. Diana had given a charming answer, one that segued naturally into encouraging his mother to talk about her pride and joy, her flower beds.

"We stopped at the old cemetery," Quinn said, as Diana was setting down her iced tea.

Quinn doubted anyone but he noticed the way Diana's tea glass slipped a mere quarter of an inch, plunking down on the wooden plank of the table just hard enough to make the ice rattle. He didn't want to upset her, but deep down, he knew—he was the only one who knew—that she was torn up at the thought of her own mother being as forgotten as the buried ranch hands. Maybe he could fix it for her. His mother knew everything there was to know about this land.

"Did those men work the River Mack, Mom?"

"No, that cemetery is part of the hundred and forty we bought from Whitey McCormick. May I give Sam his bottle, Kendry?"

Diana kept her face turned away from Quinn.

Aw, hell. His mother didn't know anything about the men in those graves. Quinn cursed himself for dimming Diana's bright smile. He didn't have her instincts, obviously. He'd thought surely his mother would know all about the cemetery.

Once Quinn's mother had her grandson happily settled in her arms, however, she picked up the subject again. "It was 1990, right after Christmas. Whitey came over here out of the blue and offered to sell it to us. He said he wanted a real family to take over his land, not a conglomerate."

"The Watersons are on the east side," Braden said. "They're a real family."

Marion MacDowell looked around the table at Quinn and his brothers. "You children were so cute, I think you sealed the deal for us before we knew the land was even for sale."

Jamie laughed at that. "I'll bet Mrs. Waterson thought Luke and Jimmy were cuter."

"Well, there were three of you and only two of them, so we had the advantage. Do you remember Whitey?"

Jamie was watching his son drink. "I was only three years old, Mom. Make sure Sam doesn't get too much air with that bottle."

"I know how to give a baby a bottle, young man."

Diana sighed a little. Quinn wanted to believe it was a sound of contentment, but he couldn't lie to himself. Diana's sigh had been wistful. Full of longing. Lonely.

Diana was relieved the conversation was turning away from the cemetery. She'd been having such a good time at this family party, she didn't want to think about the poor dead cowboys. She wanted to keep living the little fantasy in her head, the one she'd kept up the whole meal, the one where Marion MacDowell was her mother.

She wouldn't take for granted her mother's potato salad. Even if she'd eaten it every day of her twenty-seven years, Diana would still tell her mother how wonderful it was. She would already know the recipe by heart, of course. It was apparent from the conver-

sation that Marion had a health problem that brought
unpredictable bad days, so Diana would have insisted
her mother take it easy. She would have come early
today and made the potato salad for her. She and her
mother would have been very close.

"I remember Whitey McCormack," Quinn said.

Diana hoped her smile didn't slip. Did Quinn have
to intrude on her little fantasy? Did he have to remind
her about cemeteries, about her real mother's location?

"I remember him, too," Braden said. "Whitey was
old as the hills, with a long white beard."

This seemed only to encourage Quinn. "Yes, and
he always carried a staff that was taller than he was,
and you'll like this part, Diana. He had a great dog."

Braden took another brownie from the serving plat-
ter. "I remember that dog. Little scrappy thing. Runt
of the litter. I swear, the way Whitey bragged about
the runt, I assumed it was a positive word until I was
in high school. Being a runt had to be a great thing.
Who wouldn't want to be a runt? I was sad when Dad
explained that I wasn't the runt."

"Sure you were," Jamie said, with a touch of irritation to his voice.

Diana thought Braden was going on a bit too long
about runts, too. Quinn was getting those crinkles at
the corners of his eyes again, the good ones that meant
he might break into a smile at any moment.

Braden kept singing the praises of runts. "When
I called someone 'runt,' it was a compliment of the
highest order."

"You can shut up anytime now." Jamie grabbed a
beer from the cooler the brothers had set conveniently

in reach and opened the bottle by hitting the cap just so on the edge of the picnic table.

"Anything you say, runt."

Then Quinn and Braden and their mother—and even Jamie—all laughed, and Diana knew it was a family joke. It was so easy to fall right back into her fantasy of being in this family.

Sam fussed, and Jamie stood up to take him from Marion. Braden stood, too, and Diana noticed the "runt" was actually a tiny bit taller than his oldest brother. Braden was closest to Marion, so Sammy was passed from Marion to Braden to Jamie to Kendry, who excused herself, saying it was nap time and she'd have Sammy asleep in a jiffy.

In the brief silence that followed the baby's crying and the brothers' ribbing about runts, Marion turned toward Diana. "I'm sorry I couldn't tell you more about the cemetery."

"Please, don't worry about it for a second."

"It made her sad," Quinn said, "because no one remembers the men buried there."

Diana was appalled. She didn't want Marion to think anything about her picnic had been anything less than a success. Her smile wobbled. She couldn't help it. How could Quinn do this to her?

"Cemeteries aren't exactly happy places," Marion said.

Diana couldn't keep smiling when Marion said the subject wasn't happy, so she took a sip of tea.

"You have a sensitive heart, I can tell, for you to worry about men long gone," Marion said.

Diana was at a loss. She didn't know how to handle this topic at a party, so she kept drinking tea like a fool, looking over the rim of her glass at the others. Braden, Jamie and Lana all looked interested, but not upset. They didn't seem to think the picnic was ruined. Diana didn't trust herself to look at Quinn. She wanted to smack him for bringing up the subject.

Marion was watching her as she set her tea down. "I sure hate for you to leave here sad about it. Maybe you can think of it this way. Whitey knew every one of those men buried on his land. They had to have touched him in some way, and changed him, and made him the man he was. It might have been something as silly as telling him a joke that made him laugh, but every one of those men touched Whitey.

"My boys knew Whitey, and he made an impression on them. Well, Jamie was too young, but Braden and Quinn knew Whitey, and then they in turn made an impression on Jamie, and now he has a boy of his own. So you see, those cowboys' lives might not be remembered in detail, but they touched people, and those people touched other people, generation after generation. People don't walk this earth for no reason."

As she kept her hand on her cold tea glass, Diana felt Quinn squeeze her other hand under the table. She kept her attention on his mother's kind face. "Oh, that's something my mother would have said. That every experience touches us and makes us who we are in some small way."

"Well, there you have it. Jamie, refill her tea." Marion smiled at Diana, looking every inch the calm, wise and beautiful image of motherhood. "So tell me, dear, how has Quinn touched you?"

Quinn and Braden and Jamie, all three of them, exchanged a look. The silence lasted a heartbeat, and then the men simultaneously began coughing and choking and snickering.

"Yes," Braden gasped, "tell us how Quinn has touched you."

The Madonna-like Marion rolled her eyes and threw up a hand in disgust.

"Oh, grow up, gentlemen. Try to move past age twelve." But her expression wasn't as stern as her words, and Diana found herself on the verge of laughing, too, if only to laugh at the way the MacDowell men were laughing. They were doctors, for goodness' sake. She expected more from them—which made it even funnier that they were cracking up in such a juvenile way.

Marion smacked Quinn's arm—*he deserved that*—to make him sit back, so she could reach across him and place her hand over Diana's arm, where it rested on the table as her fingertips grew numb on the frosty glass. "Ignore them. I'm hoping there's at least one positive thing you've gotten from knowing my Quinn."

"I've only known him for a day," Diana began apologetically.

This seemed to silence everyone's sniggering. She felt Marion's hand jerk a little bit.

Diana bit her lip and looked around the table.

Kendry came back. "Did I miss anything?"

Marion let go of Diana's arm. "Quinn and Diana have only been together one day. I never would have guessed." She sounded astonished. Perhaps girlfriends of only a day weren't supposed to come to family picnics. Diana hoped desperately that Marion couldn't tell that she'd slept with her son already.

It was definitely time to put this party back on

track. She was willing to be the clown to do it. Everyone loved dopey, bubbly Diana.

"We met last night, at the hospital gala." Diana smiled too brightly. Even she could feel it. "If you count that as our first date, then this is really the second. Two days. We've known each other twice as long as I said. I'm so bad at math. But already, he's ruined me for champagne. I liked the cheap stuff just fine, until he gave me real champagne. Now I'll never look at sparkling wine the same way again. Isn't that terrible?"

She let go of her iced tea and twisted quickly to place the icy wetness on her fingertips on the back of Quinn's neck, like she imagined an annoying little sister should. He yelped and jumped in surprise, and everyone laughed.

Braden stood and tapped his beer bottle with a spoon, directing everyone's attention to himself—and preventing Quinn from retaliating. "Speaking of champagne, Lana and I brought the good stuff. We have an announcement to make. We're going to have a baby. We're due the first week of November."

The news was wonderful. Everyone stood to hug each other, and while the champagne cork was being popped, Lana whispered in Diana's ear, "Since we just got married two weeks ago, I'd appreciate it if you didn't do the math. It's a little embarrassing. We jumped the gun."

"I don't think anyone cares," Diana said immediately, not wanting Lana to feel badly for a moment.

"You're right. It doesn't matter how long we've been together." Lana kissed Diana on the cheek and turned to hug Kendry.

Diana wondered, just for a moment, if Lana had been trying to put *her* at ease.

She hadn't meant to make anyone worry about her. Just the opposite. Still, it was a nice idea, that first Marion and then Lana had cared about her feelings.

Quinn apparently wasn't averse to pointing out the obvious when it came to his brother. "Let's see. First week of November means you got busy around Valentine's Day. Very nice."

"Valentine's Day," Jamie agreed. "Wasn't that the weekend you skipped out on your job to go camping? In the winter? No sane person would do that. It must have been cold in that tent."

"You're a pair of geniuses," Braden said. "I couldn't have done the math without you."

Ten

They were supposed to go out for dinner and dancing.

During the entire hour-long drive back to Austin, Quinn had strategized their plans for the evening. Diana knew all the good DJs in town, and she checked her phone to see who was playing where that night. They agreed to stop first at Quinn's so he could get fresh clothes, then to go to her house so she could change for a night out. Before going to any nightclubs, they'd have dinner at a café Quinn liked. It was a solid plan, agreeable to both.

They made it as far as the elevator in Quinn's building. Again.

This time, when he carried her through the door, they only made it to the leather sofa. Afterward, they made it to the shower. Eventually, they'd made it to the phone to order some pizza, which they'd ended up eating in front of the fireplace.

"The air-conditioning is on," Diana had protested. "It's June."

"You want a fire, you get a fire."

She'd declared if they were going to do something

so silly, they should do it right, and she'd turned off every light in the place. She'd even placed a throw pillow over the glowing lights that remained on the satellite box when the television was off. While the moon lingered outside his balcony, they'd eaten pizza in his living room, staring at the fire.

At the cityscape beyond his panoramic windows.

At each other.

It had been spectacularly beautiful. He'd opened a red wine that he'd been saving for a special occasion, something he'd described as spicy and floral and hard to find. She'd worn his shirt, he'd worn none, and she'd known it was yet another perfect moment with Quinn MacDowell. She'd made sure he didn't see her tears.

The entire time, Diana had not looked at a clock. Sunday would come soon enough, and her weekend would be over.

When she woke, it was to full daylight. Sunday was here.

She rolled over to face Quinn, who was sound asleep on his stomach, his face turned away from her. He slept in the nude, warm golden skin against cool white sheets. Diana reached out to toy with a piece of his hair. It was a luxury, sheer luxury, to be able to touch him just because she felt like it. She ran her finger over his shoulder, feeling the muscle relaxed in his deep sleep, the same muscle that had flexed as he held his body over hers last night.

She'd worn him out, she thought with a smile. That was an achievement she could look back on—privately. Very privately.

I'll look back...and remember...and miss what I had...

She let her hand trail down his body, resting her palm on the large muscle of his backside, very lightly, so she wouldn't wake him. This was her moment to appreciate the beauty of a man. When he woke, would they have sex again? Would it start playfully, would it end hungrily?

It would end. That was the important thing.

Diana snatched her hand back, sudden fear making her heart feel like ice in her chest. She had to stop making memories now. This minute.

Someday, she would lie next to another man, maybe even the husband Quinn saw in her future. She'd watch him sleeping, and she'd remember Quinn, and she'd picture this moment in her memory. It would be hard to bear.

She'd made too many memories. It was time to go.

She'd say goodbye, though. Quinn had said yesterday that no one sneaked out after a night like they'd had. Well, they'd had another wonderful night, so she'd say goodbye before she left him here, in this well-designed, exclusive living space that fit him to a T.

She was just about to slip out of bed when his phone rang, jarringly. With a grunt, Quinn grabbed his phone from the nightstand and rolled over. She watched him open one eye to look at the screen before answering.

"MacDowell."

A long pause followed. While he listened, he looked at her, smiled that half smile, then scrubbed his face with one hand. "Right," he said to the caller, in a clipped tone she hadn't heard before. "That's a dihydropyridine available in Europe. It didn't cause the bradycardia."

Ah, doctor-ly stuff. She slipped out of bed quietly

and put his bathrobe on as quickly as she could. He made a grab for the edge of the robe while giving medical orders to the caller in a confident, almost cocky, tone. It was sexy in a man-in-charge way, she had to admit, but she dodged his hand and headed for the bathroom in the hall, where she wouldn't disturb his call.

She scooped up her clothes from the day before, wrinkling her nose at their wrinkled state. She'd have to leave the building in the same outfit she'd been wearing the day before. Quinn had a high-tech washer and dryer in an alcove in the hallway that could probably accomplish the same task as the local Laundromat in half the time. Her red denim shorts would have to be worn as they were, but she could wash her underwear, bra and white shirt together. Diana started the two-minute quick wash setting before bringing her purse into the bathroom.

She had her normal-sized purse with her, which meant she had a hairbrush and the disposable fingertip toothbrushes she used at work when lunch had been too much of an Austin fiesta. She decided to use the cosmetics in her purse, too. She wanted her last impression to be as good as possible. She wanted Quinn to remember her at her best, as selfish as that was.

Sunday had come so soon.

She heard water running in the master suite. His cell phone rang again, and the indistinct rumble of his voice once more had the distinct edge of a doctor to it.

She dug her own cell phone out of her purse. Maybe her friends had missed her this weekend. Maybe she had a couple of text messages to return, an invite to a Sunday afternoon get-together that would ease her back to her regular life.

Her phone battery had died.

Look at the bright side. When you charge it, you might find a half-dozen invites.

She hoped so. She was going to need something to do this afternoon, something to distract her. There was always the animal shelter. She could make other people happy there.

She left the bathroom, transferred her clothes to the dryer and headed for the kitchen. Quinn was at the stove, stopping her heart in blue jeans and bare feet, wearing a navy blue T-shirt that hugged his chest the way she wanted to. He was cooking eggs with his cell phone wedged between his ear and shoulder, but he put the spatula down to scribble something on a notepad.

Resigned, Diana took a seat at one of his bar stools. It looked like she was going to make one more memory: a handsome man cooking breakfast for her. That was another first. Darn it.

This farewell was going to suck.

Quinn hung up his call and had placed another, dialing the numbers he'd written on the notepad, when he noticed her sitting there. He did a double take, and raised an eyebrow as he checked her out with the phone held up to his ear.

"You're all cleaned up. Did you want to go out for breakfast?"

"No, thanks. Looks like you've got it under—"

He held up his finger in the standard "one minute" gesture as whomever he'd called apparently picked up. He started rattling off information that was obviously routine for him. "MacDowell, Quinn, license M nineteen eighty-nine, patient Norma Gildart, date of birth—" He paused to read the date off his notepad. "Amlodipine ten milligrams QD number seven. No refills. Instruct patient to follow up ASAP." He disconnected his call with one hand and lifted the skillet off the burner with the other.

"Sorry," he said. "Brian had asked if he could transfer the answering service over to me this morning. I said yes before I knew you. He'll pick it back up around seven."

"Oh. Well, I was saying that it's very nice of you to cook eggs for me." But Quinn's phone had started to ring when she'd started her sentence, and he gave her an apologetic smile as he took the call.

He tucked the phone between his ear and shoulder again as he opened a cabinet and took out a dinner plate, then another, then shook the eggs onto them. Diana silently got off her bar stool and found forks in the third drawer she tried. She got another apologetic smile for her effort.

She was done eating, and she was certain his eggs were cold, by the time he hung up. The lack of intimacy was welcome, in its way, considering she'd be leaving once her clothes were dry.

"What would you like to do today?" Quinn asked. "I have to be attached to this phone, but we could still go somewhere like a park, somewhere I can answer when it rings."

It was going to be up to her, then, to declare the weekend officially over. She sighed, and doodled on her plate with her fork, and tried not to get sentimental over the kindness of being served scrambled eggs.

And then Quinn stood over her where she perched,

and he kissed her, his lips warm and soft, with one hand cradling the back of her head.

She placed her palm on the soft navy cotton of his T-shirt. On his chest muscle. On his heart.

Don't forget me.

"I have to be going," she said. "It's been a great weekend, but I have to be going."

"Don't go. The phone won't ring this often all day. It comes in clusters."

Diana wondered if Quinn really thought she was leaving because of a few phone calls. She slid off the bar stool, but he didn't let go of her.

"Unless it's the answering service, I have to answer. I can let the answering service go to voice mail, as long as I call them back within ten minutes." He moved his hand from the back of her head slowly down, down to her lower back, where he pulled her close to him, body to body, bathrobe to jeans. Her bare toes brushed the inside arch of his foot. "It won't be the Sunday I'd had in mind. A badly timed call can make something turn into a ten-minute quickie when I'd rather spend an hour."

She turned her face away. He did expect her to stay for the rest of Sunday, to make love, fast or slow. She could not. Her emotions were all caught up in the sex. They had been from the first. When he whispered to her how beautiful she was, how perfect, how right, her heart kept thinking he meant her. All of her, not just her body.

"But we can make the best of it. Diana? Look at me."

She smiled first, then turned back to him with the proper expression on her face. Friendly. No regrets. "I really have to be going. It's Sunday, and we said we'd stay together until Sunday."

He did not move a muscle. Not an inch. Not for an eternity.

His phone rang. He glared at it, but he answered it, and as she backed up, he glared at her, too, and caught her with a hand at her waist. The moment he hung up, he tossed the phone on the counter and put his other hand on her waist. "I hope you're not going to hold me to that agreement. I want to see you again."

"You do?" She tried to be cautious, but she could feel the hope expanding in her chest almost painfully.

"Yes. Without a doubt."

She had doubts. They didn't move in the same circles. They had no friends in common. Their incomes were hugely unequal, their level of education, as well. They hadn't discussed their lives, where they saw themselves five years from now. Ten.

Quinn kissed her, softly at first, then with increasing intimacy, a slide of tongues that began as a slow exploration of texture, but quickly turned harder, more demanding. Her tongue answered, her body answered, and his hands gripped her waist more tightly. He lifted her onto the bar stool. Her robe fell open over her lap as his warm hand pressed her knee outward, and she felt the roughness of denim on her inner thighs as Quinn closed the space between their bodies.

"Diana, beautiful Diana, how could you doubt that I'd want to see you again? I need more of you, more of this."

This. This, that was coming to mean so much. This, that meant more every time.

"You and me, together," he said, raining hard, quick

kisses across her cheeks, her nose. "I want to know you better, to be with you, to be a couple."

She brought her arms over his shoulders and buried both hands in his hair, tugging his head to angle him for a deeper kiss.

The phone rang. Quinn made a sound of frustration against her mouth, then turned his head to answer while keeping her entire body pressed against his. She rained soft kisses on his throat while he barked "MacDowell" into the phone and started listening. This close, Diana could hear the caller, as well. A man's voice, speaking in medical terms, sounded very young as he tripped over his words.

"Slow down," Quinn ordered. He listened a few more moments. "For God's sake, if she's coding, then hang the hell up. If she's not, then report this right. Give me the presenting symptoms."

Diana eased away from Quinn, leaning back in the bar stool. Quinn turned toward the high countertop and leaned one arm on it, dropping his head and listening intently. He started outlining steps for the caller to take, Diana could tell that much, although he might as well have been speaking a foreign language. It was all Greek to her. Or Latin. Didn't doctors speak in Latin terms?

She tried to make herself laugh, but the truth was, this was horrifying. Somewhere, a woman was in trouble, and Quinn was telling a younger doctor what to do about it. He had the caller repeat back his orders, twice, and then Quinn asked for a Dr. Gregory.

During the pause that followed, a full minute at the least, she studied Quinn. He was motionless, every muscle in his body taut with tension, listening intently.

He was dealing with death, she thought, and the nausea was unexpected. She put her fingers to her lips and breathed deeply.

"Gregory. It's Quinn. You know what I'm going to say. Who the hell is that?" He paused again, then nodded at the answer. "I agree. Get him out of there. He can't keep a cool head to save his own life, let alone anyone else's."

Moments later, he hung up and set his phone down, then scrubbed both hands over his face for a moment, as if he'd rub his razor stubble away. Then he turned to Diana. "Okay. Where were we?"

She swallowed, more unsure than ever that she was the right match for this man. Would she be able to soothe that kind of tension away for him, day after day, when it affected her worse than it did him? If they were going to be a couple, she had to try.

"Are you okay?" she asked.

"Fine. That was just a first-year idiot. When doctors graduate and start working for real, you find out quickly who can hang and who can't."

"But...are *you* okay?"

"I'm fine." He looked at her closely. "I think the question is, are you okay?"

She took a breath, but it wasn't very deep. Her chest felt tight. "I'm worried about that woman. And that poor doctor—he's going to get fired, isn't he? You're acting like that call was nothing, but you were very intense a minute ago."

He cocked his head a little, studying her, and then he began to grin. "You are the most tenderhearted person I've ever known."

Diana felt a little insulted. A little hot inside, irritated that he'd be amused at her.

He took her hands in his and gave them a shake. "Don't worry. That woman is going to be fine. Her condition is very treatable, and I was listening to the nurses in the background. They weren't letting that first-year screw it up. He's not cut out for the ER, plain and simple. He may still be a good doctor someday. Maybe he'll have an eagle eye for pinpoints on film and become a stellar radiologist. You never know. But it's his job to find where he fits in. It's my job to make sure he does no harm in the meantime, so he's out of my hospital."

He gave her hands a deliberate kind of shake, one that made her arms shake, too, and her shoulder muscles loosen up, all in one expert move. "I'm used to this. I'm trained for it. You're not, so it may have seemed like a big deal to you. Trust me when I say I'm okay."

It made sense, when he spelled it out that way. She was glad to hear that the woman would survive—and the young doctor, in a way. "You don't see this as being a problem for us as a couple? Me being stressed out by your job?"

"No. It may never happen again. I don't normally try to see anyone on days I have call. Of course, if you go home now, then I won't get another call for hours. Murphy's Law. But if you want to leave, we could see each other after seven."

"You don't normally see anyone when you have call? You've got a system for this when it comes to girlfriends?"

Quinn's grin faded. "I've been a doctor for years,

so yes, I've had girlfriends in this situation. Trying to be together on call days doesn't work."

"It didn't work with them. What about with me?" Diana thought her heart would pound out of her chest. She didn't want to know about past women. She was unique. Beautiful, perfect, right—Quinn had said so. How could she only be right for days when he wasn't on call?

"You deserve all my attention, not these constant interruptions."

That was a rehearsed line if she'd ever heard one. The disappointment was sharp.

Quinn sat on his bar stool once more. He began flipping through his phone screens. "Not this Saturday, but next, I've got the whole day free. I want to spend it with you."

When she said nothing, he asked, "Do you want to spend it with me?"

He sounded just uncertain enough for her to answer him. "Of course I do." Her words came out as a whisper around the lump in her throat. He wanted to see her again in two weeks, when he wasn't on call.

That was not the same thing as being a couple. When a man needed a woman, when he wanted to know her better, he didn't wait two weeks to see her.

"Excellent." Quinn sounded relieved. Happy, even. He leaned forward on his bar stool and kissed her on the cheek.

"Did you have any other dates in mind?" She was amazed at her own ability to be a smart aleck.

"I think I can rearrange some obligations this Friday."

She must be lousy at sarcasm. He was taking her seriously.

"You should bring some things to keep here, so you can spend the night without having to pack every time. You know, a toothbrush, makeup, extra clothes, whatever you want."

"We wouldn't stay at my house? Is it more convenient for you here?"

"Your house is cute. You'll let me keep a razor there, won't you?" He grinned again, a man pleased with himself.

"And when your schedule does not permit us to get together? I assume we don't see anyone else in between these dates."

Ah, that wiped the smile off his face.

"This would be an exclusive arrangement. Very. That won't be a problem for you, will it?"

She felt her cheeks grow hot. The nausea returned, but for an entirely different reason. She looked him in his green, green eyes for the first time since he'd started laying out his plans for their future. "I'm usually so busy with my one-night stands, it might be hard to break that habit."

He didn't miss her sarcasm this time. "I meant, you're not involved with anyone else, are you?"

She gasped. "Would I have slept with you this weekend if I already had a boyfriend?"

For just a fraction of a second, he hesitated. Just a moment where she knew he'd thought that yes, some people would have a weekend fling on the side.

Not her. Never her. He didn't know her at all.

Diana wanted to leave, immediately. Quinn was ruining every perfect memory she'd made.

His phone rang. He glanced at the screen and punched it with one finger, silencing it. "It was the service. Now I've got ten minutes. Let me start by apologizing. That was a stupid question. I'm sorry."

"Thank you," she said, but her lips felt stiff and the words were forced. She jumped off the bar stool and spun toward the hallway.

"C'mon, Diana. I'm distracted with these calls right now. You can see how crazy it gets. That's why it would be better to see each other on the weekends I'm off."

"So, basically, you are asking if I'm willing to schedule booty calls on an ongoing basis."

"Booty calls?" The expression of disbelief on his face said it all. "For God's sake, I don't think in those terms. It's called dating. Dinners. Movies. Whatever you like."

He could call it whatever he liked. Putting it in sophisticated terms didn't change what it was.

She headed for the dryer. She wanted her clothes, and she wanted to get out of there while she was still furious. Tears could come later, in privacy.

Quinn followed her. "What is so awful about asking you out for a date this Friday?"

Diana opened the dryer. She reached her hand into the hot, steamy interior. Swell. Her clothes were still damp. She pulled her underwear out, anyway, and tugged it on under the bathrobe.

"What are you doing? You're getting very dramatic over this."

"Let me make sure I have this straight," she said, grabbing her red shorts off the top of the washing machine where she'd left them. She wriggled them over the wet underwear. "I get a toothbrush, a little drawer space and great sex when your schedule allows. Oh—and dinners out. I assume when you have official shindigs, I get to dress up and be your arm candy. Did I miss anything?"

She dropped the bathrobe to the floor. Let Quinn get an eyeful while she put on her wet bra. It soothed her pride to see him distracted by what he'd never have again. She whipped her shirt right-side-out, and put it on, too.

She buttoned as fast as she could. "That arm candy thing would be a challenge. I don't do elegant well."

She marched down the hall to retrieve her white sneakers from under the couch.

"Diana!" He caught her around the waist, then let go. "Your clothes are wet. Jeez."

With her shoes dangling from her fingers, she slung her purse over her shoulder and headed for the door.

He easily matched her strides. "It's ridiculous to leave in wet clothes. What's wrong with scheduling a date next Friday?"

She turned to face him with her sneakers in one hand, the doorknob gripped in the other. "Nothing, when you put it like that, with all your cool reasoning. But you got my hopes up when you said we'd be a couple.

"What if you're on call, and a phone call does upset you? Will you wait two weeks to talk about it with me? See—that never occurred to you. That's what I think a girlfriend should be. A friend. One who is around, not one who is scheduled for dinner and bed at a convenient time later in the week. What happens if I miss you on a Wednesday?"

"We have phones, you know. I'm home most nights after seven, if you'd like to call."

"Wow," Diana said, a little stunned at his honesty. She could be honest, too. "That's even more horrible than I thought. Remember that woman in the red dress? You'll see her at another big event. Ask her to dance. She'll be a good match for you. I am not."

With that, she executed another first: a grand exit, complete with the perfect slamming of the door.

Eleven

It had never occurred to Diana that a grand exit would be difficult when the guy was rich.

If the rich guy lived in a high-rise building that had an elevator, then while one waited for the elevator, the rich guy could easily stroll to the elevator bank and continue the conversation.

Darn it all.

"You've made your point," Quinn said, sounding like a stern parent from TV. "Come inside."

There were three sets of elevator doors. Diana stood in front of the one that sounded like machinery was running behind it. *Hurry up, hurry up.*

She refused to look at Quinn. She'd had her say, and she needed to stay mad for a while, at least long enough to get a taxi and get home. Lord, how long would it take for a taxi? They were pretty scarce in Austin. She might need to walk to Sixth Street to hail one.

She started to pull on one sneaker, balancing with her hand on the call button, with its arrow-pointing-down emblem. Although it was already lit, she pushed it again, anyway. *Hurry, hurry.*

One of the other condo doors in the hallway opened, and a neighbor stepped out to get his Sunday paper. "Morning, Quinn."

"Good morning," he answered, and Diana credited his unflappable manners to Marion MacDowell. She felt another pang—she'd probably never see her pretend-mother again.

The neighbor looked at her, and made no move to take his paper and go.

Quinn reached for her arm, but she warded him off with her sneaker. "Leave me alone. We've said everything there is to say."

"You're making a scene," he said through clenched teeth.

"I'm putting on a sneaker." She put her foot down and started on the second sneaker. The interested neighbor was not her problem. "You shouldn't have followed me out here. You're ruining it."

He kept his voice low, but it was seething with displeasure. "I'm ruining your attempt to run away again?"

The warmth of the dryer had left her clothes, but not the dampness. The air-conditioning in the hallway was close to making her shiver. "We're not a match. I should have left after our last dance at the gala. None of this weekend was supposed to happen."

"Ah, that last dance. That beautiful moment that will never come again. You're damned right it won't, not if you leave. Nothing can happen if you leave."

The elevator was almost to their floor. She could

hear it. It was time for the second grand exit of her life. She'd make this one kinder.

"I stayed, and we had a perfect weekend, Quinn, full of wonderful moments. I'll never forget it. Thank you."

Diana pressed a last kiss to his lips.

The elevator didn't stop. She heard it travel past them, up to a higher floor.

They stood there, staring at each other.

Quinn opened his mouth to say something, but Diana put her hand up to stop him. "Shh. We said goodbye."

She bounced on her toes a little, just to keep moving and stay warm, as they waited some more. Finally, the elevator arrived—not the one she was standing in front of. The next one over.

She kept her chin up as she walked three steps to her left.

"Goodbye, Quinn."

But as she turned to go in, another person was coming out, a taller woman, ready for an elegant Sunday brunch in slacks and pearls. Diana remembered her from the gala: Becky's stepsister, Quinn's friend in the stunning blue gown.

Patricia Cargill barely glanced at Diana as she walked into the hallway.

Diana stepped into the elevator. She closed her eyes, unable to bear the reflections of herself in the mirrors. The doors slid shut, but not before she heard Patricia's voice, as refined as Patricia herself.

"Hello, Quinn. Did I catch you coming out to get your paper? What perfect timing. It's like you were waiting for me."

* * *

Quinn resented the clock. As he let Patricia into his condo, his phone rang, flashing the time at him before he could swipe the screen to answer. It wasn't even noon. They'd agreed to be together on Sunday, but Diana had left when they still could have made love for hours.

What would have been the purpose of those extra hours in bed, before they'd go their separate ways? Sex just for physical pleasure?

A booty call.

"MacDowell," he snapped into the phone. It was the answering service, calling back because it had been ten minutes since he'd missed their last call.

Ten freaking minutes since he'd explained to Diana that he wanted a long-term, exclusive relationship with her.

Ten minutes since she'd told him his offer was ruining her idea of a perfect weekend. That made no sense. She'd shushed him, *shushed* him, and gotten on the elevator and left.

Unbelievable.

The answering service relayed five messages to him, each one nonurgent, nothing that the patients couldn't have called his nurses about on Monday. For this, he'd lost his concentration on what Diana was saying. He'd botched something up—he remembered apologizing—oh, yeah. The exclusive thing.

Patricia was helping herself to his kitchen, loading a K-Cup into his coffee machine. He watched her select a coffee mug from his cabinet, as if it mattered which drug logo freebie she was seen using. He was the only one here to see her, anyway. That was Tricia, though, fastidious to a fault. He knew her well, two years to Diana's two days.

Yet he'd known Diana well enough to know she didn't have a boyfriend. She wasn't using him to cheat on someone else. It was impossible to imagine her sneaking in a weekend fling while her regular guy was out of town. Why the hell had he said something so stupid?

He remembered an important detail: she'd already been upset before that. She didn't like that he'd developed a routine with other girlfriends while he was on call. What had she expected? He couldn't go back and undo his past.

He sat on the bar stool, feeling like gravity was too much to fight standing up. He'd give a million dollars to feel as good as he had this time yesterday. A million dollars.

Tricia slid the coffee mug under his nose. "You need this more than I do. Rough night at the hospital?"

"Fishing for info is beneath you. I know you've noticed that there are two plates here."

She laughed. "I was trying to be nice. I take it whoever she is has left the building, and I'm not in danger of getting an eyeful of any supermodel strolling around in her all-together?"

"You saw her go."

Quinn sipped the coffee. Maybe it would clear his mind, which was currently short-circuiting after the exit that Diana had made.

"That girl? I assumed she was your neighbor's little hottie. A fruity sequined shirt— Oh, Quinn." She chuckled. "Wherever did you find her?"

Quinn shot her a look, one that would have silenced

any man who insulted a woman he was with. *Had been* with. Past tense.

Patricia abruptly stopped laughing, but not from his look. She'd apparently just remembered who Diana was. "Wait—not the real estate agent from the gala?"

Quinn didn't bother answering her. He wanted to mentally review the whole disastrous last scene with Diana, pull out the details and find the precise moment it had all gone sour.

His uninvited visitor wasn't helping any. Patricia cleared away the plates and forks and put the dirty skillet in the sink, turning on the water with a quick flick of her wrist, rinsing traces that Diana had been there down the drain.

"Is there a point to this visit?" he asked. He could hear the irritation in his own voice.

So, apparently, could Patricia. "Don't take your lousy sex life out on the woman who gives you coffee."

"It wasn't lousy," he said.

She snapped the water off.

"And you can't give me coffee I already own." He took another sip after his halfhearted dig. He and Patricia had gone from acquaintances to friends since last year's relief trip, but Quinn couldn't enjoy their usual sparring today.

Patricia dried her hands and came to lean on the counter next to him. "Let's go out. I'll buy you coffee. I wanted to bounce some ideas off you about Texas Rescue. I got quite the scoop out of Karen Weaver on Friday."

"Who?"

"The new director. Honestly, Quinn, you spoke with her at length during the gala. Where's that famous head for details?" She gave his head a little push to the side with the tips of her fingers, then smoothed down the hair she couldn't really have messed up.

Diana's fingers had been in his hair just ten minutes ago. No, more like twenty now. Quinn jerked away from Patricia's hand, then pushed his own hand through his hair, trying to play off the fact that he was overreacting to everything.

"I can't go out. I'm on call."

"What's new? Bring your phone."

"Not today. I'll take a rain check."

"Karen will be at our steering committee meeting." Patricia pouted and tugged him out of his chair. "Come eat with me. I can't exactly talk about her when she's right there."

Since she had him standing, Quinn walked her to the door. "You'll find a way. I'll see you then."

By five that evening, Quinn was sick of wallowing in his own thoughts. He'd spent the day on his sofa—trying not to think about making love on it with Diana. He'd put the car race on TV—after moving the pillow she'd blocked the satellite box with. He'd drifted off to sleep a few times, only to be jarred awake by the ringing of the phone. He knew it couldn't be Diana, because they hadn't gotten around to exchanging phone numbers. Still, he was disgusted with himself for being disgusted when it was his own answering service.

None of the day's calls had been as intense as that one from the ER this morning, the one that had upset Diana.

She'd been right. That call had been more serious than the average one. As upsetting as it had been for her, her first instinct had been to find out what Quinn needed. To ask if he was okay.

He'd been an ass to laugh off that kind of rare concern. Except when it came to Diana, concern wasn't rare. She was concerned for everyone she met, and for every dog she met, too. She was concerned for men who'd been dead and buried for fifty years on a ranch.

Quinn jackknifed into a sitting position on the couch, determined to deal with this loss once and for all.

Nothing lasts indefinitely.

An ending is an inevitable part of any relationship.

I did my best.

It didn't matter how many times the loop repeated. He couldn't shake the feeling that this relationship shouldn't have died.

Couldn't she see that he was the kind of man who would put some effort into making a girlfriend feel good out of bed as well as in it? Look at how he'd tried to make her feel better about those fifty-year-old graves. He was capable of showing concern, just as she was.

Actually, his mother had been the one to really make her feel better. Hell, Patch the Second had done a great job. Quinn had given her his best all right: his mother and his dog. That was all he had to give a woman.

Quinn got to his feet, scooped a throw pillow off the floor, and pitched it at the sofa. He needed to clear his head. He didn't know why Brian had needed him to take call, but he called him on the chance that Brian could resume phone duties before seven. He could. Quinn transferred call duty back to him, stomped into his boots, grabbed his helmet and headed for his motorcycle.

The bike had been Jamie's, but Quinn had ridden it for him while he was deployed to Afghanistan. Engines that sat unused for a year got gummed up, so Quinn had agreed to drive Jamie's baby a few times a month, just to keep the engine alive. Jamie had surprised them all by returning home from his deployment with a real baby. Since the motorcycle couldn't hold a baby's car seat, and since Quinn had become accustomed to his twice-monthly motorcycle rides, Quinn had bought the bike from Jamie.

He was glad he had. It was good to hear nothing but an engine, one that was loud enough to drown out his thoughts. Most of them.

What happens if I miss you on a Wednesday?

That had been a baffling question. No other woman had ever asked such a thing.

I could have suggested she send a text. I might have been able to call her back between patients.

Even he knew how weak that sounded.

Diana didn't understand his world. She had no idea what the demands were. She sold real estate. She walked dogs at an animal shelter. If she wanted to see someone, she could drop what she was doing and go.

Quinn could not do that, and no matter what Diana thought, it wasn't because he was a jerk. If he played hooky from his job to see his girlfriend, he'd leave a staff of twenty and at least as many patients all sitting in a building he owned, wondering where the hell he'd gone. Some of those patients wouldn't get their ECGs performed and their arrhythmias caught in time. Surgeries in the hospital wouldn't take place, because anesthesiologists expected Quinn to decide if the patient's heart could withstand the procedure.

It was a lot of responsibility, but he'd asked for it. He carried that weight just fine, but damn it, when he had a Saturday free, it would have been freakin' destressing to hold Diana Connor.

That's a booty call.

Not quite. He didn't want just anyone. It had to be Diana. He'd ruined her for champagne; she'd ruined him for any other woman. Not a fair trade.

Quinn took the next entrance ramp to the Mopac. On the expressway, he drove hard and fast, concentrating on the road, listening to the engine roar good and loud at the maximum speed allowed.

Dig a little deeper.

When he thought of Diana, his first image wasn't of her between the sheets. He saw her in green fringe, saying how beautiful the ballroom was, when he could only see her. He saw her in the kitchen with his mom, watching her make potato salad like she was Michelangelo painting a ceiling.

Quinn exited the highway, stopped at a gas station in the middle of nowhere, then headed back to Austin. It was time to stop denying the truth. With Diana, he wanted the out-of-bed part, too. He wanted the pizza by the fire and the walk on the ranch. He wanted a woman who'd make him chase a shelter dog and laugh with him while he did it.

She found the beauty in everyday simplicities from sweet tea to sparkling wine, but from him, she'd expected more. He hadn't given it. No amount of rationalization was going to make the loss of Diana Connor sit easy, not when he couldn't honestly say he'd done his best.

Quinn pulled into her driveway and silenced his motorcycle.

Twelve

The sound of laughter drifted from the run-down house next door to the brightly painted blue of Diana's 1940s bungalow. From inside Diana's house, Quinn heard nothing, although he'd progressed from civilized knocking to using the side of his fist on her front door.

Her car was in the driveway. She had to be here. Either she was avoiding him, or she was unable to respond. The likelihood that she was seriously injured was infinitesimal, but he'd seen strange cases come through his brother's ER.

He pounded again, three rapid thuds, and waited. For all he knew, she'd decided to drink away the pain of their parting. It would be easy to have one too many, to pass out, to be in danger. He could walk around the house and look in the windows. If she didn't want to speak to him, that made him something of a trespasser, but if she were alone and incapacitated, he could be a lifesaver.

He raised his fist to knock again—last time, and then he was going to look in her windows—when the door opened and Stewy, sullen Stewy from the shelter, stood there, looking as surprised as Quinn felt.

"Dude, you need to chill. We moved the TV next door."

The kid closed the door in Quinn's face, since Quinn had no response whatsoever.

Okay, he had to give the kid that one. Point to Stewy.

Quinn rubbed a hand over his face, feeling the full scratch of the day's beard, as he readjusted his mental image of what Diana might be doing. He heard a screen door slam in the back of the house and watched Stewy saunter from Diana's backyard to the rear of the shabbier house.

Well, hell. Quinn walked from her neat yard through a stretch of weeds to stand on the edge of what had once been a gravel horseshoe-tossing pit. In the twilight, he watched the group gathered on the large screened-in porch.

His eye went immediately to Diana. This morning's cherry-spangled shirt had given way to a white T-shirt that had stars and hearts sprinkled across her chest, eye-catching shapes made of pink and blue sequins. She was clicking little switches on battery-operated fake candles, setting them into paper lanterns and placing them around the porch. A cluster of six or seven people sat on plastic chairs around a flat-screen television, its picture outshining the lanterns, almost painfully bright to his eyes.

Everyone laughed at something on the screen, and Diana turned to look. Her beautiful, brilliant smile lit everything inside of Quinn. He'd wanted to see her smile; he was annoyed at her smile. Not since a kiss over scrambled eggs had he felt like doing anything close to smiling. How foolish of him to think she'd been missing him the way he'd been missing her.

She seemed to be the hostess of this little party. Done decorating for the coming dark, she traded out some empty bottles for two people, even taking the foam wrap off the empty bottle and putting it on the fresh beer for one guy. Her laughter carried lightly over the others'.

Quinn's mood darkened further. He'd drag the entire party down by walking up. He wouldn't interrupt, then. He'd only come here because Diana had been so upset this morning. His mistake.

Quinn took a step back, gravel crunching under his boot. It looked like partying with the likes of Stewy was all Diana needed to enjoy life.

That's how it looks, but...

Except for the more heavily sequined shirt, Diana looked just as she had yesterday at his mother's picnic, cheerful and attentive to everyone, showing no sign that she'd been unhappy at the graves. Only Quinn had known she was hiding any sadness.

This morning, she'd been unhappy. A woman who left in wet clothes was distressed. None of these people on the porch knew she'd been that upset. None of them ever would, because Diana made it impossible to see anything but her smile.

Quinn stepped forward. He opened the screen door and walked onto the porch just as Stewy came through the house.

"That's a sweet bike out there, Di. Can I use it instead of your car to get the chips?"

"No." Quinn's answer was immediate.

Everyone turned to look at him except Diana. Two people turned back to the television immediately, uninterested in the latest arrival to the party. One guy lifted his chin in a cool greeting, as if they knew each other. They did not.

"Sorry, Stewy," Diana said, "but the bike isn't mine to give. The keys are in my car."

Without thanking her or acknowledging Quinn, Stewy went back into the house, slamming the front door seconds later.

Quinn saw the slight lift of Diana's chest as she inhaled deeply before she turned to smile at him as if it cost her no effort at all.

"Hello, Quinn. Did you come here on a motorcycle?"

What a silly question.

Diana could not ask all the others that crowded in her head. In her heart.

Why did you come?

Did you miss me?

Are you angry at me?

Why did you come, why did you come, oh, why did you come?

She smiled brightly. "Come and meet my friends." Her introductions were brief, although when she introduced Stewy's single mom and her new boyfriend, who was the only man who stood and shook hands with Quinn, she couldn't help but boast a little. She fussed with the beer bottles in their tub of ice and whispered to Quinn, "I introduced them a few months ago. They're a good match."

Quinn's grin lifted only one corner of his mouth,

but it softened the intensity in his expression, and Diana found it easier to breathe.

"Of course," he said.

Why did you come?

They were being so polite. This was nothing like their last, testy talk in his condo. Nothing like their easy walk on the ranch. Nothing like their whispers in the dark.

"So, um, we're all fans of this reality show, so I thought it would be fun to get together to watch it. If you don't know it, I can catch you up on who's who in a jiffy."

Quinn barely glanced at the TV they'd hauled from her house to this one. "No, thanks. I didn't intend to crash a party. Whose house am I barging in on?"

"It's mine." At his raised eyebrow, she explained, "I rent them both, at least for a month or two. I'm going to buy one of them."

"Which one?"

So polite. So interested, hands behind his back, navy T-shirt stretched across his chest.

Diana resolutely kept her eyes on his face, but the gorgeous green of his eyes was hardly less distracting.

"This one, I guess. I painted the other one, but then it looked so cute, the owner decided to raise the price. This one came up for rent, so I grabbed it. These bungalows are in demand. You have to move as soon as they do."

The little crowd around the TV made a united noise of outrage at the antics of one of the show's contestants.

"Do you want to show me the house?" Quinn asked.

Diana knew what he really meant. *Let's go some-*

where private to talk. He had something to say to her, and she had a feeling she wasn't ready to hear it. Then again, another ten minutes of small talk would hardly make her feel prepared, either.

"The kitchen still has a pink stove from the 1950s, and it works. Come and see."

Quinn took his time once they were inside. He actually looked at her house. She'd knocked down most of the cobwebs, thankfully. Still, her industrial broom was propped in a corner, standing guard over all the debris she'd swept out of the way so she could use the back porch tonight.

"You're renting this? I hope it wasn't priced as move-in ready."

"There wasn't a lot of room to negotiate. It is a little discouraging, especially after getting the other one up to speed, but I'm looking at the bright side. The back porch is a definite bonus in a house this size, and the kitchen could really turn out great."

The two of them stopped in the center of the tiny kitchen space. She watched Quinn's fingertips slide over the vintage pink stove. He shook his head at the rounded bubble of the chrome-and-white fridge that was from the same era. Diana thought it was darling, retro and cool, all in one.

With her back against the sink, she had nothing to do but watch Quinn and hold her breath. Her friends had glanced into the kitchen and seen a lot of work. It was crazy, how much she wanted Quinn to see through the surface to the potential underneath.

Quinn put his hands on his hips, filling the girly space with his masculine presence. "It's so you," he said, and then he was smiling and shaking his head and chuckling all at once. "It will be a huge project, but it's so you."

"I think so, too," she said, and she couldn't help but smile back. Suddenly, it was Saturday night all over again, pizza by the fireplace and the right to enjoy his words, his approval, his body. Without further thought, Diana was in his arms and they were kissing, his mouth both exciting and familiar.

They could only take things so far. Laughter erupted on the porch, reminding them they weren't alone.

Quinn took a step with her in his arms, turning her so the fridge was humming at her back when he let her go. He didn't go far, though, and kept his arms braced on either side of her. She looked up at him, and the expression on his face was so much better. Relaxed. Open. Happy.

I'm good for him.

That couldn't be right. They had chemistry, but they weren't a match, not for the long run.

She shouldn't have kissed him again. She shouldn't have let herself have another moment of pretending she belonged to him, of believing they had all the time in the world, when really, their time was up. She'd stolen a weekend with a man who wasn't meant for her, and now she had to pay for that theft.

"I'm sorry," he said, pressing a kiss to her temple.

"For what?" She didn't want Quinn to be mad at himself.

"For this morning. I offended you so badly, you ran away in wet clothes. That's for what."

"It's okay. You were trying to be nice." For both their sakes, she had to let him go. He needed to find his woman in the white gown or the red or blue, the woman who would slide seamlessly into his life, not drive him crazy the way she would.

"It's not okay. I know you like to look on the bright side of everything, but there was nothing positive about the way we ended things this morning."

He bent to kiss the other side of her face, but she ducked under his arm and retreated back to the sink. He watched her with narrowed eyes.

She cleared her throat. "You're so right. There was nothing positive about it. I'm the one who messed up the ending. It was nice of you to come here, so we could end things on better terms. Now we'll have no hard feelings."

Two hundred pounds of physically fit man was a little scary when it went as still, as deathly still, as Quinn did. Diana didn't mess with large animals that went on alert like that. Not police canines, and not this MacDowell man.

The tension lasted forever, until Diana tried to walk out of the kitchen. Quinn stopped her with a hand on her upper arm. "I didn't come here for a second goodbye. You know that, Diana. *You know that.*"

"I didn't explain it very well this morning, but this is how it should be. We really aren't a good match, Quinn. You aren't the kind of man who can give me what I need."

Quinn turned away from her in the small space. He drove his hand through his hair, making all the muscles across his shoulders move and flex under the tight shirt. "Don't tempt me like that."

"L-Like what?" Diana's heart was pounding, differently than it had been during the kiss, and it seemed like a matter of self-preservation to keep her eyes on this angry, cornered male, to track his every move.

He turned back almost violently. "Don't tempt me to show you what a lot of bull that is. I'm the man who knows exactly what you need."

"I don't mean in bed," she cut him off, feeling something close to anger herself. He wanted her now, but soon enough, he'd be wishing for a woman more like him, and Diana would become the unwanted pet, the one that was the wrong temperament, the one that was so awkward and painful to place elsewhere. "You're talking about sex. I'm talking about more."

She pushed his chest with both hands and escaped into the living room. It seemed huge, with room to breathe after the confines of that pink-and-white kitchen.

She needed that room to breathe. She never said things in anger like this. When she couldn't keep things positive, she left. Walking away took courage. It was the right way to live. She was proud of going through life avoiding ugly, angry words.

"Tell me." Quinn was right behind her.

She whirled to face him. She took a few steps back, but she couldn't really walk away.

"You were talking about *more*," he said. "I'm listening."

Diana had no words. Nothing, for a man she shouldn't have met, shouldn't have stayed with, shouldn't be so desperate to be with still.

Oh, God. If he didn't let her go, she'd end up like those dogs in the animal shelter, the ones who stood so loyally by their owners' sides while the humans they loved signed the papers to get rid of them. It was heart-breaking. It was what drove her to make good matches, every weekend, for every dog. Yet here she was, so tempted by the wrong man as he walked toward her.

"Tell me, Diana. What's wrong with me?"

"You say you love dogs, but you don't own one."

Quinn stopped short and threw his hands up, a bittersweet reminder of how his mother had reacted when she'd thought her sons were being immature. "What does that have to do with—"

She held her hand up to stop him. She was on the right track; she knew it.

"You don't have a dog, Quinn. Isn't that strange, when you've had them your whole life? You say you love dogs, but you don't. Dogs are demanding, and always present. You don't want a dog, because you wouldn't be able to keep him out of certain areas of your life. The real reason you don't own a dog is because you don't love them enough to tolerate the inconvenience. When you have a hard day, you can't tell a dog you'll let him put his head in your lap and comfort you next Wednesday.

"I'm not saying you are a bad person. I give you credit for knowing your limits. You appreciate dogs. And you would appreciate me as a girlfriend. But I don't want to be appreciated. I want to be loved when I'm underfoot. I want to be loved when it's inconvenient. I do. I want to be loved."

Thirteen

I want to be loved.

Silence followed her words.

Oh, there was the sound of the ice rattling on the porch as someone helped himself to a fresh beer, the sound of a too-loud commercial break on TV. But between Quinn and Diana, the silence was profound.

I want to be loved.

Was that what she'd been really thinking at the gala, when she'd wondered what would happen if she stopped being the life of the party? If she were the one sitting alone in the corner, wearing black, failing to reflect the light and enjoy the moment?

No one would want that somber version of Diana. No one would come to cheer her up. She knew that; she'd had to contact every person who sat on her porch right now. As long as she made them happy, they'd be her friends.

She'd never in her life intended to find out—ever, with anyone—what would happen if she stopped being positive. But she'd stopped being positive with Quinn just now. In a big way.

She put her hand to her tripping heart. "I can't believe I just said that. Any of that. I'm sorry for being so angry, for—"

"Don't apologize."

She looked up at that.

"You expressed your opinion. It's not the end of the world." He was watching her closely. "You're as white as a ghost. Is there anywhere to sit?"

She did feel kind of strange. She gestured toward the porch, where she'd carried all her patio chairs earlier today, when she'd thought she'd die of the loneliness after leaving Quinn. *Party at my place.* No one had asked her why.

"Let's go out front," Quinn said.

When she didn't move, Quinn took her hand, led her out her own front door, and gently pushed her shoulder to make her sit on the step.

She hadn't called Quinn. He'd come on his own, riding up on a motorcycle to find her tonight. Just her. Not her big-screen TV, not her chips and drinks, just her. She hadn't been positive, or friendly, or happy just now, yet Quinn was still here.

"Why did you come?" she asked. It was easier to talk in the dark.

"I came for this," he said, finding room for himself on the step next to her.

She thought he was going to kiss her. He didn't. He just sat there, staring into the night by her side.

"For what?" she asked.

"To be with you. To hear what you were thinking."

"I wasn't thinking anything nice, apparently." She wrapped her arms around her middle.

"Actually, you were thinking what I was thinking.

You just put it in different terms. My relationships have been pretty surface level. I didn't realize how shallow, until today."

He didn't say anything else. He didn't seem to expect her to say anything, either. She had no frame of reference for being with a man, with just one person, for no reason except to sit in the dark. Shouldn't she be *doing* something?

She knew her mother's advice by heart; she had every line of her last letter memorized, the letter she'd written when she was dying, to try to guide Diana through life. There was nothing in it to cover this situation.

Diana was on her own, kicked out of the nest, apron strings cut.

"I missed you, Diana. Seven hours seemed more like seven days."

"Seven months."

She felt him go still again, beside her in the dark, before he spoke. "Then let's keep seeing each other."

"I don't know where it will go," she said. "I've never had a friend like you."

He chuckled, a gentle movement of his chest. "That about sums it up for both of us."

She sighed, and dropped her head on Quinn's shoulder. The muscle was solid. Not relaxed in sleep, not flexed in passion, just solid. There for her.

"When I sigh like you just did," he said, "I know it's time for a ride to clear my head. I brought an extra helmet. Would you like to go nowhere, fast?"

She smiled, although he couldn't see it, turned her head and dropped a kiss on his shoulder.

"I'd love to."

* * *

Work should have felt good. It was everything Quinn's personal life had not been for the past two weeks: predictable, defined, controlled. He made his rounds at the hospital, listened to hearts beat, read lab results, deciphered the ECGs he'd ordered. The cardiovascular system embodied physics at its finest, a study of electricity and flow dynamics. Quinn usually found great satisfaction in fixing obstructions and restoring order in the heart and blood vessels of his patients. Usually.

Today, as he drove his truck from the hospital to his office, he was impatient. There'd been more patients in the hospital than usual, so he'd left late, and the streets of Austin were now clogged with rush-hour traffic, doubling his commute to his office. He'd begin seeing his office patients late, which meant he'd be ending his day late, which meant he'd have less of a chance to catch Diana.

Catching her was the operative term. Dating Diana was an experiment in chaos. Her actual work hours were as likely to be from five to nine as nine to five. Even then, she was as likely to be working from a laptop in a burger place as at her desk in her real estate office. Before work, or after, or during, she might disappear to take a rescued mutt to a vet or run some other errand that had been asked of her. She was generous to a fault when it came to doing favors for others.

But when Quinn could catch her…

Yeah.

Quinn caught himself grinning as he entered the building through the back entrance, smiling even though he was arriving late. He'd smiled more in the past two weeks than he had in the year before he'd met Diana at the gala. The unpredictability of their relationship bothered him, but it also kept him living an absurdly hopeful life. Maybe today they'd grab tacos and watch the bats fly out of the Congress Avenue bridge. Maybe today she'd wear her green dress to dinner at a restaurant with white tablecloths. Maybe today they'd take one look at each other and head straight for his bedroom—or hers. Her bedroom in her blue house, or maybe in the new house, which was the older one.

The woman didn't even have a set address. It drove Quinn crazy. He'd never had to work so hard to find whichever woman he was currently dating.

He greeted members of his staff as he headed down the hallway toward his office, accepting their good-natured teasing.

"Dr. MacDowell in the house. Watch out, he's got his swagger on."

Quinn remembered the first hour he'd known Diana. *I'm here to help you get your party on.* He nearly laughed at the memory.

"Someone's in a good mood…"

One time, Diana had surprised him at his desk after showing a house nearby. Only once in the two weeks they'd been dating, but it was enough to make him hope, every time he opened the door to his inner sanctum, that a woman would be waiting in his office.

"Good morning, darling. You're running late."

Wrong woman. Quinn tried to keep his disappointment from showing. "Morning, Tricia."

Patricia had made herself at home behind his desk, sitting there as if she owned it. Diana had perched on the edge for only a moment. Like a firefly, she'd flitted from there to the sofa, until she'd perched on the arm of his desk chair. He'd caught her and kept her there for as long as he could.

He picked up the day's mail, which was stacked neatly with its envelopes already sliced open for his convenience. Patricia didn't move from his chair.

"I offered you your own desk once," he reminded her.

"As your office manager?" She made a dismissive motion with one hand. "Please. I don't do hard labor."

"I offered, you said no, so now you don't get my desk."

She moved to the sofa. "Congratulations on your impending uncle-hood. I heard the news at the hospital this morning. You might have told me yourself."

"I didn't know Lana and Braden were making it public yet."

"You wound me. I'm not the public." Patricia crossed her legs. If Quinn didn't know better, he'd think she'd done it just so he'd notice her shapely legs. He doubted any man failed to notice a nice pair of long legs on any woman, but she was Tricia. She didn't need to show off for him. It must be a habit for her to sit just so.

"I heard that your little real estate girl had been there to hear the news, too."

Quinn kept flipping through the mail. "Don't tell me my brothers are turning into gossiping old biddies now that they're married."

"Kendry told me. She's an open book."

"Hardly a challenge for you, then." Quinn led with the opening jab, if only to set a more normal tone for this conversation. Patricia was in an odd mood, and Quinn was running late. Done with his mail, he stood.

Patricia remained seated. She adjusted her watch so that it was facing just the way she wanted it. "Kendry said it was so exciting, toasting Lana's baby and meeting Quinn's girlfriend. Girlfriend? Isn't that a bit much for a fling that didn't last through Sunday brunch?"

"Fishing again. Yes, I'm still seeing her, and she has a name. Diana Connor. Was there any other reason you came by? I'm getting a late start."

"I know her name, darling. My charming stepwhatever sang her praises *ad nauseam* after the gala. Thank God dear Becky's mother retrieved her the next day."

Quinn smiled—inwardly, to himself—at the power of Diana's safety pins, and her kindness.

Patricia extended her hand toward him, wanting a boost up from the plush sofa. Quinn obliged.

She took his white lab coat off its hanger on the back of his door and held it up for him. "The business portion of this visit is a Texas Rescue and Relief service announcement. We've got a meeting this weekend. It's supposed to be a busy hurricane season, and the new director is as nervous as a cat about it. I'm here to drag you to it, if I must."

"I'd forgotten." Quinn slipped his arms in the sleeves.

Patricia smoothed his collar. "No, you didn't. You were hoping I'd forget to force you to come. The forecasters might be right for once. They upgraded that tropical depression in the gulf to a named storm this morning. I can't tell if dear Karen is hopeful or worried. Anyway, since this will be only the members of the steering committee, I thought we'd hold it at my father's lake house. We can make a boating weekend out of it, if the weather holds."

"That, I definitely can't do." He had a hard enough time catching Diana during the work week. He wasn't about to sacrifice an entire weekend to Patricia and her sailboat fetish.

"Don't be that way. Everyone already agreed to it, and they're bringing their significant others. It will be fun."

The Cargill lake house was a modern-day palace on a massive freshwater lake. If Quinn could corral Diana into coming, he'd have her to himself during the long drive. Once there, she'd be all his, no dogs or people demanding her time and attention.

"In that case, count me in. I'll bring Diana."

"Are you sure? She's not exactly part of our crowd. You might want to leave your little fling at home for this kind of event."

"Let's get two things straight. First, Diana Connor is not a fling. Secondly, you're wrong about her. Take Kendry's word for it, if you don't trust mine. Diana fits in everywhere she goes. You'll like her, I promise."

"Fine. Ten o'clock sharp, then. We have to get the business out of the way so we can relax the rest of the weekend."

"Ten o'clock." Quinn gave her a peck on the cheek. "Now go harass your next victim."

Fourteen

"I'm running late."

"Late is not an option, Diana."

There was no answer on the other end of the line.

Damn it. Too late, Quinn realized the tone of voice he'd used. Diana wasn't a cath lab nurse who'd failed to hand him the proper instrument.

He tried again. "The committee meets at ten. You can't keep other people waiting for no good reason."

More silence. She wasn't an intern who needed a lecture on how the business world worked, either. But damn it, there was a meeting at ten.

The chaos that had marked the first two weeks of their relationship had only worsened since Patricia's invitation. Quinn hadn't seen Diana at all in forty-eight hours. Apparently, it was harder for a part-time animal shelter volunteer like herself to clear her calendar for the weekend than it was for a cardiologist who owned a private practice and served on staff at a major hospital.

He winced at his own thought.

Harder for a shelter volunteer than a cardiologist who needs to check his ego.

Had he always been this unbearably focused on his own life, and was only realizing it since he'd started caring how Diana perceived him?

She suddenly broke the silence, in a stunningly businesslike tone of voice. "I've got a plan. I checked my GPS, and the last errand I have to run is on the way. I'm already in my car, and so is my luggage. If you can be outside your building with your luggage in six minutes, I'll pick you up. We'll run my errand on our way out of town, and we should just make it to the lake by ten."

Quinn never knew what to expect from her, but in this case, the real estate agent who was capable of negotiating a home sale was exactly the version of Diana he needed.

The only problem with her plan, he thought, as he left the cool of his building for the ovenlike heat of June, was that he'd travel to the lake in the passenger seat of a tiny VW Bug. The car was already parked under his building's awning. He heard the trunk latch release as he walked up with his single piece of luggage.

The trunk was already full. A gigantic bag of dog food had been wedged inside. What little room that was left was taken up by a large suitcase in a jarringly bright print of cartoon monkeys. Surely, Diana wasn't making him late for a steering committee meeting of Texas Rescue and Relief because she needed to deliver some dog food. Surely.

She hopped out of the car and came up to him, wearing shorts and a tank top. Plastic gems were sewn around the neckline in a geometric pattern, and her flat thong sandals were made of gold glitter. Quinn was wearing slacks and a dress shirt. Granted, he'd skipped the tie and cuffed his sleeves, but it hadn't occurred to him to let Diana know Patricia's idea of a casual weekend meant the men didn't wear jackets to dinner. When he'd assured Patricia that Diana would fit in...

He scowled at the overcrowded trunk.

"Don't worry," Diana said, "we'll make it all fit."

She sounded cheerful. All morning, every phone call, he'd been on her case, lecturing her about promptness and meetings, and yet, she was smiling at him. She really was the most remarkably happy person he'd ever been around.

"You look beautiful." He let go of his luggage handle—what an idiot to be holding luggage when he could be holding this woman— and crowded her against the open trunk as he took her mouth the way she always seemed to inspire him to: fully. Completely. Passionately.

All weekend. He'd have her in arm's reach all weekend, and he'd have her in some undoubtedly plush bed all night. He could feel his heart beat harder. Hell, he could practically hear the blood rushing past his ears as it left his brain and headed south. He could hear...

He could hear...

The deep bass of a dog barking. A large dog. One that sounded like it might consume a gigantic bag of dog food.

He stopped kissing her. "You don't have a dog with you."

She couldn't be so...so...*clueless*. As soon as he thought it, he felt a distinct pain in his chest, a physical sensation that might have been the first crack in his confidence in them as a couple.

She kept smiling, oblivious. "There had to be a reason I had dog food in here, right?"

"Your car isn't big enough to carry the dog food and your luggage and my luggage and me *and the dog*."

She waved away his pronouncement on her car's capacity and glanced from the trunk to the tiny excuse for a backseat. "I've got it. Let's put the dog food in the backseat and the dog on top of it, like it's his bed. Then you get the front seat, and the luggage gets the trunk."

He would not acknowledge the crack. He refused to feel the pain. He could function without feeling emotions. It was a vital skill for a doctor who threaded wires into human hearts.

He hauled the dog food out of the trunk while she opened the passenger-side door and hauled the dog out of the car. It was a damned Saint Bernard, or at least mostly that breed. In a Bug. She kept the dog out of traffic with two hands on its collar while Quinn laid the heavy bag on the seat.

Quinn started to put his single, compact, efficient carry-on piece into the trunk next to her large monkey-print bag.

"Wait a second," Diana called out. With one hand on the dog, she hauled a second piece of luggage off the front seat, this one covered in a banana design. Of course. "Can you put this in the trunk?"

"Barely."

The dog was eager to get back in the car and away from the noise of the traffic. It quickly became clear that he was not going to fit on top of the dog food in the backseat. Quinn took both pieces of her luggage out of the trunk, making a splash of color on the gray asphalt.

Like putting together pieces of a two-layered puzzle, Quinn squeezed his bag and her larger one into the trunk with the dog food and slammed it shut. His dress shirt was sticking to his back in the hundred-degree Texas heat.

"See?" she said. "It fit."

"That dog and your smaller bag will both need to fit into the backseat."

In the end, they did, but only when Quinn brought his seat so far forward that he literally had to hug his knees. "Let's just get going. Please."

Diana began chatting. Quinn had seen her do it before, when she was trying to cover up an unhappy feeling. Well, he felt unhappy, too, so he sank into silence while she gabbed away.

"I'm sorry about the dog food. I made him some scrambled eggs this morning, since I was out. I usually have some in the house, but I didn't know he was coming for a visit. His owner needed someone to care for him for an extra day."

Naturally, she'd made herself available to the unknown owner. Quinn came last in her list of priorities. He was torn between feeling sorry for himself and being worried for her. She claimed to be happy when she felt needed and helpful, but Quinn thought she was being more of a doormat than she knew.

Quinn said nothing, and Diana's chatter resumed.

"We're on our way," she said, a chipper little skipper of the lime-green Bug. "I didn't have the car last night to get to the store for more dog food, so it was lucky I had a pot roast in the freezer. He loved it."

Whether two-legged or four-legged, what male wouldn't love to have Diana fawning all over him, dropping everything to make him a pot roast?

She could have called him. He could have brought her a bag of dog food. Diana shut him out of her world. Except for the volunteers at the shelter and the TV-watching crew he'd met so briefly that first weekend, Diana kept him carefully separate from her friends. From her real life.

We really aren't a good match, Quinn. She'd said it so earnestly, standing in front of her retro refrigerator.

It bothered him. If she continued to shut him out of her life, then her prediction would certainly come true.

Quinn was going to set a different tone this weekend by fully including her in his life. His friends were going to love her. Diana needed to see that her fears about being a poor match for him outside the bedroom were unfounded.

He supposed breaking his silence would be a good step toward his weekend goals.

"Why didn't you have your car last night?" he asked.

"I had to loan it to someone."

His friends wouldn't mooch off her. They'd never borrow her car. They kept their dogs at canine spa facilities.

Diana began turning down side streets. The dog's owner lived near the highway, all right. Close enough to make the property undesirable, judging by the neighborhood.

"Leave the air running, I'll be right back," Diana said. She was out of the car and coaxing the dog to squeeze out in a flash. Quinn watched through the windshield as she wrestled the animal to the door of the shabby duplex. Then she returned to the trunk and started unpacking the suitcases to get to the dog food.

The owner of the Saint Bernard was apparently content to let Diana not only buy the dog food but to haul it up the cracked sidewalk herself. Cursing inwardly, Quinn released his shoulder belt and got out of the car.

Without a word, Quinn reached into the trunk to sling the fifty-pound bag over his shoulder and followed Diana to the duplex. An unkempt man stood in the door, watching them sweat as they approached. The man couldn't stir himself to meet them halfway, apparently. Couldn't help the woman who'd watched his dog on short notice. Diana smiled and chatted and accepted his rudeness in a way that made Quinn feel close to boiling over.

He dropped the bag at the doorstep.

"What's this?" the guy mumbled around the cigarette dangling from his lower lip.

"How about 'thank you'?" Quinn challenged him.

"I don't take charity."

"Good, then you can pay Diana for this bag of dog food."

Diana looked alarmed. "Don't be silly. The dog food just goes with the dog."

The man glared at her, looking as surly as Stewy on steroids. "You keep it."

"I don't have a dog. What would I do with dog food?" She giggled and nodded as if she were making perfect sense. It was an act, of course, and Quinn could see it was an act, but Diana apparently knew what she was doing. When she said, "We'll just move the bag inside," the guy shrugged instead of keeping up his argument.

Quinn didn't like the guy's lack of gratitude. *Move it inside your damned self,* he started to say, but stopped when he saw the man was balancing on one leg. His only leg.

Quinn felt like an ass. He hauled the bag over the threshold, then turned toward the man in silent question. When the man jerked his chin toward the kitchen, Quinn obeyed and set the bag against the wall by the battered refrigerator.

The man was uncomfortable with the help. He'd already stated he wasn't a charity case, but he couldn't have much money. Diana had clearly been trying to save his pride by insisting she had no use for the dog food, so he might as well take it.

Diana said her goodbyes to the mammoth St. Bernard. She offered her hand to the amputee in a businesslike manner, another subtle way to make the man feel they were equals, not charity-giver and helpless recipient. While the man shook her hand, Quinn saw him set his other on the waist-high dog's head for balance.

Diana had made another brilliant match.

She wasn't making Quinn late by running a frivolous errand. She hadn't let herself be taken advantage of, either, but had instead deliberately spent her money on someone she deemed a worthy cause. Most of all, she wasn't clueless, and Quinn was ashamed of himself for having thought it. So how did a man go about apologizing without explaining what he'd thought?

Diana was silent as they drove out the other side of the duplex's semicircular drive. Quinn slid his seat back as far as it would go, then angled himself to watch her as she drove. She was beautiful, flushed from the heat, but she was blinking a little too rapidly. He hoped they were tears of pride in herself.

"Do you remember the morning after our one-night stand?" he asked.

She kept her eyes on the road, but wrinkled her nose at his question.

He persisted. "I said that I knew I was lucky to be with you, do you remember that?"

"Yes." She waited at the red light that would let them onto the highway's entrance ramp.

"I was right that morning, but every day, I find out that I was more right than I knew. That was a beautiful thing you did, finding a way to help that man when he was dead set against receiving help. Your instincts about people amaze me."

"Aw, shucks," she said, trying to be humorous when he could see he'd made her blush with his praise.

His silence was well-intentioned this time. She needed a minute to soak in a compliment without laughing it off.

"I hardly know what to say to that," she said.

"For me, it was a lesson in humility. I'll never doubt your errands are important, and your matchmaking skills are phenomenal."

Then, because he was making her tear up when she needed to be clear-eyed to drive, and because Diana preferred laughter, always, he tried for a little humor. "If all that weren't humiliating enough, I also have to deal with the fact that I now know I got kicked out of your bed last night to make room for a Saint Bernard."

Her laughter warmed his heart, but that crack of

doubt wouldn't go away completely. A few carefree miles passed before he put together the details.

Diana was a phenomenal matchmaker, a woman who understood others instinctively.

We really aren't a good match, Quinn.

The icy feeling returned to his chest.

Fifteen

The gas gauge was dangerously—and unsurprisingly—near empty. Diana had hoped to make it to the lake without having to run that errand. It was nearly ten when she pulled into the gas station.

"I'll be super quick."

She could have saved her breath. Quinn was already out of the car, sliding his credit card into the pump with one hand and removing her car's gas cap with the other. He didn't seem angry, just focused. Very doctor-ly. This made sense, since she was making him late to a doctor-ly meeting.

Anger, though, might have been more normal. It wasn't that she didn't appreciate his restraint, and all his kind words about how important her errands had been. After all, spending the past hour's drive to the lake in a tiny car with an angry bear wouldn't have been too pleasant for her, but she was the reason he was late to an important meeting, and she knew it.

Despite Quinn's apparent good mood, Diana was getting nervous. It didn't have much to do with making a meeting on time. It had more to do with entering a foreign world, one where everyone would focus on hard things. Natural disasters. Human suffering. How was a person supposed to look on the bright side of such things?

She couldn't, and she was afraid to spend a weekend with a group of people who were tough enough to actually seek out tragic situations.

It's just a party on a lake. It will be fun.

She ought to be more excited. Last summer, she'd had a ball at a friend's house on this same lake. They'd drunk sweet wine coolers and eaten salty potato chips on his dock. He'd owned a Jet Ski, and Diana had taken a turn on it. Maybe Patricia would have a Jet Ski, and Diana could ride behind Quinn, the way she did on his motorcycle. That would make for a fun weekend.

First, however, there would be some kind of business meeting. Quinn was wearing work clothes. No tie and stethoscope, but still, slacks and a button-down shirt didn't exactly scream "lake house weekend" to her. She wasn't part of the meeting, but Patricia would be. Patricia wasn't afraid of natural disasters.

Diana bet Patricia wouldn't be in shorts and a tank top, either.

It was too late to pack a different wardrobe, but Diana had brought a long-sleeved white shirt to wear over her bikini. If she wore it over her tank top now, she'd arrive looking a little less casual. She popped the trunk and went to find—

Nothing. Her banana suitcase was gone. She quickly checked the backseat, but only her monkey luggage was there, the one containing her makeup and hair dryer, and the bottle of champagne she'd bought for a hostess gift. Her bathing suit was in there. Nothing else to wear.

She'd taken the luggage out to get to the dog food. It was probably sitting in the duplex's semicircular driveway. Or, more likely, it had been stolen by now.

She shut the trunk, maybe with a little more force than she'd intended to.

"What's wrong?" Quinn asked, watching her as he pumped the gas.

There's enough misery in the world without me adding mine to it. Diana forced a smile. She'd already made him haul dog food in dress clothes. She'd already made him late to his meeting. She wasn't going to complain about something neither he nor she could fix.

"I hope you really, really like my outfit. It's the only one I've got with me."

The awkwardness began in earnest when they reached the iron gates. Diana rolled her window down, but before she could push the call button on the security box, a man's voice came through the speaker.

"Your name, please."

"Diana Connor."

There was a brief pause. "Are you expected?"

Quinn leaned across her. "Quinn MacDowell."

He had that tone to his voice again, the one that said he was in charge, so listen up.

The security guard did. "Good morning, Dr. Mac-Dowell. Welcome back." The gates began swinging open.

Of course. Diana Connor meant less than nothing in a place like this. She drove her little Bug several hundred yards to the edge of a cliff. Miles of blue-green water were visible beyond a modern house.

She pulled into a large parking area to the left of the house. Diana popped the trunk, but when they got out of the car, Quinn casually shut it again with one hand and took her keys. "Don't worry, they'll get the luggage."

Awkward, but interesting. Diana wondered who "they" were. The two-story house was elegant and expensive-looking with its natural stone exterior, but it didn't look big enough to hold all the people that must have arrived in the other cars. The entire bottom floor was a four-car garage. From the parking area, curving stone stairs were set into the hillside that sloped up to the top story's rather grand double doors.

As they reached the top of the stairs, one of the doors opened and an older gentleman in khaki slacks and a navy blazer greeted Quinn.

They stepped inside. Diana experienced a fleeting sense of vertigo, for they were standing in a spacious marble foyer at the top of a polished marble staircase. Beyond the iron railing, there was nothing but open space to the floor below. The lake view was spectacular through the two-story-tall windows.

Diana turned back to their host, and stuck her hand out to the gentleman. "You must be Mr. Cargill. Thank you so much for inviting us." She wished she'd thought to pull the champagne out of her monkey suitcase to give him.

The man shook her hand briefly, then let go and tucked both hands behind his back. "You are welcome here, miss, but I am not Mr. Cargill. He is not currently in residence."

Awkward. So very awkward.

Quinn put his hand on the small of her back and handed her car keys to the...whatever he was. The butler? Did people really have butlers?

The sound of a woman's heels coming briskly up the marble stairs was followed immediately by the appearance of Patricia. Well, the top half of Patricia. She stopped once she'd climbed high enough to see them. "You're here. Finally."

Quinn kept his hand on Diana's back as they started down the stairs. Her sandals didn't make an elegant clicking sound with her every step. They were completely flat, so they sounded about as glamorous as bedroom slippers as she walked down to Patricia's stair.

Patricia kissed Quinn on the cheek. Her hair was up in a French twist. Her silk navy blouse topped wonderfully flowy gray slacks, and she looked cool and sophisticated and every inch at home.

Diana felt underdressed and disheveled, like a woman who'd hauled a Saint Bernard in and out of her car all morning in the Texas summer heat.

"You remember Diana Connor from the gala." Quinn's introduction sounded so formal, but it fit the surroundings.

"Of course. The real estate agent. How nice to see you again." Without offering her hand or a peck on the cheek, Patricia turned back to Quinn and took his arm. "You're late, darling."

"Only ten minutes."

"I've held this meeting for as long as I possibly could, but we have so much to cover."

"I think Texas Rescue will manage to operate this year despite a ten-minute delay."

With that dryly delivered line, Diana knew she'd come full circle. The urbane man in a tuxedo was back, the unflappable one, the one who didn't laugh.

Or rather, Diana was back in his world.

She'd invaded this world once, naively thinking it would be a lark to go to a formal gala. She'd stolen a perfect moment by dancing with Quinn, then a perfect night, and a weekend. For three weeks, she'd been stealing moments with a man whom she never should have met. And now, in this lakeside mansion, she'd come back to the world where people wore silk and had butlers.

"Diana, do join us in the meeting room after you've had a chance to…freshen up." Patricia looked toward the top of the stairs. "I see Robert has your luggage. He'll show you to your room."

"This is all I've got," Diana said, tapping the neckline of her shirt. She smiled as she said it, so that Patricia wouldn't feel sorry for her or be concerned that her guest felt embarrassed—although her guest most certainly did. Heck, even if she'd had her luggage, Diana wouldn't have had anything appropriate to change into. Then again, that was the bright side: the forgotten suitcase gave her the perfect excuse for being so underdressed.

Quinn started shepherding them down the stairs. "We had a luggage mishap on the way here."

"Oh?" Patricia said invitingly, and Diana braced herself for a retelling of her dumb move with the dog food.

Awkward. Diana would have to laugh at her own stupidity.

Quinn didn't offer any details, however. "Since my ten-minute delay has already upset your sense of punctuality, let's go straight to the meeting. I assume everyone is in the billiards room?"

Quinn was watching out for her. She knew he was just as bothered by arriving late as Patricia was, but he was being a gentleman by not blaming Diana. The same was true of the way he hadn't said that Diana had left her luggage on the ground and driven away like an idiot. Everyone could have had a good chuckle at her absent-mindedness, but it really wasn't funny, and Diana was grateful to be spared.

But no matter how kind Quinn was being toward her, Diana was the odd man out in this house. She stayed by his side as they walked through the gorgeous great room, which was furnished with dark, carved woods and rich leather upholstery, a well-designed interior that could hold its own against the spectacular lake view. It was undeniably magnificent, but it was meant to impress, and Diana felt all the intimidation it dished out.

Patricia walked on Quinn's other side, chatting easily with him like the friend and colleague she was. Diana fell back a step, intentionally, when they reached another staircase to descend to a third level that hadn't been visible from the driveway. From her step behind them, it was easy to admire Quinn and Patricia. They looked so elegant together, moving in sync in their well-tailored clothes against the backdrop of this mansion.

They'd looked just as good together at the gala.

Patricia put her hand on Quinn's arm casually—or perhaps, not so casually. She cast one smooth glance at Diana over her shoulder. Diana absorbed all the impact of that single, well-designed look: she was the guest of a woman who didn't want her in her home.

Diana couldn't blame her. She was, after all, sleeping with the man who was Patricia's perfect match.

Awkward didn't begin to describe it.

Quinn remained standing with Diana as Karen Weaver opened the meeting with a weather update. There was one chair available, but he was half of a couple. Party of two, and Patricia knew it. Hell, he'd brought Diana at her invitation.

The billiards table had been converted into a conference table courtesy of a custom-made wood top Quinn had always admired. Matching club chairs, handmade to be just the right height, were drawn up to the table. All eight of them. But Diana made nine.

Quinn made a small gesture toward the single empty chair as he skewered Patricia with a look.

"So with these new tracking projections, New Orleans is breathing easier, but the Texas coast is not," Karen said.

Patricia stood and walked over to one of the captain's chairs that sat around the low poker table. Quinn joined her, and picked up a chair to move it closer. It was too short, but there was no other choice. He'd use it.

"Where are everyone else's guests?" he asked Patricia under his breath. The pool deck lay just outside the billiards room, but the only person he could see out there was a staff member setting rolled towels on the vacant chairs.

"Marcel took them out on the sailboat. You just missed them."

Quinn felt no need to hide his displeasure. "You couldn't have waited ten minutes to send them off? Diana's now the odd man out."

"Are you her babysitter or her paramour? Surely she can handle the disappointment of missing a boat ride."

In the split-second before Quinn could set her straight, Patricia, very wisely, backpedaled. "I'll fix it, Quinn. Take the chair."

Karen sounded distressed as she concluded her update. "Four of the five weather service models are projecting landfall on Monday." She paused to look around the table. "And we're understaffed."

Patricia addressed the room. "Then I'm so glad Quinn brought an extra set of hands. Does everyone know Diana Connor?"

With that, Patricia "fixed it" by forcing Diana to participate in the meeting for the next half hour. To Quinn, it was like watching a master class in how to be bitchy without actually saying anything rude. It started with Patricia moving her papers graciously so that Diana could have her chair, keeping her far enough away that Quinn couldn't speak to her on the side. Patricia used the short captain's chair, if standing in front of it counted as using it. That seemed generous of her, but it wasn't. From her standing position, Patricia easily took over the meeting from the seated director. Karen was no match for Patricia.

Diana seemed hopeful that the weekend would be cut short. "If you need the hospital to open on Tuesday, then will you go down now to set up, before the storm hits?"

Patricia answered in a perfectly civil way, but there was something nasty about her explanation that Quinn couldn't put his finger on. "Going down today or tomorrow puts us in the path of the storm. We can't handle casualties if we put ourselves in a position to become casualties. Besides, my volunteers will need to use Monday to arrange their schedules. Doctors cannot just leave their practices with no notice. I do hope your job is not as demanding."

"I hope so, too," Karen said. "I'd love for her to come with us."

Quinn decided he liked the new director, no matter what Patricia's issue with her was.

Diana declined. "I don't think I'd be very good in a crisis."

"Please, join us," Patricia said. "I'm sure we can use your help."

And…bitchy Patricia was back. Quinn could just *tell*. Damn it, he needed to intervene, but how did he intervene against politeness?

Patricia referred to a document in her hand. "We were looking at our areas of personnel shortage earlier this week. What can you do? I need nurses—no. Medical assistant—no. Are you CPR certified? We'd need to have an actual certification on file by Tuesday. No?"

Karen interrupted, looking as uncomfortable as the others around the table. "There is always a need for clerical work."

"Oh, yes," Patricia agreed. "Let's see. Have you any experience as a comptroller? Have you ever worked in a pharmacy? Perhaps you could alphabetize the medicines."

Diana never stopped smiling. She never showed any distress. But Diana, apparently, had had enough.

"Alphabetizing," Patricia repeated. "Shall I put you down for that?"

"That depends," Diana said, "on whether or not you need my alphabet certification on file by Tuesday. Kindergartens require more notice than one working day to send a transcript."

Sixteen

"You handled yourself beautifully."

"I offended our host." Diana thought Quinn was a little too proud of her for being less than a gracious guest.

"Your host offended you first. It was perfectly fair to hit back."

The meeting had dragged on for hours, but now the fun was supposed to begin. They'd come to their assigned bedroom to change clothes, so they were talking while Quinn wore surfer's board shorts and she wore an orange bikini. It was a strange way to have a discussion on ethics.

"I was taught to turn the other cheek," she said.

"You did turn it. Patricia wasn't going to stop until you made her. Think of her as the one dog that annoys the rest for no good reason. You made her sit and be quiet for a moment." He leaned against the footboard of the king-size bed and shook his head as he watched her brush her hair. "I can't believe your bathing suit happened to be in the monkey luggage. If it had been lost with the banana bag, we'd have the perfect excuse to skip Patricia's idea of a pool party."

"I'm not going to do anything else to hurt her feelings." In fact, Diana had spent every minute since her smart-alecky exchange trying to prove that she was normally a nice person. She'd run up the stairs and out to Karen's car to fetch some paperwork for her. When the other guests had come back from their sail around the lake, she'd shaken hands cheerfully and even brought a few thirsty guests some drinks.

"You did a great job defending yourself. How should we celebrate?"

Quinn scooped her up and tossed her on their bed, then followed by diving onto the mattress next to her, landing on his stomach like some kind of crazed baseball player sliding headfirst into home base. "We're both horizontal and nearly naked. Got any ideas?"

He was darned adorable when he was playful like that, but the man was so not getting to home base. Not now, at least.

"Everyone is out by the pool," Diana said, giving his shoulder a push, as if she could make a two-hundred-pound man roll off a bed.

"Good. They won't miss us."

"Patricia wants us to enjoy the water before dinner. You guys have a hard week ahead of you." It wasn't in Diana to deliberately offend someone who was trying to make sure others had a good time. If Patricia wanted everyone to enjoy themselves by the pool, then Diana wouldn't, couldn't refuse to go.

Quinn obviously did not feel obliged to be so obliging. He began kissing Diana, skipping her mouth and her neck and her breasts to start with her soft stom-

ach, exposed as it was in her bikini. Her soft, ticklish
stomach. Diana began to giggle and push harder at
his shoulder.

There was a knock at the bedroom door, followed
by Patricia's voice. "Hello? Is it safe to come in?"

"No," Quinn hollered.

The doorknob turned, anyway, and Diana scrambled off the bed.

The door itself only opened a few inches. "I thought
since my guest had lost her luggage, she might need
a maillot."

Diana wasn't sure what a "My Yo" was, but then a
slender hand reached through the crack and dropped
a white bunch of material onto the floor.

"See you in a few." The door shut.

Quinn cursed, and he sounded halfway serious.

Diana picked up the white material and held it up
to herself. It looked for all the world like a one-piece
bathing suit to her, but it was a *maillot*. And it was
clearly too big.

"It's a good thing I've got safety pins."

Quinn had rolled to his back and tucked his hands
behind his head. "You are not wearing that. Your bathing suit looks great."

At her hesitation, he sat up. "Seriously, your bathing suit looks *great*. Why would you put on one that
doesn't fit?"

"When someone tries to do something nice for
you," she began carefully, thinking it through as she
said it out loud, "the only proper response is 'thank
you,' and to accept it."

"That sounds like one of your mottos. Your mother's?"

He asked the question while looking at her so intently, she felt defensive for no real reason.

"She left me an etiquette book. It's in there."

Quinn stared at her a minute longer. "Let me tell you what's not in the etiquette book. Some people might give you a gift to manipulate you. And as strange as it may seem to you, some people will like you better if you see right through them and refuse to play along with their demands. Patricia respects you for the way you fielded her certification garbage today."

Diana wondered if Quinn was aware that he knew Patricia so well. Someday, he'd see what was under his nose, and Patricia would effortlessly fit into his life as his lover instead of his friend.

Until then, Patricia was Quinn's friend and Diana's hostess for the weekend, two good reasons for Diana to play nice.

"If you want to do her a favor, then don't fawn all over her." Quinn got off the bed. "Let's hit the pool before you cave in to her machinations. I will definitely be unhappy if you take off that orange bikini. No—that's not true. I'd love to see you take it off. But not at the pool. You know what I mean."

Diana laughed, but a brilliant idea had just hit her. She hadn't given Patricia that ridiculously expensive bottle of champagne yet. She could catch her and present it as a peace offering.

"You go out to the pool. I'll be right there."

Diana didn't want to walk around the house in nothing but a bikini, so she wore Quinn's dress shirt as a cover-up. After pulling the flower-painted bottle from her suitcase, she looked out the bedroom window toward the pool deck, but she didn't see Patricia. She headed up the stairs to the middle level, where the kitchen flowed into the rest of the living space.

Women were talking in the kitchen. Diana hesitated on the stairs. Their voices were not muffled at all, but sounded amplified by the granite countertops and polished stone floors.

"Don't you think it's time for you to seduce Quinn? Please? That girl has got to go."

Diana couldn't identify the speaker by her voice, but she recognized Patricia when she answered.

"If I sleep with him, then I'll be just like you. And Bethany Valrez. And all the others. You played the short game."

"That's the only game there is with him. It's a very enjoyable game, too. I don't know what you're waiting for, but I won't be able to stand having her around for the rest of the year. Do us all a favor and make your move."

Diana sagged against the banister, clutching the champagne to her chest. She was less shocked to hear that everyone expected Patricia to be with Quinn than she was to hear that Quinn had once been lovers with one of the other women. How did they stay so perfectly civilized? For the rest of her life, after she and Quinn broke up, if Diana ran into Quinn anywhere, she would blush ten shades of red and not be able to look him in the eye.

Patricia addressed her kitchen buddies like she was running another planning committee. "I'm in it for the long game. I mean more to him precisely because I haven't slept with him. When the whole game is over, I'll be the last one standing."

"Game over? You think he's ready for marriage?" This, from a third woman.

The first woman followed up. "If you think you can bring him to the altar, more power to you, but would you hurry it up? That house in Catalina will be available in October, and the guys are willing to go. If Quinn brings her, I'll gag."

"She's the last hurrah for his bachelorhood." Patricia sounded confident. "His brothers are married now. That always spooks a man at first, so he's chosen someone totally inappropriate. Someone he'd never settle down with."

Diana bit her lip, adding a little physical pain to the hurtful words. Patricia would be shocked to know that Diana agreed with her. She'd always known she wasn't a good match for Quinn, but hearing Patricia say Quinn wanted her precisely because of that made it worse.

The Catalina woman was still impatient. "I cannot be seen with a girl who wears glitter on her feet and plastic jewels on her boobs."

"I'll be engaged to Quinn within six months, mark my word. But I've got to let him overdose on her first. He won't appreciate it if I chase her away. I'm throwing them together as often as possible, in every situation. He'll be embarrassed by her sooner or later."

"Sooner, if I know you."

"By October, please."

Diana sat on the step. It cut to the bone to hear how very little the other women wanted her around. She'd been so naive, thinking that Patricia was like the high-spirited Dalmatian at the animal shelter, the one who'd pushed to be in charge constantly. That dog had never calculated how to cause the downfall of any human it knew.

Anger set in, pushing the hurt aside. She'd complimented Patricia on the house, the view, the food. She'd thanked Patricia for her hospitality, when she'd been invited only so that Quinn would see her as a misfit.

To know that the other women wanted her to make a fool of herself was infuriating. How friendly had she been to them today? Diana had memorized their names. She'd brought them glasses of water. They'd kept her hopping, no doubt hoping that Quinn would see her as some kind of underling.

She should leave. It would take courage, but it would be the right thing to do, to simply return home. In a situation this negative, what could she possibly gain by staying?

She'd make up some excuse, something to keep Quinn from being embarrassed when his date left the weekend party early. She'd get in her green Bug and drive away.

And leave him behind, with all these nasty people?

It was exactly what they wanted.

For once in her life, Diana didn't want to make people happy.

Screw them.

Those two ugly words felt kind of perfect. Diana gripped her champagne bottle by the neck, stood, and marched up the stairs. She walked into the kitchen, head high, the tails of Quinn's dress shirt fluttering behind her, and started opening cabinet doors, looking for the champagne flutes.

"Can I help you find something?" Patricia asked, in a tone so helpful, it was hard to believe it was a lie.

"Champagne flutes." She held up the bottle. "This is Quinn's favorite. I thought we'd make ourselves scarce for a little while. You know."

Patricia could have her "turn" some other time in the far, far future. Diana wanted to make it clear that for this weekend, Quinn was hers.

Patricia thought Quinn would hate an overdose of her? Diana almost laughed at the thought. He was going to love every minute.

"Oh, honey. That's not the same thing we were drinking at the gala."

Patricia reached for the bottle. Diana let it go only to avoid a demeaning tug of war.

"Good Lord, it's warm," Patricia said, and Diana saw her make a face of horror at one of her friends. She opened the glass-fronted wine refrigerator and pulled out another champagne bottle. It was also painted with flowers. "Let me help you. These come from the same *maison*, but they are hardly equal."

She set the bottles on the counter, side by side, but had barely started a lecture about champagnes that did or did not have vintage years on their labels, when Quinn came into the kitchen.

Everyone stopped staring at Diana and looked at him.

After a brief, frozen moment, Quinn looked at Diana and started to smile, one slow, sexy smile that took its time spreading over his face. Only then did he walk up to her.

"You are just the woman I wanted to see."

* * *

Quinn didn't know precisely what he'd walked into, but Diana looked a little pale and tight-lipped. It had taken him a fraction of a second to put the details together. One, he'd seen her look like that once before, after she'd gotten angry in her pink kitchen. Two, the other women in the kitchen were all angled toward her like a pack of hunting dogs. Three against one.

He was sure there'd been one of those mysterious female showdowns. Quinn didn't like the odds Diana had been facing. He hoped his deliberate smile and the way he stood next to her made it clear that he was on her side.

She looked so damned desirable in his shirt, it took him a moment to notice the two bottles of champagne on the countertop. He recognized the painted flowers. The gala. She'd tried to bring him the champagne from the gala.

He picked up the less expensive bottle, knowing she hadn't spent a thousand dollars on the other one. He had no doubt that Patricia had brought it out to show Diana that her bottle wasn't good enough.

It was more than good enough. It touched him in a way that was so sweet, it was on the verge of painful.

"You brought this for us?" he asked her.

His doubts vanished. He held that bottle in his hand, and tried not to be overwhelmed by its significance. If he'd worried that their relationship wasn't going well, this bottle proved otherwise. A woman didn't plan a private champagne toast with a man she still considered a bad match.

To hell with their audience. To hell with being civilized, with all the snarky comments and smug superiority he'd been so aware of this day. The woman who'd brought him this gift was worth having, and by God, he was going to have her.

He put the bottle down to take her face in both hands, and he whispered a simple thank-you over her lips. For a beautiful, brief moment, with a single slide of tongues that was as close to perfect as a physical act could be, he let himself enjoy the intimate interior of her mouth. He ended the kiss, slowly let his hands leave her face, and picked up the champagne.

"Let's go," he said.

The other women in the kitchen were like statues, all staring at him. He saluted them with the bottle. "Don't hold dinner for us."

As he led Diana outside, he clearly heard a woman's voice reverberate off the granite and stone.

"Do you still think he'll be yours in six months?"

Seventeen

The beautiful thing about champagne was that a man could open it without a corkscrew. With six efficient turns of his wrist, Quinn knew the wire cage would come off, the cork could be eased out and Diana would be his.

He took the first swig straight from the bottle. It was warm, and the carbonation was sharp. He'd never had anything so delicious in his life.

"What should we drink to first?"

His voice filled the tunnel-like space of the boathouse, bouncing off the cavernous wooden structure in the dark. The late afternoon sun was blindingly bright on the water beyond the garage-style door, but inside, everything was cool and dark. Jet Skis and two-person sailboats bobbed at their moorings as he and Diana stood on the wood dock that ran the length of the space.

Diana started kicking off her gold sandals, looking over her shoulder and into the dark corners of the building. Her whisper blended with the lapping sound of the water. "Are you sure this is private?"

Quinn stepped close to her, one leg brushing the inside of her thigh, and bent to whisper low in her ear. "Very private. Let's drink champagne and make love."

She shivered, a delicate movement that brushed her covered breasts lightly against his bare arm, a simple sensation that sent his body from ready to shockingly hard. He wanted Diana with an intensity that gave every caress urgency. "Hold this," he said, his voice gruff in the echoes as he pressed the champagne bottle into her hand. He pulled his T-shirt off and threw it on top of her discarded sandals. "Drink to us."

She did, tilting her head back and swallowing as he kissed her throat. His hands weren't steady, a tremor betraying his emotion, not the hands of a doctor at all, as he pushed his dress shirt off her shoulders and reached behind her neck to pull the ties of her orange top, skimming down her waist to pull the ties at her hip. The scraps of cloth fell to the floor, and the sight of her before him nearly felled him, too. He pressed her to his body, the sensation of skin on skin as shattering as he'd ever known it, and he staggered back to sink onto the boat cushions that had been stacked against the wooden wall, ready for summer days.

In the darkness of the boathouse, Diana was a vision of pale skin, a work of art, womanly and beautiful as she straddled him. Silently, she passed him the champagne so she could release his body, untying the surfer's shorts that kept him from her, slipping her hand into his pocket to find a foil packet, and then he was once more insanely, intensely grateful when she took him into her.

He would always be grateful for the gift of Diana. He knew it, had known it from the first, but this time, he allowed the truth of it into his heart. He felt it with every roll of their hips, until he had to whisper it into the skin of her chest, her neck, her ear. "I want this forever, Diana. Forever."

How could something that felt so right be so very, very wrong?

Diana rested against Quinn, relaxed, no muscle in her body remaining tense after the release of making love. Her heart beat steadily, slowing while she watched the rhythmic motion of the boats bobbing so slightly with the motion of the water in the boathouse. It was a perfect moment in time.

And yet, she felt like the terrible person she was. For weeks now, since the night she'd met Quinn Mac-Dowell, she'd worried about herself. She'd made memories with a man whom she'd known was not for her, and she'd dreaded her own inevitable heartbreak.

Not once had she worried about Quinn.

Forever, he'd said.

She wouldn't be the only one who got hurt.

Diana stared at the boats for one more minute, imprinting the peacefulness in her mind. Then she sat up. Bent over, retrieved her bikini from the dock. Started tying it on. She felt like a robot. That was good. She didn't want to feel any more emotions than a robot did.

Quinn sat up and watched her dress. Without taking his eyes off her body, he lifted the bottle to his lips and took another swallow.

"That's not the same champagne as you gave me at the gala, is it?" Diana asked quietly.

"It's better," he said. "Have some."

After pulling his shirt back over her shoulders, she

took the bottle and sat on the cushion next to him. She stared at the label. "Patricia was right."

He was frowning at her. She could feel it, although she couldn't bring herself to look at him.

"She wasn't even close," Quinn said. "That was her father's stock, not hers, and I doubt they sell that vintage at the Driskill. Don't let her start messing with you."

"She wants to marry you."

The boats bobbed, the water lapping at the edge of their dock. The sun was setting beyond the boat-house door.

Quinn took the bottle out of her hand, so Diana stared at the weathered wood at her bare feet.

"I don't want to marry her. Why are we having this discussion?"

"You should marry her. You will. Her, or someone like her. She'll glide into your life as easily as these boats come in here. You've got a good life, and she'll keep it all so perfect for you."

He made a sound like a hiss, sucking air in quickly, like he'd been punched. Startled, Diana looked at him.

"How can you make love to me and then tell me to marry someone else?"

Because I'm a terrible person.

He stood, a sudden, angry movement. He held the bottle in front of her. "Why did you give me this?"

"It was for Patricia. A hostess gift."

He reared back, actually moved his head back as if she'd taken a swing at him. Then, in a stiff and formal way, he said, "I misinterpreted it."

He paced a short distance. Two steps away from her. Two steps back. "I misinterpreted it, and you let me.

You came here with me, and you let me make love to you. Why?" He gestured toward the cushions. "What was this for you?"

She couldn't answer. Her heart was breaking, because she'd hurt him. This was worse, so much worse, than she'd thought it would be. Her tears weren't blinding enough. She could see the look on Quinn's face. The disbelief. The fury.

When she didn't answer, he repeated his question, louder, his voice echoing off the water and the walls. "What was this for you?"

He walked two steps away from her and stayed away, this time. "Was this some kind of revenge sex? Patricia was mean to you, so you showed her. You had sex with the guy she wants. My God. You accused me of idiotic booty calls. At least shallow sex is honest. But this. What the hell was this?"

"Please, please stop." The tears were falling hard now, and she dashed her cheek on her shoulder, on his shirt.

Quinn stopped, but it cost him physical effort. Breathing hard, like he'd run for miles, he came back to her. "Tell me. What has this whole weekend been about?"

She held up her hands helplessly. "It wasn't about anything. It was just another date. We've been hanging out. We've been buddies. I'm good old Diana, the gal pal, the party girl."

Quinn shoved his hand through his hair. "No, that's wrong. We're dating, because we like being together more than we like being apart. But we're not really together, are we? You only see me when you've taken care of everyone and everything else. Until this morning, I never knew just how important your work with your dogs was. You've shut me out."

She'd kept him at bay for her own protection. Why let the man invade every corner of her life, when they weren't going to be together long?

Quinn turned and chucked the champagne bottle into the nearest trash can, then grabbed his T-shirt off the dock and pulled it on. "I'll tell you what this weekend was supposed to be about. It was about that 'more' that I thought you wanted. It was about including you in my life, my whole life, not just dinners after work. I wanted you to see that you could fit into my world."

Diana felt tears prick her eyes again. He cared about her that much. Or he had cared. "I'm so sorry it backfired. I knew from the first night that no matter how I felt about you, we were too different. I'm not the right woman for you. Now you're finally seeing it."

"No, I'm not." Quinn closed the distance between them, and then to her surprise, he buried his hands in her hair and tilted her face up to his, as if he was going to kiss her. "I see the opposite. The director of Texas Rescue is ready to hire you, if you haven't noticed. Karen is grateful you can handle Patricia, because she can't. You do very well in my world."

If that was true, it was frightening. "Then here's the problem. I don't want to be part of this world. I want to make people happy, not put them in their place. It may sound weak to you, but I would rather leave than fight. I'm leaving."

Quinn was silent for a long time, looking into her eyes. "Then I'm leaving with you."

"Oh." She placed her hands on his wrists. It was so

Quinn of him, to insist on escorting a woman home. "I don't mean for the weekend. I mean forever."

"So do I."

Incredibly, he kissed her. Tenderly. Brushing his lips over hers, then over her cheek, then her temple. It didn't feel like a goodbye kiss.

"Quinn, don't you understand what I'm saying?"

"You said you weren't the right woman no matter how you felt about me. What feeling is that? How do you feel about me?"

"It's… I feel…" She wanted him. She liked him, she admired him. He made her laugh, but he also made her angry, and uncomfortable, and—she couldn't put a name to it. She spent so much time telling herself she couldn't have him, she put so much effort into not feeling too much for him, that she couldn't come up with an answer.

With his hands still cupping her face, she shook her head a little, helpless and silent.

"It's okay." He kissed her again, and let her go. "I know how you feel about me. You told me with your body, right here, while we were making love."

She wrapped her arms around her middle, feeling cold without him. Confused. "Revenge sex? I thought that was revenge sex."

Quinn knelt at her feet and held her glittery sandal so she could slip into it. She put her hand on his shoulder for balance, and he looked up at her. The darkness was coming rapidly, but she could tell that he was smiling.

Smiling.

"You weren't getting revenge on Patricia. That was a bad choice of words. You were showing her, and me, and especially yourself that you own me. That I'm yours for the taking."

When her second sandal was on, he stood and took her hand, lifting it to his lips, a formal cavalier in a T-shirt. "That feeling is right and true. It makes you, and only you, the right woman for me. We're leaving. Together."

When they reached the house, they found Karen on the phone and everyone else packing. The National Weather Service had issued new warnings. The hurricane was not obeying the predictions. It was stronger and faster, and it would hit the coast of Texas before the sun set again.

Everyone left, together.

Eighteen

Monday morning dawned gray and wet. The hurricane had made landfall hours before, damaging several towns along the coast. Its speed had enabled some of the outer bands of rain to reach as far inland as Austin, but the rain was all that was left of the storm system. As fast as the hurricane had come, it had died once it began moving over land. The Texas Rescue and Relief temporary hospital team was already on their way to the coast. Quinn and Diana were supposed to be on their way, too, to join them sometime before darkness fell.

"I'm running late."

Quinn prayed for patience.

He found it.

"I can wait," he said into the phone. He was in his truck, the pickup he used for everyday driving and disaster relief alike. The plan was to follow Diana's car to the coast. He'd much rather have Diana by his side for the three-hour drive, but policy was policy. Every member of the team was supposed to have their own transportation as well as extra gasoline.

Diana sounded upbeat. "With our separate cars, there's no need for you to be late just because I'm running late. I've got two more errands."

"Any half ton bags of dog food involved? I'm dressed for it this time." Although he'd be seeing patients on the coast as he did in Austin, he wore jeans and boots, ready for any heavy labor that was needed to get the temporary hospital up and running.

"No, nothing like that. The rain is going to slow down traffic as is. Don't wait for me."

Quinn had never claimed to read people, not the way someone like Diana could. But when it came to Diana herself, Quinn knew her better than anyone else. Her voice came across as too cheerful, too much like she'd been at his mother's picnic.

She was sad.

He drove in the rain to her house, arriving in time to see her lime-green Bug backing out of the driveway. Feeling like the worst kind of stalker, he followed her. Her first errand was to the duplex where she'd left her banana suitcase, which she put in her trunk. Simple. Logical.

Her second was to a cemetery.

Quinn sat in his truck for a long while, watching Diana wind her way between the grave markers, her blue jeans hugging her hips and her pink sequin shirt looking undimmed by the gray weather. He couldn't see her face under the black umbrella she used.

He felt all the inadequacy of their relationship. They'd taken it up a notch this weekend, it was true. He'd told her she owned him, which she did, and he'd convinced her not to run away despite his alleged friends doing their best to shut her out. But when she hadn't been able to name her emotions, he'd told her it was okay. He hadn't said how he felt about her, either.

It wasn't okay.

I failed to do my best.

And now Diana was alone in a cemetery, unaware how much he cared.

Quinn grabbed his cowboy hat from the rack in his truck cab. The rain had slowed to a drizzle, and the hat's brim kept the worst of it from rolling down his neck as he set off to find Diana.

She was sitting on a plastic tablecloth, umbrella on her shoulder, reading from a white piece of paper. She looked almost like a little girl at a tea party, with the tablecloth underneath her like that.

Quinn stopped at what he gauged to be a respectful distance, but her words reached him as she held the paper up.

"There's enough misery in the world without you adding yours to it. Not you personally, of course. You're a baby. You're allowed to cry. But I really like this philosophy, and I hope you do, too, when you're old enough to decide on your own what to believe in."

The punch to his gut was not going to pass. Quinn didn't even try to wait it out. He walked through the wet grass.

She saw him coming and stopped reading. She looked at her letter, and she looked at him, and she looked so confused, Quinn knew she'd never been interrupted before. She moved to get to her feet, but he was there first. "Don't get up. May I sit down?"

"You're not supposed to be here."

"I know."

"Did you follow me?"

"Yes."

He didn't sit beside her, but took a knee instead, keeping his boot off the tablecloth. He removed his hat and held it over his heart, as his parents had taught him since his youngest days.

"May I?" he said, as he took the handle of her umbrella and held it over them both.

He wondered how many years Diana's mother had had to teach her daughter all the ways of the world. He looked at the date on the tombstone. The first punch hadn't lessened yet, or he surely would have felt a second.

"Diana." His voice was raw, little more than a whisper. He cleared his throat. "What year were you born?"

She sighed and put the paper in her lap. Her letter, her precious letter.

"She died the day after I was born. There was some complication with the pregnancy, and they told her she'd have to stay in the hospital for the last four weeks before I was due. On the second day, she wrote my letter."

Diana affected a slightly different voice, the one she must have imagined her mother used. "It's so incredibly boring here. I think I'll use the news hour to write you a letter every day. I'll pick one topic, and try to tell you what I know. That will be so much better than an hour of doom and gloom on this hospital TV."

Diana looked down at the letter in her hand. Not the original letter, Quinn realized, but a photocopy, much folded.

Diana talked in her usual voice. "In the first letter, she wrote about happiness. The next day, she suffered a stroke or an aneurysm or something. My grandpa just called it 'an attack.' She never regained consciousness. I was born by C-section two weeks later, and they took her off life support."

"Good God." He bowed his head.

She was quiet until he opened his eyes again. "You're a doctor. Don't you see things like this all the time?"

He hoped his voice wouldn't fail him. "No. Those cases are rare. You can't help but feel the loss."

"Don't start crying, okay? It will make me cry."

"Okay." Quinn cleared his throat again.

After a moment of silence, Diana looked at him out of the corner of her eye, as if she were shy. "But you do think some of the doctors might have cried when she passed away? Maybe a little?"

"I know they did."

These punches were killing him. The hair on the back of his neck practically stood up, so strongly did he feel that he was seeing a glimpse of a very young child in Diana's shy question.

By the time she'd been old enough to ask about her mother, those who'd known her would have had years to adjust to her mother's passing. Diana had probably been told the story in the same straightforward way she'd just told it to Quinn. All of her questions through the years must have been answered matter-of-factly.

It must have seemed to her as if no one mourned her mother. Maybe it still seemed that way to her.

"I guarantee you that when Leslie Diana Connor died, all the nurses wept. And when the ones who hadn't been on duty came to work later that day, they wept, too, when they saw a new patient in her bed. Every doctor had to take a few moments to step into an office or a bathroom or a broom closet so that they could get themselves together before calling on their next patient. Your grandfather was torn up, so much so that he still found it hard to talk about years later, so he probably didn't talk about it much at all. But everyone—every single person, Diana—everyone wished they could have saved your mother for you."

He couldn't look at her. The tombstone in front of him was a wet blur, and if he looked at Diana, he would surely cry when she'd asked him not to.

"Thank you," she said, breathless. "That was the best story, ever."

He ditched the umbrella and hauled her to her feet and pulled her into his arms. She was crying, and she squeezed him back as tightly as he was hugging her.

"Thank you," she repeated, "thank you, thank you."

"Yeah," he said, and he kissed her soft hair and her wet cheeks, then held her a little longer as he read the tombstone once more. "Happy birthday."

Diana couldn't cry anymore, not here, not in what was left of this coastal town.

It was her birthday, and all around her, everywhere she looked, people were devastated. Their houses were gone. Their shops, their roads, their lives, all damaged. They kept coming to the medical tents, carrying their belongings in a suitcase or pillowcase, wearing clothes that were tailored or torn, signing in, asking for help.

Diana couldn't help.

Blood made her faint.

She hadn't known this. She'd never been around blood before, or at least, not around this kind of blood. This wasn't a scraped knee or a finger-prick kind of blood, but the kind that caked around a broken bone that poked through the skin. That made her faint.

When she fainted, she made everyone's jobs harder. On this birthday, she'd been labeled a fainter, and had become a burden to the hospital. Not to the town's real hospital, with its shattered windows and the roof that had been peeled back and ripped halfway off. Not that hospital, but the one housed in white tents that had been set up in its shadow. The one Texas Rescue ran. The one where Quinn worked, and Patricia, and Karen, and everyone except Diana, because she was a fainter.

There's enough misery in the world without you adding yours to it.

Diana wouldn't cry, not when everyone had a better reason to be sad than she did.

Patricia would show her no mercy if she cried. While Diana had been alphabetizing the medicine, a little boy had been wheeled past her as he spit blood from his broken teeth and then proudly, gleefully, viciously smiled at every adult he passed. Diana had felt light-headed for one second, and then she'd been on the floor with little plastic pill bottles raining down on her.

The alphabetizing had begun again without her. Patricia, disgusted Patricia, had sent her to the X-ray tent to hand clipboards and paperwork to waiting patients. That had lasted less than five minutes. Diana had cracked her elbow hard on her way down during that faint, and her shirt had caught on something that pulled the right thread to cause a line of pink sequins to start falling off, one by one. She'd insisted her elbow would be okay, but still, she'd been almost grateful to be kicked out of the X-ray tent.

So, she was spending the rest of her birthday in the

parking lot, in a chair, sitting in a tent with its flaps down. She was sweltering, but no one wanted to risk having the new girl catch a glimpse of any gory injuries among the people who waited in the line for medical attention. She kept track of the walkie-talkies. Local cell-phone towers had been knocked out, so the hospital ran on battery-operated handheld devices. When someone came to change out their battery, Diana wrote down the serial number on a clipboard.

In other words, the hospital ran just fine without her.

Diana sat alone, hour after hour, and felt the full weight of her uselessness.

The one touchstone in her life, her mother's letter, seemed frivolous in the face of all this disaster. *Find moments of beauty.* Where? Light and reflection and sparkle meant nothing here, nothing. Ice was used for injuries, not to fill tubs of drinks for friends. Candles were used as an inferior source of light when batteries died. Dogs were used to find corpses in collapsed buildings.

Where was the happiness?

The flap of the tent opened behind her, and Quinn walked in.

She turned, took one look at his face, and knew she wasn't the only one having a bad day.

Nineteen

Quinn had left the main treatment tent with a mental list of things he needed. He needed to find Patricia, so that she could light a fire under someone to source more nitroglycerin. He needed the second generator fixed, because they could only keep one set of equipment charged without it. He needed better lighting, now that the sun was going down. He needed a fresh battery for his two-way radio.

When he lifted the white flap and saw Diana with her whiskey-colored hair, every other need became secondary.

She walked straight to him, and gave him a hug.

Damn. It was still a little alarming, the way she did that, but it was exactly what he needed. He slid his stethoscope off his neck and tossed it on the table, then wrapped both arms securely around her. She leaned into him, so he could lean into her, too, and they stayed that way, taking some of the weight off each other.

Quinn closed his eyes.

In the wake of any natural disaster, an unfortunate spike in the amount of heart attacks occurred in any community. Quinn could deal with that. It was why he was here. Most MIs required stabilizing medicines and transportation to the nearest city whose hospital was still in working order. Today, two patients had needed more.

Quinn had performed CPR on the first patient, applying the hard and deep compressions with the heels of his hands and the force of his entire upper body, while the team had scrambled to find the portable defibrillator in a room not yet completely ready. It had taken a long, long time, an eternity, and Quinn would feel the effort tomorrow in his triceps, he knew, but the patient had survived.

It wasn't the first time he'd had a human's life in his hands—literally, under his hands—as he forced a heart to pump. It wouldn't be the last. But it wasn't a normal part of his routine; he was an interventional cardiologist, not an emergency physician.

Diana felt so good in his tired arms.

The second patient had died. Quinn had thought of Diana's mother, and he'd thought about the way he was leaving too much unsaid with her daughter.

Quinn started to let go, but Diana held him tightly. He put his arms back around her. She owned him. If she needed him, then she could have him.

"Is this for you, for me, or for us?" he asked quietly.

"I think we've both had a hard day."

She kept her cheek pressed against him. He brushed her hair back with his hand. "You do know there is an 'us,' right?"

She frowned, a tiny movement of her brow. "Yes, of course."

"In the boathouse, when I said you owned me—"

"We're exclusive. We're dating."

"No." He ran his thumb over her cheekbone. "No, there's more to us than that. I love you, Diana."

She picked her head up and looked at him, just looked at him, for the longest moment. She was beautiful. Quinn wanted to look at her forever. He planned on looking at her, forever.

"I can't think of anyone who deserves to be loved more than you, Diana. I don't think you've had enough of it in your life."

"I deserve it?" she asked. "Everyone deserves to be loved. I'm nothing special."

"You are extraordinary."

She looked down, fingering the edge of her sequined shirt, his compliment making her shy.

"Please, let me go," she said.

Something was bothering her. He relaxed his hold so she could slip out, but her next words froze his heart.

"Let me go this time, when I leave. I'm not the right woman for you."

She wasn't shy. She just didn't love him.

Every crack he'd felt in his heart, every hint of ice, came at him at once, a barrage of freezing shards.

"I'm so sorry," she whispered, and she took a step backward.

He worked hard to push through that first punch. This didn't make sense. He knew this woman. He knew her. She had strong feelings about him.

"You're sorry for what?" he asked.

"I'm sorry I let you talk me into staying every time I tried to leave. I shouldn't have been your lover, not when I knew we weren't a match."

"Not a match." He recaptured her, and pulled her tightly to him, so her jean-clad legs brushed against his. "That's a lie."

The tent flap opened and a man walked in. Diana pushed away from Quinn and stood at a little distance, crossing her arms over her chest.

The man held up the battery for his radio and gestured toward the storage rack. "So, I'll just…uh. Right." He grabbed a new battery and left.

The tent was stifling. Quinn didn't know how she'd stood it all day. "Come take a walk with me."

He pushed aside the back flap so they'd avoid the busiest part of the tent city. The edge of the parking lot bordered a drainage ditch. It was nearly overflowing, full from the hurricane's downfall, but the water was moving, draining, slowly returning to normal. The coming twilight promised some respite from the heat.

Diana stepped up onto a concrete parking barrier, fidgeting rather than facing him.

Quinn hoped she was listening. "I respect your matchmaking intuition, more than you do. Think about that very first night. The very first moment you saw me, you noticed me, didn't you? Every instinct inside you must have sent you toward me. You wanted to be my friend. You wanted me to be happy, from the first minute we met."

"I try to cheer people up all the time." She stepped off the barrier and put her hands into her front pockets. "I left you at the gala. After I found you a good match, I walked away."

"And I came after you."

"You shouldn't have."

"I've got instincts, too, and every one told me to

hold on to you. *Don't let this one go.* We belong together, Diana." He reached for her arm and ran his fingers from her elbow to her wrist, so that she removed her hand from her pocket. They faced each other, so close, but touching only those two hands.

After a long moment, she took her other hand out of her pocket and placed it over his. "This is so hard to say, but Quinn, we have no future together. Don't you see? You're thinking with your heart, but I'm being realistic. I know the limits of my matchmaking skills. I've seen so many first loves turn sour. Do you remember Stewy's mom? I think her new boyfriend is right for her, but I thought that six months ago, too, with a different guy, and I was wrong. The animal shelter is full of sad endings. It's frightening, when you see someone leave with a new puppy, so very happy, and they come back in a few months or a year, convinced that it's impossible to live with that dog one more day."

She was so tenderhearted, Quinn had no doubt that she felt the pain of every abandoned dog. "I'm in love with you, Diana. That's not going to change."

"We're like…we're like a Yorkie and a rancher. It doesn't matter how much the rancher is taken with the Yorkie. It doesn't matter if he thinks the puppy is cute and fun. If he takes that Yorkie home, he's still not going to have the help he needs to bring the horses in from the pasture, is he? It's not a good match. He may keep that dog until the day he dies, just like you might keep me around, but they won't live the happy lives they could have had, because they were paired up with the wrong partner."

She dropped his hand only to press her palms flat on the muscle of his chest. She rose on her toes the tiniest bit, and she kissed him gently, beautifully on the mouth.

She stepped back. "I won't do that to you, Quinn. Goodbye."

Diana tried to find the beauty in the heartbreak. She took another step back. The sunset was spectacular. The water edging the asphalt looked like a silver pond.

Quinn MacDowell looked furious. *"Don't you ever kiss me like that again."*

Diana started walking in the general direction of the farthest corner of the parking lot, where the Texas Rescue personnel had parked their vehicles.

Quinn followed, his boots loud as they struck the asphalt. "You're really going to walk away, aren't you? You're going to live the rest of your life as a martyr. You're going to tell yourself you did the right thing, the noble thing, and let me go on to find someone more suitable."

It was exactly what she'd had in mind. She walked faster. "Don't make this more difficult than it already is."

"Difficult? You want to know what difficult is? It's being crazy in love with a woman, and hearing what a low opinion she has of herself. Your Yorkie analogy sucks."

Diana flinched a little at the way the word *sucks* ricocheted off the asphalt. The parking lot for the damaged hospital building was huge, like a shopping mall's. They had acres to go.

"You're not a dog, damn it. You are a human being with the power to change, the power to affect the world around her, the power to make her life anything she wants it to be. That Yorkie crap is a cop-out. It gives you the excuse to never change. It's easy to say, 'This is how I was born, this is how I have to stay.'"

She wished he would be quiet. He was ruining her moment. Her heart hurt because she had to leave him, but she couldn't give in to the pain, because Quinn was right beside her, and he wouldn't shut up.

"Let's try your analogy with humans in it. If you decided to live with the rancher, then you could become one, too. If he needed help bringing the horses in from pasture, you could learn how to do it. If you didn't enjoy it, you could say, 'Hey, honey, let's hire a ranch hand to do this.' There's an option your Yorkie didn't have.

"Your little analogy doesn't address the real problem. You're not selfish enough. You're so busy trying to make sure everyone else is happy, you forget to go after what you want. You give away your home and your car and your time and your talents. You would rather leave than fight for something that you want, just so someone else won't be unhappy for even a moment."

And that was the last straw. Diana stopped walking and rounded on Quinn.

"It's good to make other people happy. It's bad to make them miserable. That's what my mother said." Quinn had seen her letter at the start of this endless, horrible day, and now he was insulting it. Her mother's letter.

She hated the tears that pricked her eyes.

Quinn spoke with a little less heat. "I know, and she was right. It's noble and honorable to wish nothing but happiness for those around you, and you do. But when it comes to your happiness, you have to be greedy. This is your life, and if you want to be happy, then you might have to demand it for yourself. Start small. If your talents aren't being used in an asinine walkie-talkie tent, then go find yourself a position you'll enjoy."

"You're asking me to throw away every philosophy I've built my life on."

"No. Your mother's letter says it takes courage to be happy. Maybe she didn't mean the courage to try bungee jumping or to go solo to a ball. Maybe she wanted you to have the courage to take what you want. I can love you, Diana. But you've got to get greedy. You've got to keep me for yourself."

Be greedy. Be selfish. And then, she'd become happy? It went against everything she knew.

"You have choices to make," Quinn said, and he sounded kind. "So do I. I choose not to stand here and watch you drive off into the sunset. It won't make me happy."

Quinn turned and started the long trek back to the hospital. Diana watched him go.

Then she walked slowly the rest of the way to her car, curled up in the backseat, and read her mother's letter until it was too dark to see.

If the backseat of her car couldn't hold a Saint Bernard, then Diana had been foolish to think it could hold her. By the time dawn sent rays of light through her car window, she ached in every muscle. Dragging her banana suitcase behind her, she returned to the hospital.

Feeling a million times better after brushing her teeth and changing her clothes, she went to find Patricia in the administration tent.

Quinn had said it would be starting small, but it felt like a big step as she faced Patricia over a collapsible conference table.

"I need a different assignment."

Patricia didn't glance up. "You're not qualified to do anything except clerical work, and those spots are filled right now with people who do not pass out at the sight of blood."

Patricia's workstation was in a tent with a generator and an air cooler, Diana noted. But Patricia worked hard, there was no denying it.

"There must be something I can do to help," Diana said.

"Look, you may think I'm being a bitch, but I'm not. I've got responsibilities. When you passed out in the X-ray tent, the techs told me you missed cracking your head on the corner of the table by a fraction of an inch. I don't knowingly put volunteers in harm's way. It isn't how I operate."

"I'm glad to hear it," Diana said mildly. She doubted she'd ever be friends with Patricia, but she could still think of her as a Dalmatian, particularly when Patricia tilted her head just the right way.

Patricia stood and picked up her two-way radio and her notebook. "I don't have time to find a new spot for you. Keep yourself busy today or go home, I don't care."

She left her usual uncomfortable silence in her wake, as the other volunteers in the tent stayed busy. Diana turned to the friendliest-looking one. "Are there any dogs around here?"

The woman shook her head. "No, but we've got kids out the wazoo."

"Are they bleeding? Not that I wouldn't want to help, but I kind of go 'timber' when I get around that stuff."

The woman laughed. "Oh, I heard about you yesterday. No, the recovery ward should have them all nicely bandaged up. Here, I'll show you which tent it is."

The only way to tell the area was pediatric was that the patients were children. Otherwise, it was all white walls and white bed linens. The patients had white bandages, but there was no blood. A few had IV needles, but that didn't bother Diana in the least.

Parents were attempting to entertain the kids with varying degrees of success. Portable electronic devices had died. Card games seemed to be more successful, but there was a shortage of games. There was a shortage of everything.

Most especially, there was a shortage of happiness.

"I was thinking of having a party," Diana said casually, when she noticed a few children looking at her as she stood in the door. "What kind of party do you think we should have?"

The news started filtering into the adult treatment area around eleven o'clock.

More nitroglycerin had been located, purchased, transported and stocked in the pharmacy, and the nicest young woman had taken over the pediatric recovery area.

Everything she did was described as darling. She herself was darling. The sock puppets she'd made for the kids were just darling. She was also generous, clever and creative. Long before Quinn heard the first male gossip, that she was the hot chick who'd fainted twice yesterday, he'd already known the darling they were talking about was his.

He hoped.

It was nearly three before he could escape to the pediatric recovery ward.

Quinn stood in the doorway and took in the scene. Where yesterday there had been fear and worry, today there were sock puppets. Dozens and dozens of them, one for each hand of the children in beds and the children running around. Some for the parents to use, so their puppets could talk to their children's puppets.

The eyes were made of plastic gems, and their bodies were made from the material of various pieces of Diana's wardrobe. Quinn recognized the sequined cherries. She must have run out of socks and started cutting up her shirts to keep the supply of puppets going.

He saw her before she saw him. She was leaning against a bed, using one of the curved needles from surgery to sew her next creation, and she was beautiful. Her shirt was plain white with no gems remaining on it, but she was still dazzling, full-color Diana.

She looked good in pure white. The last bachelor MacDowell didn't find the thought frightening at all.

"Hey, mister. Are you going to listen to my heart?"

Quinn looked down at the young boy who was pointing at the stethoscope around his neck. "Not today."

"Are you here for the party?"

Quinn kept his eyes on Diana, waiting for her to look at him. Just one look, and he'd know if this new venture meant she'd decided to be selfish about him as well as her job.

She looked. She smiled. And she bounced on her toes, just a little bit.

Quinn walked straight to her and gave her a hug.

She clung to him, hard, and he could feel her laughing in his arms. Or crying. Or both.

The boy had trailed him across the room. "So didja come for the party?"

"Yes. I'm here to get my party on."

"Oh, it's not just a party," Diana said. "It's a dog party."

A dozen little puppets started barking, their high-pitched operators making little "arf, arf" noises. Quinn raised an eyebrow at Diana, who was wincing. "You find this worse than the real barking at your shelter?"

"A hundred times worse. And it was my idea." She picked up a tube sewn out of cherry-sequined material. "Stick out your hand. Can you tell what kind of dog it is?"

Quinn couldn't hazard a guess.

She wriggled it onto his hand differently, and tufted up some strips of material in the center of its head.

"It's a Yorkie. They're super cute, and I hear guys who own real ranches really like them."

Then Diana murmured in his ear, "But I'm much, much better to have around. I love you like crazy, Quinn MacDowell, and I'm gonna make you one happy man."

Epilogue

Quinn had the whole family in on the secret.

Diana thought he was still working on the coast with Texas Rescue, but he'd been home for two hours now. Two hours that he'd spent having not enough time to set up the party and too much time to second-guess his sanity.

Diana's real birthday had been Monday. She'd told him she loved him on Tuesday—thank God. She'd left with only the de-jeweled clothing on her back later that night, because she'd had to go back to work here in Austin. Today was Saturday, and Quinn had decided that a mere five days wasn't too late to throw her a birthday party.

The part of the equation that made him question his sanity was this: he'd met Diana four weeks ago. Four weeks and one day. Was it too soon to propose?

Jamie, who'd eloped after knowing Kendry for four weeks, had said the timing was irrelevant. Braden had too wisely pointed out that only Diana could decide if it was too soon. Both brothers had given him their blessing to offer Diana their grandmother's engagement ring. They'd chosen different rings for their brides, each for special reasons.

Quinn hoped the girl who valued everything she'd been handed down from her mother would value the ring from his father's mother.

She would. Of course she would. She'd say yes.

Quinn cleared his throat and looked out the front window of Diana's house—the blue one—and waited for the lime-green Bug to make its appearance.

In the end, the surprise went off without a hitch. Diana was thrilled with his mother's cake, Lana and Kendry had managed to buy her gifts in her size, a feat Quinn wasn't certain how women accomplished, and both of his brothers had covered for him when he'd gone outside to add the finishing touch to his proposal.

"Come out in the sunshine with me," he said, taking Diana's hand to give her a boost out of the armchair. She looked like sunshine herself in a bright yellow sundress. Quinn wished he'd changed from his jeans and blue shirt, suddenly. He should have worn a suit and tie for the occasion.

As soon as they were out of his mother's line of sight, Diana whispered in his ear. "Have I told you how delicious you look? I love you in blue."

Quinn decided he should stop trying to figure out how she knew what he needed to hear.

And then they were outside, and the sky was blue, the grass was green, and the whole world consisted of only the two of them.

She immediately noticed the clothesline he'd strung up, of course. From it fluttered a dozen homemade children's cards with a dozen childish variations on the spelling of "Happy Birthday."

"When did they make these?" she asked, going down the line and touching each one.

"The day after you left. Crayons arrived in a Red Cross package."

She stepped back to take in the whole clothesline. He watched her profile as she nodded, just once, in approval.

"It looks very happy," she said.

"It looks like you. This is what you bring to my world, Diana. This is what you bring to everyone's world, but I'm selfish enough to want you by my side at the end of every day. I've missed you this week. Four days without sunshine felt more like four weeks."

"Four years."

He got down on one knee and revealed the gray velvet box he'd been keeping in his hand. The speech he'd so carefully prepared flew out of his mind, so he said what seemed right for the moment. "Will you please marry me? Will you please bring dogs into my home and chaos into my life? I love you, Diana. You're color and sunshine and everything good in the world. You're my happiness."

Diana nodded and nodded, then began fluttering her hands in front of her cheeks and blinking her eyelashes. "Oh," she choked out. "I don't want to cry."

"I don't, either. Please say yes."

"Yes! Oh, yes, of course. I'm sorry, I didn't think. I couldn't talk, and—"

Quinn stood and kissed her swiftly on the mouth. A round of applause came from the side of the house—

so much for privacy—and his family joined them with crystal champagne flutes as they toasted the good life, with the good stuff.

* * * * *

We hope you enjoyed reading

YOURS AND MINE

by #1 *New York Times* bestselling author

DEBBIE MACOMBER

and

THE BACHELOR DOCTOR'S BRIDE

by

CARO CARSON

Both were originally
Harlequin® series stories!

⊕HARLEQUIN®

SPECIAL EDITION

Life, Love and Family

"Lydia Grant, assistant manager," he read, then lifted a
questioning glance to her. "Is that you?"

Her head made a quick bob, causing several curls to
plop onto her forehead. "That's me. Assistant manager
is just one of my roles at the *Gazette*. I do everything
around here. Including plumbing repair. You need a fau-
cet installed?"

"Uh, no. I need a wife."

The announcement clearly took her aback. "I thought
I misheard you earlier. I guess I didn't."

Enjoying the look of dismay on her face, he gave her
a lopsided grin. "Nope. You didn't hear wrong. I want to
advertise for a wife."

Rolling the pencil between her palms, she eyed him
with open speculation.

"What's the matter?" she asked. "You can't get a wife
the traditional way?"

As soon as Zach had made the decision to advertise for a bride, he'd expected to get this sort of reaction. He'd just not expected it from a complete stranger. And a woman, at that.

"Sometimes it's good to break from tradition. And I'm in a hurry."

Something like disgust flickered in her eyes before she dropped her gaze to the scratch pad in front of her. "I see. You're a man in a hurry. So give me your name, mailing address and phone number and I'll help you speed up this process."

She took down the basic information, then asked, "How do you want this worded? I suppose you do have requirements for your…bride?"

He drew up a nearby plastic chair and eased his long frame onto the seat. "Sure. I have a few. Where would you like to start?"

She looked up at him and chuckled as though she found their whole exchange ridiculous. Zach tried not to bristle. Maybe she didn't think any of this was serious. But sooner or later Lydia Grant, and every citizen in Rust Creek Falls, would learn he was very serious about his search for a wife.

Don't miss
THE MAVERICK'S BRIDE-TO-ORDER
by Stella Bagwell, available September 2017 wherever
Harlequin® Special Edition books and ebooks are sold.

www.Harlequin.com

H HARLEQUIN®

SPECIAL EDITION

Life, Love and Family

Save **$1.00**

on the purchase of ANY
Harlequin® Special Edition book.

Available wherever books are sold, including
most bookstores, supermarkets, drugstores
and discount stores.

Save $1.00

on the purchase of any Harlequin Special Edition book.

Coupon valid until November 30, 2017.
Redeemable at participating outlets in the U.S. and Canada only.
Not redeemable at Barnes & Noble stores. Limit one coupon per customer.

52615098

Canadian Retailers: Harlequin Enterprises Limited will pay the face value of this coupon plus 10.25¢ if submitted by customer for this product only. Any other use constitutes fraud. Coupon is nonassignable. Void if taxed, prohibited or restricted by law. Consumer must pay any government taxes. Void if copied. Inmar Promotional Services ("IPS") customers submit coupons and proof of sales to Harlequin Enterprises Limited, PO Box 31000, Scarborough, ON M1R 0E7, Canada. Non-IPS retailer—for reimbursement submit coupons and proof of sales directly to Harlequin Enterprises Limited, Retail Marketing Department, 225 Duncan Mill Rd., Don Mills, ON M3B 3K9, Canada.

5 65373 00076 2   (8100)0 12305

U.S. Retailers: Harlequin Enterprises Limited will pay the face value of this coupon plus 8¢ if submitted by customer for this product only. Any other use constitutes fraud. Coupon is nonassignable. Void if taxed or restricted by law. Consumer must pay any government taxes. Void if copied. For reimbursement submit coupons and proof of sales directly to Harlequin Enterprises, Ltd 482, NCH Marketing Services, P.O. Box 880001, El Paso, TX 88588-0001, U.S.A. Cash value 1/100 cents.

® and ™ are trademarks owned and used by the trademark owner and/or its licensee.

© 2017 Harlequin Enterprises Limited

NYTCOUP0817

Return to Blossom Street with
#1 *New York Times* bestselling author

DEBBIE MACOMBER

for a heartwarming story about finding love
where you least expect it.

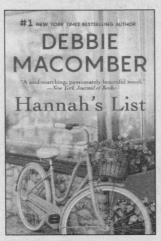

On the anniversary of his beloved wife's death, Dr. Michael Everett receives a letter Hannah had written him. In it she makes one final request. An *impossible* request. *I want you to marry again.* She tells him he shouldn't spend the years he has left grieving— and she's chosen three women she asks him to consider.

During the months that follow, he spends time with each of these three women, learning more about them...and about himself. He's a man who needs the completeness only love can offer. And Hannah's list leads him to the woman who can help him find it.

Available now, wherever books are sold!

THE WORLD IS BETTER WITH

Romance

Harlequin has everything from contemporary, passionate and heartwarming to suspenseful and inspirational stories.

Whatever your mood, we have a romance just for you!